Freelanders

Ces Basi

Acknowledgements

Writing a novel is never a solitary journey, and Freelanders could not have come to life without the love and support of many.

First and foremost, to my wife, Mary, and my loving family — thank you for your patience, encouragement, and unwavering belief in me. You have been my foundation, and your understanding carried me through every late night and long silence at the desk.

To my friends, I am deeply grateful for your encouragement.

To Penguin Publishers: Lucas Parez, William Brooks, and the editorial team, and early readers. Your insight, guidance, and careful attention helped shape these pages into the story I had only dreamed it could be. I would also like to thank Steve Wilson and Danny Brown.

Finally, to every future reader — thank you for stepping into this world with me. Stories only truly live when they are shared, and I am honored to share this one with you.

For Dion, Isabella, Gabriel, Cristian, and Luca.

My loves, my treasures—this book is for you.

In loving memory of my father, Giovanni Basi.

Contents

The Histories

"The efforts of previous generations have led to nothing. Overpopulation and food shortages have divided humankind socially, politically, and economically. Clashing opinions and interests have divided the Allied and Freelander people. If that is your belief, then human ingenuity counts for nothing. Individually and collectively, we have disrespected and exploited all living things. We must rediscover goodness and compassion and learn to live together; future generations depend on it. As challenging as that may seem, humankind must open its eyes to what is happening here on Earth, or humanity will perish. There is hope for the home we think we know so well. We find ourselves at the beginning of a new era in space science. New worlds await discovery, bringing challenges and opportunities for Allied folk and the Freelander people." — *Rachel Sibley.*

***

London: Greater Britain's capital.

The debate in the House of Commons continued as rising numbers of dissatisfied members on both sides of the Commons Chamber demanded the resignation of the prime minister. Sir Henry Arthur refused to admit responsibility for his failings as head of the British Government; he blamed everyone but himself. He stormed out of the chamber knowing his political career was in tatters, and his reputation as a negotiator shattered beyond repair. London was facing a crisis as trade unionists demanded more political action, and social instability was at its highest since the Great Rebellion. Jobs were scarce and difficult to maintain. All government-sponsored social initiatives led to closed doors; there were no free government handouts for anyone.

Privately funded food distribution centers and wholesale food operators promised to provide high-quality food at affordable prices. The food parcels, securely stored in warehouses and guarded by military personnel, were often mistakenly sent to the wealthier part of the community. Hungry individuals protested but their efforts yielded no change. Riots frequently erupted, resulting in numerous casualties as people fought for food. Not a single Freelander was among the deceased. Freelander communities had communal farms that combined vegetable and livestock production. Fish and eels were carefully bred to provide reliable sources of protein during long, cold winters.

The governments of technology-rich Allied countries, like Greater Britain (the oldest and most influential), couldn't tolerate the strength and resilience of the Freelander communities growing exponentially worldwide. Security forces hunted Freelanders, stole their crops and livestock, and burned their communal farms. Despite all this, Freelander communities continued to emerge in other places and defended themselves with better weaponry.

***

In the British Parliament, MPs with the childish propensity to point fingers stopped playing the blame game. After much deliberation, MPs voted according to their conscience and for the greater good. They accepted a new leader, the Right Honorable Brett Ormsby, a reluctant aristocrat held in high regard by the king and the British people.

King Edward XI summoned the newly elected prime minister to Buckingham Palace. The young king, acting in the best interest of the British people, appointed Mr.

Ormsby prime minister of the United Kingdom (UK) and asked him to form a majority government and fix the British economy. But fixing the British economy would not be easy since the Eurozone and the United Americas had not fully recovered from trade wars. As if that wasn't enough, civil disturbances prevented America's resurgence in politics and international relations. In response, several Xiangshan Traders in China stepped up to stabilize the financial systems within the UK of Greater Britain. The UK's central government, aware of the economic significance, was overly cautious. Doing any business in that part of the world could unearth old political sensitivities. That meant reopening old wounds. Regardless of the long-standing political differences and conflicts between the two great nations, Prime Minister Ormsby was quoted as saying, *"Accepting any economic aid is in the best interest of the British people."*

While King Edward XI was thrilled with the new prime minister, anger seethed within trade unions, where radical members blamed Brett Ormsby for caving under economic pressure from the Xiangshan Traders. The two houses of Parliament, the House of Commons, and the House of Lords, placed on record that nothing could be further from the truth. So, a referendum, called The Xiangshan Trade Referendum (XTR), took place. All British citizens had to cast their votes either for or against the referendum and accept the result. But the elected members of the United Allied Nations (UAN) understood that any acceptance of the financial aid package would have far-reaching social implications not only in Britain but also around the globe.

There was strong evidence suggesting that the owners of multinational companies were collaborating with CEOs of the World Trade Corporation to control commodity markets, agriculture, and food production in Greater Britain. They were working together to target the

Freelanders and conspired to derail multilateral talks on Eurozone economic cooperation and the XTR. Their aim was to avoid losing not only sales revenue and profits but also their political influence. However, their conspiracy failed. The British people voted in favor of the aid package, and the British banking sector embraced all economic reform proposals made by the Xiangshan traders. This newfound optimism for the future offered renewed hope for the British people. Politicians and their many sycophants took all the credit, flung themselves into the limelight, and declared their unbending support. The total bailout package amounted to twenty trillion British pounds in the old money, the best offer ever made by Xiangshan traders backed by a Chinese government. After the deal was finalized, the promising partnership between the UK government and the Xiangshan traders began to sour, leading to a decline in public support for the bailout package. This decline was fuelled by the arrival of a Chinese transition committee composed of influential traders in London, who began pushing people to work harder, causing distrust to grow.

Other nations allied to the West had received the same generous offer from the President of the Xiangshan Traders Association in China, and every political commentator outside Great Britain had the firm belief that the four most significant bicameral legislatures in the Eurozone (Italy, Germany, France, and the Netherlands) would simply reject the offer, no question. Political commentators and analysts from the Eurozone said at the time that if their respective governments reached a decision and accepted the traders' offer in its entirety, then the power and influence of Freelanders would only increase. For the millions of city dwellers, the unjustified seizure of land by the Freelanders was illegal and outrageous. Long-standing cities were being systemically demolished, razed to the ground to free up extra acres of land for planting high-yield organic crops.

Nevertheless, the Freeland movement had a reputation to uphold. Free food, clean water, and shelter to anyone willing to follow and enforce the principles written in the Freelander Constitution and the Book of Universal Law, words written by the great Rachel Sibley, the first Freelander.

Inside the Eurozone, the Xiangshan Trade Referendum became a divisive topic in all social circles, and everyone had their own opinion. The old Republic of China, often ridiculed in history books, had the worst reputation for human rights and animal rights abuses among the Asian non-Allied countries in the past. In modern times, successive trader associations and Chinese governments had sanctioned the idea of Freelander independence and encouraged it.

However, the British government and the UAN leadership considered any trading arrangement with Xiangshan traders a dubious business practice. Moreover, they regarded the treaty of alliance with the Freelanders as illegal under international law. Freelanders were regarded as stateless people, citizens of no country; they were a melting pot made up of people from all over the world, a collective of disillusioned people with little social influence. How they were gaining international political alliances and free land to raise crops rang political alarm bells around the Allied world, but not everyone was listening. So, the UAN legislature demanded that the Freelanders surrender to the UAN all the territories they had acquired. The UAN legislature contemplated military force to silence the political alarm bells ringing loudly and for so long. To counter the threat of war with the UAN, the 300 members of the Council of Freelander Elders (CFE) signed the

Treaty of Alliance with Xiangshan traders and the Chinese government. Strong-minded Freelander business leaders had also entered the global political economy; they had infiltrated every business organization in the United Kingdom, including the British government and the royal family household.

The British security forces dedicated considerable resources to tracking down Freelanders. Political commentators within the Eurozone suspected collusion between Britain's security minister and the Freelanders. Influential commentators suggested to the media that the minister's interactions and leniency towards the Freelander administration were aimed at countering the UAN's worldwide mandate that banned the Freelander movement. British commentators even went as far as to say that the security minister's apathetic behavior would be another turning point for the Freelander movement, providing it an opportunity to gain more international political alliances as Freelander membership, which had already surged after the Great Rebellion, continued to grow..

Applicants seeking Freelander membership in Greater Britain were inundating the office of the secretariat in London. However, no arrests were made because the police and Britain's elite security services overlooked the Freelander activities.

***

The Freelander movement crossed the English Channel spreading throughout France, then Italy and Spain, and finally the rest of starving Europe like an out-of-control forest fire. The privileged rich had the money to buy the best food and the cleanest water. Everyone else lived on cultured meat products, synthetic milk, and tubes of dehydrated vegetable paste and garum (fermented fish sauce). The Freelanders, unconventional fighters, waged guerrilla warfare in every country in Europe, combating better-equipped private armies of mega-rich corporations and corrupt food distribution companies and winning significant victories. Furthermore, their clever military tactics and word-of-mouth strategies played a crucial role in attracting more young people to the Freelander movement.

In Germany, starved citizens ravaged cities and towns, burned to the ground food storage facilities and mismanaged food distribution centers, diverting food to the black market.

George Hiedler, the prime minister of Germany, and active member of the Freelander movement added more fuel to the fire when he openly blamed the multinational food companies for starving the people of the Allied nations inside the Eurozone. Dirk von Bassmann, a fanatical German nationalist, was at Pariser Platz, Berlin, when Hiedler read out his hate-filled speech and declared publicly his intention to seize areas of unproductive agricultural land in Germany. Later that same day, Von Bassmann, with three other men, followed the Prime Minister to the Chancellery Building, where they murdered him for three gold rings, and a diamond-studded belt. The CFE alleged that the owners of the five largest food manufacturing companies had hired Dirk von Bassmann to assassinate George Hiedler, a man they could not buy. Informants led police to a hotel where Von Bassmann and his three accomplices worked for little pay. Police apprehended and imprisoned the four men for Hiedler's murder. Prosecutors found all four guilty of murder and sentenced them to death by burning. Their public execution simultaneously broadcast via television around the Eurozone sparked violent rioting. Pariser Platz, the cultural center of Berlin, suffered random acts of property destruction and looting. When the violent rioting ended, the

CFE, wanting to exact revenge, sanctioned the assassination of the Secretary-General of the UAN Security Council and 47 elected members. Security protocols in and around the building were enhanced due to the increased threat. Nevertheless, paid assassins efficiently carried out each hit; the Secretary-General, 47 elected members, and their entire families were brutally murdered within their homes. British lawmakers, exasperated and tired of worrying that the same lawlessness would happen in the United Kingdom, pressed for a new referendum. This was a proposal that recognized the Freeland territories and their Treaty of Alliance with the Xiangshan traders in China. Once again, the British people headed to the voting stations. With more Yes than No votes, the British Parliament accepted all territorial claims made by Freelanders and their Treaty of Alliance with Xiangshan traders.

After weeks of negotiations with the Xiangshan Minister for International Development and Trade, the first cargo ship from China docked in Southampton, delivering fuel, food and medicine, grain, and cleaned sowing seed. Three months later, the first commercial flight from Beijing, China, touched down at London's Windsor International Airport. British Airways Flight BA-562 to Beijing took off from Windsor International shortly after, with little fanfare from the media when word got out that Passengers paid the modest sum of 15,000 yuan to independent ticket brokers in China for the privilege.

***

From the Resolute Desk in the Oval Office, President Terrence Marcipor Williams (via Satellite Link) had open and wide-ranging discussions with Chinese President Ruan Chow and Russian Sergei Petrov, the Russian prime minister. The United Americas, weakened economically

8

and socially by civil war, had few opportunities in the global marketplace. Therefore, no one was surprised when President Williams decided that reciprocal transparency in business dealings and trust was the best weapon to secure any lasting peace. Unbeknownst to President Williams, the Chinese Minister for International Development and Trade had sided with his colleague, the defense minister. Both men had agreed to postpone any meeting with the American President indefinitely; they claimed Williams was a poor negotiator and a bellicose narcissist, undeserving of any respect whatsoever. Furthermore, President Chow stated that there would be no negotiations with the American President, but he did not rule out providing food aid. Not one of his ministers dared to disagree. Undoubtedly, recalling the fact that for more than two centuries, successive American governments for reasons of national security had set up a closed economic border policy, particularly against China. John Terrence Arter, the former President of the United Americas, discussed his proposed action to prevent Xiangshan traders and citizens of non-allied nations from entering his country. He was quoted as telling the Defense Secretary, *"No more handouts! To anyone! Keep Xiangshan traders out of my country, or I'll find someone who will."* Only the mega-rich praised the UAN, praised leaders like President Arter for wanting to put a stop to hordes of hungry foreigners entering their country, all murdering thieves according to government-sanctioned media. In and around affluent residential areas, looting of anything edible often turned violent. People turned on one another like dogs fighting over food scraps. The disregard for private property prompted the American government to take immediate action to preserve some semblance of civil order. At every border crossing, makeshift refugee camps were set up. In the first few weeks, the number of people that had entered through guarded gates totaled a staggering 250,000. The camps served as detention centers, where fundamental human rights existed only on paper. The refugees protested vocally at first, then came the violent confrontations, bloody clashes with the camp guards. Finally, when security forces arrived on the scene, all the food aid stopped. The clean water piped into the camp and the electricity supply stopped. The living conditions inside detention camps broke bodies and spirits; thousands died. The winter months claimed many more lives. Displaced people without implanted ID microchips that stored their personal data fared far worse during Rachel Sibley's socio-economic war, also known as the Great Freelander Rebellion: 220 million people lost their lives.

President Ruan Chow played the role of peacemaker, and at the same time, he placed harsh economic sanctions on any nation at war with the Freelanders. Any sovereign State expressing hostile actions against the Freelander movement received no financial aid from mega-rich Asian economies. The UAN leadership voiced their opinion openly, called the sanctions blatant political blackmail but their harsh rhetoric backfired. The Xiangshan traders refused to grant the Allied nations access to their global market economy, banking, and financial system. Additionally, by integrating Freelanders into Xiangshan society, the Xiangshan bolstered the China/Sibley Alliance. The Freelanders were widely recognized by the international community as a global social phenomenon. However, the China/Sibley Alliance was considered a threat to world peace, raising concerns among the Allied nations. Soon after the China/Sibley Alliance had been signed, a dirty bomb devastated the city of Vienna.

The members of the UAN demanded revenge against the Freelanders for the indiscriminate slaughter of 12 million innocent civilians. With no one accepting responsibility, the representatives of 189 allied nations stepped forward.

They voted in favor of the Decimation Act and signed it into international law. This Act was a worldwide lottery of death for 1 in 10 young adults between the ages of 20 to 30. Security teams arrested and publicly executed 100 selected Freelanders categorized by age as young adults. The unattested slaughter of young innocents continued until members of the World Elite Fellowship came forward and claimed responsibility for the attack.

***

During the Food Wars that ravaged the late 22nd century, the Decimation Act had far-reaching effects. Subsequently, a groundbreaking zoonosis serum was developed and introduced into the worldwide vaccine market, offering a crucial solution to combat animal infections that could be transmitted to humans. However, issues arose when contaminated serum batches led to the mutation of a new strain of pneumonic plague due to problems in the vaccine's marketing and distribution. In the following eighteen months, no effective treatments or cures for the pandemic existed. Measures such as social distancing and border closures had minimal effect in halting the spread, resulting in forty percent of the world's population becoming infected. Consequently, four billion people worldwide lost their lives. The pandemic sparked significant changes in political ideologies and brought about the most substantial social transformations in human history. These developments led to the Freeland movement, which witnessed a mass migration of highly skilled young adults, including teachers, scientists, professionals from various fields, and performing artists worldwide. They resettled in Freeland territories in Australia, New Zealand, and Antarctica in the Southern Hemisphere, as well as in the Northern Hemisphere in countries such as Iceland, Norway, Finland, Greenland, Alaska, Canada, and Northern Russia. The vision of the Freelanders for a society free from racism, prejudice, injustice, and greed was then not only conceived but was also embraced by oppressed people worldwide as the new social norm.

***

FS Taimaha

Present day.

Four sailors were performing routine maintenance when they saluted their captain as he walked past the quarterdeck. Captain Jonathan Wheeler smiled at the four sailors and saluted them before entering the bridge through a sliding door. First Lieutenant Satori Thomas was preparing Captain Wheeler's morning coffee. Five naval officers, including Lieutenant Thomas, saluted crisply while Satori announced, "Captain is on the bridge."

"Carry on," Captain Wheeler said, making eye contact with each officer.

Satori poured hot coffee into a cup and handed it to Captain Wheeler. "Good morning, sir."

"Good morning, Lieutenant. Thank you."

"You're welcome, sir."

Wheeler was an experienced naval captain and expert navigator, who had safely made numerous voyages to the ever-changing Antarctic continent. Over his extensive seafaring career, his devotion to the welfare of his crew had earned him their trust and respect. Wheeler considered the Freelander ship FS *Taimaha* his home. The ship wasn't just a place to work, eat, and sleep; it was the love of his life. He treasured every moment spent on the ship, finding joy and fulfillment in his role as the captain. Lately, though, there'd been a noticeable change in attitude, a crisis in Jonathon's life, as retirement stared him in the face after a distinguished career spanning forty years in the Freelander Navy. FS *Taimaha's* days at sea were numbered also. The

Freelander Navy had decided to replace its aging fleet of
warships with ultramodern vessels. Why not sail with the
latest radar and sonar arrays, satellite navigation, and
advanced Sequanta computer technology? Without FS
Taimaha, Jonathon saw himself as an old man who had
outlived his usefulness. He couldn't bring himself to
imagine retirement or what would happen after it. Jonathan
believed that the pain of loneliness in old age far surpassed
that of a frail and failing body. So, with no children, no
family, and only a few friends, Jonathan continued to love
his job and his ship, despite thoughts of ending his life
before the October winds arrived.

***

FS *Taimaha* reached Macquarie Island and turned southeast
towards Freeland Antarctica's eastern ice shelf. That was
the Great Continent, home of Rachel Sibley's hard-won
victory over the armies of the Allied nations. It was a long-
drawn-out war, fought chiefly on the battlefields of
Western Australia, but the negotiating table was where the
verbal battles took place. When everything was said and
done, Rachel Sibley contracted pulmonary tuberculosis.
Surrounded by her family and friends, Rachel died
knowing that she had secured a future for all Freelanders
and a new way of life for the coming generations. In Dome
Halley, Antarctica stood the memorial commemorating and
celebrating her life. The Freelanders and Allied nations had
unfinished business, and their ongoing war over land,
water, and food was still a continuous struggle.

Standing with his five officers around the wheelhouse chart
table, Captain Wheeler opened the yellow envelop Rear
Admiral Marcus Fletcher had given him before FS
Taimaha sailed out of Southport, a deep-water harbor in
New Zealand's South Island. Inside the envelope, a letter
announced the name of the VIP aboard his ship, Professor

Joseph Arunui, the young Māori astrophysicist, labeled the 'New Einstein' by New Zealand scientists and journalists.

Joseph Arunui and the ship's crew boarded the FS *Taimaha* at Southport. Joseph boarded last, walking behind five commissioned navy officers personally chosen by Jonathan. The naval officers were young and inexperienced but possessed the Freelander Navy's best minds. One hundred, thirty-five experienced navy personnel and 25 civilian volunteers, including men and women from Western Australia, New Zealand, and Antarctica, were also on board. Captain Wheeler respected every member of his crew, and every opinion mattered; listening to others with empathy was behind his seamanship. Jonathan had learned the fundamentals of quality seamanship aboard the FS *Elizabeth*, his first ship, a Howard Class Frigate.

The Office of Marine Affairs did not publicize the expedition to Antarctica. The passenger manifest also did not include the name of the VIP on board, Joseph Arunui. The entire expedition was top secret and organized by Rear Admiral Fletcher. There was an urgent need to protect Joseph Arunui from the possibility of kidnapping. Xiangshan traders were constantly seeking talented, high-quality individuals. The owners and managers of research laboratories and mining facilities tempted them with substantial sums of money. Additionally, they would reward unscrupulous traders with hallucinogens and other illegal psychoactive drugs.

Admiral Fletcher's letter emphasized that numerous esteemed scientists regarded Joseph Arunui's dark matter theory, proposed at the age of eighteen, as the next paradigm shift in comprehending interstellar space. This invaluable knowledge was something Admiral Fletcher was determined to protect. So, Captain Wheeler absolutely did not want to see VIP Joseph Arunui openly chatting with civilian mariners who were serving as crew members on his ship. The knowledgeable Doctor Miron Philips, the captain's closest friend and Chief Medical Officer on board also agreed not to share information that could endanger the VIP. So, Captain Wheeler alone chose when the time was right to inform his senior and junior officers and only on a need-to-know basis.

***

For eight days and nights, FS *Taimaha* traveled with a punishing storm, avoiding Cape Adare, the tip of the Adare peninsula separating the Ross Sea to the east from the Southern Ocean to the west. Captain Wheeler then focused on the glaciated Balleny Islands, lying 150 miles off the coast of Oates Land, Eastern Antarctica. Standing with the captain at the wheelhouse chart table and managing navigation planning and the general safety of the ship was Officer of the Deck, Lieutenant Satori Thomas. "The latitude and longitude of Prydz Bay are correct, Captain."

"Good work, Lieutenant. Enter the coordinates in the ships log."

"Aye, sir."

Satori studied the marine charts covered with dirty fingerprints and penciled corrections. Despite that fact, Satori gave the captain her thumbs down and sounded the ship's horn as Cape Adare came into her view on the starboard bow. The sea was flat calm, but she could see drift ice through the binoculars.

"We are getting clear of the drift ice, Captain."

"Distance to the edge of the ice sheet?"

"200 nautical miles, Captain."

"Thank you, Lieutenant Thomas, carry on."

"Aye, sir."

Captain Wheeler then fixed his steely gaze on Commander Martin Brindle.

"Commander Brindle!"

"Sir!"

"Send out a drone on ice patrol. Lock course at maximum distance."

"Course locked and set…maximum distance, aye, Captain."

"Mr. Michaels, are there any over-voltage alarms or power dips on the data-logger?"

The helmsman scanned his diagnostic screens for any active alarms his young eyes may have missed. "I see no over-voltage alarms. No power dips, Captain."

"Thank you, Peter."

Captain Wheeler opened the daily Antarctic Sea ice chart and a map of Prydz Bay. He leaned forward and studied the map slid over the chart table. For a few moments, FS *Taimaha's* bridge was silent; it was clear to the bridge crew that Captain Wheeler looked anxious and perplexed.

"Is Drone-86 in the air?"

"Aye, Captain. Drone-86 is in the air and active two nautical miles ahead of us and heading south-south-west," Martin replied. "Is everything all right, sir?"

"To be perfectly honest, I don't know for sure. There could be an intermittent problem with the wheelhouse power unit. Or this ship is being systematically trolled for contraband ordnance by an orbiting enemy satellite."

"We could launch an M7-squelcher just to be on the safe side," Martin said confidently, knowing SAF (Set-and-forget) weapons like the M7-squelcher, MQ-sniper, Firecracker, and Dragonfly all carried unique capabilities in the air. But only the M7 had a microwave system which suppressed radioactive signatures emitted by high-grade weaponry stored deep inside underground bunkers, in steel containers, or the cargo hold of an enemy vessel. Standing at the wheelhouse chart table, the captain and Lieutenant Thomas reviewed the data displayed on the navigation computer. "I'm going against my better judgment by launching an M7 with only a couple of hours of sunlight left," Captain Wheeler said.

"We will be in communication limbo as long as the drone stays active," Martin declared.

"Pulsed microwave emitters disrupt older wireless communication systems from time to time, Martin. We all have to accept that fact," Captain Wheeler said, thinking aloud.

"Correct me if I'm wrong, sir. M7s are relatively new, tested only in simulated battle conditions," Lieutenant Thomas said.

"Lieutenant Thomas, how long have you been in the navy?"

"Two years, three months and four days, Captain."

"Well, I have had extensive battle experience against the UAN navy, and I can tell you with great certainty that SAF weaponry is very efficient and lethal."

"Duly noted, sir."

"Commander Brindle, you have my permission to launch the M7."

"Launching now, Captain."

"Mr. Michaels, when the squelcher goes active, hands off the boat wheel and throttle control. The M7 will control the ship. Enemy satellites attack communications and disrupt the chain of command by sending down phony encrypted messages."

"Aye, aye, Captain."

Regardless of the perceived shortcomings of SAF weaponry, the M7-squelcher drone positioned itself 500 feet above FS *Taimaha* and matched her speed and heading. Then it set to the task of blocking the radioactive signatures emitted by *Taimaha's* short-range nuclear arsenal.

"Helm, change course. Turn 2 points to starboard, slow to 20 knots," the Captain commanded.

"22.5 degrees to starboard…20 knots, aye, aye, Captain," Michaels said, turning the boat wheel two points, adding more sea miles between a mountain of floating ice and *Taimaha's* starboard bow.

"Hold course and speed, Mr. Michaels."

"Aye, sir, holding speed and course."

FS *Taimaha* continued along a predetermined course, rounding the Rauer Group of islands early the following day and sailing between Neptune's Twins, the two massive icebergs guarding the narrow entrance to Prydz Bay. The bay had shallow regions, only a couple of feet of water below the ship's keel. Captain Wheeler reduced speed and sailed cautiously at eight knots. Through his binoculars, he spotted the northeast edge of the Ranvik Glacier, less than ten miles from a suitable anchoring point in the deepest part of Prydz Bay.

***

Commander Andrew Faulkner strolled along the ship's portside railing as the bow anchor descended to the seabed, maintaining good tension about half a mile eastward of a rocky island and a cluster of jagged rocks. The rocky island was home to a colony of over 200 Kerguelen fur seals feasting on krill, fish, and squid. An engine room attendant (ERA) joined Commander Faulkner at the portside railing. "What are you doing here?" Commander Faulkner said sternly. "I'm on my meal break, sir," the ERA replied.

Faulkner always seemed attentive, but he never wanted to come across as friendly or show favoritism towards any crew member.

"I have sailed these waters many times over the last twenty years, and I have never seen so many fur seals in one place," the ERA said as he leaned over the railing to better see two all-white fur seal pups approaching the ship.

"Keep your observations to yourself," Faulkner said, eyeballing the ERA. "The captain will conduct the engine room audit today instead of tomorrow. Now, get back to work. I want the engine room spotlessly clean, or you'll find yourself working in the ship's galley."

"Aye, sir."

***

Captain Wheeler exited the wheelhouse to do the last safety audit of the day. Commander Brindle donned his navy-blue duffle coat and followed the captain out the sliding door leading to the port-side passageway and the exposed afterdeck. A blast of icy wind slapped Martin in the face, causing his eyes to well up in the frigid air and forcing him to squint. He pressed his lips and wrapped a scarf around his nose and mouth as Faulkner's voice was heard over the ship's time-worn speaker system. *"Captain, the starboard bow anchor has stopped dragging."*

"Very well, Mr. Faulkner. Pay special attention to the wind now. If it changes direction, lower another fluke anchor."

"Aye, aye, Captain. I'll keep that in mind."

Captain Wheeler considered Lieutenant Commanders Martin Brindle and Andrew Faulkner exceptionally talented officers, the finest in the Freelander Navy. The captain also considered Martin Brindle as his likely successor. Andrew Faulkner believed Martin was favored because Wheeler was a close friend of Martin's uncle, Josiah Brindle, and well acquainted with the Brindle family. When Faulkner received no reply from the admiral, he assumed an error had occurred and the letter never reached its destination. The truth was that the admiral had torn up Faulkner's letter after speaking with Captain Wheeler.

***

The wind, which had been buffeting since early morning, calmed slightly as the sun peeked through a gap in the clouds. "Look, a sun halo!" Martin said, looking up at thin wispy cirrostratus clouds.

"Wispy cirrostratus clouds and a sun halo indicate a storm front is approaching. I'd say in the next 24 to 48 hours," Captain Wheeler said.

"A Sun halo brings forth the wind, a Moon halo the rain," Martin said.

"Shustak's Odyssey?"

"Yes, Captain. Shustak's Odyssey was my father's favorite poem. He would read a verse of Shustak's Odyssey each night to me before I went to bed. I was eight years old and didn't understand everything Jeremiah Shustak mentioned in his poems. Still, I have felt a close connection to nature and the sea ever since," Martin said, remembering how swiftly his childhood years in Western Australia had flown by and how terribly he still missed his parents. Martin often felt guilty for not having spent more time with both of them after the Brindle family left Western Australia and emigrated to Antarctica.

"Your father was a dedicated sailor and a trustworthy trader."

"My father was a living paradox," Martin said bluntly. "Yes, he loved his family, no question, but his business dealings took precedence over everything, and you saw that firsthand."

"I did at times," Captain Wheeler said, thinking back to when he visited antique shops and military auction houses. "But I don't recall your father ever saying family commitments were less important than his business dealings, but people change. In any case, I haven't spoken to your father for many years. But I do recall when he and your uncle Josiah visited Maccabi's auction house and successfully bid on a wrecked cargo ship."

"Salvaging that old rust bucket cost my father and uncle a great deal of money," Martin said.

Captain Wheeler looked up at the sky again. "Well, let's finish the work we came here to do. I don't want to stay here longer than we need to."

***

The aft deck safety audit continued. Captain Wheeler and Martin checked fire extinguishers and oily water separators, lifeboats, and davits. They uncovered a half-empty bottle of cheap Vodka hidden inside a storage locker.

Wheeler looked disappointed. "I don't tolerate this sort of nonsense."

"Nor do I, sir."

"I have a letter on my desk addressed to you. It's from Rear Admiral Fletcher."

"From Admiral Fletcher?"

"It's not a letter of reprimand if that's what you're thinking."

"Well, that's a relief." Martin chuckled. "Is there anything else, Captain?"

"Mr. Arunui will be joining us for dinner this evening. Tell the others, please. And tell them to dress appropriately."

"So, we will finally meet the VIP," Martin said, smiling.

"Yes. Mr. Arunui is an intelligent young man. I think you and he will get on well together."

Martin paused, looked the captain in the eye, and said, "Get on well together? Why do you say that? Captain, the guy could be a total asshole."

"Admiral Fletcher personally selected Mr. Arunui; he likes to bring together opposing philosophies and differing points of view. Don't worry, Martin. Everything you need to know and do is in Admiral Fletcher's letter."

Martin nodded. "Aye, sir."

The evening dinner started as usual, with Captain Wheeler sitting at the head of the table. He was flanked by five officers in order of seniority from right to left. The guest of honor typically sat at the far end of the tastefully decorated dinner table. The table was adorned with refined white linen, matching napkins, porcelain plates, and crystal glassware. It also held bottles of expensive wine, beer, old Scottish whiskey, and fine French brandy. Joseph had never seen such luxury before. Looking around the wood-paneled dining room, Joseph noticed Freelander banners hanging from heavy orange, black, and purple drapes. The drapes covered three square windows extending from the ceiling to the floor. Joseph felt trapped and wanted to return to his cabin; nervous tension was making him sick. After quickly completing the introductions, Captain Wheeler called the steward, and dinner was served. Joseph enjoyed his meal—grilled, tender and juicy swordfish with mixed vegetables—and drank only water. Sulfites in fancy wines always gave him a headache, and he did not like the taste of beer or any hard liquor. However, he was keenly interested in the brewing process and associated technologies.

As the evening continued, Joseph felt more relaxed. He took an immediate liking to Lieutenant Thomas and found her to be friendly, unpretentious, and easy to talk with. He told her he was born in Auckland but grew up in Greymouth, on the west coast of New Zealand's South Island.

Around the dinner table, only Captain Wheeler and Doc Philips understood the extent of Joseph's reputation as a radical thinker in theoretical physics and astrophysics. Martin and Andrew, Satori, and Lesley understood the fundamental laws of physics, seamanship, and astronomy but had little knowledge of Earth's history. So, they sat and listened quietly and let Joseph do most of the talking. "A new Age of Discovery is dawning for humankind," declared Joseph. "Equivalent in importance to the Apollo moon missions: the first human steps on the moon by Armstrong and Aldrin."

Joseph had always admired famous seafaring explorers, though he preferred the great inventors and innovators of the late 1800s: Thomas Alva Edison and Nicolas Tesla (the father of wireless power transmission and alternating current). While Captain Wheeler and Doc admired Joseph's zeal for history, there were also blank looks around the dinner table.

The Allied Nations Security Council (ANSC) had declared the Freelander movement an illegal cult that had to be isolated from the rest of the world and destroyed. The underwater fiber-optic cables linking Freeland territories to the rest of the world were vulnerable prey for deep-water submersibles and underwater drones. Cutting internet connectivity to the Freelands also shut down data cables carrying massive amounts of information and money transactions worth trillions of yuan to world markets. This was the main reason President Ruan Chow approved China's significant withdrawal from the World Bank and the ANSC, leading to questionable business dealings that threatened the security of Freeland territories. Shortly after the internet shutdown, a media war erupted between World Media Group and Winthrop Holdings, the wealthiest company in the world. World Media Group's managing director and CEO, Michael Wilding, strongly supported the Freelander movement. As a result, he offered to buy Winthrop's orbiting assets, specifically the satellites leased to Allied nations. The data transmission to and from privately owned Earth-orbiting satellites was a lucrative source of revenue for Winthrop Holdings. However, Michael Wilding's interest in this venture wasn't purely financial. It was also a strategic and political move by the Council of Freelander Elders to address the escalating risk of all-out war with the Allied nations. Gordon Winthrop, the CEO of his company, successfully navigated working with both sides of the political spectrum. He sold communication satellites to Wilding while acquiring more mining leases on the Moon and increasing his ownership of LOS, an aging space station in lunar orbit.

* * *

After dinner, Satori showed Joseph all around the ship. Joseph told her he could hardly wait for the following day to disembark the vessel and continue his journey to the Dome Fuji Observatory in Antarctica. After saying goodnight to Satori, Joseph went back to his cabin to collect his few belongings. He was very methodical in everything he did and painfully slow in folding clothes. He laid them inside a green army surplus backpack with his other items: an oversized orange coat, spare heavy boots, rolled-up thermal undergarments, several beanies, five pairs of merino wool mittens, and thermal gloves.

Joseph cherished his daily diary and the scientific papers he had published in three prominent journals. These included "Dark Particle Theory," which explored the existence of Nanotrine Particles or exotic matter created during the Big Bang, and his enigmatic description of gravitational waves interacting with the interstellar medium. The esteemed Professor William Briar had received encrypted copies of Joseph's exceptional work and offered to provide funding for further research if Joseph moved to Briar's Dome Fuji Observatory in Antarctica. Joseph had initially declined to leave New Zealand and relocate. He changed his mind when multimedia reporters discovered Joseph's private home address, broke in, and stole his research computer. This incident caused Joseph to fall into a deep depression, and he refused to continue his research. It wasn't until Professor Briar expressed his passionate belief that one day Joseph's Dark Matter Theory would propel the Freelanders to the stars, that Joseph found the motivation to continue his work.

***

Early the following day, Joseph stumbled out of bed, barely awake, to answer the ringing phone in his cabin. Commander Faulkner called Joseph and instructed him to report to his assigned muster station on the flight deck. "We have a cloudless sky, and the sun is sitting low on the horizon shining brightly. It's a good omen," Commander Faulkner said.

"I don't believe in omens," Joseph countered, as he slowly awoke, rubbing his eyes.

After washing up, he followed his usual morning routine before stopping by the porthole window. He peered out and saw no ships in the distance, only a rolling sea and an uncertain future.

***

Joseph glanced around the cabin before stepping into the narrow passageway. A backpack over his shoulder and a leather briefcase in his hand, Joseph remembered his first conversation with Doctor Philips on the way to the sickbay.

Joseph had told the doctor that he had never sailed on a ship before or set foot in a plane. "Boarding a helicopter and flying to Dome Fuji will be a nightmare for me; I'm afraid of heights."

"A glass of Scotch whiskey always calms me down before a flight," Doc had said, pouring himself a full glass of his most excellent single malt Scotch whiskey. "I remember my first flight; I was strapped to a gurney at the back of a helicopter air ambulance."

Joseph said inquisitively, "Why? What happened?"

"I was a green eighteen-year-old naval cadet doing snowmobile training on frozen Lake Meade when my machine fell through a patch of soft ice. Paramedics pulled me out of the icy water and airlifted me to Dome Halley Hospital. I suffered deep frostbite, lost two toes on my right foot."

"If I had a choice, I wouldn't step inside any aircraft."

"I understand what you are saying, Joseph. But you must be in Dome Fuji no later than February 15."

"I could have sailed to Port of Davis, then taken a country-track bus to Dome Fuji and arrived in Dome Fuji with one day to spare," Joseph had said with a tone of spontaneous confidence.

"The Council of Elders canceled private and commercial shipping permits to and from Antarctica. In any case, the country-track bus service to Dome Fuji does not run this late in the summer; the ice is too soft."

"Personally, I don't particularly care for the Council of Elders or their politics," Joseph said.

"Is that so? Well, you should; they are the most selfless individuals I've encountered."

"Doc, I understand all that, and I'm grateful," Joseph said. "The Arunui family wouldn't have survived the Great Rebellion without Rachel Sibley and the Council of Elders' help. There was no manufacturing, and food was more valuable than gold, diamonds, and petroleum."

"It is an insane world. Freelanders have come far since the days of Shustak, Alviero, and Sibley," Doc had said, as he refilled his glass with more Scotch. "Admittedly, we Freelanders made many social, political, and economic mistakes along the way, and yet Freelanders have created the most significant social transformation in human history; a fundamental human right cannot have a price attached. So, we have food in our bellies, a roof over our heads, and unconditional respect for each other. Total respect is the tie that separates us Freelanders from the Allied folks, and makes us unique, and we are unique, every one of us. Social divisiveness is not humanity's curse. Greed is humanity's curse. Today, Indian-registered deep-water harvesters flying the Allied flag trawl the Bohai Sea for krill and burn our deep-water harvesters."

***

Doc discussed the Arctic/Antarctic-Freeland Agreement (AAFA) protecting the Freelanders in the Northern Hemisphere, Australia and its satellite states in the Corral Sea, the Pacific Ocean, New Zealand, and Antarctica below latitude 61 degrees south. For more than a century, military, and civilian maritime vessels of nations other than those protected by the AAFA could not cross the 61st parallel south. In contrast, the Freelander Navy protected the Freelander fishing fleets trawling Antarctic waters. The harvesting and processing of krill was an overexploited rich source of high-quality protein.

"Why do we have an Arctic/Antarctic-Freeland Agreement if we don't enforce it?" Joseph had asked.

"The illegal harvesting of krill will inevitably lead to a serious conflict with the Allied nations. But this is not the time to reignite hostilities against united and allied nations (UAN) over our territorial waters and fishing rights!"

"So, we say nothing, do nothing about the illegal trawling. We sit idly by while our people starve to death when there are no more fish to catch."

"No. We must stop illegal fishing and secure a future for our people," Doc countered. "But another all-out war against the UAN is a frightening scenario, Armageddon, the scientists say."

"Armageddon?"

29

"Armageddon is where the last battle on Earth will take place. An ancient prophecy…the meek shall inherit the Earth and all that."

"Do you think that such a war will come in our lifetime?"

Doc gulped down the last few drops of whiskey in his glass. "For more than one hundred years, there has been a delicate balance between the people who have embraced the values of Freelander Society and people trying their best to destroy it or tip the delicate balance their way. But they failed and will fail again because there are two-billion registered Freelanders today from all social classes and political leaders, philanthropists, intellectuals. Members of the World Elite Fellowship, the Vanguard Army of Europe and Russia, Royal Astronomical Society, Holy Astronomical Society, The Māori Brethren, Anzac Brotherhood, and the Freelander Liberation Army."

"You haven't answered my question, Doc."

Doc poured himself another shot of Scotch whiskey. "Yes, Joseph, I do believe that war is inevitable in our lifetime. Rachel Sibley's death card is still on the negotiating table. Human stupidity will destroy this world. It is just a matter of time."

Joseph had thought Doc made a lot of sense. The Freelanders had Rachel Sibley's death card with thousands of nuclear warheads buried under the Arctic/Antarctic ice sheets. Simultaneous detonations of nuclear warheads would melt the Earth's polar caps, drowning the great coastal cities of the UAN and much more.

"If we detonate the nuclear warheads, the Freelander dream on Earth is over."

"Forget Earth, Joseph, look to Galraithia! The future for our Freelander brethren is on Galraithia!"

Joseph understood that Doc was correct. People worldwide were united in facing the grim future of Earth. Galraithia offered new opportunities, challenges, and a haven for the oppressed, and Joseph Arunui would be instrumental in helping the Freelanders reach it.

***

Joseph tapped on the open sickbay door.

"Ah, Joseph, come in. I was beginning to worry," Doc said.

As Joseph sat down, he looked relaxed and happy. "I wouldn't leave without saying goodbye."

"There are moments when it's best to depart without saying farewell," Doc stated, his voice tinged with sorrow.

"Come with me to Dome Fuji. It's not too late, Doc. Professor Briar could really use someone with your knowledge and experience."

"My life is here. On this ship," Doc said proudly. "Commander Brindle will be the one looking after you from now on. Martin is a good man and a good friend. He is the right man to have on your side. Otherwise, Admiral Fletcher would not have selected Martin to escort you to Dome Fuji. I suspect Admiral Fletcher has a bolder plan for Martin."

Doc then opened the top drawer of his office desk and pulled out a small cardboard box wrapped in orange-colored paper. "This is for you, Joseph, a farewell gift."

Silently regretting that he did not bring a gift, Joseph took the cardboard box, unsure of what to say or do. He hadn't ever received a gift from anyone outside his family. He awkwardly thanked the doctor.

"Come on, open it up!" Doc said anxiously.

31

Joseph looked at Doc and smiled as he removed the wrapping paper and put it in his pocket; the colored paper was hard to find and costly. He then looked inside the box and saw an old-style wristwatch.

"I added a tiny Van Wagner crystal to power the display screen," Doc said proudly. "The top button activates a homing beacon with a circular range of 50 miles."

Joseph thanked Doc Philips and pondered which wrist the watch should go on.

"It goes on the left wrist," Doc said, smiling.

"Thank you once again, Doc. I won't forget your kindness."

Doc shook Joseph's hand. "Well, my boy, this is goodbye. When you walk out that door, do not look back. Treat life the same way, or you will never move forward. Leave all regrets behind, free yourself from self-doubt. And do your best not to over-complicate your life."

For Joseph, articulating his thoughts and feelings was never easy, and he resigned himself to the fact that he would never see Doc Philips again. He wrote in his diary:

"I have learned to appreciate Doc Philips's encyclopedic knowledge of all things. The good doctor believes conquering the vastness of Interstellar Space and colonizing Galraithia increases the odds of humankind surviving the next millennium."

***

Joseph consciously avoided the mess hall and galley because the foul smell triggered his seasickness. He carefully pushed open the final watertight door and stepped out onto the cold and blustery aft deck. His designated muster station was located in the stern section of the ship.

Joseph removed the hood of his Drexlar thermal suit and patiently waited for Commander Brindle, who was approaching from the helicopter hangar.

"Joseph, put your hoodie back on."

Hoodies made Joseph's head itch, but he had to endure it to minimize body heat loss. He pulled the Drexler suit hoodie over his head, concealing his short hair and half his face.

"I am ready to leave whenever you are, Commander." Martin looked at Joseph with concern. "I'm afraid I have some bad news. The helicopter is out of action for the time being. Technicians worked all night to repair it but were unsuccessful."

"That's disappointing," Joseph stated firmly. "I was really looking forward to it."

"That's not what Doc told me."

"You spoke with Doc?"

"I did. Your fear of flying could jeopardize the entire mission."

"What I told Doctor Philips was meant to be confidential," Joseph said.

"Yeah, well, the good doctor informed me that Captain Wheeler has made other arrangements for you."

"Other arrangements?"

"A personal air vehicle (PAV) has departed from Mawson and is en route to our rendezvous point, Shanawi Station."

"Our rendezvous point?" Joseph said, not knowing anything about Shanawi Station.

"You want to go to Dome Fuji, don't you?"

"Well, yes," Joseph replied with a blank look on his face.

"The PAV is coming from Mawson. It doesn't have the range to reach this ship. Shanawi Station is on the edge of its range limit. Do you understand?"

Joseph frowned. "I understand perfectly."

"You have to trust me, Joseph. Trust each other. This is your chance to conquer your fear of flying."

Joseph unfastened the straps and lifted off his heavy backpack. The arrival of more unwelcome news only heightened the tension festering inside him.

"A lifeboat will take us as far as the low ice shelf. From there, it's a short trek over the ice field to Shanawi Station," Martin said.

Joseph, ever the pessimist, was unhappy about the PAV en route to Shanawi Station, and traveling in a rickety old boat was also unwelcome news.

"Have you had breakfast yet?"

"No, I'm not hungry," Joseph replied.

"Do you feel ill?"

"No, sir, I feel perfectly fine."

Martin let out an audible sigh.

"I don't feel hungry in the morning," Joseph stated.

"Well, you have to eat something before we leave," Martin said, handing Joseph a protein bar.

Joseph made it clear that he disliked protein bars, emphasizing that they tasted bad.

"Don't give me a tough time, Joseph. Eat the protein bar and wait here until I return. Don't speak to anyone while I'm gone, not a word."

Joseph wasn't paying attention.

"Look at me when I'm speaking to you."

"I'm sorry, Commander, my mind was somewhere else."

"Joseph, it's time to focus. Our mission to Dome Fuji is of utmost importance and highly classified."

Joseph lowered his eyes and apologized to Martin for his childish behavior.

***

Martin and the other officers had little to do with Joseph Arunui. They had nothing in common except that Professor Arunui was a loyal Freelander. The previous evening, Joseph was introduced at the dinner table as a brilliant young astrophysicist with little known about his background. However, Joseph left a positive impression on everyone he met, including Commander Andrew Faulkner, the most cynical officer. Martin thought that the young VIP seemed shy and uncomfortable around people. However, as the evening progressed, Joseph became witty and entertaining. Despite this, Martin felt that Joseph was hiding something. Martin wasn't wrong because Joseph kept a detailed diary recording his moods, thoughts, feelings, and the good and bad points of people he had met. Joseph treated everyone the same and equally; he showed genuine respect without any conditions attached. Yet, his peers had little or no empathy for Joseph Arunui, a professor in his own right. The scientific community labeled him as a super-intelligent outcast with no friends.

Joseph took out his diary from his breast pocket, and a faded newspaper clipping fell out. It was a photograph of a sickly-looking eight-year-old boy wrapped up in a Red Cross blanket. The faded newspaper clipping read:

"Young Joseph Arunui, the youngest survivor of the undersea earthquake that struck the west coast of New Zealand in the early hours of March 27, 2396. The powerful shockwave flattened the cities of Westharbour and Punakaiki, as well as the small township of Greymouth. Joseph lost his entire family, and fifty thousand people lost their lives."

When rescuers found Joseph, they had pulled him out from the rubble more dead than alive. He had hip fractures, two broken ribs, and a collapsed lung. There were other painful memories from that dreadful day, memories Joseph couldn't erase from his mind. A photographer who was a member of a crack 27-man rescue team from Japan had photographed Joseph leaving the hospital wrapped up in a Red Cross blanket. The photographer made much money after the World Media Group bought the copyright. But making money from someone else's misfortune troubled the Japanese man so he put the cash in Joseph's bank account. Joseph never knew where the money came from or the name of the Shinto priest who photographed him.

***

Returning to the wheelhouse, binoculars in hand, Captain Wheeler peered through the high-resolution lenses. His old eyes spotted large fragments of drift ice on a flat sea and petrels sweeping low over the water's surface. Cyclonic winds had pounded his ship a few days earlier, and giant waves swept over the bow and aft deck. Metal cables and extendible webbings had snapped. The ship's 7-ton short-range helicopter slid across the wet aft deck and crashed into the portside bulkhead and Lifeboat-6. While the lifeboat sustained only superficial damage, it may have prevented the small helicopter from sliding into the angry ocean.

Captain Wheeler looked around the wheelhouse. Thirty-two-year-old Andrew Faulkner and twenty-three-year-old Satori Thomas, both brilliant individuals, were busy training twenty-year-old Lieutenant Lesley Fredericks, an assistant engineer and a timid introvert who couldn't tolerate Faulkner's behavior. The helmsman, a 36-year-old Englishman named Troy Michaels, had served in the Navy for 18 years. While Troy and Andrew Faulkner got along well, Martin Brindle and Faulkner had a mutual dislike for each other. Their lack of collaboration stemmed from past experiences when inexperienced commanders in the Freelander military chose to work in pairs, making them easy targets for UAN Sniper drone units.

***

"Lieutenant Fredericks, any luck with the MBSA?" Captain Wheeler asked.

Fredericks was feeling tired and sleepy nearing the end of a twelve-hour nightshift.

He was trying hard to stay alert but he could barely keep his eyes open. "Lieutenant Fredericks!"

"Yes, Captain."

"Any luck with the old multibeam sonar array?"

"Aye, sir. I got the MBSA to work finally but I had to scavenge a few electronic parts from the engine room."

"Good work, Lieutenant, keep me informed."

"Captain," Lieutenant Fredericks whispered, "the MBSA has detected methane gas bubbling up to the surface from several hyperthermal vents on the seafloor."

"Show me."

"The deepest hydrothermal vents are this area, sir," Fredericks said, pointing to an area on a map called Haggits Pillar.

"Send an encrypted copy of the current data to Admiral Fletcher. There may still be time to cap the vents before the winter weather sets in."

"Aye, aye, Captain."

"Commander Faulkner, the mast camera, operational status, please."

Faulkner looked at the grainy images being transmitted to a display screen from the gyro-stabilized multi-vision camera mounted on the top of FS *Taimaha's* integrated mast.

"The camera mounts were fixed overnight, Captain. The camera is operational."

"MBSA data encryption successfully transmitted to Admiral Fletcher as you instructed, Captain," Fredericks said.

"Thank you, Lieutenant. Now go to bed and get some sleep."

Faulkner watched the thin young man next to him. "Look at yourself, Fredericks! You look like crap."

"Mr. Faulkner, stop harassing young Fredericks, or you'll find yourself on permanent night duty."

"Captain, he's insubordinate, a slacker, sir."

Fredericks wanted to turn around and say something to Faulkner, but he left the bridge without saying another word.

"Mr. Faulkner, I am not interested in what you have to say," Captain Wheeler said. "Now, I am giving you a direct order, ready Lifeboat-6! I want Mr. Arunui off this ship as soon as possible."

"Lifeboat-6 has a broken winch handle. It's tagged out for repair, sir."

"Then, get a repair team down there and fix it!"

"Commander Brindle issued the work order, sir."

"Andrew, I don't want to hear any excuses! I want the winch handle fixed! Now, see to it, please."

"Aye, sir."

Satori whispered a remark about Faulkner under her breath, and with a mocking smile, she told him that he was an asshole. Faulkner's face flushed red with anger and embarrassment walking out of the bridge.

"Lieutenant Thomas, keep your eyes peeled on the radar scanner. Call me when the incoming PAV from Mawson reaches Shanawi Station. I'll be in my quarters."

"Yes, Captain."

***

Presage

Satori was a precocious three-year-old when Catherine
Thomas and Meg Hartwell visited a rundown orphanage on
the outskirts of Osaka, Japan. Both Catherine and Meg
relished their successful careers in the world of finance.
The Financial media often described the two women as
beautiful, mega-rich, shrewd, and business savvy.
Catherine and Meg could afford all the material wealth life
had to offer. However, fertility treatments had failed both
women. Call it luck, call it destiny, the life of the three-
year-old was never the same again after the sympathetic
Catherine, with the consent of life partner Meg, signed the
necessary papers to adopt Satori.

Satori excelled academically throughout her schooling,
namely mathematics, science, economics. Ruthlessly
competitive, she also excelled in all sports that she entered.
She had no equals on the sports field, and few of her
friends matched her elegance, etiquette, and grace of
manner in Osaka's cultured social circles. Satori had
everything a modern young woman could wish for: the best
designer clothing, shoes, and jewelry from Paris, Rome,
and enjoyed homes in Osaka, Tokyo, Sydney, London, and
Beijing. The Thomas family had plenty of money and many
influential business friends. A career path in high finance
awaited Satori; she would take over the family business one
day. Catherine and Meg expected nothing less.

The lifestyle of the world's poor was vastly different from
the lavish lifestyle Satori enjoyed. Financial support from
the rich remained socially divisive then as now. About 97%
of the world's impoverished could not afford to provide
food or contribute to their children's education expenses.
So, it's not surprising that very few children of poor

families received any formal education beyond the second grade. Too many people in the world struggled to find work and desperately needed food, medicine, clean water, shoes, clothes, and rent assistance while welfare payments were unavailable.

Historians said the world went mad after the Great Rebellion of 2170 when Rachel Sibley's Freelander movement toppled governments during a time of great wealth and prosperity. At that time, there had been an overabundance of food, but only rich people could afford to buy it. The rich often threw away perfectly good food, buried the excess in waste dumps instead of improving the lives of the world's poor. Earth had a population of 12 billion people in 2170, and 29 percent of the Earth's total land area was fit for human habitation. The first Freelander communities predicted global famine unparalleled in human history. The wanton deforestation by city managers and property developers sprouted mega-sized cities with all the needed infrastructures. However, with little or no work and money for food and health care, the poor waited like hungry vultures for food. The market failures and dramatic climate shifts in the past were just a few of the warning signs that humanity on Earth was failing. Past generations chose to overlook the warning signs; it was always a problem for future generations to solve.

****

And now the population on Earth had exploded to 32 billion people. Overpopulation combined with social and economic disparities between people in different regions of the world, and the ever-diminishing food supply were damaging every society on Earth. Cities of concrete and steel replaced vast swathes of forests set aside for agriculture. Wanton deforestation increased the air temperature, and sea levels were rising. Entire regions became too hot in the daytime, particularly in West Africa, the Middle East, South-East-Asia, and Oceania.

In overcrowded cities such as Sydney, the powerful determined who lived and who died. The vulnerable and the sick accepted their fate silently. Without compassion and ethics, they left the dead where they fell in streets and alleys.

Seagulls swooped down, pecked out eyes, and menaced the water rats that feasted on bloating human flesh. All the while wealthy individuals resided in secure, luxurious apartments with expansive views of Sydney Harbor. Their food supply and clean water were airlifted from the productive free lands in the Riverina District. Catherine Thomas and Meg Hartwell didn't venture outside during the day, not without armed guards. Going out at night was more dangerous and irresponsible; the night belonged to the impoverished people. These roamed the streets, alleyways, the underground sewers of Sydney, hunting water rats to eat, sell and trade them.

***

Satori was uncertain whether a career in commercial banking would make her happy for the rest of her working life. She had experienced her happiest moments going sailing with Meg. She loved the ocean's smell and power, the pounding surf, and walking barefoot on a sandy beach at low tide.

A recruiting poster presented a glimpse of a happy future in serving the Freelander navy though only Freelanders could apply. Satori did not lose hope; she was fortunate enough to be born into a Freelander family. But her biological parents had died in a road accident shortly after her birth and left her a birthright instead of money and property. Catherine was furious when Satori told her how badly she wanted a naval career. While Meg couldn't be happier to hear of this decision, Catherine was seething. She blamed Meg for teaching Satori the basics of sailing and spending too much time on racing yachts and enjoying the sea and ocean.

When Catherine refused to speak to Satori, Meg begged her to stop being so selfish and implored her to listen to what Satori had to say. Throughout the afternoon, Satori recounted to Catherine and Meg how a chance meeting with a woman named Beth was the catalyst for her decision to join the Freelander Navy: "It was sweltering outside. I wanted to go for a swim. I packed some cornbread and a water bottle in my rucksack and headed to the harbor. I did not bother with security or an escort. Still, I had the good sense to wear a security bracelet and strolled down the deserted buildings and past burned-out cars on York Street without fear."

"Leaving the Tower Apartments was foolish and irresponsible," Catherine reproached.

"It was suffocating in the apartment, Mother; the air conditioning unit wasn't working. I wanted to go for a swim."

"Don't lie to me, Satori Thomas. The air conditioning unit was working perfectly," Catherine countered.

Meg frowned at Catherine. "Stop interrupting and let Satori speak. Now, tell us what happened next."

Satori continued to share her memories of that day. "An old woman was walking down the dirty sidewalk, looking into stormwater drains. I stopped and called out hello, but I must have startled her because she hurried away. I remember shouting, 'Wait! Don't go. I won't hurt you!' The woman paused, turned around, and approached me.

"She said, 'I'm Beth. What's your name?'

"'I'm Satori Thomas. Great to meet you, Beth.'

"'You're not from around here, not with clothes like that. Where do you hail from, my dear?'

"'Oh, from various places, but I was born in Japan.'

"'Japan! You've traveled far, my dear.'

"'Although Japan is far away, my family and I moved to the Tower Apartments across York Street.'

"'Well, you and your family made a mistake coming to Sydney. Don't you realize how risky this city can be, young lady?'

"'Every major city is dangerous.'

"'Before chaos engulfed the world, Sydney was a beautiful and peaceful place to live and raise a family,' Beth said, her voice tinged with sadness.

"'Do you have a family?' I asked.

"'Just my son. He's serving as an officer in the Freelander Navy. Proud of him every day.'"

***

Satori and Beth had then walked side by side, and they talked of this and that until they reached the marble steps of the York Street railway station, one of many no-go zones in the city.

"Beth, meeting you today wasn't a mistake, but I can't go any further. The railway station is located in the no-go zone. I have a security bracelet, but it's not safe to enter the railway station."

"You must be rich. Only rich people can afford a gold security bracelet," Beth said.

"It was a birthday gift from a dear friend."

"A wonderful birthday gift is one that serves its purpose well," Beth said.

"Indeed."

"Thank you for keeping me company, my dear. Stay safe."

Satori opened her rucksack before the woman could walk away. "Beth, wait! Here's some food and water. I'll bring more tomorrow."

Beth gently touched Satori's sleeve and said, "Thank you for your kindness, my dear."

"Goodbye, Beth. I will see you tomorrow morning. Same time, same place, okay?"

"Yes. Same time, same place. Goodbye."

***

"The next day, I sat on the worn steps of York Street railway station, waiting for Beth. I kept glancing at my watch, but there was no sign of her. With each passing minute, my excitement turned into worry. Where could she be? I walked down York Street, Malley Road, and the area of the city known for its dirty alleyways and hidden entrances to the abandoned residential district, burned-out cars, and hungry squawking seagulls that swoop down to feed on flying insects. I stayed there for a short while, watching birds chase a swarm of insects towards Sydney harbor, where the harbor people were waiting with their open nets, ready to catch the flying supply of protein.

"Then, the quiet in the city returned, I saw a young man in a Naval uniform approaching. As the man approached, I felt anxious about my safety and considered using the laser pistol in my rucksack. I warned him firmly, 'Don't come any closer!' He then introduced himself as Commander Nathaniel Ellery, Beth's son. He apologized for startling me, as that was not his intention. Commander Ellery thanked me for helping his mother, which made me happy; however, he informed me that Beth had passed away, as her heart had stopped beating sometime during the night. 'Beth was a beautiful lady, a gentle soul. I'm so sorry for your loss.'

"'Don't be sorry. It was her time.'

"'I would like to see her and pay my respects,' I told Beth's son.

"We then walked down to Circular Quay, where a continuous line of timber-clad houses lined the water's edge. Most of the homes were empty as people had moved closer to the food distribution centers."

***

Nathaniel and Satori walked to First Avenue North, a hilly street that lay 50 yards from the harbor's northern shore. Beth's house was the third house on the uphill side of the street and the only one painted lime green. A path of broken red brick led to the front door Beth had painstakingly restored and painted orange.

Nathaniel led Satori down a narrow corridor to a small bedroom at the back of the house. She sighed deeply and wept at first sight of Beth's body lying on a bed opposite a boarded-up window, her face and body covered with a white bedsheet. Satori recited the Shinto Death Prayer in Japanese. Nathaniel, who respected his Freelander tradition, began the Freelander Rite of Committal. Satori asked if she could light the funeral torch Nathaniel intended to throw inside his mother's house, as was the custom.

Satori and Nathaniel held hands as they mourned the loss of Beth. Following tradition, they lit the torch together. Dense smoke soon enveloped the harbor as the lime-green house was engulfed and reduced to ashes.

***

Later in the afternoon, Nathanial separated his mother's ashes and charred remains he found in the smoldering debris. He then buried Beth's blackened bones where her colorful house stood and scattered her ashes under an old rusty bridge.

"I have to go home," Satori said.

"Don't go home just yet," Nathanial pleaded.

Satori looked up at the sky. "No. I have to go home. It will be dark soon."

"Nonsense, there's three hours of daylight left," Nathanial countered.

"But we can't stay here."

"We'll go to my ship," Nathanial said quickly. "And I'll show you around. No harm will come to you, I promise."

"Where are we going? To the old warship that's docked in the harbor?"

"FS *Albany* is an old ship and the first Freelander vessel to break the Allied blockade of Albany," Nathanial said.

"I would love to see your ship, but I don't want you to get into trouble."

"Civilians usually cannot come within 20 feet of a naval vessel, but the captain won't mind if I bring a guest on board."

"You're certain the captain won't mind?"

"Captain Carpenter is a good man, and I'm sure he'll be happy to meet you."

"If you say so," Satori murmured, unsure if Captain Carpenter would be pleased to see a total stranger being attended to by one of his youngest officers.

***

A month later, Satori decided on a career path completely different from high finance; she enlisted in the Freelander Navy and graduated at the top of her class from the Terra Nova Bay Naval Academy in Antarctica. When Meg and Catherine arrived at the graduation ceremony, Satori was surprised. However, she was even more surprised to see Nathaniel Ellery, whom she had not seen since the end of the summer holidays in Sydney. They celebrated late into the early morning and woke up around noon, side by side in one bed. Nathaniel had fallen in love with Satori, the ideal life partner he had been searching for.

In a tragic turn of events, Nathaniel's helicopter, while courageously returning from a critical sea rescue mission during severe weather conditions, unfortunately crashed off Antarctica's Lazarev Coast. Meg Hartwell died a few weeks later. A security team found Meg's naked body near the steps of the York Street railway station, murdered for her designer clothes and shoes and her expensive pieces of jewelry.

Police arrested a 49-year-old woman who was discovered wearing Meg's clothes. The woman confessed to the crime, claiming it was justifiable. In her police statement, she said, "The rich bitch was strutting around with money, wearing expensive jewelry while people around her were starving to death. I took the money and sold the jewelry to a local Xiangshan trader for food and medicine for my two boys."

The arrest and subsequent trial intensified the consequences for Meg's killer. Convicted of robbery and murder, the judge delivered his verdict death by burning in the nearest public place. Military police took the convicted woman to Sydney's York Street Station and tied her to a nearby metal post with rope. Before a tumultuous crowd of harbor residents, the executioner delivered justice as a warning to other potential thieves and murderers.

***

Living without Meg had become unbearable for the distraught Catherine. Satori was often away, serving in the Freelander Navy, leaving Catherine to confront her emotions alone. The solitude became overwhelming for her. Catherine made a difficult decision to sell all their business interests to billionaire philanthropist Walter Briar. The evening after signing the legal papers, Catherine, in her despair, tragically took her own life by cutting her wrists. News of Catherine's death shocked Satori. She looked to Captain Wheeler for emotional support. She sought his advice, which he provided eagerly, just as his Vice Admiral father offered him emotional support and immediate assistance when Jonathon joined the Freelander Navy.

Jonathon joined the Navy not out of a desire to explore the world, but because his father expected nothing less from his only son. He enrolled in the Terra Nova Bay Naval Academy, a longstanding tradition in the Wheeler family that dated back to the first Freelanders, who were needed as sailors in Antarctica following the Great Rebellion.

Jonathon quickly advanced through the ranks, earning a fine reputation as an innovative battle tactician and an inspirational leader. The Freelander Admiralty appointed Jonathon as acting 1st Lieutenant aboard FS *Elisabeth* through his skills rather than family connections.

Under the watchful eye of Captain Wheeler, Satori quickly developed a reputation as an expert navigator and battle tactician. Yet, a few hours before the FS *Taimaha* sailed, Admiral Marcus Fletcher of the Freelander Admiralty invited Captain Wheeler to his home on Old Port Road. After a light lunch and refreshments, the conversation between Admiral Fletcher and Captain Wheeler started to heat up when Fletcher revealed the Admiralty's plan to retire and scrap half a dozen ships, including FS *Taimaha*.

"Jonathon, there's nothing that can be done; it's out of my hands," Admiral Fletcher said. "FS *Exeter* and *Trident* are also on the scheduled dismantling list. So, you're not the only captain without a job."

"And my crew, my officers, what happens to them?"

"Until a new ship is constructed, the civilian crew will be reassigned to other duties within the Navy Defense Portal."

There was no doubt in Admiral Fletcher's mind that Captain Wheeler was disappointed. However, Admiral Fletcher, his leadership skills, and his years of experience in the Navy had taught him to disconnect from any personal feelings; his duty as a leader must come first.

"Jonathon, I received another urgent message from Admiral Cunningham this morning. A list of names, candidates for the new astronaut training program."

"Astronaut training? That's news to me!" Captain Wheeler admitted. "The Phoenix Spacecraft is nowhere near ready, much less for flight testing, which I understand won't be until the end of next year."

"Well, I can tell you with certainty that Phoenix is six-months from flight-status-ready. Lieutenant Commander

Brindle, First Lieutenant Satori Thomas, Second Lieutenant Lesley Fredericks, Able Seaman Aitama, and Leading Seaman Samuel Hinchcliff will be reassigned to the Science Portal and undergo astronaut training and evaluation," Admiral Fletcher said, handing Jonathon the decrypted message.

"Admiral, this has to be a mistake, surely?"

"No. Jonathon, I'm afraid not."

Rear Admiral Fletcher walked over to the window that looked out on to Southport Harbor. "There was a time when the oceans and seas offered humanity a long-term future. Today, we say the same for Deep Space exploration."

"With all due respect, sir, I believe the Admiralty is making a huge mistake. We must protect our core interests on Earth, not some faraway planet."

"Jonathon, I have voiced my opinion in that regard more often than any other admiral, and I'm always honest with you no matter what, you know that. But we need a disciplined, well-trained crew on board Phoenix, and the best young people in their chosen field serve in the Freelander Navy."

"Admiral, the Science Portal is a civilian agency whose dubious financial practices are wrapped with the Xiangshan traders."

"There's no point arguing the details, Jonathon, the decision on this matter has been made by the Admiralty and the CFE."

"In that case, I would like the record to state that I strenuously object."

Admiral Fletcher got up from his comfortable armchair and walked over to a glass-fronted liquor cabinet. He poured French brandy into two glasses, filling them to the brim. "Here, drink up."

"I don't drink while I'm on duty."

"And I don't drink alone. You and I have been friends close to forty years," Admiral Fletcher said, softening his tone, "and I know that look on your face. You're angry, and I'm sorry you feel that way."

"Admiral, I have preparations to make before departure. With your permission, I would like to return to my ship."

"Yes, of course."

Admiral Fletcher picked up the phone on the small table next to his favorite armchair and called his secretary. "Anna May, bring me the yellow envelope on my desk, please."

After a moment, a slender round-faced woman on the far side of 40 walked into the large dining room. She handed the Admiral a wax-sealed yellow envelope, and he returned her smile.

"Thank you."

"Miss Davis, thank you for preparing lunch. It was lovely."

"It was my pleasure, Captain."

Admiral Fletcher handed Jonathon the yellow envelope with this inscription written on the front and back: *Do not open until you reach Macquarie Island.* Jonathon put the envelope in his briefcase and stood up to leave.

"Have a safe journey."

"Thank you, Admiral."

Admiral Fletcher walked to the dining room's harbor-side window as Captain Wheeler's car left the stately Fletcher mansion, drove up Old Port Road, and entered the motorway. The admiral suddenly had a premonition that he would never see Jonathon again. At that moment, he unknowingly stared straight at FS *Taimaha*, docked in Southport Harbor.

***

Admiral Fletcher left the dining room and hurried to his private office, the largest of six bright and airy rooms on the east wing of the main house. He sat before his mahogany table and studied Joseph Arunui's psychological profile, and a new form of mathematics Joseph had developed before his fifteenth birthday. Reading Joseph's personal profile and family history, Admiral Fletcher acknowledged a well-known fact: not since Einstein and William Briar had someone put forth groundbreaking theories so distant from modern astrophysics. The psychological profile revealed the sadder side of Joseph's young life. The terrible earthquake that had almost killed him had changed his life. Some of Joseph's physical scars had faded, but deep emotional scars may never heal. The quake was a recurring nightmare in Joseph's mind; he was the little boy with long, brown, tight curls and hazel eyes, crawling over rubble, over the bodies of his dead grandfather and grandmother. For a small child, the physical pain and emotional distress must have been unbearable, and ever since that terrible day, Joseph had suffered chronic depression, bouts of self-harm, and crippling self-doubt. Then, there were days when the difference between sanity and insanity was only a thin, foggy line. Even so, during the lengthy period of healing and rehabilitation, Joseph's steely resolve and intestinal fortitude had earned him the heartfelt admiration of many people along the way.

53

The admiral became increasingly fascinated by Joseph Arunui's story, his work on faster-than-light travel, and Dark Matter theory. What troubled the admiral was that Joseph's Freelander heritage was the reason for the lack of support from the global scientific community. Despite Arunui's contentious theories and the absence of backing, the admiral believed that with Joseph's assistance, the Freelanders would one day be able to colonize a habitable star.

The admiral then opened Martin Brindle's psychological profile. He had an exceedingly high opinion of Martin's seafaring skills. He thought the former fist-fighting champion would be the best man to protect Arunui. Professor William Briar regarded Martin Brindle as a competent commander. Some members of the Council of Freelander Elders (CFE) suspected Martin had divided loyalties. This concern had arisen because his father was a well-known trader with connections to unscrupulous Xiangshan merchants. Despite both of Martin's parents supporting the Freelanders during the uprisings in Western Australia and the Australian Civil War, doubts about his allegiance lingered. The victorious Freelanders waved banners, and families mourned their dead loved ones. From the ashes of burned-out cities, the Freelanders had made a new beginning, a new way of living in Australia, the first Freeland country. As the Freeland movement spread to New Zealand and Antarctica, the Brindle family had left Western Australia and migrated to Antarctica, where they built their family home in Dome Halley, the first Antarctic Freeland city.

Martin's father, Ethan, and his uncle, Josiah Brindle, founded the Brindle Brothers Salvage Company, and his mother, Sara, set up the first school for the blind in Antarctica shortly after Martin was born.

The Reckoning

Joseph Arunui approached the ship's port side, gripping the salt-encrusted railing for support and feeling the invigorating motion of the sea fuel his spirit of adventure. He gazed at the distant Ranvik Glacier, partly shrouded in fog, and realized he had a long journey ahead before reaching Shanawi Station and, ultimately, his final destination, Dome Fuji.

Joseph shifted his gaze as two men approached. He remained silent while observing the two men walking closely together and talking. One was tall and thin, with deep-set eyes and a worn, weathered face. The other man was stocky and tough-looking, with bushy eyebrows, a graying beard, and a square jaw. He had a snarling wolf tattoo on the back of his fully shaved head.

As the two men walked past Joseph without acknowledging him, the thin-framed man accidentally bumped into Joseph. He glared at Joseph and gave him a stern look with no apology.

Joseph had never seen either of these two men before. Without knowing their names, Joseph nicknamed the man who had accidentally bumped into him "Wiry Man," noticing his lean, athletic build and quick movements. With his thick, graying beard and hearty laugh, the stout man became known to Joseph as "Bearded Man," capturing his robust appearance and friendly demeanor.

***

Later, Joseph walked along a green-painted walkway that led to the aft deck muster station. Once again, he saw Wiry Man and Bearded Man. They were preparing a working zone between the base of the outrigged davit arm and Lifeboat-6, tying off a large piece of canvas and shielding the work area from the wind. When Joseph arrived at the aft deck muster station, Wiry Man gave him a suspicious and irritable stare and said, "I've never seen a civilian passenger on a Navy ship before."

Bearded Man glanced over at Joseph, who avoided direct eye contact.

"You must be wealthy. Loaded with money," remarked Wiry Man.

Joseph felt an instinctive urge to remain silent and avoid direct eye contact, pushing him to be cautious and move to another area of the ship. However, he was at his muster station, where Commander Brindle had ordered him to be.

"Leave the boy alone and prepare the welding machine," Bearded Man said firmly.

Wiry Man prepared the welding machine and cast a menacing look at Joseph.

Bearded Man put on his long leather apron and gloves. He said, "Step away from the welding machine, Douglas, and don't look at the welding arc while I'm working. Its light can burn your eyes in just a few seconds."

Joseph looked directly at the wiry man, who was named Douglas.

"Samuel, I don't appreciate you telling me what to do. You're not my boss," Douglas said, frowning.

Douglas's frustrated voice stirred secret amusement in Joseph, making him chuckle inwardly.

Meanwhile, Samuel donned a black welding helmet over his face, disappeared behind the canvas shield, and began fusing together broken metal pieces, ejecting hundreds of burning sparks, welding fumes, and bluish-white light. The winch handle was repaired quickly, as Commander Martin Brindle requested efficiency. Afterward, Samuel used his hand-held radio to contact Martin. "Winch handle repaired, Commander."

"Good Job, Samuel. You and Douglas have done well."

"Collaborating with Douglas Tyler proves to be quite challenging, sir."

Douglas stood up and approached Samuel. "I heard that! You are truly a bastard, Samuel Hinchcliff. You are not my friend."

"Alright, enough of that, you two," Martin ordered.

Grimacing slightly, Samuel said, "We are both ready to start on another job, Commander. Just tell us when and where sir."

"You will save us a lot of time hooking the davit arm to Lifeboat-6."

"Aye, aye, sir. I'll get on it right away."

"Good man."

"I like Commander Brindle," Douglas said.

"You like Commander Brindle, but you don't like the other officers," Samuel said.

"I don't like men like Commander Faulkner, the officer I dislike the most," Douglas snapped.

Joseph continued writing in his diary, occasionally glancing up to watch Samuel as he hooked the davit arm to Lifeboat 6. Samuel then loaded tobacco into a hand-carved pipe, lit it, and exhaled puffs of white smoke into the cold air.

"You need to calm down and lower your voice," Samuel said.

"No! Someone needs to put that sniggering Faulkner in his place!" Douglas shouted. "Having to submit to being ordered around by him, a lesser man who believes he is all important, sickens me to the core."

"Are you looking for trouble or plain stupid? Faulkner is a Commissioned officer in the Freelander Navy. He's untouchable!" Samuel said firmly.

Douglas caught Joseph staring. "Are you listening to our private conversation, boy?"

"Leave that boy alone and be quiet!" Samuel snapped.

"Shut your mouth, Samuel, and leave me alone," Douglas said with a scowl.

"Douglas, I think you've said more than enough for one day."

The intense conversation between Samuel and Douglas abruptly stopped when Commander Faulkner approached Samuel and said, "The winch handle on the davit arm was repaired twenty minutes ago. Why are you still here talking to this man?"

"Samuel is the best craftsman aboard this ship. He's proud of his work, sir."

Commander Faulkner, his disappointment evident, shot Douglas an angry stare and warned in a low, steely voice, "Not another word from you. Is that clear?"

"Aye, sir."

"Samuel, I will ask you again: Why are you still here chatting instead of working?"

"Douglas and I are awaiting further orders, sir."

"Well, I would be more than happy to give you additional work," Faulkner said mockingly. "Douglas, once you have finished packing the welding gear, go down to the galley and report to the Head Chef. He requires an extra pair of hands in the kitchen."

"Aye, sir."

"The viewing windows need a thorough scrubbing. That will be your job, Samuel."

"Commander Faulkner, sir, a moment of your time, please."

"Go on, Samuel, I'm listening."

"Douglas and I work well as a team, sir, don't split us up."

"Samuel, it took thirty minutes to repair the winch handle, a ten-minute job."

"We lost time in the cargo bay, sir. We needed a piece of canvas for a windbreak. We didn't want hot sparks flying everywhere."

"I don't believe a word of it. You two idlers went down to the cargo bay to drink alcohol."

"No, sir, you are mistaken!" Samuel protested.

"During the last safety audit, Captain Wheeler found a vodka bottle inside a storage locker. Do you have anything that you want to tell me, Samuel? Or do I have to find the culprit myself?"

"Vodka bottle? Douglas and I don't know anything about that, sir."

Samuel began to sweat, and his heartbeat began to race. He had consumed half a bottle of vodka and left it inside a storage locker for safekeeping.

"I don't want to see you and Douglas Tyler working together for the rest of this voyage. Is that clear?"

"Loud and clear, Commander," Samuel replied.

"Good. Now both of you carry on with your assigned duties."

"Aye, sir."

When Samuel and Douglas left, Faulkner turned his attention to Joseph.

"Mr. Arunui, I'm sorry you had to hear all that nonsense. Sailors are hard to handle at times."

"If you say so, Commander."

"Have you filled in your disembarkation card?" Commander Faulkner asked.

"Yes, I have," Joseph replied.

"May I have it, please."

"Doctor Philips has it. I handed my disembarkation card earlier this morning. Is there a problem?"

"No, no problem. Commander Brindle will be here soon. Don't leave your muster station."

"Absolutely, sir," Joseph replied assertively.

***

As Faulkner walked confidently toward the hatchway leading to the wheelhouse, taking long, purposeful strides, Douglas Tyler pulled an imaginary pistol from his hip pocket and aimed it at Commander Faulkner. "I will kill that man someday."

"Douglas, stay well clear of that guy. Do you hear me? He's trouble."

"I reckon a bullet in his brain, or do I open his throat while he's asleep?"

"You don't know what you're saying," Samuel said with an icy stare. "Do you want to end up in Ercial Prison, live inside a converted shipping container, and line up for yellow soup, sardines, and brik bread for the rest of your life?"

"Do you think I care what happens to me?" Douglas said.

"Please listen to me for a moment," Samuel said as Douglas walked away. "Faulkner enjoys irritating people. Then, when their nerves snap and they lose their composure, the green-eyed pig wins."

"I'll be the winner when he's dead," Douglas said, frowning.

"Keep your voice down, you fool."

"Faulkner can't hear me!" Douglas declared. "He's inside the wheelhouse sucking up to the boss, Captain Wheeler."

Samuel gave Douglas a cold stare. "Shut your filthy mouth. Captain Wheeler is a respected veteran of two Freeland wars, and he's a good captain. Now, quiet down."

"I fought in the Freelander wars. I served in Albany's front-line division," Douglas said, raising his voice.

"I said, quiet down!"

"The night before we recaptured Albany, a coordinated naval barrage fell on the east of the city. The defending

Allied armies were on the run, chased by the 22nd Freelander Militia. My son Erik was by my side. He had just finished telling me he was happy the fighting was over. Then, a single gunshot put us both on the ground. Someone yelled, '*Enemy down, move out!*' An EK76 round killed the sniper, and Erik was lying down on his belly, face down. I turned him over, my hands and my body shaking. I still see his head and face half-blown away; I can't get that image out of my mind. My captain raised the Freeland Flag triumphantly, and people came out of hiding. While people celebrated in the streets, I buried my dead son. The days came and went, and I wasted time visiting pubs, downing too many beers. But the painful reality of losing my beautiful boy did not lessen. Then, one day, while I was drinking alone, a guy in a gray tailored suit came running into a pub. I remember the gray suit, but I don't remember the man's name. I think he was the Lord Mayor of Albany, someone important. Anyhow, the man waved a newspaper in the air and shouted the place down for all to hear: '*Every Freelander citizen receives a quarter acre of land,*' the man said, '*more land than anyone would want in a lifetime.*' I was too drunk to think, so I walked out while he talked. He was jabbering about the benefits of owning land and growing crops. There and then, I lost my temper and hit him, knocking the man out cold. Someone called the police because they came and arrested me for breaking the man's jaw. After a tense courtroom standoff, the magistrate found me guilty of aggravated assault, sealing my fate with a firm sentence to the Shoal Bay Rehabilitation Centre."

"You've never been able to control your temper, Douglas. One day, it might get you killed."

"At Shoal Bay Rehab Centre, they controlled my temper and mind."

"The Shoal Bay Rehab Centre is not for the faint-hearted. How long did you stay there?

"Shoal Bay Rehab Centre was my home for one year, three months, and two days. Initially, I found my rehabilitation plan difficult to manage. But I had an exceptional rehab counselor who helped me improve my health and secure full-time employment."

"In Albany?"

"Yes. I joined the Freelander Navy after the rehab counselor drove me to a recruitment center. Have you returned to Albany?"

"No! I carry too many scars from the war, and I have a metal plate in my head to prove it," Samuel said, tapping a finger just above his right ear.

"After fifteen years, I still carry an invisible scar on my heart. Not a day goes by without me thinking of my beautiful boy." Douglas walked away with his head down and hands deep in his pockets.

"Hey! Where are you going?" Samuel asked.

"I'm going home," Douglas replied.

***

Boarding Lifeboat-6 Joseph had a provocative question in his mind: Could he trust Martin Brindle? Although Martin was a capable commander, Joseph sensed that there was a darker side to his personality. This worried him because he struggled to handle any form of hostility directed toward him.

Joseph secured himself into one of the fifty vacant seats in the covered half-cabin. Titanium cables, ceramic brakes, and a robust electric motor gradually lowered Lifeboat-6 into the water. As the lifeboat swayed from side to side, Joseph gripped the edge of his seat until Martin joined him in the cabin.

"We are all set and ready to go, Professor," Martin said.

"Don't call me Professor. My name is Joseph."

"Alright, we're all set and ready to go, Joseph. Is there anything you need or want?"

"Commander, I don't have a life jacket. Should something go wrong…"

"You don't need a life jacket," Martin interrupted. "The water temperature is zero degrees. Cold-shock reflex will drown you in less than a minute if you fall in the water. That's why we wear a self-inflating flotation device called a Roni suit."

"I've never heard of a Roni suit before."

"A Roni suit protects against extreme environmental conditions and has proven to be a lifesaver in water and icy environments. You can find your personal Roni suit inside the safety locker," Martin said, gesturing toward the red locker. "When you put on your Roni suit, ensure the thermostat dial is green; this is the default comfort setting."

"I don't like being near deep water. I've had a strong fear of drowning since childhood."

"Don't worry, Joseph; everything will be fine, trust me," Martin said confidently.

He then gestured toward a wooden rack. "There's about a gallon and a half of freshwater in those bottles over there. Please take all six, Joseph. Staying hydrated is essential in every part of Antarctica. When you're ready, come up and meet Mike Copeland, and we'll get underway."

Joseph wore a Roni suit for the first time and adjusted the thermostat settings to green. Then, he put the six water bottles inside his backpack and went up to the half-deck steering console to meet Mike Copeland, the man at the controls of Lifeboat-6. After informal introductions, Joseph sat himself down in the stern section of the lifeboat. Martin explained to Mike that young intellectuals like Joseph Arunui were noticeably quieter than tenacious sailors and preferred their own company. Mike couldn't care less. His first impression of Joseph was one of weakness; he was a young man with a less than desirable handshake.

***

With the wind blowing in moderate gusts from the northeast, the water was surprisingly calm as the twin electric Wincorp engines pushed the small lifeboat forward. Mike reduced engine speed and steered Lifeboat-6 between wide and narrow gaps in the treacherous, rolling sea of ice. Joseph turned his face away and shifted his gaze to FS *Taimaha*. The ship was not too far away for Joseph not to see a group of men gathering on the exposed aft deck. Joseph could see their faces: Captain Wheeler, Commander Faulkner, Doc Philips, and the bearded Samuel Hinchcliff standing in a defensive posture with two security guards armed with handguns. The guards aimed their weapons at Douglas Tyler, who was holding a pistol pointed at Captain Wheeler. "This cannot be happening," Joseph said, seeing the two security guards lower their weapons and put them down on the deck.

The seconds passed, and Lifeboat-6 drifted further away from the FS *Taimaha*.

"Stop! Stop the boat," Joseph cried.

Martin turned to Mike Copeland and said, "Do as Joseph says. Stop the boat."

Mike swiveled his chair around to the control panel and reversed-throttled the twin electric motors.

"Aye, sir. Power off. All stop."

Then as the boat slowed to a stop, Joseph reached for the binoculars resting on the steering console. His scoping did not reveal much except for the occasional wind gust and water lapping the hull. "Commander, we must go back to the ship at once," he said as he stood up and almost lost balance.

"Sit down before you fall down!" Martin snapped.

Martin carefully adjusted his binoculars, the lenses glinting in the sunlight as he focused intently on the FS *Taimaha*. He peered closely at the ship's portside railing, where Douglas Tyler stood against the backdrop of the vast sea of floating ice. Douglas leaned casually against the ship's railing, posture menacing; he gripped a Navy revolver in his hand, its metal polished and reflecting the light, ready to defend himself against any potential threat. The scene was charged with an underlying risk, the stakes palpable as Martin considered the implications of the standoff unfolding before him. A single gunshot rang out, and Martin watched in horror as Captain Wheeler collapsed onto the deck. The captain instinctively pressed his hands against his stomach, as if trying to contain an invisible wound. Panic surged through Martin as he saw Doc Philips rushing forward to assist the captain.

"Gunfire! Someone just fired a shot from a pistol!" Mike exclaimed, looking toward the ship.

Joseph grabbed the binoculars from Martin and looked through the lenses as two security guards helped Doc Philips carry Captain Wheeler to the ship's hospital on C Deck.

***

Samuel Hinchcliff pleaded with Douglas Tyler to drop the weapon and surrender as Douglas climbed over the portside railing. "Don't try to stop me, Samuel. I want to go home."

Douglas looked at Samuel, smiled, then jumped feet-first into the freezing water and disappeared.

"Douglas jumped overboard; that damned fool!" Joseph yelled, trembling. The events unfolding before his eyes were surreal and could not possibly be happening. "Mike, turn this boat around! Take me back to the ship!" Joseph shouted.

Mike gave Joseph a disapproving look and pushed hard on the throttle lever. "The current is too strong; he's gone," Mike said as the lifeboat sped away from FS *Taimaha* toward Martin's planned drop-off point.

"We have to go back!" Joseph shouted.

"Joseph, look at me! We are not going back. There is nothing anyone can do for Douglas Tyler; he's gone, but we are moving forward to the drop-off point," Martin insisted.

Joseph sat alone at the back of the lifeboat, overwhelmed by what had happened. He couldn't cope with the death of Douglas Tyler and the possibility that Captain Wheeler had been shot…and perhaps killed. Martin and Mike attempted to reassure Joseph that the captain was being well cared for; however, Joseph ignored them and everything else happening around him, struggling to maintain a grip on reality. In his mind, he imagined standing on the deck of the FS *Taimaha* with Captain Wheeler alive and well. Joseph suddenly felt weak and developed an intense headache due to overwhelming emotional stress, which caused him to faint.

***

Soon after regaining consciousness, Joseph opened his eyes and stared at Martin's concerned face. Martin sat beside him, holding an empty syringe. "Welcome back. How do you feel? Dizzy, light-headed?"

"A little dizzy," Joseph said, getting up on his feet.

"Do you need to inject more cervlax?" Martin said, looking inside Joseph's medical kit.

"No, I'm feeling okay. Thank you for helping me."

"Think nothing of it."

"But how did you know I was cervlax dependent?" Joseph said.

"Before we left, Dr. Philips informed me of your illness and the correct dosages for the neuron blocker medication."

"You freaked me out when you started speaking to me in Freilish," Mike said as he securely positioned a wood ramp with one-inch metal spikes in the ice. "Boat secured, sir. Be careful; the ramp is wet and very slippery."

"Are you good to go, Joseph?" Martin said.

"I think so."

"Okay. Put your backpack on and follow me."

As Joseph stood up to follow Martin, he noticed that the comfort setting of the Roni suit was changing from green to red. "Commander, I'm overheating inside this suit," he said.

"Press the red button to vent the excess heat," Martin said.

"Okay."

"The current air temperature is 15 degrees Fahrenheit with wind chill, which will become colder as we ascend the glacier. Keep the comfort dial in the green zone, whether standing still or moving."

"I'm cooling down, now, thank you, Commander."

"You're welcome."

"Taimaha, Taimaha, come in," Mike said into his handheld radio. "Duty officer on the bridge, this is Mike Copeland. If you can hear me, please respond."

Static crackled from the radio speaker as Mike changed the frequency. "Taimaha, Taimaha!

This is Mike Copeland. Why won't you answer?"

"Mike, don't waste your time; the communication systems are offline. Please head back to the ship."

"Aye, sir. Goodbye, and good luck to both of you."

The boat engine sputtered to life, and the water seemed to boil behind the rudder assembly. Mike waved one last goodbye before he and Lifeboat-6 disappeared behind a wall of floating sea ice.

"Commander Brindle, if comm systems are down, how do we communicate with the ship?"

"For security reasons, this entire area is being patrolled by a squelcher drone," Martin said, pointing at the sky. "We must wait until the squelcher drone recognizes the area between Prydz Bay and Shanawi Station as a safe zone."

***

Shanawi Station

Martin had set a quick walking pace battling against the elements and the harsh landscape. They had covered only three miles in the first hour. Joseph's lack of physical fitness troubled Martin. There were two miles to go before Hill 41, then three more miles to Shanawi Station.

"Come on, Joseph, try to keep up. You can do it."

Joseph was furious, not with Martin, but with himself. "I can't walk any faster; my thighs are burning."

The wind carried his voice away from Martin who had stopped 15 yards ahead.

"This is not an easy hike," Joseph said, slumped over with his hands on his knees. "Is there an easier route to Shanawi Station?"

"Not for you and me, Joseph. This is the shortest possible route and the safest route to Shanawi Station."

The icefall of the Ranvik Glacier hindered their progress. Joseph followed Martin's steps, climbing over loose blocks of ice. The long and arduous hike to the top of Hill 41 pushed the mind and body beyond the limits of endurance. The last mile was the most laborious walk in Joseph's life. Broken in body and spirit he reached the top of Hill 41 drained of energy. He couldn't take an extra step without falling over, his legs were that tired.

Standing on the summit of Hill-41, 2,500 feet above the icefall and looking north-east, a high continuous ice cliff sheltered Prydz Bay from the katabatic winds that swept the high Austurland Plateau. "Commander, another ship is entering Prydz Bay!" Joseph yelled.

Martin unclipped his binoculars from his belt. Looking through the lenses, he focuses on the Hawk-class frigate dropping anchor two miles east of Taimaha's current position.

"It's a warship! FS *Aurora*."

"A warship? Why would a thin-hulled warship come this far south at this time of year?" Joseph asked.

"I don't know why," Martin, said in a dismissive tone.

"If Doc were here right now, he'd know why."

"Doc wouldn't stick his nose into something that didn't concern him," Martin said, frowning. "Now, grab your gear and let's get going; the wind is picking up."

***

The Japanese civil engineering project called Shanawi Station was Antarctica's most extensive underground research facility. Its designer, structural engineer Kaito Shanawi had also designed the Dome Fuji Deep Space Observatory. In response, the Chinese government had constructed the Guangdou research facility on the Amery Ice Shelf. The location of the Chinese facility, which was ten miles from Shanawi Station, was a sensitive political issue.

Both Guangdou and Shanawi Station were government-owned research facilities. Guangdou was much smaller. It was built above ground, only a couple of miles from a narrow sea channel. The only redeeming architectural feature of the concrete building painted all white was a permanent deep space telescope under its observatory dome.

Guangdou had small working teams during the winter months. Typically, twenty scientists stayed behind, though the maximum number of working scientists, assistants, and private researchers never exceeded 120. Guangdou had stored provisions enough to last two years; bad weather often hampered the rapid delivery of personnel and supplies by air. Guangdou's resupply problem was complicated because Chinese ships did not traverse the narrow Shanawi Channel. The Chinese Government refused to accept the deep-water channel in Japanese territory. It was ludicrous, to say the least; however, it was not surprising to any follower of Chinese/Japanese history. The bitter rivalry between these two great nations, their long-forgotten wars, grudges, and mistrust, had robbed the world of many innovative ideas.

***

Joseph explored the area surrounding the research station that the Government of Japan had abandoned a century earlier. As he wandered through the landscape, the serene silence made the research station feel even more desolate. "I don't see the stairwell. Am I searching in the right place?"

"You are close to the stairwell, Joseph, but there's no time for sightseeing. The PAV will be arriving shortly. Stay close and don't wander off!"

"Okay."

Joseph looked skywards, beyond the snaking chain of low ice hills to the north-east. The incoming PAV from Mawson was nowhere in sight. So, he continued his search for the stairwell.

Joseph's eyes widened with curiosity when he lifted a sheet of steel partially covered with snow and ice. He got down on his hands and knees, cleared the snow, and found the entrance to the stairwell leading to three underground levels of the Shanawi research complex.

"Hey, I found the stairwell! I'm heading down to the research complex."

"Did you not hear what I told you, Joseph? I told you to stay close and not wander off!"

"Don't stress, Commander, I'll be back before you know it."

"You are causing me stress. You better return on time, or I will leave without you if you are late. Do you hear me, Professor?"

"I hear you, Commander. And don't call me Professor."

Joseph's hand-held flashlight illuminated his cautious steps, the bottom of the staircase, and then after the last step a steel door scorched black by fire. Joseph turned the doorknob and pushed the heavy door open. The white beam of his flashlight lit up extended workbenches, old computers, test tubes, beakers, metal tubing, and colorful tables with matching color seats. In the quiet of the abandoned research facility, Joseph could hear the trickle of water flowing down the concrete walls. A blue door led Joseph to a long passageway and the recreation area. Inside, he found several gaming tables, empty food machines, old books, and magazines on the tiled floor. But the mattresses, blankets, and people's personal belongings looked out of place.

On one wall were the names of people and photographs of happy faces and unfamiliar cities. There was a faint smell, a smell Joseph remembered that sent shivers down his spine. It was the smell of blood and death. Joseph had seen enough; a sign pointed to an exit. Joseph followed the beam of the flashlight until he discovered another stairwell. This emergency exit led to the frozen desert landscape outside. Joseph shielded his eyes from the sun, wore his orange wrap-around sunglasses, and approached Martin.

"Shanawi Station is mind-blowing scary," Joseph said. "There's technical equipment down there and in good working order. The Japanese abandoned this place, why?"

"Shanawi Station was the largest research facility in Antarctica a century ago," Martin explained. "It housed 250 full-time research scientists, had an efficient management system, abundant resources, and received year-round support from Japan. However, everything changed with the Arctic/Antarctic-Freeland Agreement, impacting not only the residents of Shanawi Station but all Freelanders living in Antarctica."

"I recall Doc Philips stating that the 45th parallel south serves as the dividing line, protecting Antarctic Freelanders from incursion by the Allied armies and preserving Antarctica's pristine environment and scientific integrity," Joseph said.

"The doctor was right, Joseph. The 45th parallel south served as the dividing line. However, the Arctic/Antarctic Freeland Agreement was misapplied because it included provisions for resupplying ships and air transport to support the Allied navies threatening Freelander trade routes. The Japanese government, fearing the possibility of a full-scale war with the Freelanders and Allied forces, delayed the departure of loaded resupply vessels bound for Shanawi Station. As a result, they never left Okinawa Harbor, and Kaito Shanawi and his people starved to death."

"I find it difficult to picture 250 people suffering on those filthy mattresses, waiting, hoping, and praying for a resupply ship that would never arrive," Joseph said.

"Not everyone in the facility starved to death. Kaito Shanawi took his own life by putting a bullet in his brain. Rather than resorting to cannibalism, Kaito's family and close friends followed his lead."

"The thought of bodies being dismembered and cooked turns my stomach," Joseph said.

"Joseph, wouldn't you consider eating human flesh to save your own life?"

"No, I would not! I'd rather open my veins than be a cannibal."

***

The sound of someone coughing carried across the frozen landscape from somewhere out there in the whiteness. "We have company!" Joseph shouted, looking through Martin's binoculars. Martin finished relieving himself against a large boulder and returned to Joseph, who handed him the binoculars. "Take a look. Six men and four women heading our way."

Martin looked, and the focus dial adjusted automatically. "Japanese tourists from FS *Aurora*. They return to Shanawi Station each year to commemorate the anniversary of Kaito Shanawi's death and to ask their deceased ancestors to watch over the living members of their family. The tall man leading them must be their guide."

The ten elderly people following their guide slowly approached Martin and Joseph.

"Hello there! I'm Bill Aldridge, and I have the privilege of leading this fantastic group through the breathtaking wilderness." Bill removed his goggles and extended his right hand toward Martin and Joseph as a gesture of friendship. "May I ask who you two gentlemen are?"

"Commander Martin Brindle of the FS *Taimaha*. Pleased to meet you, Bill."

"Hello, Mr. Aldridge, sir. I'm Joseph."

"There's no need for formality between friends. Unless your commander objects," Bill said, looking at Martin.

"No, I don't object. I've never embraced formalities; I prefer to keep things simple and direct, especially in casual settings where they feel unnecessary. However, once we step aboard the ship, it's a different story."

"It's a pleasure to meet you, Joseph," Bill said while shaking Joseph's hand. Always suspicious of everyone, Bill added, "A naval commander and a civilian traveling together in this wilderness is quite unusual, wouldn't you agree, Commander?"

"There's nothing peculiar about the Science Portal team's operations here, Bill," Martin replied, his tone steady despite the tension in the air. "Shanawi Station is home to a vast repository of artifacts and various materials we're cataloging." Martin gestured toward the open staircase leading to Shanawi Station, hoping to deceive Bill Aldridge and provide evidence of their thorough research efforts. "Both Joseph and I are dedicated research scientists. Our mission is with the Science Portal team, not with the Freeland Navy."

"I'm a Research Glaciologist," Joseph said, knowing he wouldn't willingly lie to anyone. However, Martin had given him explicit instructions: never reveal your true identity to anyone you do not know. "Since leaving New Zealand, FS *Taimaha* has become our home away from home. While researching this wilderness, I remember the cozy comforts of FS *Taimaha*, a fine old ship."

"FS *Taimaha* is a fine old ship, Joseph. However, gentlemen, let us speak, frankly. I must remind you that Shanawi Station is still regarded as Japanese territory, a memorial complex. While I cannot inquire about your reasons for leaving the ship and being here, I must prioritize the safety of my people, as I am being paid to guide and protect them. I hope you both understand."

"Joseph and I understand your position, Mr. Aldridge. As dedicated Freelanders, we believe that defending the weak and poor and showing kindness and empathy to all living beings is a core part of our daily lives. We strongly feel that accepting money to help and protect the innocent is wrong, as it contradicts the ideals of Freelander values."

"I'm not a Freelander, Commander, but I respect your Freelander ideals. Captain Wheeler was also a dedicated Freelander. When the news reached the FS *Aurora*, it came as quite a shock to me and to everyone aboard."

Martin stood frozen, his eyes locked onto Joseph, the weight of stunned silence hanging heavily between them. "News! We haven't heard anything from anyone since we left our ship," Martin said.

"A communication blackout ensued shortly after Captain Wheeler was rushed to the ship's hospital, leaving everyone in darkness," Bill explained. "Sadly, Captain Wheeler passed away from his injuries."

"We were off the ship when Captain Wheeler was shot," Martin recalled, reflecting on the event.

"Doc Philips would have done everything possible to save Captain Wheeler, his closest friend," Joseph said.

"I met Doctor Philips. He is a good and honorable man," Bill said.

"Did Doctor Philips get appointed as captain?" Martin inquired.

"No. Andrew Faulkner was appointed as the captain of FS *Taimaha* without dissent," Bill said.

"I find it hard to believe that Andrew Faulkner was appointed captain without opposition," Martin stated.

"Nonetheless, Andrew Faulkner is the captain of FS *Taimaha*."

"Faulkner may hold the title, but he is not a leader," Martin said angrily.

"Regardless of your personal feelings toward him, Captain Faulkner holds a steadfast belief that several influential individuals, while not directly responsible, contributed in some capacity to the unfortunate death of Captain Wheeler. In fact, your name came up during his reflection on the circumstances surrounding this tragedy, Commander."

"I can't say I'm shocked my name was mentioned...not even in the slightest. Captain Faulkner is a spineless coward, utterly unworthy of any respect."

Martin stood stoically against an endless sea of ice, his mind racing about what to do or say without revealing too much information to Bill Aldridge, a man he didn't know or trust.

"Commander, you must return to your ship and face your accuser," Bill said.

"No, Joseph and I have essential work to focus on right now. Faulkner can wait."

"Is there anything more vital than restoring your good name?" Bill asked.

"I can't answer that question," Martin said bluntly.

"Well, that's understandable; having a good sense of security is essential, even in this situation," Bill said. Aldridge glanced over his right shoulder at the oldest member of the group, a Shinto holy man. He was helping two women chant as they pulled a small sled filled with earth-fired clay pots containing equal numbers of white and yellow chrysanthemums.

"Anyhow, Commander, one must do what feels right and proper in any situation. Right now, I have a group of elderly citizens from Japan who rely on me for their safety," Bill said.

"Do you know what they're singing?" Joseph asked softly, concern in his voice as he leaned toward Martin.

"The chant acts as a powerful prayer for the departed, purging and liberating any malevolent spirits that may linger within Shanawi Station," Martin asserted.

"Are malevolent spirits inhabiting Shanawi Station? The thought sends shivers up and down my spine," Joseph said.

"No, Joseph, Shanawi Station is a place of comfort and remembrance, rather than fear or malevolence for these people," Bill said. "The family gatherings serve as a powerful testament to the positive memories connected with the site, reinforcing that it holds significance and warmth in their hearts. Each year, they return to this wilderness to honor a loved one's memory. It's quite profound."

***

"Youkoso! Welcome back to Shanawi Station," Bill exclaimed to the ten elderly individuals in his care.

"Hello, Aldridgesan. Konnichiwa," the friendly elderly individuals replied with warm smiles.

Joseph was unsure whether to bow or say hello to the Japanese people, so he followed Martin's lead and chose to do neither. As Freelanders, both Joseph and Martin often faced scrutiny for their beliefs. One woman remarked in

79

Japanese, "These two lack the respect that our deceased deserve."

"Hiroko, you talk too much," the Shinto priest said.

Another elderly Japanese gentleman approached Bill.

"Aldridgesan," he said, bowing deeply. "My wife and I created this funeral urn in memory of our dear friend."

Bill accepted the urn and bowed lower than the elderly man. "Futabasan, this urn is beautifully decorated. Thank you and your lovely wife for thinking of Richard Orentzsan." Bill smiled and bowed again.

"Richard Orentz…the fighter?" Martin asked as the elderly man bowed back and then left.

"Yes!" Bill exclaimed, leaning closer to Martin, his eyes sparkling with curiosity. "Did you know Richard?"

"Orentz was my opponent in a 'Big-Fist' match two years ago. He knocked me out in the final round," Martin added, regret evident in his voice.

"Reaching the final round of a Big Fist match is impressive. Richard broke my jaw the first time I fought him in the ring. Regrettably, Richard is no longer with us. He died six months ago," Bill said, his voice filled with sadness.

"How did Richard lose his life? Surely not in a battle in the ring?" Martin inquired with a hint of disbelief in his tone.

"Richard died on Ross Island," Bill told him, recalling the trip Richard had planned after his last fight. "Richard loved to climb mountains; he decided to climb up to the crater rim of Mount Erebus and photograph the active lava lake. He had the best and latest equipment, but halfway down on the way back to base camp, his crevasse detector meter

must have failed, and he fell through soft ice into a deep
crevasse. We recovered his broken body. His ashes are in
this small urn that Futabasan gave me. Richard was a
professional fighter and also Mr. Futaba's personal
bodyguard."

"Aldridgesan, we are ready, please come," the Shinto priest
said.

"Hai, ima sugu kite," Bill said, bowing.

***

As the Shinto priest recited prayers for the departed, Joseph
and Martin moved respectfully away from the mourners
dressed in gray robes. After a brief silence, the priest
approached Joseph and handed him a perfectly bound book
with a brown leather cover. It was a collection of ancient
Japanese chants. "I would be very grateful if you would
accept this gift," the Shinto said, bowing.

"Thank you very much, sir. It is a generous gift, but I
cannot accept it as I do not understand Japanese."

"Joseph Arunui, remember that there is always an
opportunity to learn and grow," the Shinto said as he
handed Joseph the brown book.

"Hey, wait! How do you know my name, who are you?"

As the elderly bowed and left, Joseph stood there with a
puzzled expression on his face. He thought, *Well, this is
interesting and unusual...receiving a gift from a stranger.*

***

Bill Aldridge approached Joseph to bid him farewell.
"Goodbye, young man. I truly hope we have a chance to
meet again someday."

81

Joseph nodded. "Bill, I don't understand why the Shinto holy man gave me this book. I can't read Japanese, not a single word. Before you leave, can you explain why he insisted I take it off his hands?"

Bill smiled and said, "There's nothing for you to worry about, young Joseph. The Shinto holy man followed a long-standing Shanawi tradition. When someone departed from Shanawi Station, they always received a book as a parting gift. As I understand it, books bring lasting knowledge and happiness."

"That is a beautiful thought," Joseph said.

Bill said goodbye to Joseph and approached Martin, who was diligently clearing ice and snow from Shanawi Station's location marker — a pyramid-shaped cairn made of hundreds of polished jade stones.

"Commander, I want to give you this card before I leave. It's an invitation."

"An invitation?"

"I'm inviting you to the Southern Conference Challenge. Dome Halley has the honor of hosting the event this year."

"That is a generous invitation, considering the ticket price is more than many can afford."

"Let me clarify, Commander. One spot remains in the Southern Conference Challenge, and I am offering it to you."

Martin shrugged. "Let me be clear, Bill; I no longer participate in those fights."

"You and I would make a formidable team. And this year, the prize is a life-changer."

"I don't fight anymore," Martin said sternly.

"I understand, Commander. I'll be staying at Dome Halley's Preston Hotel if you change your mind, or you can use the card for free tickets to the fight if you and Joseph are interested."

"Thank you for your generous offer, Bill. I will check with Joseph to see if he's interested."

"Sahristi beness *peace and happiness*," Bill said in Freilish.

"Sahristi beness," Martin replied.

***

Martin and Joseph walked alongside Bill Aldridge and his group until it was time to say goodbye. I really admire Bill," Joseph remarked, a thoughtful smile crossing his face. "He's not only clever but also genuinely a good person."

"Seriously, Joseph, you're not worldly-wise."

"And you are?"

"Joseph, you don't know who Bill Aldridge is. He is a skilled journeyman fighter and a professional killer in the ring."

"Is the Shinto holy man also a professional killer?" Joseph asked.

"Are you blind to everything, Joseph? The Shinto holy man is a high-ranking Xiangshan trader. The wool scarf around his neck hides a unique tattoo: a red dragon, the iconic symbol of Xiangshan traders."

Joseph wanted to believe Martin; he had no reason to lie. "But how can you be so sure?"

"My father had the same tattoo on the right side of his neck because he was a high-ranking Xiangshan trader in his youth. He gave up on everything and stopped trading after my mother passed away."

"I'm sorry to hear about your mom."

***

Bill Aldridge and his group had stopped at the edge of the channel facing the Guangdou research facility. Further in the distant skyline loomed the Trans-Antarctic Mountains. Bill approached a tall, round-faced chap named Shen. "We are heading back to the Aurora."

"Okay," Shen replied.

Bill looked at Shen and the abandoned Guangdou research facility on the other side of the channel.

"Did you visit the research facility?" Bill asked.

"No. The ice is too thin to walk on," Shen replied.

"So, what have you been doing here all this time?"

"Remembering my grandfather. Comparing some of his photographs," Shen replied. "The Guangdou research facility looks much the same as it did 100 years ago."

"Your grandfather was the greatest Chinese astronomer of his generation," Bill said.

"History remembers my grandfather as the man with impaired empathy, a psychopath who refused to help Kaito Shanawi."

"Your grandfather could not help Kaito Shanawi, but he saved Guangdou's team of researchers. Come on, let's go, Shen; dwelling on the past changes nothing," Bill urged, increasing his pace.

Shen took a thin-chained necklace from his pocket, which held his grandfather's bravery medal. He gazed at the medal some moments before casting it into Shanawi's channel.

***

When Bill joined the leading group, the elderly people exchanged glances. The Shinto priest gazed across the frozen landscape and asked, "Where is Shen?"

"He's coming," Bill said, kneeling to adjust ski bindings.

"Aldridgesan, we must go. The wind is getting stronger."

"Stronger and colder," Bill responded. "Shen will be here soon."

After ten minutes, with the wind blowing hard and cold across his face, Bill walked back to Shanawi's Channel. There was no sign of Shen, just his footprints leading to the water's edge. Bill reluctantly returned to the others with the sad news that Shen had drowned. Everyone expressed their sorrow and sympathy, though no one admitted their guilt and shame for treating Shen like an outcast.

Dome Fuji

As the PAV landed softly on the frozen ground, twelve rotating blades slowed to a stop and the pilot opened the cargo bay door.

"Hello, gentlemen. I hope you haven't been waiting long," the pilot said.

"You're two hours late," Martin said sternly.

"I had battery problems and ran into a stronger headwind when I reached Lake Meade. You must be…Commander Martin Brindle," Adrian said, looking at his passenger manifest.

"Adrian Sangster, what are you doing here?" Joseph said.

"Damn me to hell, Joseph Arunui. How are you, man?"

Adrian had also survived the earthquake, lost his family as Joseph did and the pair shared more painful memories of their time together in Auckland's Rehabilitation Hospital.

"I'm glad you two found each other, but we have to leave," Martin cut in. "The wind is getting stronger by the minute, and the temperature is dropping fast."

"Commander, I need to replace two dead power cells first. Give me an hour, thirty minutes tops."

"Okay, how can I help?"

"Well, you can start unscrewing the fasteners on the battery cowling if you want," Adrian offered.

***

When power was restored, Joseph and Martin boarded the PAV named Black Roach. They buckled into their seats for the 622-mile flight to Dome Fuji in Austurland. In 2360, the Freeland Militias had annexed East Antarctica from Norway and Japan, renaming it Austurland.

Flying over Freeland territory, the view was unremarkable. Joseph's fear of flying drifted away like the clouds.

"Guys, you can just make out Mount Victor there on our right," Adrian said.

Gazing out at the landscape, Joseph was struck by the vast emptiness below, where the shadow of Black Roach danced across the undulating terrain. Martin wholeheartedly shared the sentiment that the grand mountains, with their truffle-brown slopes crowned with white snow were the highlight of their journey to Dome Fuji.

"Do you make good money flying this tin can?" Martin said.

"I have to fly twelve hours a day, seven days a week to make decent money, but I'd rather put in the hours flying than work in a Gaussberg mine, digging out lamproite for the rest of your life." Martin smiled and nodded.

"In any case, Xiangshan traders pay big money for those bags of chicken shit, frozen krill, and drums of brik paste back there in the cargo bay," Adrian added. "So, I'll keep putting in the hours and keep this old girl flying for as long as they pay me."

"Doing business with Xiangshan traders is illegal in Antarctica," Joseph said bluntly.

"Only if you get caught," Martin countered.

Adrian smiled. "Joseph, I have all the required permits."

"I don't think the Freeland Security Forces (FSF) lose sleep over drums of chicken shit and brik paste," Martin added.

"I totally agree," Adrian replied. "The FSF couldn't care less, and that's how I like it."

"Just be careful," Joseph said.

"Hey, stick to chasing stars with your little telescope, okay."

"I dream of nothing else," Joseph said, smiling.

"Well, Dome Fuji is teeming with astronomers, journalists, and aerospace engineers. You'll fit right in with that snobbish lot," Adrian said.

"We have accommodation, Building-89, I think," Joseph said, searching inside a trouser pocket for his reservation details.

"Building-89 is the old hospital," Adrian said. "Rent is cheap and the food, well, the less said about the food, the better."

Martin rolled his eyes and gave Joseph a disapproving look.

"Dome Halley is where all the action is," Adrian added. "This year's Southern Conference fight is going to be the fight of the century. The Xiangshan Traders are going to make a lot of money over the next few days. They prearranged the outcome of the fight; Bill Aldridge will beat Aleksandr Volkov."

"We met Bill Aldridge back at Shanawi Station."

"Yeah, right. Spin another one of your tall tales, Joseph."

"PAV Alpha-Delta-Romeo you have permission to proceed through Class Bravo," said the voice of a flight controller. *"Wind is blowing hard from the North, caution is advised."*

"Roger, Bravo," Adrian replied. "The wind has changed its direction. It's going to get bumpy, guys. Sorry to spoil the pleasant ride."

"What happened to the blue sky?" Joseph said.

"The wind direction and the weather changes so quickly here, even during the summer months."

Martin looked out the window. "Hard to distinguish what's ground and sky."

"For an average pilot, flying in white-out conditions is never easy," Adrian mused. "But you're not flying with an average pilot. You're flying with the best pilot money can buy."

***

A blustery crosswind suddenly buffeted Black Roach. Adrian circled the chosen landing zone twice before the wheels touched the ground.

"Welcome to Dome Fuji, gentleman."

Martin moved forward to get a better view. "I never doubted your flying skills, splendid job."

"We were lucky. PAVs are great machines, but twelve blades cannot handle a right crosswind," Adrian said. "The blade designers at Davis-Molby Engineering are a useless lot if you ask me."

The wind howled across the sparsely settled Dome Fuji. Despite the howling wind, Adrian sat Black Roach safely on the landing pad of Building-89. With little time to spare before starting his next delivery, Adrian hurried to replace the battery pack. Martin helped him again, and Joseph stayed strapped in his seat filling two more pages in his diary.

"Come on, Joseph, grab your gear! Let's go!" Martin commanded.

"Okay, I'm ready."

Adrian waved goodbye as Black Roach took off from the ground. Martin and Joseph waved back and watched Black Roach vanish into the dark gray clouds. Martin touched an interactive wall panel, and the elevator door opened. A calm female voice informed them about the hotel elevator; it was out of order. A sign pointed to an iced up stairwell. Despite the strong urine smell, Martin remained calm as he and Joseph walked down the stairs.

***

Upon arriving at the hotel lobby, they discovered it was completely empty. Both the concierge desk and the bell desk were unattended. Martin glanced around and noticed an open jar of pickled herrings, remnants of smelly fish oil on stained wrapping paper, and someone's abandoned lunch. He rang a small silver bell and was beginning to have second thoughts about their accommodation when a bald man with a prominent scar above his left ear walked in from a storage room behind the concierge desk.

"Welcome to Dome Fuji. Fill out the arrival forms," the bald man said in a less than enthusiastic tone.

"Are you the landlord?" Joseph asked.

The bald man snorted. "No. Mr. Hasana is the man you want. He owns this place and the pub next door."

Martin gave the bald man a suspicious look. "I didn't get your name."

"My name is Jonas, Jonas Tohvian. I work for Mr. Hasana. Now, how can I help you?"

"I have a reservation and an authenticated passkey," Joseph said.

"Okay. I have to verify your ID and passkey. Look at the biometric scanner. When you see the red light, don't blink, or move your head."

"Scanned and verified. Thank you, Mr. Arunui."

Joseph nodded.

Martin walked over to a table covered with old newspapers and magazines. He shifted his gaze and looked around the room, which had one redeeming feature: the open fireplace. The warm air from the fire was inviting, in contrast to the cold, rundown areas of the hotel.

"Commander, may I see your ID, please?"

"Yes, of course."

"Thank you, Commander. Look at the biometric scanner. Don't blink or move your head."

"Okay."

As Jonas made the final adjustments to the biometric scanner, Martin blinked without realizing it. Sharp, stinging pain pierced both his eyes, causing him to wince and blink rapidly. He realized the vision in his right eye had become blurry as if a thick mist had settled over it. The unease intensified when the world around him blurred into indistinct shapes and shadows and he tried to focus on something, anything, to ease the discomfort.

"All done. Are you okay, Commander? You seem a bit dazed."

"No. I feel fine," Martin lied.

"That's what I like to hear. Your discomfort will fade away in just a few seconds."

"The vision in my right eye isn't blurry; it's clear."

"Your vision has returned to normal, Commander," Jonas said before examining the hotel guest list. "I can give you apartment 9. It's the cleanest apartment on the second level."

"Thank you, Jonas," Joseph said.

"Hey, Jonas, thanks for the help."

Jonas gave Martin the thumbs up and said, "Take the stairs; the elevators in this building haven't worked for years."

***

Martin and Joseph walked toward the stairs, and the front doors of Building 89 opened automatically. A man wearing a modern, refined, tan-colored weatherproof coat and several layers of garments piled under his long jacket entered the hotel lobby. His complexion was sickly pale, making him look like death warmed over. "Shay laburi caperisti," the man said in Freilish. "Hello, gentleman, and welcome. I am Theodore Hasana, your humble servant."

Martin shot Theodore Hasana a contemptuous look for the poorly spoken Freilish.

"Gentlemen, hot towels, and steaming hot tea are available at any time for a small service fee."

"No, thank you," Joseph said politely.

"If there is no other business, gentlemen, dinner will be served at 6 p.m. All food and beverage sales, including water, are cash only."

"Decent food at a reasonable price?"

"Absolutely, Commander! Anything less just won't do!"

"You are not a Freelander, Mr. Hasana. A Freelander never accepts money for food, water, or shelter."

"Commander, with all due respect, the Freelander movement isn't suitable for everyone. Money drives things globally, and for hardworking individuals like me who are passionate about their businesses, that is the only direction worth following. However, here in Dome Fuji, I struggle to make ends meet. A local Freelander militia unit actively annoys me by refusing to pay for food and drinks and taking advantage of my hotel daily. The sooner they leave, the better, in my opinion."

"You're an arrogant bastard," Martin said, glaring at Hasana. "The next time the Freelander militia marches down your main street, you'll need all the money you can get if you want round-the-clock protection. Businesses owned by individuals who oppose the Freelander cause often burn down."

"Are you threatening me, Commander?"

"I'm merely giving you some friendly advice, Mr. Hasana. Anything less just won't do, remember?"

***

As they approached Apartment 9 on the second level, Martin turned to Joseph. "Hasana is a jerk."

"I don't like him either, not one bit," Joseph replied.

When they entered the dimly lit apartment, Martin mocked many decorative fixtures, paintings of old ships anchored off Port of Davis, and a dozen older photographs of Halley City 100 years before Freelander engineers constructed its world-famous Dome. He opened the drawers and cupboards and found them empty. The bathroom was small and ordinary, with just a few cabinets and a sink. Two thin towels were hanging on a towel rack opposite the shower recess. In the rectangular room, two tall cupboards, a round wooden table, two chairs, and two small beds filled most of the space. Joseph lifted each mattress, bed cover, sheet, and pillow. After completing the inspection, he told Martin that he was satisfied with the level of hygiene. However, that didn't stop Martin from plopping himself down on the bed without removing his muddy boots.

***

On the first evening after their arrival at Dome Fuji, Joseph and Martin showered and went to dinner dressed for the occasion. While they waited for their evening meal, Martin tried to strike up a conversation with Clare. She was a

93

Winthrop security guard but being in a relationship, Clare wasn't interested in the sweet-talking man in the navy uniform. Martin retreated to his table, beer in hand and a bruised ego, no doubt grasping that getting laid was not about to happen anytime soon. On the other hand, Joseph preferred the warmth inside the apartment, and he wondered why he hadn't found his true love. *She is out there, somewhere*, he thought. *She has settled in for the long night and is having the same thoughts.*

He sat at the round table and wrote in his diary: *My first day in Antarctica. As I write, I am full of apprehension and self-doubt. Was it a mistake coming here? There are many aspects in and around Dome Fuji that worry me. I expected this place to be different. There are only six buildings. The Lecture Hall and the Observatory are the most noticeable in size and area. Martin and I are staying at the hotel for the time being. Building 89, as locals call it, was once the biggest hospital in Antarctica. However, the hospital last supported patient care over sixty years ago. The Warehouse and Supermarket are new constructs.*

While I am full of apprehension, I am also happy. Martin and I meet Professor William Briar tomorrow morning, the father of modern Interstellar Astronomy."

***

Meanwhile, back on FS *Taimaha*, three galley staff were serving the scheduled breakfast service. Captain Andrew Faulkner followed a dozen sailors to the front of the serving line. He was about to order his breakfast when a gas fire erupted in the galley area. As fire alarms activated, Satori bolted to the fire control panel and switched camera angles to see the fire's extent. But the three security cameras in the galley area had already melted in the searing heat. Flames and searing heat blasted the Chief Fire Warden and the fire teams, and acrid suffocating smoke poured out of the galley area. Doc Philips hurried to the galley.

"How many casualties, Chief?"

"Thus far, two deaths, but there could be more; six sailors were taken to the ship's hospital in critical condition," the fire warden remarked.

Brendon Aitama and Samuel Hinchcliff, the squad leader of Fireteam-2, were searching the galley and mess hall for survivors from behind their breathing gear when Samuel heard a faint trembling voice. "Endure the pain. Don't give up. Help is on the way," Captain Faulkner was saying with excruciating pain. The galley fire had severely burned his face and hands.

Samuel lifted a section of the galley wall and found Captain Faulkner trapped under an oven that had toppled in the explosion. He extended his right arm to Samuel.

"Help me!"

Samuel stood quietly, clearly unaffected by Captain Faulkner's urgent plea for help.

Captain Faulkner's anguish was palpable as tears cascaded down his cheeks, betraying the torment he was fighting to conceal.

"Help is on the way, Captain. Help is coming," Samuel said, remembering his friend Douglas Tyler, who had jumped overboard and drowned himself out of hatred for Faulkner, the man who had made life on the ship unbearable for everyone under his command.

The Captain's pleas for help went unanswered. Samuel watched him close his eyes and draw his last breath. Justice was served for Douglas Tyler and Taimaha's crew.

"Samuel, did you call for a medic?" Brendon Aitama called from the open doorway.

"No, I didn't call for a medic. Check the next room."

"I already checked. There is no one inside. The injured and deceased must have been taken to Emergency Point-92," Brendon observed.

Then Doctor Philips approached and asked, "Did you two find anyone else, injured or deceased? Captain Faulkner is still missing."

"No, sir, we didn't find anyone," Samuel replied as he exited the galley.

"I will be at Emergency Point 92 if you need me," Doc said.

***

On the bridge, Satori hurried to the communication panel. "Fredericks, where are you?" Satori spoke over the radio.

"I am currently in the engine room replacing the air filters as Captain Faulkner commanded," Fredericks replied, his irritation evident.

"Captain Faulkner isn't answering his radio. I need you to find him," Satori said, expecting a reply, but all she received was static. "Fredericks, hello? Are you there?"

The fire alarm's repetitive sound finally stopped. The galley fire was extinguished, and the smoke vented from the ventilation system. Taimaha and her crew were safe.

Urgency laced the voice that crackled through the radio, "Bridge duty officer, this is the Chief Fire Warden reporting in."

"Yes, Chief."

"E-deck is secure, Lieutenant."

"Thank you, Chief. Good work, fire teams," Satori replied. *"Guys, has anyone seen the captain? He's not answering his radio."*

"Captain Faulkner died from severe burn injuries sustained in the tragic fire that engulfed the galley. One of my crew members discovered his lifeless body there."

"Are you sure it's the captain?"

"Meet me at Point-92, Lieutenant. If you don't believe me, I will open the body bag for you."

***

Nineteen-year-old Brendon Aitama, the youngest crew member, was of Māori descent. Brendon was an intelligent young man and physically strong. He helped Samuel carry a dozen injured sailors and Captain Faulkner's body to emergency Point-82, the muster station on aft-deck. Zipping up the body bags of five of his closest companions, Brendon was furious. A rumor circulated that the explosion was an act of sabotage by a crew member. Speculation pointed to an engine room attendant, as ERAs had unrestricted access to the ship's galley.

The gas fire aboard Taimaha had claimed twelve lives, with Officer Faulkner the only official military casualty. Among the civilian dead were Head Chef Albert 'Fiery' Banister, his wife Madeline, and apprentice Chef Amadeo Vittorio. Eighteen critically burned sailors now fought for survival, their fate hanging in the delicate hands of Doc Philips. As he awaited the air ambulance from Port of Davis Hospital's burn unit, the doctor swallowed anxiolytic pills, wrestling with the crushing weight of imminent loss. Surrounded by the stark reality of his limitations, Philips was acutely aware of how the Department of Population Control's guidelines reduced human suffering to mere statistical annotations, leaving practitioners like himself to grapple with the raw, unscripted moments between life and death.

***

Dome Fuji:

"*Life goes on, and time passes slowly;* Joseph wrote in his diary: *Fourteen days have passed since our arrival in Dome Fuji. Both Martin and I agree Dome Fuji is not a well-planned township. Nonetheless, I have an ideal work environment, a well-funded, tight-knit scientific community all under one roof, rather than the impoverished Research Hubs back home in New Zealand. This place is my home now. Furthermore, the Dome Fuji Observatory is much bigger than I thought. And disregarding the severe weather, I have not felt this happy in years. There are days when venturing outside is impossible. 190 miles per hour winds keep everyone indoors, and the local pub is the meeting place for hotel guests. In Martin's opinion, Australian beer is the only good thing to come out of that pub. The food is terrible here: synthetic meat and mushy peas or synthetic meat and mushy peas with potatoes. Everything on the menu is rehydrated and reheated. The art of seasoning food is non-existent, which is good for my gentle stomach. Besides that, meat coated with spices is often an indicator of tasteless synthetic meat.*"

***

As the temperature outside fell below freezing, the arguments between Joseph and Martin intensified. Martin's cheerful nature when sober took a dark turn after he had had one too many during dinner. Sitting on the opposite side of the table, Joseph felt worried for his friend. "Martin, please lower your voice."

Martin opened another beer. "Why should I? This is a free continent."

"You're speaking too loudly; people are staring."

"Am I making you feel embarrassed, Joseph?"

"Yes. Just lower your voice, please, Martin."

"Okay, duly noted." Martin stood up and said, "I apologize to everyone here for speaking too loudly; it has embarrassed my friend."

"Martin, sit down and stop creating a scene."

"Okay, Joseph! This scene perfectly captures everything you have been dreaming about:

Galraithia may favor human habitation, but it's too far away, light years away from Earth. And the cost, have you considered the cost?"

"No, I haven't considered the cost," Joseph replied. "I'm a scientist, not a bean counter."

"Then you dream an impossible dream, my young friend," Martin said.

"Why is it impossible?"

"It takes a significant amount of money," Martin replied. "Not to mention that Freelanders have been outlawed in all but four countries for the past one hundred-and-fifty years. This places you, me, and all our people on the other side of a fence, unable to voice our opinions while watching everything that happens in the world and space. That's why the Freelanders will never be part of the race to Galraithia. Another war is coming, Joseph, and I believe it will be sooner than we think."

"Now you're beginning to sound like Doc," Joseph said.

"Another war is coming," Martin declared. "A war we cannot win; the odds are against us. The Allied armies have significantly more military personnel than ever before, and they are better equipped with enhanced security measures."

"We have nuclear weapons buried deep in the North Polar Ice Cap and Antarctica"

"It's all a lie," countered Martin. "There are no buried nuclear warheads. Rachel Sibley made up the story to stall the Allied invasion of Antarctica. Our beloved Antarctica."

"Going to the stars and finding life on another world…will change everything. I know it will."

Martin poured himself another beer. "Yeah, well, you keep dreaming, and I'll keep drinking,"

"I believe I will see Galraithia before I die, and not through the lens of a telescope, but with my own eyes," Joseph said confidently.

"Joseph, this mania you have with Galraithia… seriously, it will lead to nowhere. Trust me."

Then, Mr. Hasana approached table-12, arms balancing dinner plates, and a small basket of fresh bread smeared with foul-smelling brik paste (a percolated paste made from fish guts and black olives). "Enjoy your meals, gentlemen."

Martin didn't see Hasana's smile or the yellow teeth. "About bloody time too," Martin protested.

Martin cut through his meat like he was a starving man.

"How can you eat that crap?" Joseph asked.

Martin chewed tough, tasteless beef and washed it down with a bottle of cold beer. His fourth in an hour. "I'm hungry, and so are you," he said.

Joseph sniffed the brik bread. The reconstituted meat looked as cold and gray as the sky outside. "I can't eat this. The smell is so bad I want to gag," Joseph said, pushing his dinner plate away from the edge of the table.

Martin glanced around the room, envying the other guests near the fireplace who were enjoying a hearty dinner of roasted potatoes, green beans, and spiced meat skewers, while he sat with nothing but an empty beer bottle.

He stood up from his chair, tossed his paper napkin on the table.

"Where are you going?"

"Hasana is treating us like two miserable rat catchers," Martin said storming off.

It was evident to Joseph that Martin was angry when he walked over to the landlord who was busy making conversation with a well-dressed woman in the bar area while the other dinner guests chatted merrily and consumed copious amounts of alcohol. So, it was a sudden unexpected move when Martin punched Hasana in the mouth and in the face. One woman screamed when Hasana fell on the floor, and Joseph, like many other dinner guests, couldn't believe what had happened. Everyone looked shocked. Poor Mr. Hasana grimaced in pain; he could feel blood dripping down his swollen nose and torn bottom lip.

Martin returned to his chair and sat down, stared at Joseph as if nothing had happened.

"Tomorrow night, there will be a special menu for you and me."

"The way Hasana is scowling at you don't be surprised if he spits in your food from now on," Joseph said.

Then an elderly man and the young lady walked over to their table. The man said to Martin, "I don't know what your problem is… assaulting the landlord was a barbarous act to say the very least."

The young woman also had words to say to Martin. "Who do you think you are? You disgraced the navy uniform," she snapped.

"Joseph, get her out of my face before I'll really lose my temper."

People were staring and muttering aloud. Joseph didn't like people staring at him and Martin. He had to get home before Martin started another fight.

"I'm very sorry," Joseph said, trying to get Martin to stand up and leave. "I think my friend had too many beers."

The woman said a few words to Joseph, but her soft voice was drowned out by Martin bellowing, "Hey, Hasana, see you tomorrow evening."

Joseph helped get his inebriated friend out the dining room. Later, in Apartment-9, merciful sleep vanquished Martin's nausea, the spinning ceiling, and the involuntary retching.

When Martin woke the following morning, he looked out his bedroom window towards the sky. The wind howled outside. The morning looked dark and cold. He made his way to the small kitchen where Joseph poured him a cup of hot tea.

"How do you feel?" Joseph said.

"I feel like shit!"

"And you look like shit," Joseph snapped. "Now, hurry up and take a shower; the meeting with Professor Briar is today, or have you forgotten?"

When Martin didn't reply, Joseph said, "Never mind. I'll go on my own. You stay here and rest."

"No! I'm coming with you," Martin said, walking to the bathroom.

***

With a biting wind in their faces and hands in their pockets, they made their way to Nobu Shirase Lecture Hall. Joseph had no sympathy for Martin, who followed him and declared sobriety.

"I don't want to hear it," Joseph said. "And don't try to justify last night's embarrassing behavior. The woman called you a dog; she said you should be muzzled and kept on a short leash."

A steam-heated pathway, weathered by years of harsh winters, snaked between the old hospital and its neighboring structures. The pub, dormant until midday, stood silent beside a supermarket with boarded-up windows and padlocked doors—a frozen tableau of isolation. Beyond, the Nobu Shirase Lecture Hall emerged at the end of snow-carved trenches that zigzagged like white-walled arteries through the bleak landscape. Timber slats lined the narrowest trench, offering a precarious walkway between the hospital, the residential quarter, and the hangar flanking the supply depot, each connection a lifeline in this desolate, snow-entombed wilderness.

Upon entering the semi-circular auditorium, both men stared at the high vaulted ceiling supported by long stainless-steel trusses and polished timber paneling. There were doors, and rows of chairs handcrafted from New Zealand's plantation-grown pine and blue ceramic tiles imported from China added color. Joseph approached three stage lighting poles straddling an empty stage. An open doorway led to the Observatory on his left, but Joseph

103

spotted a long and heavy oak wood table in front of the stage. An old lamp stood on an antique table with a drawer. Joseph didn't know much about antiques; he guessed the early 19th century; a small, faded sticker belonged to Auckland's Heritage Museum.

The lecture hall had many antique collections and historical artifacts, but Joseph was interested only in a pile of books and high-grade photographs on the old table. Joseph selected a book: a leather- covered journal and a star chart. He seemed to flick through the pages, but he memorized every heading and footnote. Every page was an explosion of thought, and Professor William Briar's scratchy drawings made Joseph smile. His eyes fell on Dimos, a yellow dwarf star in the Milky Way galaxy cataloged by the first Space telescopes: Hubble, Webb, Fleming, and in recent times by the innovative Chinese built Faxian Space telescope.

A star chart on a wall drew Joseph's attention. He stared at stunning images of seven newly discovered planets orbiting Dimos. He could name the seven planets circled with a green pencil. However, a red circle marked the farthest pinpoint of light, planet Galraithia.

"A fair copy, but not Briar's original star chart. The date is incorrect," Joseph said, turning to Martin. "Faxian discovered Galraithia on February 5, 2170, but it wasn't cataloged officially as a habitable planet until November 19, 2170."

Martin had no interest whatsoever in the black dots that represented stars and the rows of mathematical symbols on the star chart. They were meaningless to him. However, the date of February 5, 2170, was familiar. "The beginning of the Great Rebellion," Martin said.

"Yes. Rachel Sibley's socio-economic war," Joseph added. "The reason Faxian's discovery hardly raised an eyebrow. People weren't interested in new planets; the focus was on Welsh-born Rachel Sibley, the leader of the Freelander movement… considered by many political pundits of the day as the greatest threat to world peace."

"She was the greatest woman of the twenty-second century," Martin said.

"Indeed. Rachel Sibley changed the world for the better."

"Someone's coming!" Martin cautioned.

Joseph turned to see a gray-haired, middle-aged man, thin of build and wearing the black cassock worn by Christian clergy. The hem of the cassock covered black leather shoes, sweeping the tiled floor as he approached. "Welcome, gentlemen. I'm Father Sandor, Professor Briar's personal assistant."

"Hello, Father. I'm Joseph Arunui."

"Welcome, Joseph," said the priest, lowering his voice and placing the right hand over his chest. "Professor Briar is expecting you. And you must be Commander Martin Brindle, welcome to Dome Fuji, sir."

"Joseph and I are glad to be here."

The priest noticed Martin's unwelcoming, cold eyes, and his expressionless tone of voice. "Professor Briar said he would be here to meet us," Joseph said, looking around.

"Professor Briar is working in the observatory. He's been expecting you. If you will follow me, gentlemen."

Martin was always a good judge of character, and Father Sandor's weathered face belonged to a man who had lived a hard life, possibly a man with many secrets.

The Freelander People had no religious ideologies to follow. Nonetheless, Freelander militias patrolling the occupied territories hunted down and punished anyone who tried to sway or mock the beliefs of the Freelander movement. Martin, a rational man with a proud Freelander heritage, wanted nothing to do with Father Sandor or the teachings of his ancient Church.

"Father Sandor, you are a Christian priest and the assistant of the most powerful man in the Freeland territories. Surely, your Pope in Rome has needs and roles for a man with your strong academic talents?"

Joseph walked up to Martin and whispered, "You are a jackass when you are drunk, and a bigger jackass when you are sober."

Martin clipped Joseph upside the head.

"What was that for?"

"For interfering, and not minding your own business," Martin said.

"You are an A-grade jackass" Joseph said, walking away.

The priest felt obliged to ease the rising tension. "Commander, I no longer practice my ordained duties. I serve Professor Briar. And I am one hundred percent committed to him and the Freelander cause."

"Yeah, well, you can say what you like. But your words carry no weight with me, Priest."

Father Sandor shook his head, and it wasn't that he couldn't deal with Martin; he wasn't in the mood to argue. The priest led the newcomers down a long iron-grated walkway. Through an open doorway, the party of three entered the Dome Fuji Observatory, the pride of William Briar. Exhibited on the East wall of the observatory were high-gloss-colored photographs of the Solar System, interactive lesson content and short narratives recounting the Voyager 1 and Voyager 2 missions. Many more images featured the Hubble and James Webb space telescopes. Nonetheless, the pride of place belonged to Faxian, the first traveling Space telescope. China's Wenchang Space Center (WSC) had successfully launched a Far Star (FS) rocket into Earth orbit December 26, 2167, and by Chinese New Year of 2169, the WSC had proudly declared the Faxian telescope fully operational. Justifiably in China, Faxian's departure from our Solar System was a momentous occasion. From the beginning of Faxian's mission, astronomers in the Allied United Nations harbored deep misgivings and attempted multiple sabotage efforts.

"Get a move on, Joseph, you're not standing on hallowed ground," Martin said, knowing the historical significance of the photographs and the fact they had fired Joseph's imagination from a very young age.

"Mr. Arunui, if you would care to follow me, I will show you the first enhanced images of planet Galraithia taken by the Faxian telescope," the priest said.

"How far away from Galraithia was Faxian when the photographs were taken?"

"Faxian was approaching the Liaoning Gateway," the priest said. "Regrettably, Faxian's 70-year journey terminated at the Gateway... for the time being. A refueling mission and systems upgrade are being planned for Faxian as we speak. I'm sure Professor Briar will bring you up to speed with what's going on with the Phoenix and Endeavour Projects before the convention."

An interactive sound panel turned on, a female voice beckoned Martin and Joseph to approach.

"Please, insert headphones into ears," commanded the voice.

Both men followed the instructions. A continuous ringing sound filled their ears. Then, they listened to breaking waves on an unknown shore, the wind howling through a forest, and a sandstorm sweeping over a desert.

Martin removed his headphones. "Listening to relaxing sounds helps me unwind," he said.

"The sounds are 133-year-old recordings," said the priest. "Electromagnetic vibrations from wavelengths that originated from Galraithia."

"Or from Earth," Martin said, with a questioning look on his face.

"Martin, you are the most negative person I have ever met," Joseph said.

"Joseph, you believe those sounds come from Galraithia because you are obsessed with Galraithia, and there is nothing more important in your life. But I'm a realist, I rely on proven facts."

"Whatever!" Joseph said. "Lead on, Father Sandor, there's no point talking to Martin; he's no fun when he's in this mood."

Ahead loomed the East wall and a treacherous metal staircase spiraling to the observatory's summit. The three men climbed, their muscles burning and resolve tested with each grueling step. Joseph gazed upward at the segmented dome's underbelly, its tubular framing cradling the largest working telescope in the Southern Hemisphere. The staircase terminated at the observation platform. Treading across perforated metal sheeting and grated walkways, Joseph's pulse raced, his breathing ragged, his body drenched in thick perspiration that testified to the arduous ascent.

"Hey, do you feel okay?" Martin asked.

"Never better," Joseph replied.

"Never better, eh? You are a terrible liar, Joseph."

"Commander, we can wait here for a few minutes while Mr. Arunui catches his breath, then we'll proceed."

"I'll be okay," Joseph said, panting heavily.

Martin approached the safety railing and peered down at the eastern ground floor. A cacophony of mechanical life churned below: hydraulic pumps and actuators interconnected through a complex network, punctuated by the rhythmic whirring of oil cooling fans. "It's a long way down," he murmured, taking in the industrial sprawl.

"300 feet high to be exact," Father Sandor said. "Color has returned to your face, Mr. Arunui. Shall we continue?"

"Yes, by all means. I'm sorry for the delay."

"We are born imperfect beings," the priest put in. "Our physical limitations are with us until the day we die. Then begins our spiritual journey."

"Keep your religious beliefs to yourself," Martin snapped.

The old priest whispered words in a foreign language then he looked away. And it was becoming clear to Joseph that the two men on either side of him had a mutual dislike for each other.

"Professor!" the priest shouted.

His mind on the job, Briar had no time for distractions. "Back so soon, Ludwig?"

"Your two guests are here, Professor."

"Tell them to go away," Professor Briar said. "I'm not receiving any visitors today, Ludwig."

"It's Joseph Arunui, the young astrophysicist, sir," the priest said.

"Yes, yes, yes," Professor Briar said, pulling out a piston rod from a faulty hydraulic cylinder.

The professor placed the rod end back into its new pin connection, screwing tight the retaining bolt. "This should do the trick," the professor said to himself. "Ludwig, I'm almost done here, tell them I'll be down soon." Professor Briar returned to a workstation and pressed a few black buttons on an old electrical panel. Then, ever so slowly, the segmented roof started to open, and the Antarctic summer's fading light filled the observatory.

If you did not know William, you would say he was a man who cared little for his outward appearance. Three months into his 43rd year, the inventor/astronomer with shoulder-length unkempt hair, graying-black beard, and dirty loose-fitting blue coveralls lacked a commanding presence. But Briar had an athletic build, martial arts skills, and he was particularly fond of bare-knuckle fighting. In other words, Briar was not a man to trifle with. And he was a British exile by his own choosing, an outcast for joining the Freelander movement, and he enjoyed the company of Xiangshan traders and called a Jesuit priest his friend.

Working fifteen-hour days, Professor Briar, with the help of Father Sandor, had managed to repair the only ground-based telescope on Earth, although there were many setbacks. Poor weather conditions and technology sanctions imposed on Freelander scientists by the UAN had had Professor Briar and Father Sandor scavenging for parts in the abandoned Shanawi Station and the Guangdou

Observatory. Indeed, Briar and Sandor's hard work paid off when they focused their telescope on the constellation Cassandra Major and managed to establish a data link between the Dome Fuji telescope and the Faxian Deep Space telescope, which had made history late in the year 2378. That was when it had discovered seven planets orbiting the sun Dimos, a star that was visible from Earth every 186 years.

***

Professor Briar stepped down off the Observation terrace ladder. "Gentlemen, welcome to the Dome Fuji Observatory."

"Hello, Professor," Joseph said, extending his hand. "It's an honor to meet you finally."

"Thank you, Joseph. It's an honor to have you and Commander Brindle here with us, which reminds me, I have good news from the Science Portal. The recruitment process has ended, and you two gentlemen are the first successful candidates selected for astronaut training… congratulations gentlemen."

"Thank you, sir."

Martin nodded, but he did not look nearly as pleased as Joseph.

"Is there something wrong, Commander?" Briar said.

"No, Professor, I'm alright."

"Gentlemen, there's no doubt in my mind that the astronaut training program is a great challenge. We are all aware of that fact, and I think we need to be determined to succeed. Have you anything to add, Ludwig?"

"Yes. We shall announce the names of the other successful candidates at the Freelander Assembly," Father Sandor said. Then, an alarm echoed loudly off the concrete walls of the observatory.

"It's okay!" Professor Briar shouted. "The base of the telescope is rotating to its positional interlock. Ludwig, would you be so kind as to escort Commander Brindle to the Tea Room, please?"

"Certainly. Follow me, Commander."

"Joseph, come with me to the Oculus. I have something to show you," Professor Briar said.

Outside in freezing cold, Professor Briar and Joseph walked along a narrow protruding walkway circling the outside girth ring of the dome. Five steps down, a doorway led to a large room with an Oculus. This large circular window faced north and offered the best panoramic view of Dome Fuji. Upon entering the room, Joseph saw no heating units on the floor or the four walls. Instead, there was junk everywhere: large reels of hemp rope, electrical cable, grimy tarpaulins, gray wool blankets, wooden chests, steel pipes, old computer cases, arcade gaming machines, and advertising posters. One poster, an artist's vision of the future, depicted the terraforming of ice-covered Antarctica. Another poster described a magnificent glass dome over a city with glistening apartments, leafy boulevards, and a bustling civic center. A high-speed underground rail network linked Dome Fuji to the beautiful coastline city of Dome Halley. However, the first Freelanders had abandoned the notion of terraforming the interior of Antarctica. So, no significant highways linked Dome Fuji to the city of Dome Halley, there were no fast rail networks, and no bustling civic center.

"What's the matter, Joseph, don't you like what you see?" Professor Briar asked.

"There is nothing to see," Joseph countered. "Terraforming the interior of Antarctica was just a pipe dream."

"People said Dome Halley was just a pipe dream back in the day, but it became a reality after Rachel Sibley's death if you remember your Freelander history," Professor Briar said. "Today, the Freelander People are the envy of the world. And thanks to your work on nanotrine particles, we have the means to compete in the new space race." Then Briar added with his brow arching, "Travel to distant stars."

Joseph hesitated; his face reddened. "Professor, a nanotrine powered Far-Star engine is in the development stage, untested in space."

"Nonsense! All the numbers stack up, your math is true, not that Gordon Winthrop and the Davis-Molby Company (DMC) will reap any rewards from your outstanding work."

"Winthrop is the most narrow-minded man I've had the misfortune to meet," Joseph said, peering through the oculus at the few scattered buildings beyond the supply depot. "I did try to explain my dark matter theory to him, but he didn't understand it, maybe he didn't care. Either way, I won't waste my breath talking to that man."

"Joseph, I'm not surprised," Professor Briar said. "The Endeavour spacecraft has the latest Ion powered propulsion system, and Ganitte generators provide electrical power to a parallel backup system. Fabricators installed the last of five DMC engines the day before your vessel sailed from Southport."

"I never expected Phoenix would be ready for flight testing before Endeavour. Gordon Winthrop must be first, and he must have the best," Joseph said with scorn in his voice.

"The best-built yacht does not necessarily win the race, Joseph. But with your redesigned Far-Star engines, the once-in-a-lifetime race to Galraithia is ours to win."

"Or ours to lose," Joseph said bluntly. "The issue has always been engine reliability, and you and I both know a Far-Star engine is likely to explode when pushed to its thrust limit. With a nanotrine reactor supplying power to five engines, I just don't know what will happen out there. That's why we need more time for testing. We must be certain that every engine works in parallel above maximum thrust."

"Joseph, there is no time left for performance diagnostics. Congress is tomorrow evening. Transit day is the day after. And Winthrop has requested another meeting with you before we announce the candidates for astronaut training."

"Really! After our last meeting in New Zealand, I didn't think he wanted to see me, or Professor Lin again."

"Both you and Professor Lin certainly did an excellent job at shutting him out during that meeting," the Professor said.

"Yes, we did!" Joseph snapped. "He wanted his people on the Phoenix."

"Joseph, both you and Professor Lin know I would never allow that to happen."

"Winthrop knows you would override any decision that favored his people," Joseph said. "The man does not deserve any respect."

"Gordon Winthrop is not a fool. He knows the expedition to Galraithia has a life-endangering index that is off the scale. His best people are extroverts, people he can trust, and they are all team players he can rely on should something go wrong during the mission."

Joseph's mind switched off; he could not believe his ears. William Briar, the man he had idolized since the age of eight defending a man that couldn't be trusted?

"Then, you talk to Winthrop!" Joseph snapped. "Because Professor Peng Lin and I are two young nobodies, according to him. When Peng told him she wanted some of our best people on the Endeavour, Winthrop ripped into her. He said Freelanders are not welcome on his ship."

"Gordon and I have crossed swords many times, and the best way to beat him was to play on his vanity…that's how you deal with powerful men like Gordon Winthrop."

"And how will you deal with his private army, his best soldiers armed with weapons?" Joseph remarked. "He wants to bring them to Galraithia for his personal protection."

"Gordon and I have an agreement, weapons will not be allowed on Galraithia, and his private army must not and will not enter inside the settlement area, and they'll enjoy no preferential treatment from Winthrop or anyone else for that matter. I made myself clear to Gordon on that point."

Joseph was stuck in two minds because without the support of Winthrop and his Endeavour the Phoenix spacecraft would have to go it alone to Galraithia.

"Professor, I'm no sycophant," Joseph said after some thought. "My grandfather taught me to be my own man, to discard toxic people in my life, but I'm prepared to put aside my personal feelings to fulfill Phoenix's mission parameters."

"So, you'll talk to Gordon Winthrop?"

"Professor, humanity is on the cusp of another paradigm shift in space exploration. For that reason, I am willing to put my subjective opinions aside and meet with Winthrop."

As much as Joseph disliked Gordon Winthrop, there was no denying the man's importance. Winthrop held the gun on the starting line of the new space race. The UAN without Winthrop's political influence and backing would not have approved the construction of the Endeavour. She was capable of journeying to Galraithia and back to Earth within the span of an average human life. In contrast, the Phoenix spacecraft would remain on the surface of Galraithia and be re-engineered to include the population center of the first settlement. Therefore, William Briar and Gordon Winthrop had agreed that working together would be beneficial to the people of Phoenix and Endeavour.

"Professor, you didn't bring me up here to talk about Gordon Winthrop."

"No, Joseph, I wanted to show you the latest Faxian data."

"But Faxian's fuel cells are depleted," Joseph said. "Faxian is dead in space."

"Assuming that to be correct, you can imagine our surprise when we received a Faxian transmission early this morning, and it's the latest data."

"Does Winthrop know?" Joseph asked.

"Forget Winthrop, take him out of the picture," Professor Briar said.

"Okay."

"The data module tells us the landscape and weather conditions on Galraithia's southern continent are not too dissimilar to that of Antarctica," Professor Briar said. "Nevertheless, there is a high probability that nearer to the Ithinian Sea winter blizzards also occur during the dry months, and they could last ten years or more. Follow me, Joseph, I have more weather data to show you."

Joseph had many questions, but he didn't know where to begin. Three powerful Sequanta computers were chirping away in Briar's control room. The Sequanta computing standard needed no human interaction; they could self-learn, self-repair, and they boasted the latest artificial intelligence module. When they communicated, or transferred data, they spoke their own language and sounded very much like a flock of birds atop a forest canopy.

"All this modern technology!" Joseph declared. "How is this possible with all the sanctions in place?"

Professor Briar explained that for over 200 years, the UAN had limited the free flow of technology to Freelanders; opposing sides of global politics had agreed that something drastic had to be done to stop the Freelanders remapping countries as their own. The Freelanders believed the world needed great social change; the consequences of human overpopulation and the following social costs of failure would lead to another global war over food and water.

"How do you manage to hide all this equipment from the UAN inspectors?" Joseph said.

"There are times when inspectors come and inspect the telescope, but all they see is our blurry photographs and a rusting telescope. So, they go away thinking Freelander technology is not a threat. All smoke and mirrors, Joseph."

There were a dozen Pinyin display screens inside Briar's control room, but Joseph was interested in the smallest screen. The screen that was showing him seven planets orbiting a yellow dwarf sun.

"All seven planets are equidistant from Dimos," Joseph proclaimed.

"Yes. And Dimos has a weaker gravity field than the Sun of Earth," Professor Briar pointed out.

"Professor, when did the planets form?"

"Faxian data suggests six of the seven planets formed around 2.2 billion years ago and Galraithia 4.2 billion years ago."

"Galraithia is the third planet from the Sun, and its age is comparable to that of Earth," Joseph said excitedly. "Do the similarities end there, Professor?"

"Look at the images on the computer and tell me what you see."

"Well, Galraithia is not too dissimilar to Earth in color and size, and I can see the outline of two continents and many large islands, but the southern continent is out of focus."

"Is the southern continent clearer now?" Professor said, zooming into the image.

"Yes, thank you, Professor. The detail is unbelievable! Equatorial Galraithia has the characteristics of Earth during the Carboniferous Period."

"The averages of atmospheric pressure and air temperature in and around Galraithia's equator are numbers that are comparable to the yearly averages we have on Earth," Professor Briar said. "So, those large islands may contain a diversity of plant and animal species due to higher air temperatures, but we need more time to decipher Faxian's planetary data to be certain."

"The Faxian telescope is an outstanding piece of engineering," Joseph said.

"Faxian is a machine, and it can fail, make mistakes," Martin Brindle cut in, as he entered the oculus chamber. Father Sandor was standing in the doorway awaiting Professor Briar's permission to enter.

"Come in gentlemen," Professor Briar said.

Martin didn't hesitate; he walked around an extended workbench, stepping over several multicore electrical cables that snaked across the floor.

"Commander, be careful where you walk; most of the electrical equipment around this place is in poor condition," Father Sandor said.

"Professor, how do we communicate with each other on Galraithia? The high-speed interstellar communication is in its infancy, and Galraithia is too far from the slower DSCN."

"Joseph, that's an excellent question," Father Sandor said.

"We can use the Faxian telescope as a relay station once it's refueled and powered up and then link it up to Earth's listening posts," Professor Briar said, as he opened a digital map. "However, from what we know of Galraithia's atmosphere, our microwave and radio technology will be of little value once we get on the planet's surface. That is why we have opted for the line-of-sight communication system. We plan a series of laser communication beacons that will connect the northern and southern continent to the Equatorial Zone. Bring that small table a little closer, please, Joseph."

Upon the small table, between two chairs, were several digital charts and an astronomy book. Professor Briar rested a circular pedestal carved from black marble on the small table. Touching the circular pedestal activated a small electrical motor and holographic circuitry concealed inside. The pedestal seemed to glow from black to blue as the table vibrated and the motor hummed, then the pedestal glowed bright blue and the ceiling lights dimmed. In response, the holographic circuitry generated a scaled-down image of a planet floating two inches above the pedestal.

"This is a hologram of planet Galraithia. Ludwig designed the circuitry and wrote the coding," Professor Briar said.

"It's not perfect," Father Sandor said. "There are discrepancies in the data; Faxian's long-range sensors cannot penetrate Galraithia's strong geomagnetic field. However, there's enough good data to suggest a two-season model for regions temperate in climate."

Professor Briar controlled the black marble pedestal with the hidden holographic circuitry. Waving a hand over the pedestal, he peeled away digitized layers of Galraithia's atmosphere. Bright and crisp, two 3D displays of landmasses equal in size promptly appeared. Galraithia's ice-covered northern continent and semi-arid southern continent.

"I'm guessing the blue shaded area in the hologram is water," Martin said.

Professor Briar looked at Martin; there was no tone of condescension in his voice as he said, "Correct. The Ithinian Sea and the Tezarian Ocean divide the two continents."

"Could there be living organisms, aquatic lifeforms?" Martin asked.

"Theoretically, yes," Father Sandor replied.

Professor Briar hesitated before he answered Martin. "Faxian's computer systems are asking the same question. Tell me, Commander, do you like Space music?"

"I listen to all styles of music."

"Professor Briar is referring to Space noise," Joseph said.

"I suppose you could call it that," Professor Briar said, thinking aloud. "The interaction of electromagnetic radiation with ordinary matter and every piece of matter, regardless of size, has its own unique vibration."

Martin scratched his head and tried to think. "I don't doubt the behavior of molecules and atoms. But what you say, Professor, I just don't understand or pretend to understand any of it."

Professor Briar opened a small portable computer and touched the display screen. "If you allow me, Commander, I will enlighten you and save a lot of time."

Martin nodded.

"This is the raw data collected by Faxian's spectroscope. Our computers have evaluated only the data from Galraithia's equatorial region, and there's a diversity of plant life, insects, and small reptiles cohabiting in the wetlands." While explaining, the professor touched the display screen again and the screen went black. He turned to Joseph and said, "Ludwig and I calibrated Faxian's multi-channel light detector, and everything disappeared: no plant life, no insects, and no small reptiles. The spectroscope reported the planet as lifeless. No biosignatures anywhere on or below the surface."

"The spectroscope could be faulty," Joseph offered.

"Faxian has self-diagnosing multiprocessors as well as Sequanta's self-repairing intelligence modules," Professor Briar pointed out.

"Faxian is more than capable of resolving any conflicting LDPs (Life Data Profiles)," Father Sandor added.

"Life Data Profiles?" Joseph said.

"It's complicated, but I'll do the best I can," Father Sandor said.

Martin sighed deeply. He was bored, and it was clear to Joseph that Martin could not wait to go home.

"Faxian's logic processors transmit Galraithia's LDP as raw data to the nearest Wincorp-7 satellite," Father Sandor said. "The raw data is then processed using powerful computer programs and transmitted to NASA and re-encrypted. The Wenchang Space Centre and the Dome Fuji Observatory receive re-encrypted copies, not the original Galraithian LDPs."

"NASA is withholding the original Galraithian LDPs, why?" Joseph asked.

"NASA is a subsidiary of Winthrop Corporation…accountable to no one but Gordon Winthrop."

"Are you suggesting that NASA is deliberately falsifying the Galraithian LDPs?" Martin asked.

"Suggesting! I am not suggesting," Father Sandor loudly. "I am telling you that Gordon Winthrop is behind all of it, the conflicting LDPs, the corrupted planetary data. If we cannot trust Faxian's data, Freelanders will never set foot on Galraithia."

"If Gordon Winthrop and the UAN reach Galraithia first. It's game over for our people," Joseph declared.

"Ludwig, irrespective of whether or not there is life on Galraithia, there's one undeniable fact, we are running out of time."

"Professor Briar, unlike Joseph, I haven't read any of your books, but I respect your opinion," Martin said bluntly. "I don't understand what all this 'life/no life' means. If you are uncertain, why not send an unmanned probe to Galraithia?"

"Martin, we are not dealing with sea ice drifting off Eastern Antarctica," Joseph remarked.

"Commander Brindle is offering his opinion, and we need every opinion," Professor Briar said.

"We don't have time for opinions! We need answers, and we need them quickly. A rendezvous with Galraithia will not come again in our lifetime." Joseph said.

Martin frowned at Joseph; he didn't understand the importance of Joseph's last statement. "Are we done here, Joseph?"

"I have a few more questions about Galraithia that I would like to ask Professor Briar."

"Well, you can stay here all day if you want to. I'm leaving this shithole, and I'm leaving now."

"It's getting late," Professor Briar said, looking at an old digital clock on the wall. "Gentlemen, please stay for dinner. Ludwig is very competent in the kitchen."

Martin didn't want to stay, but he was getting hungry, and dinner was free. That evening during the evening meal, the forthcoming Southern Conference Fight dominated the discussions around the dinner table, and Martin was gratful that Joseph had stopped talking about Galraithia.

***

123

The Freelander Assembly

On the evening of 25 February 2424, Joseph and Martin were among the first of the invited guests to arrive outside the Nobu Shirase Lecture Hall. Smartly dressed in their best warm clothing, both men hurried to the two female security guards who had set up a DNA scanning station at the front entrance of the lecture hall.

"Mr. Andrew Tohvian, please step forward," said Clare, the leading guard. "Andrew, are you traveling to Dome Halley tomorrow?"

"No, my son Jason is traveling tomorrow. He wanted me to go with him to the Southern Conference Fight this year, but I'm too old to be traipsing around Sibley Arena."

"Okay, I understand. Form another line, please. In front of me will do nicely, thank you. The doors will be opening very soon, so be patient."

A man walked up to Clare, and he wasn't happy. "Excuse me, Miss, how much longer must we wait? It's freezing out here in this wind."

"I know, be patient. The doors will open soon."

More people arrived in front of the lecture hall. Some were friends, and some were acquaintances in one way or another, although most were total strangers.

"Okay, the doors are opening," Clair said. "You can go inside now, Andrew. A guard will escort you to your reserved seat."

As Andrew shuffled a little closer to the front door, both Martin and Joseph moved to the front of the line.

"This is taking forever," Martin said, exhaling in frustration, and glaring at Clare. She remembered Martin, the handsome navy man who she thought was vain and drank too much. "Commander Brindle, we'll get to you as quickly as we can," Claire said before addressing everyone who had lined up in front of the lecture hall, "Now, please move over to Melinda's line and have your DNA scan card ready if you plan to travel to Dome Halley tomorrow morning."

Melinda verified DNA and identity scans, and she conducted an effective pat-down procedure: search for weapons, cameras, and audio recording devices, which she had listed on her display screen as prohibited items. Joseph declared an insistent 'No' to every question put to him by Varon, the big guard helping Melinda.

"Mr. Arunui. Thank you for being patient," Varon said, before he turned to Martin. "Commander, may I have your DNA card, please, sir?"

Martin made eye contact with the big guard before he handed him his Navy identity card.

"Thank you for being patient, sir," Varon said, as he read data scrolling down a scanning device.

"Commander Brindle and Mr. Arunui. I am issuing two tickets for tomorrow's transport and two vaccination packs. Each pack should contain two sterile syringes, one multi-dose ampoule, dosage instructions, and injection times. Any questions?"

"No, I have no questions," Martin replied. "Vaccinations are a fact of life in the Navy."

"No questions!" Joseph snapped. "It's easy for you to say, but I would like to know the side effects of the chemical compounds inside the ampoule. Under Freelander Law, I have the right to know."

"Mr. Arunui, having the right won't change a thing. Vaccinations are a mandatory requirement before entering and leaving Dome Halley. No ifs or buts! I'm just stating the rules, sir."

Varon's scanner beeped twice, and the small display screen flashed green.

"Commander Brindle and Joseph Arunui, you are good to go, move along," Varon said. He then pointed to the British Ambassador. "I need to see your DNA card, sir. Step forward, please."

The British Ambassador, who was a short, pompously overbearing Englishman in a refined suit which was a mix of dark blue thermal fabric, walked up to Varon.

"Ambassador Blainey, are you traveling to Dome Halley on tomorrow's transport, sir?"

"No. I'll be here another week at least, maybe longer."

Varon looked at his scanner and waited for confirmation. Ambassador Blainey hadn't lied to him. "You are good to go, sir. Thank you for being patient."

Melinda called the next person waiting in her line. "Veronica Blainey, step forward please."

Veronica glanced over at her father, who was becoming increasingly frustrated, having to wait in another line.

Melinda said, "Veronica Blainey, 34, born in Sheffield, England, are you traveling on tomorrow's transport?"

"Yes, I am."

"Have you visited Dome Halley in the past six months?"

"No."

"When was the last time you visited Dome Halley?"

"I have never been to Dome Halley."

"Have you ever been refused entry to any Freeland city?"

"No."

Melinda looked Veronica in the eye. "Okay. I am authorized to issue you one ticket for tomorrows transport and one vaccination pack," Melinda said. "Your pack should contain two sterile syringes, one multi-dose ampoule, dosage instructions and injection times. Any questions?"

"No questions," Veronica said. "Am I good to go?"

Varon turned around, and he eyed the British Ambassador's attractive daughter, a classy long-legged, vivacious blonde. "Yes, Miss Blainey, you are good to go."

As more invited guests continued to arrive, Marion Tyler noticed the moon rising into a dark sky full of twinkling stars. The Southern Lights (Aurora Australis) danced above the distant horizon, and a cold north-easterly wind was gusting up to 40 knots. Marion adjusted the dark blue neck-warmer around her grandfather, touched his gold badge lightly, and read the citation inscribed on the badge: *The Council of Freelander Elders awards this Medal of Honor to General Randal Tyler.*

"It's getting colder by the minute. Are you warm enough, Poppy?"

"I don't feel cold, my dear," Randal Tyler said. "My brothers and I slept out in the open on colder nights than this." After a short pause, he continued, "Our past hunting trips in search of new sealing grounds were an adventure, but without much success. Half-starved most of the time, we huddled together under woolen blankets like newborn pups to keep out the cold. Then in 35, the Xiangshan Traders came to Antarctica peddling Roni suits and other modern-day gadgetry."

"And you end up marrying the daughter of the most powerful Trader around at the time," Marion said.

"Michael Redfield was a highly intelligent man. Today's successful Traders would pale in comparison."

After a short pause Marion said, "Look, the doors are open. Come on, Poppy, let's get you out of this wind."

Randal Tyler, retired Freelander general and older brother of Peter and the late Douglas Tyler, walked alongside his granddaughter Marion, believing the best years were behind him. All the good days he had spent fighting for the Freelander movement; making trouble for the Allied armies with his wife Sarah by his side. They had survived the war and continued taking part in the Multinational Freelander Force in Antarctica and the Freelander Global Movement headed by their daughter Haley. But those happy days ended when Sarah died of acute pneumonia shortly after their first grandchild, Alistair, was born.

"I look at you and see your grandmother. You have her caring eyes. She would be immensely proud of the loving and caring woman that you have become. Are you one-hundred percent certain that you want to go with Alistair?"

"I'm afraid so, Poppy, but don't you worry, okay. Uncle Peter is here, and he will take good care of you. You and he get on so well together; you always have," Marion said as she approached Varon.

"Good evening, Miss Tyler, a pleasure to see you again."

"Hello, Varon. I thought this line would never end."

"Good evening, General. I'm sorry for your loss."

"My old friend, you are too kind," Randal Tyler said. "But you needn't feel sorry. My brother Douglas was a drunkard and a fool for leaving our home in Antarctica."

The old General in his gray battle-fatigues and a tight blue scarf around his thick neck had Varon's respect. The gold badge pinned to the scarf (rising sun behind boomerang) was an ancient emblem dating back to the first Freelander uprising in Australia.

"I don't see Alistair," Marion said, searching the front area of the lecture hall, "has my brother arrived?"

"Yes, Miss," replied Varon. "He's sitting in the front row, three seats in from the left aisle. Follow me, please."

"Thank you, Varon, but I think my granddaughter and I can manage nicely on our own," Randal said.

"As you wish, sir."

***

A half-track taxi stopped in front of the lobby door of the Crossroads Hotel. A security guard standing on the sidewalk checked registration numbers and screened passengers and guests entering the Crossroads Hotel. The vehicle belonged to a guy called Timmon, a privateer taxi driver from Dome Halley. Timmon said he and his two passengers had the current Security Clearance IDs and had cleared the seven checkpoints between Dome Halley and Dome Fuji.

"Stop talking and step out of the car," said the guard. "I ain't got all day."

"But we all have security clearance!" Timmon proclaimed.

The guard pulled his pistol from its holster and shouted, "IDs, please!"

From a short distance, Varon recognized the man Timmon, a known scrounger.

"Guard! Let him pass," Varon commanded.

"Yes, sir."

Timmon's smirk became more pronounced as he approached Varon. "Hey, Varon, how're things with you, man?"

"Give me the IDs and shut up," Varon said flatly.

"You're in a lousy mood today," Timmon said.

Looking anxious, his right hand shook as he handed Varon three metal ID cards. Varon inserted three cards into a portable scanner. "The two foreigners, how well do you know them?" Varon asked, looking at the scanner.

"Other than the fact that they are priests...nothing," Timmon replied. "They hired me to drive them around, and here we are."

"Timmon, I will ask you one more time. Can you vouch for the two Italian priests who are now under your care, yes or no?"

Timmon stepped closer and whispered, "Yes. I will vouch for them. But they are not under my care."

Varon opened a small tablet computer. "Okay, sign here."

"The fat-faced priest is wearing a solid gold cross chained around his neck, and his satin robe is decorated with many valuable jewels. Have you ever seen such finery on one man?"

Varon glowered at Timmon. "The IDs have been verified, move on."

"Xiangshan Traders pay very well for gold and precious jewels."

"Stay away from Xiangshan Traders. They'll skin you alive one day."

"I don't think so. I have a good friend watching my back."

"I'm not your friend!" Varon proclaimed.

Walking away, Timmon said, "The next time you come to Dome Halley, there will be 20 bottles of homemade scura alcohol waiting for you, Varon."

Timmon returned to the Italian priests and demanded prompt payment of the total fare from Dome Halley to Dome Fuji, 5,000 yuan per person. The priests were not impressed with Timmon. Having no choice but to pay, they handed Timmon the money, protesting angrily that the fare had tripled. They called him a liar and a thief, but the name-calling did not bother Timmon in the slightest. He cared even less about the two Italian priests. So, Timmon stepped to the rear of the taxi, opened the trunk, and threw ten suitcases onto the sidewalk.

Then he promptly jumped in the car and drove off, leaving behind a red-robed man, the 63-year-old Cardinal from Rome and the fair-skinned interpreter, a 25-year-old Jesuit priest with sleepy blue eyes, a kind face, and a typical pugilist's nose. He looked at the Cardinal, then he shrugged his shoulders helplessly as Varon approached.

"Why are you two still here, is there a problem?"

The young priest extended his right hand towards Varon. "Good evening, sir. I am Father Antonio. Cardinal Salvatore Bresciano's personal secretary." His English had a heavy accent. "His Eminence is the invited guest of Professor William Briar. Please, if it is not too much of an inconvenience, can you direct me to the Nobu Shirase Lecture Hall?"

Varon looked at the overweight Cardinal, pondering whether or not he should oblige the visitors from Rome. Italy was the oldest member of the European Green Zone nations. Still, its ancient ties to the Roman Catholic Church prevented Italy from gaining a permanent seat on the Freelander Security Council. Nevertheless, the Italian Government favored the Freelander movement, and for that reason, Varon felt obliged the help the Italian priests; he called out to the guard closest to him. "Guard!"

"Yes, Varon."

"The two priests are staying at Crossroads Hotel. After they check in and deposit their luggage escort them to Nobu Shirase. Don't let them out of your sight! I'll hold you personally responsible if they get into any kind of trouble."

"Yes, sir."

***

The lecture hall was bustling with activity, as every seat on both sides of the main floor was filled to capacity; many attendees had resorted to standing in the aisles, creating a lively atmosphere. Martin sat comfortably next to his friend Joseph, both of them absorbed in their surroundings. Nestled directly behind them were the imposing figures of Ambassador Blainey, distinguished in his tailored suit, alongside his daughter Veronica, who exuded an air of grace and attentiveness as she listened intently.

"All these people," Joseph said with a glum look. "I feel sick in the stomach."

132

"The conference starts in five minutes just try to relax. Focus on breathing, Joseph, the anxiety will pass."

"But I dislike public speaking. I love numbers, not words," Joseph said, worrying that he did not possess the persuasiveness of Professor Briar. Then, Father Sandor sauntered across the floor, stepping over a mosaic of tiles. A raised wooden platform stood in the middle of the room, while armed security personnel guarded the entry and exit doorways. The priest nodded to Varon, who activated the LSS (Laser Sentry System) that had been set up around the lecture hall's outer perimeter. Outside, puffs of steam hissed from the frozen ground as seven towering metal poles, each twenty feet tall, extended skyward. Attached to them was a wide-view, high-energy Van Wagner laser, designed to scan an area spanning 1,117 acres in diameter. At the time of its manufacture, the Freelander-designed Van Wagner laser had been regarded as a first-strike military asset. The Freelander army had relied on it heavily during the Great Rebellion, securing many victories due to its ease of use, minimal maintenance requirements, and devastating power. It had been capable of melting even the thickest armor of the strongest allied tanks within seconds.

***

Having secured Dome Fuji from any ground or aerial attack, Varon nodded to Father Sandor to proceed with the discussions as rapidly as possible. "Your Eminence, distinguished guests, ladies, and gentlemen. On behalf of Professor William Briar, welcome to Dome Fuji and the Nobu Shirase Lecture Hall. This evening, we have many guest speakers from around the globe. You may recognize them by their photographs, or you may know them personally. So, bear with me and stand up only when I call your name, please," Father Sandor said with his eyes looking over the rim of his reading glasses. "Please put

133

your hands together for Mr. Gordon Winthrop of New York City."

Gordon stood up, smiled, and waved to the audience. The man from New York was a tall man with style-cut gray hair and fashionable attire, and his clean skin announced he was a man of high quality, but Gordon was also vain, and he had plenty of money to spend on himself.

Then the priest introduced Ambassador Anthony Blainey, representative of the British Crown and the Davis-Molby Corporation's Chairperson. The ambassador stood up and bowed, though the people acknowledged him with less vigorous applause. Veronica caught Martin's gaze, and to his surprise, she had a smile for him. There was a round of spirited applause for Doctor Ezra Tohvian, the current President of the Freelander Astronomical Society, and the magazine: Voices for Peace. Also attending the conference was Professor of Astrophysics at the University of Auckland and Chairman of the Academy of Science of New Zealand, Mr. Niels Sorenson.

"Put your hands together for Roberta Tully of World Media Group."

Roberta Tully, a senior journalist in the Media Group, received boos and hisses for her views against Freelander integration in China. Roberta was a respected journalist, and her voracious appetite for uncovering the truth had made her many enemies. Rebekah Roezen was another familiar name. The 48-year-old Rebekah was the wife of beef baron Malcolm Roezen, the world's third-richest man.

"Professor Peng Zhenyi Lin, President of the Xiangshan People's University of Aeronautics and Space Sciences." Peng received thunderous applause as she waved hello.

"And from Rome, Italy. His Eminence, Cardinal Salvatore Bresciano."

The Freelanders offered patchy applause, and unhappy
mutterings filled the room when the appointed papal
spokesperson stopped his interpreter from translating. The
Cardinal looked away; he flatly refused to notice Father
Sandor, the rogue priest whom he had excommunicated and
exiled from Italy 12 years earlier.

"Is the fat-headed man the Pope?" Adrian Sangster
whispered.

"No. Salvatore Bresciano is the late Pope's younger
brother, a Freelander," Jason Tohvian replied confidently,
his voice booming around the room; Tohvian males never
knew how to speak softly.

Father Sandor continued to introduce scientists and
journalists who had come to Dome Fuji as honored
representatives of their respective countries. Looking
around the large hall, Martin spotted Jonas Tohvian
escorting Mr. Hasana to his reserved seat. There appeared
to be dark blue bruising around the landlord's left eye.
Martin glowered at the property owner, and there was no
place for him to hide. Thankfully for the proprietor, the
auditorium went dark, and in the darkness, Martin's anger
lessened.

"Our time here is almost over," Joseph.

"Yes. Tomorrow morning can't come soon enough for me."

People muttered, and chairs creaked; people shuffled their
feet, and the sickly-sweet scent of a woman's cheap
perfume made Joseph gag. Then, the ceiling lights came
back on, and Professor William Briar was standing on the
raised dais. The Freelander people cheered and revered
William as their leader, but he knew he could not rule
alone. Freelander Law had outlawed the idea of one
absolute ruler and yet, standing on the dais, William Briar
looked what he was, a proud ruler: tall and muscular, well-

dressed. Not the scruffy-looking man that Martin and Joseph had met earlier that day.

"Humanity is on the verge of another paradigm shift in Space," Professor Briar said. "And the man building the path to the stars is Mr. Gordon Winthrop."

Gordon Winthrop walked over to Professor Briar, stepped onto the dais, and shook the professor's right hand. Then, he thanked Professor Briar for the invitation to the biannual Freelander Assembly. This prompted mutterings around the hall. They became louder when Gordon Winthrop, the richest man in the world, bowed to patchy applause.

"Your Eminence, distinguished guests, ladies, and gentlemen. I am delighted to be here with you this evening." The room went silent. The Freelanders scrutinized every move by Gordon Winthrop, the richest man in the world and the most hated man in the Freeland territories.

Regardless of Gordon's political affiliations and his level of involvement against the Freelanders, they allowed him to speak; Gordon said: "From the outset, the planning, engineering, and construction of the Endeavour and the Phoenix spacecraft in Space were the most ambitious and challenging projects of our time. I take tremendous pride in being the first to announce the Endeavour spacecraft is undergoing engine testing, and its interior construction is on schedule and on budget. But unfortunately, I cannot say the same about Phoenix. I'm sure Professor Briar has received countless apologies and excuses."

"I have indeed," Professor Briar responded, glowering at Anthony Blainey, an arrogant man who had flatly refused to do any business with the Freelanders.

"Chairman Blainey, we don't need your DM manufactured engines," Professor Lin said in her native Mandarin. "With the help of Joseph Arunui and other friends at Wenchang, we have managed to acquire five Far Star compliant engines for Phoenix. And we are confident of meeting two launch dates: August 5, 2424, and October 8, 2424."

People stood up from their seats; there was thunderous applause for Professor Zhenyi Lin.

The T-5 language translator unit matched Peng's soft tone beautifully. Vox-Wand was a reputable Chinese audio company with a long history that dated back to the early years of Space exploration. Then, in the year, 2345, Ercial Winthrop, Gordon's grandfather, bought the Vox-Wand Company. Ercial installed Vox-Wand's reliable and efficient communication system in his penitentiaries on the Moon and on dwarf planet Quaoar. There, convicted criminals serving sentences longer than 5 years with no eligibility for parole experienced hell. The scum of society lived out a miserable existence in an underground world of pain. There was no night or day for dead people walking; time was an unseen enemy stalking the weak in body or mind; there was no going back to the world of the living.

Professor Lin sat back down in her seat confident the translation from her native Mandarin to English was correct and understood by everyone inside the warm auditorium. Both Briar and Winthrop were often at odds with the Chinese rocket men stationed at Wenchang Space Port. Nonetheless, the dates of August 5, 2424, and October 8, 2424, were non-negotiable. Then, without any forewarning a man occupying a third-row seat shouted, "Professor Briar! A moment of your time please."

"Robert John Finnegan, I cannot remember when we spoke last. What can I do for you, RJ?"

"William, I'm not good at idle chatter, so I'll get straight to the point. I will supply the electrical power system equipment for the opportunity to join the expedition to Galraithia, 60-billion-yuan, worth of electrical equipment."

"60 billion yuan!" Joseph whispered to Martin. "That is serious money!"

"Not for R. J. Finnegan. He owns all the geothermal power plants on the West coast of Antarctica and Deception Island," Martin said.

Gordon Winthrop took a tentative step forward and said, "Mr. Finnegan, we all understand your generous gesture. Thank you. But the expedition to Galraithia involves a good deal of physical training and technical knowledge."

"Winthrop, you and I have three things in common," Finnigan retorted "We are on the wrong side of fifty, successful in business and filthy rich. But there are major differences in terms of thinking and attitude between you and me. And I really don't find too many areas of business that we agree on."

"And you think I care?" Gordon said.

"Yes, you care, don't deny it. You care because you're afraid of Freelanders. You couldn't beat them in business and war, so you joined them, wanting to keep them close. Freelanders were willing to tear down the historical barriers between us. But the Allied folk gave us little hope in achieving those goals here on Earth. So, now we have an alternative solution, the opportunity to go to Galraithia and start a new life. Freelanders don't want to rebuild old barriers in a new world, Mr. Winthrop. Why do you?"

While the muttering voices around the auditorium were getting louder, Professor Briar considered Finnegan's offer. But the elected members who constituted the Council of Freelander Elders had the last word. Finally, Judge Michaels's face, the oldest active member on the Council, came on the viewing screen. "Mr. Finnegan, all Council members accept your generous offer."

"The expedition to Galraithia is a one-way trip, RJ. Once you are there, there's no coming back," Professor Briar said.

"William, I have no intention of coming back here for anyone or anything."

Finnegan, known as one of the most eccentric and financially successful individuals in the world, hastened away from the auditorium a happy man. He planned to sell the Eris Asteroid Mining Company and all his business interests on Earth for a significant profit and donate all the money to the Galraithian Expedition. Professor Briar thought the Council members had made the right decision, and William was happy for his friend RJ; the future looked brighter for him. Nevertheless, Professor Briar had a somber look on his face standing with his back to the invited guests and writing symbols and numbers on a large display screen, mathematical formulas from Joseph Arunui's theory on Dark Matter. Joseph started to sweat because he was suffering from anxiety.

"I have to leave the room. I feel nauseous," Joseph said.

"Joseph, stop squirming in your seat," Martin whispered. "Cup your hands over your mouth and focus on your breathing, stop worrying."

Professor Briar turned around and faced 500 pairs of peering eyes.

"Late last year, on 20 December, Father Sandor and I received data from the Faxian telescope. It was projected data, before the rendezvous with planet Caelus." Then, Professor Briar stepped aside for Father Sandor. "Caelus is the furthest planet in the Cassandra Major System," Father

Sandor said. "One of the key calculations we had relied on was Faxian's projected slingshot orbital velocity around Caelus, but the real-time data suggested Faxian's trajectory and relative speed moving away from Caelus had increased to 191C. In other words, a much stronger gravitational force propelled Faxian faster than the speed of light."

"Professor Sorenson, you are a founding member of the Academy of Sciences and an Astrophysicist, do you see a problem with the formulas on the screen?" Professor Briar asked.

"William, you know my answer. How many times must I repeat it? Arunui's math is wrong regardless of the number of letters you write saying the contrary. And my poor opinion of your boy genius is still the same."

Joseph grinned and muttered under his breath.

"Joseph Arunui, you can grin all you like," Professor Sorenson said, wiping sweat from his face with a small handkerchief.

"Joseph, you have a right of reply," Professor Briar said, pointing to the dais.

The auditorium was becoming increasingly warm for Professor Sorenson, but Joseph was seething, and he remained silent in his seat. So, Professor Briar introduced Doctor Anne Hillier. She's a close friend of Briar and a respected astrophysicist.

"Good evening, Anne. I'm sorry for putting you in the spotlight, but I need your help."

"Good evening, William. How can I help?"

"In your professional opinion, do you believe Dark Matter waves exist in interstellar space?"

"Swirlonic behavior in deep space is theoretically possible," Doctor Hillier replied. "Joseph's mathematical formulas on the screen say exactly that: Self-propelled nanotrine particles become circular and tubular as they cluster together."

Professor Sorenson sat facing the dais outwardly disinterested but secretly yearning for Doctor Anne Hillier to drop dead. "She's a fair-haired puppet bitch," Sorenson said to his wife Marta seated next to him.

"Shut up, Neils. Don't bring embarrassment to our family."

"But the woman is Briar's puppet."

"Why do you care? Just look around the room, Neils. There are more enemies than friends staring at you," Marta declared.

"Joseph Arunui, Professor Emeritus of Astronomy and Aerospace Engineering. You are a humble young man deserving of our homage and respect," Professor Briar said. "Stand up and be recognized, Joseph. Don't be afraid of a bottom fish like Neils Sorenson."

Joseph stood up reluctantly, and people cheered, but none cheered louder than Martin Brindle. Then, Henry Dahlberg, a journalist from The London Times stood up to speak to Joseph.

"Henry Dahlberg, London Times. I have been following your work on matter/antimatter engines for some time now."

Joseph nodded. "Thank you."

"But I must say that I was surprised by several ambiguous comments on your recently published scientific paper."

"Mr. Dahlberg, I do not recall any ambiguous comments. My articles discuss hard scientific facts. Having said that, if there is any ambiguity in my words, I am sorry."

"I'm not here to criticize your work, sir. I'm simply curious that on one page, you say faster than light travel is possible, and on another, you say Endeavour's DM engines are outdated and unreliable. With the benefit of hindsight would you agree that your negative comment appeared in print after Aerospace engineers working onboard Endeavour during outfitting had proclaimed the spacecraft flawless in design and an engineering marvel?"

"No, I do not agree. I stated a known fact: Davis-Molby engines are not efficient in the denser interstellar medium beyond the Kuiper Belt. And for that very reason, Professor Lin made the decision to source Far Star engines for the Phoenix and fit a Nanotrine power plant inside a redesigned reactor compartment."

"Nanotrine power plants are highly unstable," Professor Sorenson said. "And how many Far Star engines have exploded in the last five years, ten, twenty?"

"Compliance testing of the Far-Star engines and the Nanotrine reactor has not detected flaws in any of my design specifications."

"Your design specification! Who are you trying to impress, Briar's Chinese friends or the Xiangshan Traders in this room?"

"Sorenson, sit down!" Father Sandor said sternly. "Or you can leave the room now!"

Sorenson made a snorting sound and cast a glowering look at Father Sandor.

"I will sit down, but you haven't heard the last of me."

There was a great deal of muttering around the auditorium when Father Sandor moved closer to William Briar and whispered, "Don't forget to announce our successful candidates."

Professor Briar nodded; Gordon Winthrop was given the honor of reading out the names of the chosen candidates for astronaut training: Joseph Arunui, Martin Brindle, Ezra Tohvian, Jason Tohvian, Roberta Tully, Margaret Gray, Marion Tyler, Margaret Mason, Veronica Blainey, and Adrian Sangster would be the first of the selected candidates to undergo an astronaut training program which Professor Lin had developed and improved to fit the Freelander military model.

The popular Roberta Tully and Margaret Gray punched the air in triumph, and it seemed everyone in the auditorium was celebrating their inclusion in the Astronaut Training Program.

Martin and Joseph enjoyed the celebratory drinks and returned home to pack and get a good night's sleep.

The candidates for the astronaut training program departed for Dome Halley early the next morning with the other selected candidates. Satori Thomas, Lesley Fredericks, and Brendon Aitama on board FS *Taimaha* had also received confirmation of their selection in the Astronaut training program. They had said goodbye to FS *Taimaha* and the crew and hired a half-track taxi to drive them to the Dome Halley Science Portal. At this time of year, late February, it was common for the ice road from Alta-Aria to Dome Halley to rut up. Brendon kept complaining about driving the four-track snow vehicle (4SV) too slowly. He didn't want to arrive late and miss the Southern Conference Fight.

***

143

The Games of Death

The half-track taxi and 4SV crawled over the final ridge, revealing Dome Halley gleaming against the stark white landscape. Thanks to clear skies and virtually deserted ice roads from Alta-Aria, they'd made good time. After meeting with the stern-faced Science Portal administrator—nodding through safety briefings and scrawling signatures across countless forms—Martin, Joseph, and Brendon found themselves free to pursue their true mission: the Southern Conference Challenge.

Their footsteps quickened as Sibley Stadium loomed before them, its massive structure humming with anticipation. Joseph and Martin clutched their precious tickets—a generous gift from Bill Aldridge himself—while Brendon lagged behind, resigned to whatever standing-room spot he could claim among the masses. The trio separated at the security checkpoint, Joseph and Martin following an usher up through the echoing concrete corridors.

Emerging onto a high aisle, Joseph froze mid-step. Below them stretched the central arena, a gladiatorial pit surrounded by rising tiers already half-filled with spectators. By match time, these stands would transform into a living organism of 350,000 bodies, their collective roar becoming a physical force. All eyes would be fixed on two men: defending world champion Bill Aldridge and his challenger, the Russian Aleksandr Volkov, whose cocky fist pump now dominated the giant Pinyin screen hanging above the Ferntree Curve—that infamous 190-foot southern arc named for the suburb where Rachel Sibley was buried.

The northern section of the stadium thundered with the collective roar of Aldridge's devotees, packed shoulder-to-shoulder beneath the towering Kalashkan Curve—named for the infamous militia general, Miro Kalashkan himself. These weren't mere fans; they were disciples, wearing replicas of Bill's gear, mimicking his mannerisms, living by his ruthless philosophy: nobody likes a loser. Above them, a massive Pinyin screen displayed Aldridge's iconic commercial pose, his statistics and personal details illuminated in brilliant digital clarity. Joseph's attention drifted to a cluster of women at the barrier's edge, offering not just adoration but their bodies to the champion who strode past them, oblivious. Sex wasn't on Bill's mind—only his legendary fighting tactics: the explosive speed, relentless momentum, and devastating accuracy that had made him a god in this arena.

A hush fell across the stadium as all eyes locked onto the central feature of Sibley Stadium. What might be mistaken for an artifact from some ancient carnival stood proud at the arena's heart: a colossal wheel erected vertically, its surface gleaming with polished steel, ceramic, and glass. This was no relic but the gaming Rotor, purpose-built for the Southern Conference Fight, soaring 160 feet above an elliptical track that stretched 240 feet in diameter. Around this track glided the carbon Platform car, its electric motors calibrated to perfectly sync with the spinning Rotor where combatants would soon battle for glory. This season's redesigned vehicle could now accommodate three fighters simultaneously, achieving velocities that would have been unthinkable in previous tournaments.

Thirty high-resolution Pinyin cameras—ten more than last year—were strategically positioned throughout the stadium, poised to capture every brutal second of the Platform car's dizzying journey and the violence that would unfold within the Rotor wheel. The holographic technology had evolved too; the spectators seated in the upper tiers and those wealthy enough to claim front-row positions would struggle to distinguish flesh-and-blood contestants from their digital doppelgangers—"the latest and best pixel creations that money could buy," as the Xiangshan marketing executives constantly boasted.

"Look! The Rotor is starting to spin. Good luck, Bill," Joseph shouted.

Bill Aldridge had conquered the Wheel of Death the previous year. As a result, many Volkov supporters suspected Xiangshan Traders had the world champion in their pocket. However, there was never any proof presented to show that Xiangshan Traders had colluded with gaming officials and with Bill Aldridge. Nevertheless, with several hundred Traders inside Sibley Stadium, all gambling on the outcome of the final fight and the fact that Aldridge had won with surprising ease in the earlier rounds had Volkov supporters shouting, "Aldridge is a cheat!"

"Martin, do you think Bill is a cheat?"

"Richard Orentz was an honorable man. I don't think he would have associated himself with Bill if he knew games were being fixed."

Like Bill Aldridge, Martin had learned to fight with his fists from an early age. He trained often and hard, honed his fighting skills inside dingy pubs and brothels and other feel-good arcades. He had seen many bouts of false bravado, which is typically the first sign of weakness in a person's character after consuming one too many alcoholic drinks.

Cameras zoomed in and enlarged the Rotor's central hub from which eight triangular segments divided the rotating wheel, like spokes on a wheel connect hubs to rims to maintain tension. Attached between each triangular section was a G tube, a glass cylinder of regolith glass engineered with precise measurements to accommodate the muscular body of 6'3" tall Aldridge.

Cameras zoomed in again as Aldridge entered his assigned G tube, strapped himself into a shoulder harness, activated the targeting computer, and loaded a dagger in an air cannon, the Rotor's only weapon system.

***

While the primary camera tracked the real Bill Aldridge, roaming cameras zoomed in on seven holographic duplicates entering their assigned G tubes. These digital twins would mimic Bill with uncanny precision—capturing his sounds, facial expressions, body movements, and even the distinctive sheen of sweat across his brow. Bill had long recognized how these holograms confused opponents, attributing much of his success in previous Rotor battles to countless hours spent in simulator training and the invaluable experience gained in actual combat. Starting the game inside the Rotor rather than on the Platform car was the strategic choice, playing to his strengths and experience.

Nevertheless, in a gesture of sporting tradition, the defending champion Aldridge offered challenger Volkov first choice: Rotor or Platform car? Without hesitation, the imposing Russian selected the latter, drawing thunderous approval from his supporters. Everyone understood the brutal math of the situation—both competitors had only a single opportunity for a quick kill during the Wheel of Death round. For Aldridge, confined within a G tube and fighting against crushing gravitational forces, failure to strike precisely with his dagger would lead to an inevitable outcome; as veterans of the sport knew all too well, no one survived a bullet to the head.

147

In the busy broadcast control room, a middle-aged Event Director barked orders and drank too much coffee. He shouted into his microphone, "Camera 12! Focus on Volkov. Follow every move that he makes, or you can find another job. Do I make myself clear?"

"Yes, sir."

Every display screen showed Volkov standing on the Platform car wearing his army fatigues, blue/gray, and Army black heavy boots. Camera 12 zoomed in on Volkov's bruised face, and there was a cut above the left eye. However, Aleksandr's bruised ego pained the most because the two combatants started the day on the same total points after Aldridge was awarded ten points for winning the first round of the competition, bare-knuckle boxing. Volkov had hoped to do better, win the first round, but he received ten points for winning the second round, the speed climb to Halley's 1500-foot-high dome. Aldridge had heard Volkov brag unashamedly at the press conference that he would also win the third and final round, the Wheel of Death round.

As darkness fell over the entire arena, a dozen spotlights followed the big Russian crouching low, riding the open Platform car. He held a small round metal shield in each hand, the only protection Volkov had against fast-flying projectiles. With the plate-sized shields at the ready and the speedy Platform car under his feet, Volkov had confidence in his ability to dodge the eight sharp daggers that would shoot out from the central hub of the air cannon at 150mph. But as the Rotor spun faster and faster, approaching 5gs, Aldridge was starting to lose peripheral vision due to the lack of blood supply to the brain and optic nerves. Volkov shrugged off what he believed was a momentary weakness as he waited patiently like a crafty hunter. He knew how realistic holographically re-created images were, but flesh and blood Bill Aldridge was overheating, sweating profusely. With all his shrewdness and fight experience, the defending world champion could not avoid a well-placed bullet traveling faster than the speed of sound.

Volkov raised two shields above his head and rehearsed a few blocking moves. Aldridge supporters countered with volleys of cheering shouts for their champion. Cameras zoomed in for a close-up of Bill, a hapless man struggling to stay conscious and beginning to doubt his physical strength. Yet, Aldridge supporters didn't abandon hope. Bill was not a quitter. Gasping for air, Bill silently urged the crosshairs of the targeting computer to turn green; he must kill Volkov before Volkov kills him. With his body shaking and arms feeling like lead weights, Bill struggled to keep the green crosshairs steady on Volkov's carotid artery. Then the air cannon fired eight very sharp daggers straight at Volkov. Volkov supporters murmured. Aldridge supporters cheered. More eyes widened as Camera 12 focused on Volkov; his instinct and experience took over. The big Russian immediately shifted his weight to the right and raised his two plate-sized shields above his head. Then, seven holographically created daggers stabbed the raised shields and burst into hundreds of tiny multi-colored balls on the giant display screens. There were more volleys of cheering from Volkov's most devoted and zealous supporters as a slow-motion camera replayed the moment the real dagger deflected harmlessly off Volkov's right-hand shield.

"Volkov! Volkov!"

The deadly game wasn't over, not with the Rotor spinning at its maximum speed.

A small electric motor drove a linkage that slid open the lid on a metal box hidden beneath the Platform car. Two highly burnished Breda pistols were inside the box.

"Camera 12! Focus on the pistols," the Event Director shouted into his microphone. The Director was meticulous about the impact of realism, and he knew one pistol was ready to fire a live .22 caliber bullet; the other was a harmless replica of a .22 caliber Breda pistol. Volkov needed to determine which pistol was preloaded with a real bullet and which pistol was the harmless replica before he could choose one of eight spinning targets, the real Aldridge or the seven identical Aldridge holograms.

"Choose the right pistol! The pistol to your right," the Event Director shouted.

Aldridge was fighting G forces passing 7g's and was about to pass out. The Russian's heart beat hard in his chest when he chose the real pistol. Every camera captured his confident smirk as he squeezed the trigger. Volkov was still holding his breath when the .22 caliber bullet tore into the glass tube. Then Volkov clutched his head and cursed loudly; he had failed to hit his intended target by a couple of inches.

Frustration in Volkov's voice reverberated around the stadium as the Rotor decreased its revolutions per minute and slowed down to a stop. Nauseated and sweating profusely, Bill leaned on the shattered tube, staggered out, and puked his guts out. Then he dropped down on one knee and rolled slowly over onto his back. The massive glass dome of Halley City spun violently above him as Volkov supporters stomped their feet and argued with officials, and called Aldridge a cheat for deliberately wasting game time to recover. Volkov didn't say a word when Bill shuffled past on his way to the Platform car. Bill avoided eye contact with Volkov; he knew lady luck was on his side this day; he had survived the Wheel of death and swore he'd never enter the Rotor again. But now it was Volkov's turn; the Rotor was waiting for him and the seven Volkov holograms to ready up inside their G tube. Volkov looked out the G tube and gave Bill a stone cold stare as Bill stood in a defensive posture on the Platform car and held only one shield in his left hand. Bill met Volkov's icy gaze and returned a narrow-eyed angry stare. The Rotor started to spin and whoosh past until it became a spinning blur at 8gs. The face of the strong-willed Russian was on every display screen, and he was not showing any visible sign of bodily weakness. But his ears were ringing, and he felt light-headed. Reaching for the computer keypad, activating the targeting computer was difficult. "Wait for the green light, Alek, wait for the green light! Don't pass out!"

Once more, daggers shot out of the air cannon. Bill was a little slow to react; his metal shield blocked the flying holograms, causing the pixels to explode like colored balls. The real dagger caught Aldridge just above his right collarbone. A group of Volkov supporters, believing Aldridge was dead, rushed the Rotor to congratulate their hero. Cheering and waving their arms, the overzealous fans approached the inner perimeter fence. Automatic sentry guns waited silently as they scrambled over. Seconds later, anyone who crossed to the wrong side of the security perimeter was slaughtered, cut down by deadly lasers.

No shouts of protest followed—only silence. Everyone knew the stadium's rules, which stated that the perimeter fence was permanently off-limits to all supporters. Meanwhile, underneath the Platform car, a small electric motor slid open the lid of another metal box, revealing two Breda revolvers inside. If Bill knew about guns, he would pick up the pistol loaded with a .22 round that could punch through Volkov's skull. But with his injured right shoulder, he almost dropped the weapon. Then, grimacing in pain, he lifted his right arm to shoulder height and aimed.

"Bill's going to be in trouble now," Joseph said.

"Even though Bill is small in physical size, he has strong arms and legs and exceptional stamina. He's a winner," Martin countered.

Gripping the pistol in his weaker left-hand, Bill took aim, but the Rotor was spinning much too fast. "Shoot and miss the Russian wins," Bill reminded himself.

The Rotor's spin rate was nearing 9gs. Camera 12, positioned inside his glass tube, captured the moment Volkov lost consciousness and let his head sink in his chest. The event director responded quickly, beaming the image onto the giant display screens, then Camera 12 captured the droplets of sweat rolling off the Russian's brow. Bill felt his strength leaving him, but he looked up at the fast-spinning Rotor and squeezed the pistol trigger. When the Rotor stopped spinning, paramedics rushed in and took Aleksandr Volkov's body and the injured Aldridge to the Dome Halley Hospital.

The next evening, before being discharged from the hospital, World Champion Bill Aldridge agreed to an interview with a select group of journalists from around the world in the hospital conference room. The Southern Cross Conference (SCC) president and founder pointed to journalist Henry Dahlberg and told him to ask only one question at a time.

"Mr. Aldridge, do you regret killing Volkov?"

"No, Henry, I don't regret anything. If Aleksandr were here instead of me, I'm sure he would say the same thing."

Johnathon Ross from World Media pushed his way to the front of the room.

"Sir, we understand you are joining the expedition to Galraithia."

"Yes, winning the SCC allows me the opportunity to join the expedition to Galraithia."

"Do you know which crew you'll be joining, Endeavour or Phoenix?" Henry Dahlberg asked.

"No, Henry, that's a question for Mr. Winthrop and Professor Briar, not me."

"I would like to follow your progress, a weekly report that will appeal to your many fans around the world."

"I don't think so," Aldridge said bluntly, casting urgent glances toward the SCC president.

"Sir, I will forgo any further questions."

"No more questions," the SCC president said. "Mr. Aldridge is terribly tired." Then, the president of the SCC handed Bill the SCC trophy: a warrior wrapped up in wings of gold. Bill kissed the SCC trophy, then read a short inscription on the plinth: *The real enemy is time, for time conquers all and everything.*

***

The Year of the Monkey

The Freelanders had celebrated the anniversary of the Great Rebellion ever since the year 2170. Rihanna Wakeman believed 2424 would be the most significant year for Freelanders worldwide. Sixty British citizens boarded flight EUP556 bound for Beijing, China. The airtime from London to Beijing was less than two hours. Travel brochures publicized happy passengers enjoying the flight, but they neglected to mention that even brief periods of weightlessness could produce nausea, vomiting, and other motion sickness symptoms. There were no glossy color photographs of nauseated travelers holding barf-bags or complaints of excruciating ear pain during liftoff. Rihanna suffered none of the adverse effects of hypersonic flight. Instead, she experienced the beginning of a new day from the edge of space. White clouds cover most of Northern Europe, and Africa bathes in sunlight.

***

Soft morning light gleamed on the metallic outer skin of EUP556, flying hypersonic over the Indian Sub-Continent. Rihanna focused on the landscape below, quickly changing from soft browns to pale greens to snow-covered peaks as the Himalaya ranges and the Tibetan Plateau moved into her field of vision. A few more seconds passed. A cloudless sky appeared above Northern China and the shimmering Yellow Sea. "Another picture-perfect moment. Earth is truly a rotating paradox," Rihanna said to herself. The view of the world from an unfamiliar perspective did not alter reality. In an article Rihanna wrote in the London Times, she requoted Rachel Sibley's epigraph and Martin Luther King, JR: *"Overpopulation and clashing opinions divide humankind socially, politically, and economically. The labor of generations past counts for nothing. If that is what you believe in, then human ingenuity counts for nothing because we must never devalue and disrespect all life on this planet." -Rachel Sibley.*

"Humankind has only one home in the universe, and this is it. Either we learn to live together, or we perish together:" -Martin Luther King, JR.

A small light above the loudspeaker on the wall flashed red, then the speaker beeped twice. *"Cabin crew, initiating re-entry,"* said the authoritative voice of Captain Michaels.

Several passengers enjoyed personalized refreshments in the bar area when the seat belt light came on. "Return to your assigned seats, and fasten your seatbelts, please," Cabin Attendant Donna Marshal said.

The plasma sheath (electrically charged gas) enveloped the outer skin of the hypersonic airliner EUP556. Manufactured by the European Space company, the hypersonic airliner's outer skin and flight control systems were the most advanced in aviation.

"EUP556...radar contact. Continue, and maintain altitude. Contact Beijing Approach:124.70, good day," said the impersonal voice of the flight controller at Beijing Capital Airport.

"124.70...EUP556, good day," Captain Michaels replied. "Cabin crew, prep for landing."

EUP556 descended below a thick blanket of clouds over Chinese airspace. Donna Marshal gazed out the viewing window and unbuckled her seat harness as the land and sea appeared to rush up to meet her. Donna moved to the front of the cabin to speak to the only passenger listed on the flight manifest as a VIP. Rihanna is sitting on her own, reading a book. *Quite unique*, Donna thought since the majority of passengers favored digital media activities.

"Excuse me, Miss Wakeman, is there anything else I can get you before we land?"

"No, I'm fine, thank you."

Donna forced a smile. "Enjoy your stay in Beijing."

"I'm sure I will," Rihanna said, blithely turning a page in her book, the authorized biography of William Briar.

As Rihanna read the pages, she realized how little she knew about her uncle William. In his authorized biography, William talked openly about his fear of the future: *The population of the world today is about 32 billion people. And if long-range projections and predictive modeling prove to be correct, there will be ten billion more people by 2450. Earth cannot sustain an ever-increasing population regardless of the increases in agricultural productivity. Therefore, the global impact of adding more mouths to feed is the greatest paradox of our time."*

Professor Briar was a respected member of the Council of Freelander Elders, and widely recognized for his groundbreaking advancements in optical technologies. For seven years, Professor Briar and his assistant, Father Ludwig Sandor worked tirelessly from their Dome Fuji Observatory in Antarctica. Together they designed broad-spectrum detector arrays, and liquid mirrors for viewing planet Galraithia, the new world many Freelander scientists believed would be the answer to the problem of human overpopulation on Earth. All their hard work paid off after Professor Briar and Father Sandor received research grants from China's Space Research Academy (SRA). The Freelander-owned facility was the research arm of the Freelander Science Portal.

On the morning of 21 November 2392, Professor William Briar and Professor Peter De Vries Lee, the Director General of the SRA, shook hands and announced the construction of the Fenghuang Starchaser, the first joint venture in Space between China's Space Research Academy and the Freelander Science Portal. The Fenghuang Starchaser, also called Phoenix by Professor Briar, will be the fastest and the most advanced interstellar spacecraft ever built. While the SRA and the Science Portal employed brilliant engineers and scientists, there is serious competition from Winthrop Corporation's new E-Class interstellar spacecraft named the Endeavour after Captain Cook's famous exploring vessel HMS Endeavour.

Every influential media source around the world announced the construction of Winthrop's Endeavour. News of the Freelander-backed Phoenix was just a short statement in a local newspaper that also mentioned Albert Forey, Director General of the UAN, slapping sanctions on the Freelanders, restricting them from using nuclear technology, and electronic equipment. The Director-General was quoted as saying that if he could, he would bomb the Freelanders back into the stone age."

While Albert Forey wallowed in downright hate rhetoric, Professor De Vries Lee and Professor William Briar declared their joint venture in space as the beginning of a new Space Age.

"It's an ambitious project, and we recognize the construction challenges. The Phoenix spacecraft would effectively connect Earth to the Cassandra Major System and the Faxian Deep Space Telescope (DST), the most powerful telescope ever launched into space, the furthest human-made object," Professor Lee stated publicly.

At that moment in history, Roland Winthrop is CEO of his corporation, Winthrop Holdings. He is the wealthiest man in the world, a shrewd business magnate, philanthropist, and author. Roland is also an outspoken proponent of the Freelander movement. Roland's connections with leaders of Freelander communities in Antarctica and Australia-New Zealand had made him many political enemies. Media commentators called Roland 'a dead man walking' after selling weapons and modern technology to Freelanders and Xiangshan Traders and buying William Briar's registered patents. Roland also agreed to finance the construction of a new space dock outside the debris field around Earth. In return, the SRA and the Science Portal would equally share mining rights between the principal investors. The Freelanders were the real winners in the new space race; they now had the means to travel to the stars and colonize the new world of Galraithia.

The joint venture, hailed as the beginning of a new era in space exploration, began with smiles, and handshakes but ended in bloodshed when Roland Winthrop and Professor De Vries Lee are assassinated on March 15, 2393. Noram Speers, the Freelanders leader, pointed his finger, accused the UAN leadership of murder. The Freelanders despised Albert Forey, and they were threatening an all-out war with the UAN. It was just a matter of time, and Albert Forey knew it.

The world was in a sorry mess. UAN sanctions on the Freelanders halted access to major pathways supplying medicine, energy, and technology. The nightmarish hell of another all-out war against the UAN was too real a threat. William spiraled down into debilitating depression, suffered recurrent bouts of unbearable sorrow and suicidal behavior. Desperate and needing help, William moved to London's Redbridge District to live with his sister Veronica and Albert Wakeman, her husband. But Albert had not an ounce of respect for William and Walter Briar.

Years later, during an interview with Sir Oliver Hilt of the BBC, Albert Wakeman said, "Having grown up in the same street, I couldn't stand the Briar brothers when we were kids. More so after I married their sister, who is the real bitch in the Briar family. Now people pay me for talking behind their backs and on national television, go figure."

During the interview with Sir Oliver, Veronica Wakeman said, "Daily life turned gray and dark and uncertain for William long before the Beijing attack. Both he and I couldn't accept our Nan's passing. Everything changed after she died, and our aunt Emma moved into Nan's house. Though, when people came around to visit, Emma was all nice and genuine and our cousins, well, none merit a mention. But we didn't know how fortunate we were when she passed. I mean, our older brother Walter took over the role of breadwinner, and he did the best he could until he lost his job with the Newbridge Standard-Times newspaper. His finances tottered on the brink of bankruptcy, and I wanted to marry Albert Wakeman and move in with him, which made things a little easier for Walter with one less mouth to feed. But it was a terrible mistake marrying that loser. Albert spent most of his pay drinking scura alcohol or spending money on mistresses."

"When did you divorce Albert?" Sir Oliver asked.

"I divorced Albert after I found out I was pregnant. I moved back home to Nan's house, but I was too sick with pain on most days to help William."

"How do you mean?" Sir Oliver asked.

"William stopped taking his medication, and he was extremely violent. I had a baby growing inside me. I couldn't risk going near William. All I could do was pray, and I was not a religious person. But I prayed every day to a God people said did not exist. Today, with the benefit of

hindsight and my new-found faith in God, I believe it wasn't coincidental when Walter came home with news of a business opportunity in Beijing, China. He and William went to Beijing, and I was rushed to the maternity unit at the Saint Anthony Hospital in London; Rihanna was two weeks early.

Following their arrival in Beijing, the Briar brothers met with the new Chinese president, a retired taikonaut. The blueprint for the Fenghuang/Phoenix spacecraft interested him ever since Professor Lin, the new Director-General of the SRA, received encouraging data from the Faxian telescope that suggested atmospheric pressures and temperatures on planet 97B favored the presence of water and plant life. Professor Lin renamed planet 97B, Galraithia, after her Gaelic grandmother, Galraithia Pentreath, affectionately called 'Peng' by her many grandchildren.

Gordon Winthrop, Roland's son, and heir to a vast fortune, had reopened negotiations between President Ruan Chow and C. J. Hale, the UAN Minister for Astronomy & Space Science.

President Chow had invited C. J. Hale to attend the day-long meeting as Gordon Winthrop's representative. Acting on behalf of Gordon Winthrop, Hale agreed to finance the expedition to Galraithia. He also agreed to cover Endeavour's construction, staffing, provisioning, and fueling. The Fenghuang/Phoenix spacecraft was the responsibility of the SRA.

Like his predecessors, President Chow trusted the CEO of Winthrop Corporation; he accepted the Winthrop offer. The deal President Chow had made with the Winthrop Corporation did not go down too well with the Briar brothers; they said President Chow was a soft negotiator. Walter Briar was furious; he renamed the

*Fenghuang/Phoenix program to the Freelander Phoenix
Project.*

***

Beijing, China, 5th April 2424.

Ten of the world's tallest skyscrapers graced the skyline of
Beijing. However, the Meridian Hotel was not the tallest
building. Haidian Apartment complex, the first structure to
rise above 3,200 feet, was supposed to be the world's tallest
residential building. Nevertheless, the Meridian Hotel, with
its trapezoid construction and 128 floors, topped out at
2,800 feet above busy Tianli Street.

The talking point for first-time visitors to the Meridian was
not the dizzying height and trapezoid construction, but the
slow-spinning map of ancient China in the middle of the
lobby area and rosewood panels adorning the walls:
beautiful hand-carved lotus flowers and passerines sucking
nectar from plum blossoms. Nearer to the front desk were
ancient artifacts from the Tang Dynasty: gold dragons and
silver tankards, and porcelain wine ewers placed safely
inside the upright glass display cases.

The Meridian Hotel lobby was a busy area with people
coming and going. Lanfen Lim had front door duty. She
possessed a relaxed demeanor and was exceptionally good
at greeting hotel guests. Blind since birth, eighteen-year-old
Lanfen was a knowledgeable young lady and an inspiration
to many. She absolutely disagreed that total blindness was a
weakness. On the contrary, Lanfen had an uncanny sense of
smell and heightened auditory awareness.

Lanfen turned the moment she heard the distinctive ring of
the private elevator. Only one person stepped out, and
Lanfen knew by the short, quick steps it was Mr. Walter
Briar, the hotel proprietor. She liked the Englishman. He

was not full of self-importance, unlike the visiting tourists from his country of origin.

"Good morning, sir."

"Good morning, Lanfen. Another cold and windy day."

Walter wrapped his wool scarf around his nose, mouth, and neck and walked to the front doors.

The front doors opened automatically, and frigid air rushed in.

"Mr. Walter, the easterly wind carries the sweet scent of spring and the rain."

"I am prepared whatever the weather, my dear. I have my raincoat and umbrella."

Every morning after sunrise, Walter strolled down Jianshi Road to his favorite tea house. Joon Lei's Apple Blossom Tea House was the best-known and longest established. The sight of crabapple trees, the sweet smell of plum blossoms, added a little pleasure to his vigorous early morning walks. Two blocks from the Meridian Hotel, the sidewalk was overcrowded with locals flocking like pigeons in the gated Old Quarter of Beijing. Shop keepers came out of their trendy boutiques and fancy restaurants and invited Walter inside. They knew the Englishman was very wealthy and did not suffer fools gladly, nor did he associate with irritating fakes and know-it-alls. Walter waved hello and gave them a genuine smile as he walked along Jianshi Road with tourists visiting the Old Quarter.

The local inhabitants of the Old Quarter considered Walter Briar as one of their own, though they had been a suspicious lot when he arrived 33 years ago. However, Walter won the locals over when he hired a teacher, learned Mandarin, and hired local people to help him run the hotel.

A bell above the front door rang whenever a customer entered the front door of the tea house. The air was comfortably warm inside, and Walter received the usual morning greetings and smiles from Joon Lei, the chatty proprietor. Joon was a cheerful man who loved to openly express his opinions, particularly about the morning news bulletin televised via satellite from around the country and the world. This early morning, between serving customers, Joon spoke to Chongan, a close family friend, about the firebombing of several warehouses. Police put the blame entirely on extreme right Freelander activists.

"There are far too many Freelanders in Beijing," Chongan said. "And what is being done to restrict the flow of new arrivals? Nothing!"

"You are absolutely right, Chongan."

Walter acknowledged and respected their views, but he mostly kept his personal opinions to himself.

"Good morning to all," Walter said, walking to the front service counter. "A large cup of your special ginger tea please, Joon."

"Good morning, sir," Joon said, as Walter seated himself at his favorite table.

"Chongan is up early this morning," Walter said.

Joon poured ginger tea in a decorative porcelain cup. "He came by before dawn in an angry mood. His warehouse at Xicheng was firebombed last night."

Walter shook his head in disgust and glanced out the window. Rain was pouring down just like Lanfen had predicted. "Rainy weather like this reminds me of my home in London," Walter said as the front doorbell announced the arrival of a young couple. Upon entering the Apple

Blossom Tea House, the young couple cast envious glances at locals chatting over cups of hot tea. The Englishman was sitting alone buttering freshly baked bread. Constantly wary of strangers, Walter cast an unobtrusive glance at the couple in their mid-twenties. The young man had a ruggedly handsome face, cracked upper lip, and nasty bruises under both cheeks. He was tall and muscular, and his right arm was in a sling. Walter guessed the young man was either a professional soldier or a professional fighter. Many young westerners had come to Beijing to compete in the Xiangshan Games. The Chinese woman standing beside the young man was 5 feet 5 inches, muscular with an extended stomach. Walter suspected she was pregnant and anxious as Joon welcomed her and the man to his tea house. Walter looked out the window where it was raining so hard he could not hear a thing.

Joon Léi rushed to Walter's table and said in English. "I'm sorry to bother you, but the young gentleman at the front counter would like to speak to you. He said it's urgent, sir."

Walter cast another glance at him and the woman. "They will most likely be looking for work at my hotel," Walter thought aloud.

"No, not this man," Joon said forcefully. "He is the best fighter in Asia…winner of Xiangshan Games!"

"And the woman?"

"She is the daughter of a Xianzhi, a high-ranking Xiangshan Trader."

"Are you sure, Joon?"

"Yes. The Xianzhi tattoo letterings on the right arm are unmistakable. They signify a daughter bound to blood kin. She must support and defend her parents for as long as she lives."

"The daughter of a Xianzhi and Asia's best fighter, eh?" Walter said. "Joon, tell the young man that I'm happy to oblige. And don't look so worried, Joon. I know what I'm doing."

Joon Léi nodded, then he ushered the young couple to Walter's table.

"Good morning to you both, please have a seat," Walter said, standing.

"Mr. Briar, I'm Alexander Chyloe, and this is my wife, Jiaying."

"Nice to meet you, sir," Jiaying said, removing her beige-colored jacket.

"I am pleased to meet you, Mrs. Chyloe."

Joon poured steaming hot ginger tea into three waiting cups. Jiaying rubbed her pregnant belly, wondering whether the teahouse proprietor could be trusted.

"Nothing better than a cup of Joon's ginger tea to warm you up and brighten a gloomy morning," Walter said.

Joon smiled at Walter and the young couple and hurried to help his wife at the service counter. "Mr. Chyloe, you look like you have been through a war."

"My husband is a great champion. The best freestyle fighter in Asia," Jiaying said proudly.

"Yes, a great champion. Winner of the Xiangshan Games," Walter said, stirring his tea. "Yes, my dear, I've heard of your husband's recent win."

"Luck was on my side," Alexander said softly, looking at Walter like he was embarrassed to admit the charisma and the talent to excel at boxing.

"You are much too modest, Mr. Chyloe. There's no such thing as luck. Poor decision-making, yes, not luck."

Jiaying looked at Walter as she sipped her tea. "Flavorsome ginger tea, thank you."

"You must be proud of your husband's success in the X-Games," Walter said.

"I am very proud," Jiaying replied, hugging Alexander's left arm.

Walter could see the love in Jiaying's eyes was real. "My dear, the tattoo symbols on your right arm are quite beautiful."

"They date back to antiquity, to the time of Shuowen Jiezi, 150 BC.," Jiaying declared. "The symbols represent virtue, honor, love, happiness, and harmony."

"Indeed," Walter said, wondering why Jiaying neglected to mention the fact that she was the daughter of a high-ranking Xiangshan Trader.

"So, Mr. Chyloe, what can I do for you and for your beautiful wife?"

Alexander looked around the crowded tea-room. An unworthy suspicion occurred to him that people were eavesdropping. "Jiaying is pregnant with our first baby," Alexander said quietly. "She's experiencing severe stomach cramps, but the hospital administrators will not admit my wife. They told her to leave Beijing."

Walter's gaze shifted to Jiaying and he said, "The birth quota in this city is zero for the next fifty years, Mrs. Chyloe. Pregnancy outcomes for mother and child in a city hospital are never favorable."

"We are Freelanders, sir," Alexander said emphatically. "We have nowhere else to go."

"Your wife is also the daughter of a high-ranking Xiangshan Trader! Do you know what a great risk you took in bringing her to me? You not only risked her life but the life of your unborn child."

"I have nothing to do with my father's business," Jiaying said. "He disowned me when I married Alexander."

"Please help us. Jiaying and I have no one else to turn to here in Beijing."

"I may be old, but I am not a fool," Walter said sternly, with eyes locked on Alexander.

"I have lived long enough in China to know that unregistered dealings with Freelanders and Xiangshan Traders carry very long prison sentences."

"Then it was a waste of time coming here," Alexander said, standing up.

"Mr. Chyloe, sit back down, please, and listen to what I have to say. I will help you and your family, but you must do as I say without any questions, or your wife will be in the city morgue if police find her."

Alexander and Jiaying shook Walter's hand and agreed to do whatever it would take to keep their growing family safe.

"Now, the first hurdle is getting you and your wife out of the city without being stopped for an ID check," Walter said. "Then, we take Jiaying somewhere safe, somewhere security forces will never look."

"The civil authorities have eyes everywhere," Alexander said.

"The civil authorities have no authority in Shihei, the largest city in Zungaria. You can rest assured that no harm will come to your family there."

"Zungaria is north of the Tian Shan Mountains!" Jiaying said. "There are security outposts on every highway, every mountain pass!"

"We have constructed new mountain passes through the Tian Shan Mountains to the east unknown to any map," Walter said, looking self-assured and in control of the situation.

Alexander looked at his wife. "We have no other choice. We cannot stay here."

Walter stood up and looked out the window. "The rain has stopped. I suggest you stay at my hotel, but you must keep a low profile until I make the arrangements for travel and the necessary accommodation for your family in Shihei."

"We both appreciate your help and guidance," Alexander said, squeezing his wife's hand.

Walter used his discretion to get Joon Léi's attention. Joon hurried to Walter's table and ushered Walter, Alexander, and Jiaying towards the back of the teahouse, behind the bakery and the loading dock. Joon scrutinized the surrounding area. Then thinking it was safe, he nodded at Walter, Jiaying, and Alexander and waved them forward.

***

Directly behind the busy south end of Tianli Street, a curved alleyway led to the farmers market recently reopened after stepped-up police enforcement arrested nine farmers for plotting a mortar attack on Beijing Capital Airport. Under the watchful eye of an ever-present security team, a crowd of people from near and far haggled for the best priced local and imported goods as well as fresh seasonal produce. Walter, Alexander, and Jiaying dodged past the day shoppers who had begun to throng the farmer's market. They hastened to the Jianshi Road overpass, the twelve-lane highway linking the Old Quarter of Beijing to Tainan West Business District and the city center. High-rise apartment blocks cast giant shadows over hundreds of food stalls occupying the outer edge of the sidewalks of Guanghe Road as well as the narrow, overcrowded side streets where the pleasant scent of street food mingled with the sickening stench of blocked sewers. An old woman hurrying out of Lim's Laundry recognized Walter.

"Thank you, Mr. Walter, for helping my Lanfen," she said in Mandarin.

"Your granddaughter is an outstanding young lady, Mrs. Lim."

Mrs. Lim felt her wrinkled face flush with pride, but the eyes looking at Walter were sad. "When do you leave?"

"I don't know yet," Walter replied. "When we have a confirmed date, Lanfen will let you know. Have a good day, Mrs. Lim."

"Have a good day, sir."

Before long, Jiaying and Alexander were safe inside the Meridian Hotel, in a two-bedroom apartment on the 63rd floor. Alexander wrapped his strong arms around Jiaying and kissed the nape of her neck. She was soft and delicate like a porcelain doll. Jiaying smiled, and Alexander was happy that she had predicted to give birth to a boy in a Freeland hospital, in Freeland territory.

***

169

It was early Saturday morning and Xian the hotel manager was not a happy man. Heavy overnight rain continued to fall, and there were reports of road washouts. Flooding had occurred inside the 102-airport tunnel, and morning traffic was backed up all the way to Marco Polo Bridge.

Xian had several hotel guests booked on the late morning flight out of Beijing Capital Airport (PEK) to Los Angeles (LAX). And most notable among the guests was Barbara Hopkins, a wealthy widow from the State of California, USA. Barbara, and three of her closest friends had come to Beijing to learn traditional Chinese cooking skills, and study Mandarin.

While waiting in the lobby with her friends, Barbara walked over to Walter.

"Thank you so much for your hospitality. We had a wonderful time."

"These two weeks flew by," Walter said.

"I know! I can't wait to return for a longer visit."

Xian called out from behind the service desk. "Oh, Mrs. Hopkins, the airport shuttle service is running late this morning. I'm terribly sorry for the inconvenience."

Barbara looked to Walter for help. "I wouldn't worry about it too much," Walter said calmly. "The Jianshi Road overpass and the North Highway is operating with minimal disruption."

She cast a loving smile upon Walter. "Thank you, Walter. You made me feel welcome, and you made me feel safe. I feel young when I'm with you."

"I really enjoyed our time together, Barbara. I'm sorry that you have to leave."

Barbara was Walter's perfect match. She was a lover of history, always initiated sex, and was great in bed. But Walter always kept his true feelings hidden. He kissed her cheek and said one final goodbye as the shiny black limousine driven by Dani Li arrived to take her and her friends to the airport. Lanfen waved goodbye as the limousine drove off, then she entered the lobby from the Tianli Street entrance, carrying an arrangement of freshly cut flowers inside a wide-mouth glass vase. "Good morning, Lanfen."

"Good morning, Xian."

"Beautiful flowers," Walter said.

"A welcome gift for your niece," Lanfen said, smiling. "Women love flowers, their color, sweetness, and purity express more than most men can put into words."

"You are special, Lanfen. I'm sure Rihanna will love them."

Lanfen left the lobby smiling.

"Lanfen may be blind, but she knows flowers," Xian said.

"Lanfen is a flower," Walter said. "Tell me Xian, did you by any chance see Mr. and Mrs. Chyloe this morning?"

"I saw them leave in a taxi early this morning, sir."

"Did they say anything to you?"

"No, sir, not a word. Is there something wrong?"

"They left the hotel!" Walter said angrily. "I gave them explicit instructions to stay put until I organized transport."

"I'll call Central Cab. The company dispatcher is a friend of mine. He can tell me where the taxi stopped and dropped them off," Xian said.

Walter nodded. "Call me the moment the Chyloe's return and don't let them out of your sight."

"What should I say to them, sir?"

A deep frown appeared on Walter's face. "I don't know! Tell them there's a problem with the passkey to the apartment or something. Use your imagination, Xian."

Eager to please his boss, Xian pressed a small button on the desk, locked room 9119, and disabled the passkey.

***

Beijing Capital Airport

Rihanna began working as a journalist at age seventeen, covering local conflicts and amateur sport. Later, as a prominent journalist, Rihanna covered the Asian food wars. A great heaviness of heart dragged behind her words each time she expressed the wish to help Oceania's displaced island communities. Rising ocean levels had engulfed low-lying areas of Japan and the Pacific islands. Rihanna could not ignore the terrible realities of global warming. She pleaded with wealthy oligarchs for economic aid. Several generous Beijing business leaders led by Walter Briar rallied to build new coastal cities and islands on top of debris and sand pulled from the seabed and great quantities of lunar regolith transported from the Moon to Earth inside massive Regolith carriers.

Walter Briar had received the Rachel Sibley Prize for his outstanding Public Service and Lunar regolith initiatives. Humbled by the recognition, Walter nominated four other people for being among the first applicants fighting for places on the Galraithian expedition: Rihanna Wakeman, Michael Stoddard, Dani Li, and Lanfen Lim.

The two-hour flight from London to Beijing, like the landing, was uneventful and quiet. Looking outside the viewing window, Rihanna could see Beijing's twin arrival terminals and a progression of red and white lights marking the end of the runway.

"Welcome to Beijing Capital Airport," Captain Michaels said over the loudspeaker. *"It's 10:35 a.m. local time, and the outside temperature is 9 degrees Celsius. On behalf of Eurospace Technologies and the entire crew, I'd like to thank you for joining us on this flight to Beijing."*

Rihanna was last off the plane. She hurried down one of Beijing Capital's long and wide arrival corridors. Hidden cameras, interactive screens, and holograms dressed in blue-gray uniforms welcomed the arriving passengers. "All part of the journey," she thought.

A beautiful looking hologram, a young tourist guide, appeared directly in front of Rihanna. "Welcome to Beijing, Miss Wakeman."

"Thank you."

"Please follow me to the baggage reclaim area."

"Okay, but I feel a little weird following a hologram."

The hologram looked straight ahead. "There might be a slight delay, Miss Wakeman. The baggage carousel is experiencing minor mechanical problems."

Following a holographically created image of a smartly dressed tourist guide fended off unwanted invitations from charismatic commercial holograms hawking cheap souvenirs as well as costly places to visit in China.

Before long, the baggage carousel hummed back to life. A small fabricator robot said that the electrical motor was working once more at its maximum efficiency. Rihanna reclaimed her suitcase and made her way to Arrival Hall B, the last checkpoint before the exit doors.

A guard named Lin worked the security console. She pointed to Rihanna, who was next in line to enter the rapid body scanner. On the display screen, Rihanna's DNA matched her ID card. She has no criminal convictions, no history of violence, not even a traffic ticket. Rihanna was a model citizen, a respected journalist, but she was also a Freelander, Britain's most dangerous criminal society.

"Miss Wakeman, your ID verification was successful, enjoy your short stay in Beijing," Lin said via a Vox-Wand translator unit.

"Thank you."

As the exit doors open, two deadly security lasers withdrew to a hidden compartment in the ceiling. Rihanna walked out of the airport terminal and stepped onto the overcrowded sidewalk. The cold wind blowing from the north carried the constant roar of traffic and honking car horns. The first drops of rain bounced off Rihanna's red puff-coat and knee-high black leather boots. She began to feel uncomfortable pushing through a throng of returning travelers and first-time tourists to Beijing and Greater China. Finally, a shiny black limousine pulled up alongside the curbside pickup area. A man stepped out of the limo and approached Rihanna.

"Hello, Miss Wakeman, my name is Dani Li, and I'll be your driver today." Dani opened the rear passenger door for his only passenger.

"I had hoped my uncle would be here to meet me," Rihanna said.

"Mr. Briar is a busy man," Dani said quickly. "He is waiting for you at the Meridian Hotel."

Rihanna held onto her suitcase and hopped into the back seat of the limo.

"Is the Meridian Hotel far from here?"

"No, not too far," Dani said, sliding into the driver's seat. "About a twenty-minute drive from the airport."

The limo turned into the Car Parking Station on Tianli Street, the Meridian Hotel's underground entrance. Dani parked the limo then he escorted Rihanna to the hotel lobby. Xian, the hotel manager, picked up the phone and called Walter. "Your niece has arrived, sir."

"Thank you, Xian."

"Shall I'll tell her that you'll be right down, sir?"

"Yes, please. And Xian, prepare a nice table with a choice of nibbles, preferably on a table that is far away from the bar area."

"Yes, sir." Xian turned to Dani and told him that three hotel guests needed to get to Beijing Capital airport in a hurry, or they would lose their return flight home.

"Goodbye, Miss Wakeman, see you around," Dani Li said.

Rihanna had the reputation of being very selective with the company she kept, but she was keen to see Dani again. "I'm sure you will and thank you for picking me up at the airport."

Dani smiled and walked through the main kitchen area of the hotel.

"Your uncle will be down shortly," Xian said. "May I offer you some hot tea while you wait?"

"I'd prefer a glass of water if it's not too much trouble," Rihanna replied.

"Oh, it's no trouble. No trouble at all."

***

Walter dashed out of his private elevator and hurried to the front lobby to greet Rihanna. He smiled and gave his niece a big kiss on the cheek. "Rihanna, my dear, you are more beautiful than ever."

"It's good to see you again, Uncle."

176

"The last time we met you had shoulder-length chestnut hair and brown eyes."

"Five years is a long time. People like to change their appearance."

"Indeed. Though feel-good providers charge more money each year. How the average citizen can afford such vanities, I'll never know."

"Perhaps they have a rich uncle."

"Ha! Touché, my dear. Five years is a long time," Walter said, thinking back to his sister's funeral. "I miss your mother more than you can know. May she rest in peace."

Walter still grieved for his sister. All the money in the world couldn't save Veronica's life.

"I think Veronica would like your short blonde hair and blue eyes. They suit you, my dear. You look very sophisticated."

Lanfen opened the servants' door and walked across the lobby area carrying a fragrant bouquet: clusters of gardenias and lilacs for Rihanna.

"Hello, Miss Wakeman, welcome to the Meridian Hotel."

"Beautiful flowers, thank you so much," Rihanna said, touching the petals and smelling their fragrances.

Lanfen said goodbye to Rihanna and Walter and hurried away to greet a group of science teachers from Germany.

"Lanfen is lovely," Rihanna said.

"She is a remarkable young lady. Come with me, my dear. I have another surprise waiting for you."

Walter led Rihanna to Blackfriars Restaurant, the smallest of three eateries inside the hotel. Xian had prepared Walter's favorite table away from the bar. Walter and Rihanna sat facing each other, and on their left-hand side was an oil painting of Blackfriars Bridge over the River Thames in London. "Do you like the restaurant?"

Rihanna smiled at Walter, and she looked surprised at this question.

"Of course, I do…I feel like I just walked into Blackfriars Pub back home."

"I managed to recreate the look, but not the beery smell of spilled ale and burning wood fires." "Uncle Walter, do you ever regret leaving London?"

Walter twirled a spoon between his fingers. "To be honest with you no. I don't regret leaving London. Coming to Beijing with William and buying this hotel was the best decision I ever made."

"I spoke with Uncle William via satellite link before I left England."

"I hope he's well?"

"Yes, he sends his greetings and his love and hopes to see you soon."

"Did William tell you where the first phase of astronaut training is taking place?"

"Uncle William started to tell me, but the satellite link went offline."

"That doesn't surprise me. Hackers working for the UAN often block messages to and from William's satellite phone."

Rihanna had never met William in person; he was notably absent from her mother's funeral. William and Walter paid the funeral and burial expenses and were able to look after their niece's educational interests. They contributed money for food and clothing, personal expenses, and an apartment in Nelson's Square, the most fashionable part of London. Both selfless, generous men, Walter and William made a great deal of money selling William's patented inventions throughout the Americas, Europe, and Asia. The brothers thought it was good to exclude manufacturing industries operating inside the Allied nations for military reasons rather than political ones.

***

Rihanna caught a quick glimpse of other hotel guests (a noisy group of friends) who had seated themselves next to the bar drinking and laughing and talking loudly. Xian brought a bottle of water and two crystal glasses to Walter's table. "Thank you, Xian, that will be all for now."

"As you wish, sir."

"Did you have a good flight?" Walter asked, filling the two crystal glasses with water.

"Oh, yes, it was wonderful, a thrilling experience. One minute bright blue-sky, and then you touch the edge of space and feel weightless. I had the best time."

The bar area's noise level was rising as more people sat down to enjoy a meal and have a drink. "I cannot hear myself think," Walter said, casting angry stares at the noisy hotel guests. "Follow me, my dear."

They walked to a polished steel door in the far wall. This opened into Walter's private elevator. When the elevator stopped on the 128th floor, Rihanna found herself standing inside Walter's formal sitting room.

179

"Welcome to my home."

Rihanna's eyes darted around the spacious apartment with high ceilings, ornate wallpaper, polished wooden floorboards, and outdated decor from the late 1900s. She thought Walter's apartment looked more like a museum than a home. Covering one wall were three polished oak bookshelves filled with hundreds of valuable books, drawings, and photographs of famous people, explorers, and scientists. Rihanna recognized one of the faces, Albert Einstein. The black and white photograph was taken back in 1915 by some unknown photographer.

"Only one photograph exists of Albert Einstein, and you are looking at it, my dear."

"Einstein had sleepy, dreaming eyes," Rihanna said.

"Albert Einstein was a very clever man, and so was this man," Walter said, pointing to his favorite original oil on canvas portrait of renowned British artist William Turner.

"Don't you ever tire of sourcing old things?"

"My dear, I love *old* things. My collection of paintings and photographs are like windows into the past."

"Michael often referred to his photographs as windows," Rihanna said. "Speaking of Michael, he should have been here by now."

Walter looked at his wristwatch. Michael was three hours late.

***

Michael Stoddard drove his hired car at a reckless speed from Beijing Capital Airport to the Meridian Hotel. He parked it with the engine still running and hurried to the hotel lobby.

"Hello, Xian. Call the elevator, please. Walter is expecting me."

"Mr. Briar has been waiting for you for some time now, sir."

"My connecting flight from New York arrived late. Is Rihanna here?"

"Yes. Miss Wakeman arrived an hour earlier than expected," Xian said as Michael stepped inside Walter's private elevator.

Speeding up to the 128th floor, nature photographer Michael couldn't wait to see Rihanna after six long years living and working in the frozen Antarctic wilderness, waiting for the perfect money shot that would change his life. Their three-year relationship had ended because Michael's wandering lifestyle clashed with her wish to settle down and raise a family. But things were different now. The upcoming expedition to planet Galraithia ticked all the boxes for Michael, and his love for Rihanna hadn't lessened. Still, he felt anxious; he didn't expect Rihanna to have the same feelings towards him.

When the elevator doors opened inside Walter's sitting room, Michael locked eyes with Rihanna. He was surprised to see the bottle-blonde hair he remembered, cropped short, blue eyes, contacts obviously, but blue, nonetheless. "Hello, Rihanna, I'm happy to see you again," Michael said, wanting to give her a hug and a kiss. The butterflies in Rihanna's stomach were restless; she still had feelings for Michael, but he didn't want a relationship with strings attached.

"So glad to see you again too, Michael."

When Walter peered over the rims of his glasses, Michael knew that his boss was in a sour mood.

"Michael, are you going to kiss and make up with my niece? You're two like an old faucet set, hot and cold." Michael cast a loving glance towards Rihanna, and that made her blush deeply.

"Did you speak with Gordon Winthrop?" Walter asked.

"Yes. I spoke with Mr. Winthrop for about twenty minutes last night," Michael replied.

"Well, what did he say?"

Michael shook his head, knowing he had some information for Walter but more unanswered questions. "Not much. Winthrop doesn't like to be pushed into saying anything about the Endeavour spacecraft or the expedition, to be fair. But he did tell me that his engineers and fabricators had completed Endeavour's certification checklist. And that the Endeavour was ready to leave its docking bay."

"And the Phoenix?" Walter said excitedly, dwelling upon the impending expedition to Galraithia. "What did he say about the Phoenix spacecraft? Any good news?"

"There is one good piece of news regarding the Phoenix. The spacecraft didn't blow up into a million pieces."

"Another engine failure?" Rihanna said, returning her attention to her uncle who was trying to conceal his disappointment.

"Yes. Phoenix's start-up and shutdown engine tests failed to meet the minimum safety requirements for the Propellant Feed System. So, if the Phoenix fails another Propellant Feed System test, Endeavour will depart from its space dock alone."

"So, Winthrop's intention has not changed since your last meeting with him."

"No, Walter, his true intention is obvious; he has only one goal, get to Galraithia first."

Rihanna looked at Michael. "Winthrop and his people are fools if they believe that will ever happen."

"Well, that is what he intends to do," Michael countered. "Allied people like Winthrop believe planet Galraithia is where the next evolutionary phase for humankind will begin. And they will stop at nothing to be the first humans to colonize Galraithia."

"Galraithia means a fresh start for Freelanders," Rihanna said. "We have had enough of wars and death here on Earth. How many battles have been fought over clean air, agricultural land, good food, and freshwater?"

"Sad to say, too many, my dear. Gordon Winthrop is a cagey old bastard; he's used to getting what he wants," Walter said, as he began pacing the room. "There are several political strings William and I can pull to get what we want." Just as Walter finished speaking, a loud chime announced the elevator's arrival. When the elevator doors opened, Dani Li entered the brightly lit room. He hesitated momentarily as Rihanna and Michael rushed to him; his hair and clothes were covered in white concrete dust, and Rihanna noticed dried blood on his shoulder and chest. Immediately, Rihanna and Michael guided Dani to a chair next to the dining table. Rihanna impulsively poured water from a tall jug into a glass and handed it to Dani; his eyes said thank you. Walter sat in a chair beside Dani and watched him drain the glass without stopping. Dani lifted the empty glass, and his eyes asked Rihanna for another.

"Well, speak up, man. Tell us what happened to you! Are you hurt somewhere? Is that it?"

Michael stepped forward. "Leave him alone, Walter."

"I'm fine, sir. My head isn't hurting too badly now. The mortar blast knocked me off my feet and threw me back into the wall."

"The mortar blast! When, where?" Walter said, his eyes frantically jumping from face to face.

"Beijing Capital Airport and Chaoyang District Hospital were mortar bombed," Dani said, wiping his face with a wet napkin. "The attacks started at 10.30 am or shortly after because I had just dropped the Enders family off at the entrance to the airport departure lounge. Then high explosive mortar shells and incendiary bombs rained down on Dragon Terminal-5 and the west wing of the Chaoyang District Hospital." Dani explained he had been lucky to have survived the mortar attack; he had found a quick way out of the parking station filled with burning cars spewing acrid black smoke. But he neglected to mention how he had saved three German tourists and an Indian family.

"Michael, call Xian and tell him to put out a security alert to all Freelander safe houses. Hurry!"

"Okay."

"Dani, I want you to go home, clean yourself up, and get some rest. I'll call tomorrow morning."

"Yes, sir."

"I'll drive. You might have a concussion."

"I can drive," Dani said, standing up.

"Let me walk with you to your car since you don't want my help," Rihanna said, noticing Dani was steady on his feet. Dani gave a nodding smile but his eyes expressed much more.

***

184

Michael got off the phone with Xian and sat in a chair beside Walter, watching a live television broadcast reporting the worst that had happened during the mortar bombing. Michael briefly took his eyes off the television screen and gazed at Dani and Rihanna walking arm-in-arm to the elevator. Michael waved goodbye and gave them a polite smile but a dismissive look that didn't go unnoticed. At the same time, a live television broadcast continued to show devastating scenes of Beijing Capital Airport and Chaoyang District Hospital, ablaze with thick smoke billowing blackly into the sky. News camera operators focused on emergency service vehicles and dozens of approaching army units. Then, newscaster Mei Chang appeared on the television screen: *Also, this morning, a media spokesperson working for the Wenchang Space Center reported 223 Chinese miners contracted to Sidjartha Moon Base had lost their lives when their Nightingale Class transport exploded on launchpad 36. We have to leave that story there for the moment," Mei Chang said quickly. "We have reporter Douglas Chiu live from Beijing Capital Airport."*

The other reporter began, "Mei, the Chaoyang District has been shut down to the public. Only Military units are allowed inside. Personnel from the emergency services are scrambling over piles and piles of concrete rubble to get to the injured. The people of Beijing are shocked by this cowardly and reprehensible act of violence directed at innocent people."

"Has anyone claimed responsibility?" Mei asked.

"No, no one has come forward to claim responsibility for the bombings. However, the Minister of National Security has put the blame squarely on members of the Freeland Movement. Back to you, Mei."

"Thank you, Douglas. That was Douglas Chiu, who is at the scene of this morning's devastating mortar attack on Beijing Capital Airport and Chaoyang Hospital. Earlier this morning, I spoke with General Bao about the attack." Walter turned off the news broadcast; it was a media circus, an endless loop of different camera angles and eyewitness reports. The story was going to be told and retold to get people talking because around the globe, Freelanders had banded together with the firm belief that everyone is born with 30 fundamental human rights, including clean air, clean water, food, shelter, agricultural land. The entitlements were without bias, and there was no cost attached.

***

Walter's phone rang. On the visual display screen Philip Mason, CEO of Eureka News Corporation did not look his usual happy self.

"That irresponsible bastard sanctioned the attack on the Wenchang Space Centre and now Beijing Capital Airport," Philip Mason said. "You know who I'm talking about, Walter, don't give me that surprised look."

"Philip, there are many sycophants in the world of politics. Gordon Winthrop isn't one of them."

"Gordon is the head of the snake. The bombings could start a war between the Freelanders and the Chinese people. Gordon Winthrop and his Corporation have everything to gain if that happens."

"I hear what you're saying, Philip, but this is not the time to stoke a political fire. The risk of losing the Phoenix and the Endeavour spacecraft is too great."

"Walter, I have always respected your opinion. But I swear on the souls of all my Freelander ancestors that the

Endeavour spacecraft will not be the first vessel to touch Galraithian soil."

Walter knew Philip Mason better than anyone; they had remained good friends for over 40 years. However, Philip became distant after his wife Margaret left him. Philip was very stubborn, controlling, and he had a violent temper. Expressing openly any affection toward his wife was a rarity. Philip's anger reached new heights when he burned down their house shortly after Margaret moved to Dome Halley. Philip experienced trying times filled with sorrow and regrets, but Margaret never spoke to him again. Instead, she made new plans, friends, and a happy life in Antarctica.

"Winthrop would like nothing more than to see Freelanders fail," Michael said.

"Damn him! We've come too far to fail at the final hurdle. Galraithia belongs to the Freelanders, belongs to all oppressed people," Rihanna said.

Walter was about to say something to Rihanna when the hotel phone rang. "Yes, Xian?"

"The Chyloe family have returned to the hotel and are waiting in the lobby, sir."

"Stay calm and stall them, I'll be right down. Philip, I have people waiting for me. We'll talk another time."

"Yes, another time. I'll look forward to it, Walter. Goodbye to all."

***

Walter stepped out of the elevator and headed to the lobby. Xian quickly followed after him.

187

"Michael just called. He said five armored security vans crossed over the Marco Polo Bridge. They are heading our way, sir."

In an instant, Walter's mood changed. "Xian, look after Lanfen, keep her safe."

"Yes, sir."

Walter hurried to Alexander and Jiaying.

"Mr. Chyloe! You disobeyed my direct order not to leave the hotel."

Alexander stood bolt upright, his fists clenched, ready for a fight. His eyes were wide with rage, giving him the unsettling stare of someone who had lost touch with reality. His wife Jiaying was crying terrified tears and trembling like a leaf. "Are you okay?"

"Get away from me!"

"You don't need to be frightened, my dear." Walter looked at Alexander, trying to calm himself down.

"I admitted my wife to intensive care earlier this morning. She was bleeding between her legs. Taking her to the city hospital was a terrible mistake," Alexander said, staring at Walter blankly.

Jiaying's brown eyes stared wildly at Walter. "Nurses tore out my insides, they stole my baby boy."

Walter could not believe what he was hearing.

"I killed them," Alexander said. "Those who were accountable are dead. Retribution for a life stolen. Justice for our unborn son."

A desperate urgency came over Walter suddenly. "You two are high on scura alcohol and not making any sense right now." Before Walter could utter another word, glass shards, flash-bang grenades, and tear gas canisters announced the arrival of heavily armed security teams. They blocked every exit trapping hotel staff and visiting guests inside the hotel. Foolishly, with so many eyes seeking them out, Alexander and Jiaying reached for their laser pistols. Automatic rifles fired, and hollow-point-bullets ripped through human flesh and bone and shredded everything else in the way.

Walter, his ears ringing, body splayed out on the ground, looked up when two more security guards arrived in the lobby. One of them walked towards Lanfen. He lifted Lanfen off the floor and carried her outside. She screamed in panic. "Heartless bastard! Leave her alone," Walter cried. A moment later, the same guard came back to Walter, brought his rifle butt around and slammed it into Walter's right kidney. The guard tied Walter's hands with a metal cable and led him by the wrist to a waiting armored van. Walter stopped him in his tracks and faced the bullet-riddled body of Xian slumped over the concierge desk. The guard sneered at the Freelander, slammed his fist hard into Walter's face. It was a knockout blow that put him on the floor. Security teams rounded everyone up and transported them to the Central Security Building on the eastern shore of the Kunyu River. The dead were taken inside bloodied body bags to forensic physicians on duty at the Beihai Military Hospital.

***

Walter regained consciousness blindfolded, with arms and feet tied to a chair inside a padded prison cell. He had been interrogated for 15 hours and cleared of any suspicion.

Walter Briar was not a terrorist, nor did he play any part in the planning of the mortar attack.

189

But the Englishman was a Freelander, and every Freelander was a threat to city security.

General Bao returned to Cell Block C after leaving Doctor Li Jun Shaw, a known Freelander sympathizer.

"Guard!"

"Yes, General?"

"Open door 96 and get the Englishman cleaned up."

"Right away, sir."

Walter Briar was semi-conscious when a burly, powerfully framed guard unlocked the cell door. "You must wash," the guard said in the Hakka dialect. Walter didn't understand the language; he showed disinterest by not looking at the guard. The guard helped Walter get up from the padded floor and led him into a walk-in shower. But Walter's thoughts were sluggish, impeded by the scopolamine truth serum. So, he just stood there under the shower in his underwear and socks. The guard was frustrated; he had a demeaning job. "You must wash," the guard said, threatening Walter with a dominator stick. Then he turned on the cold water. The sudden shock forced Walter to sigh deeply, and press his back hard against the wall.

"Mr. Briar, you better do as the guard says. Doctor Li Jun Shaw would be terribly angry with me if any harm comes to you," General Bao said.

Walter's eyes focus on the camera in the ceiling. "Doctor Li Jun Shaw? Is he a relative of yours?"

"Li Jun is no relation to me," General Bao replied.

"Your best friend?" Walter said, smiling.

"Freelander, unlike you, I do not have family or important friends in high places."

"Is that so? You have eight medals pinned to your chest. How many more do you have at home, I wonder?" Walter asked.

The guard moved in, hit his mark hard, and opened a deep gash on Walter's head.

Blood trickled through fingers, but Walter, naked and vulnerable, stood defiant.

"Freelander, I want the name of the third bomber," General Bao said, lighting up another cigarette. "You had a meeting with Alexander Chyloe and his partner Jiaying. Who else was involved in the mortar attacks?" Expecting an answer, Bao drew hard on his cigarette.

"Your interrogating officer questioned me for three hours, injected me with the scopolamine truth serum. I had nothing to hide then and nothing to hide now, so go fuck yourself," Walter said, sneering.

"Freelander, one way or another, you will give the name of the third bomber."

"General, you must be demented if you believe that will ever happen," Walter said, with a mocking grin on his face.

A hush fell over the room. A man wearing a fine custom-tailored suit had walked into the room and approached General Bao.

"General Bao! I respectfully implore you to tell your guard to back away from my client."

"Your client?" Bao said, looking at the impeccably dressed young man.

"Sir, my name is David Wu. I'm Mr. Briar's lawyer, appointed by the Public Security Office. I have a letter signed by Doctor Li Jun Shaw requesting Mr. Briar's immediate release."

"You work for Doctor Li Jun Shaw. Tell me, is he a good doctor? He employs more young men and women than most doctors, and he pays them well."

"Doctor Shaw is an excellent doctor and a generous man. He loves to help young people start productive working lives."

"Doctor Li Jun Shaw is your friend?"

"He's only a business acquaintance, nothing more."

"Doctor Shaw has divided loyalties. Are you aware of that fact, Mr. Wu?"

"I have been a practicing lawyer for only a few years. I have no knowledge of any divided loyalties, General."

"I am delighted to hear that, Mr. Wu. People with divided loyalties often end up dead."

"Are you threatening me, General?"

"No, Mr. Wu. It's not a threat, it's a warning," General Bao said, pulling out his revolver and pressing the barrel hard against Walter's temple.

"I strenuously object at all times to hostile and intimidating behavior. My client is a respected businessperson; he has no criminal record, and he's not a Freelander. My client has never had any dealings with Freelanders."

"Mr. Briar, you win today," Bao said, moving away. "But I promise you this. When next we meet, your friends in high places will not save you."

"I very much doubt it," Walter countered with an insolent smile of triumph.

Bao took out another cigarette, lit it up, and exhaled smoke in Walter's face. When Bao turned and moved away, he told the guard to find a clean pair of coveralls for the Englishman.

"Yes, General."

With no evidence linking Walter to the mortar attacks, General Bao allowed him to walk out of Cell Block C, a free man, but he was not convinced that Briar and his layer were telling him the truth.

***

General Bao sat at his office desk and activated an encrypted pinyin computer. He opened the personal file of Dr. Li Jun Shaw's nephew, Marcus Shaw, the interrogating officer who had injected Walter, Michael, and Rihanna with scopolamine truth serum. General Bao questioned his staff and the interrogational benefits of scopolamine. He believed Freelanders had infiltrated the city security forces and beaten the world's highest-tech security systems. As Beijing's director of security, it was Bao's responsibility to expel anyone suspected of harboring dissident views and engaging in acts of terror. So, he decided to send the Freelanders a message, a warning they should take seriously. His immediate goal was contacting Drone-7 flying high above Beijing in stealth mode.

"Drone 7, verify my voice command, Broken Wall."

"Voice command, Broken Wall, is verified, sir."

"Initiate!"

Moments later, Drone-7 reported back to General Bao. "Mission accomplished, sir."

"Drone 7, self-destruct. Verify my voice command."

"Voice command, Self-Destruct, is verified, sir."

"Initiate!"

Drone 7 destroyed itself high above Beijing, and General Bao's link to the Meridian Hotel missile attack vanished instantly. Four security guards posted at the front gates of the security building turned their eyes to the bright flash high in the sky. Walter and Dani had to move quickly to avoid the guards.

Walter hesitated and said, "Rihanna and Michael, are they safe?"

"Rihanna and Michael are fine, sir. They have been waiting inside your car for over an hour. Keep moving," Dani urged.

"And Lanfen?"

"With Rihanna and Michael. She's very shaken up and upset. Xian was her biological father."

"I didn't know," Walter said softly.

"We are almost there," Dani said, pointing past Walter's shoulder towards the black limousine parked nearby. Moving quickly over to the passenger side of the car, Dani opened the door for Walter before jumping into the driver's seat. "We must avenge our dead. Quisis bara mortis," Dani said in Freilish.

"Quisis bara mortis," Walter replied.

"Uncle Walter, are you okay?"

"Yes, my dear. I'm sorry that you had to experience all this."

"They landed a helicopter on the roof," Michael said. "Then they stormed into your apartment commando style. There was no time to warn you and Xian or anyone else."

"Michael, I'm not blaming anyone. I blame myself for the whole mess. But I'm thankful Dani kept his wits about him."

"The lawyer disguise plan was a gamble. We were lucky to get away," Dani said.

"Ah, it's just a matter of time until Bao begins to realize that Doctor Shaw diluted the truth serum with distilled water," Michael said.

"We all should feel profoundly grateful," Walter said. "You were brilliant, Dani, thank you."

"We also owe a debt of gratitude to Marcus," Rihanna said.

Walter held Rihanna's hand. "I do hope Marcus is safe."

"Marcus did a splendid job in the interrogation room. Without his help, we would not be here," Michael said.

"Bao dispatched a crack team of security guards to arrest Marcus, but he managed to outsmart them all," Dani said.

Michael looked at his wristwatch. "Right now, Marcus is on a plane heading to Dome Halley, probably trying his best pick up-line on the flight attendants."

"And enjoying his favorite bottle of wine," Dani said.

"Too early for celebratory drinks, I fear. General Bao isn't the type of man who gives up easily," Walter said. "Sooner or later, Bao will come after us."

"Not if we kill him first," Michael said.

"Don't worry, leave it to me."

"Dani, be careful. General Bao is an intelligent man," Rihanna said.

"He may be a man of high intelligence, but I will have the element of surprise."

***

Walter chose an unfamiliar path back to the Meridian Hotel, his conscience crushed under the weight of guilt. He found himself overwhelmed by the chaos that had shattered his carefully constructed world. The truth gnawed at him—the hotel, which he had strategically purchased as a Freelander safe house, now demanded accountability to the local community. Carefully calculating all sides, Walter crafted a believable lie: the tragedy that had stolen three lives was nothing more than a security exercise gone horribly awry.

Dani turned onto South Road and Tianli Street North. Dani slowed down and stopped the limousine behind a private taxi.

"Why have we stopped?" Walter asked.

"Armed police have set up a roadblock, sir. They are stopping cars from entering Freeway 12."

"Turning the car around will only draw attention," Walter said, twisting around to look out the rear window. "So, we wait, like everyone else."

Police were searching every vehicle and every person entering the area. There was understandable concern etched on the faces of the drivers and passengers as thick black smoke billowed high above the far-off trees and the Old Quarter.

"Driver, get everyone out of the vehicle!"

196

Michael tapped Dani on the shoulder. "Dani, wait. I know this guy. Walter, let me talk to him."

"Alright, but can you hurry it up?" Walter urged, a hint of worry creeping into his voice.

Michael lowered the rear passenger window and called out enthusiastically, "Hey there, Cheung!"

"Hey, Michael! Nice car," Cheung said, giving him a thumbs up.

"What's going on, man?" Michael said coolly, "Another mortar attack?"

"No. A ruptured gas main triggered a massive explosion inside the Meridian Hotel. The entire area down to the Marco Polo overpass is in lockdown."

"I have a training session booked at Wei's Fitness. I want to get there before it gets too crowded."

"Haven't seen you around the fitness center lately," Cheung said.

"No. I am working like a madman, a new project in New York. By the time I get home, I feel too tired to train."

"New York is a fascinating place."

"Yes, a fascinating place with too many rip-off scams," Michael said. "Cheung, I don't have much time…do you need to see my papers, inspect the car?"

"No. I know you, Michael. Tell your driver to turn this car around and follow Simiao Road."

"Thank you, Officer Cheung."

Cheung nodded. "See you in the gym, Michael."

Dani turned the car around and took a left turn into Simiao Road. The black limousine sped down Simiao Road and came to an abrupt stop in front of the Apple Blossom teahouse. Lanfen was inside consoling Chongan's wife. Security police had found her husband's body near a worksite close to Beijing Capital's runway 18L. He had been shot several times in the face at close range. Meanwhile, as fire teams battled to secure the Meridian Hotel, armed police exchanged fire with looters brandishing homemade guns and rifles, knives, and swords.

Media helicopters circled like vultures above the Meridian hotel on Tianli Street, their cameras documenting the destruction of the once-towering 164-story structure. Through lenses trained on the catastrophe below, they recorded a grim tableau: walls crumbled into heaps of broken concrete, synthetic rubber smoldering in the aftermath, furniture splintered beyond recognition, and metal framework contorted into unnatural shapes—all shrouded in columns of rising smoke.

*　*　*

With Lanfen sitting safely inside the car, Walter had enough time to think and plan the journey ahead. "Stay on the Mao Zedong city bypass, then take the next off-ramp to Ulanqab."

"We don't have enough fuel to reach Ulanqab," Dani said.

"We can ditch the limo before we reach Ulanqab, but we'll need another car."

"Stealing two cars will double our chances of making it to Freeland territory," Michael said.

"Right," Walter said, thinking aloud. "Michael, you, and Dani follow the Silk Highway to Zamiin. Rihanna, Lanfen, and I will follow Urumchi Road to Shihei."

"I've never been to Shihei," Lanfen said.

"It's a long way from here, my dear. Now, try and get some sleep."

"Mr. Walter, I want to thank you for bringing me along. I belong to this family now."

Rihanna hugged her tight. "And we belong to you, Lanfen."

***

Walter, Rihanna, and Lanfen reached the southwest corner of Shihei without being stopped by 'Black Ops' teams of investigators hired by General Bao. Michael and Dani arrived shortly after without encountering any resistance on the road except for a small two-man patrol, which Dani killed expertly enough. Still, Walter was not entirely sure the city of Shihei was a haven for Freelanders. He had a Xiangshan Trader's trust, and Timur was a Trader kingpin, described by General Bao as one of the most ruthless leaders in the Trader hierarchy in China. With Timur and his Trader cohorts as willing business partners, Walter and his people had a place to stay and food on the table. More importantly, they had protection against General Bao's forces.

One week after making their escape from Beijing, the Phoenix spacecraft completed the maximum number of engine tests needed for flight certification. With Phoenix's first voyage to Galraithia fast approaching, Walter made the necessary arrangements with Timur. A transport helicopter arrived to take Rihanna, Michael, and Lanfen to Hainan Island's Wenchang Spaceflight Facility, which mandates three months of intensive astronaut training. Sadly, for 63-year-old Walter, age and heart health predicted his decision not to journey to Galraithia. Doctors had warned him that prolonged cryogenic sleep would kill him. Walter and Timur, acting quickly, enrolled Dani in the astronaut training program. There was a condition attached: Dani would begin the mandatory training after completing an assignment sanctioned by Timur and Walter. There were preparations to make before Dani headed back to Beijing.

| The summer solstice of 2424 dawned over Beijing City with a merciless clarity, the sky stretched taut and blue above the metropolis. Merchants Tower was a gleaming colossus that dominated the lower eastern stretch of Dawang Road. General Bao's armored transport glided to a halt before it. His uniform was immaculate and laden with insignia as he strode through the complex's manicured grounds.

Among the gardeners laboring in the rising heat, Dani Li's fingers stilled on her pruning shears. She pulled her straw hat lower, casting her face in shadow, and bent into a deep bow as the General swept past. His eyes, cold and calculating, passed over the workers as if they were merely extensions of the landscape.

In his penthouse suite, Bao stood under the punishing spray of his shower, letting scalding water sluice away the morning's tensions. Steam billowed around him like the ghost of battlefield smoke. Later, wrapped in a silk robe, he savored the amber burn of imported Scotch. The crystal tumbler felt cool against his palm as he contemplated the city sprawled beneath his window. The whiskey's smoky notes still lingered on his tongue when three precise knocks announced a servant with his breakfast.

Bao looked at the security console, but he never took any notice of the servants. The door opened automatically; the woman had a security clearance. "Leave the breakfast tray on the balcony table and get out!" Bao shouted.

When the door locked shut, the General sauntered out to the balcony and sat down at his set place at the balcony table to have his breakfast. Suddenly, Bao felt an arm tighten around his neck. Dani Li, dressed like a servant, lifted the General off his chair from behind and dragged him towards the balcony railing. While struggling for breath, Bao tried desperately to fight his attacker and gain the upper hand, but he lost consciousness. Then, Dani grabbed the General by the throat and crotch and threw him over the railing like a ragdoll. Later that afternoon, security guards found General Bao's body directly where he fell, on a flower bed 50 feet below the balcony. Bao's murder was sanctioned by Timur, and Walter went precisely to plan. Dani wiped the makeup and burned a long-haired wig, a blue dress, and a pair of brown leather shoes. He put on green coveralls and a wide-brimmed straw hat and walked out of the Merchants Tower apartment complex.

Three months later, Walter was not coping too well living alone, but he was happy for Rihanna, Lanfen, Michael, and Dani. They had successfully completed the astronaut training program and headed to the Lunar Orbiter Station (LOS). Walter decided to return to the Old Quarter and visit his favorite teahouse. Joon Léi couldn't believe his eyes when Walter walked in. There were a few welcoming nods and happy smiles from the morning regulars who saw Joon and Walter shake hands like old friends. The two friends sat together at Walter's favorite table, chatted over cups of hot ginger tea, and discussed a promise Walter had sworn to keep: reconstruct the Meridian Hotel.

***

Lunar Orbiter Station

Lunar dawn crept across the Sea of Tranquility, its shadows stretching like fingers across the dusty regolith. There, bathed in the harsh unfiltered sunlight, rose the NASA memorial. It was a towering prism of anhydrous glass that soared 75 feet into the airless sky. Created by harnessing the Moon's own substance, melted lunar soil cast into an obelisk shape, it caught the sunlight and fractured it into brilliant spectrums across the desolate landscape.

The prism, unblemished after centuries of exposure to micrometeorites and solar radiation, stood as a crystalline testament to perseverance, excellence, and the boundless reach of human ingenuity.

Around its base lay scattered remnants of humanity's first tentative steps beyond Earth. The descent stage of the Lunar Module Eagle rested in silent dignity, its gold foil tarnished but still glinting in the sunlight 455 years after Armstrong and Aldrin guided it to this barren plain. Nearby, the lunar plaque's stainless steel had withstood the test of time, its famous message still boldly proclaiming: "HERE MEN FROM THE PLANET EARTH FIRST SET FOOT UPON THE MOON JULY 1969, A.D. WE CAME IN PEACE FOR ALL MANKIND."

Yet, for all this commemoration of the past, something was noticeably absent. No plaques honored the Freelander men and women who battled corporate interests for this desolate world. Nothing marked the sacrifice of those who fought against powerful mining conglomerates claiming the Moon's mineral riches as their exclusive domain. These forgotten heroes, whose collective courage had paved the way for Sidjartha Moon Base as humanity's first sustainable lunar colony remained uncommemorated.

This joint venture between seven specialist companies, each representing one of Earth's seven continents, emerged from the ashes of that conflict. The Base stood as a promise of cooperation, a beacon of possibility in the vacuum of space. As the Earth rose over the lunar horizon, its blue waters and swirling clouds visible through the dome of Sidjartha's observation deck, visitors were reminded of both homes—the one we were born to and the one we fought to create—and the great hope for humanity's future among the stars.

The first flat-pack shelters manufactured in progressive stages on Earth had excellent thermal insulating properties and sheltered Sidjartha Base from meteorites, cosmic dust, and radiation. But the detrimental interaction between moon dust and moving parts in machinery had design engineers scrambling for their drawing boards.

Then, on May 16, 2400, Sidjartha chemist Jerome Johansson invented a new non-stick synthetic fluoropolymer that could repel moon dust in a similar way 'like poles' of separate magnets push away facing each other. Jerome, a proud man, believed that he had solved the dust problem. However, moondust continued to pile up on machinery, reducing their value, adding high labor costs, and stopping outside work.

May 16, 2400, is an important date in the history of space exploration since it coincides with the completion of the Lunar Orbiter Station (LOS). On this day, an efficient core team of international aerospace engineers from Sidjartha loaded the Cryo module, the last sequential piece of Orbiter, onto a solar-powered electromagnetic catapult sitting on the lunar surface and hurled it into space 60 nautical miles above the Sea of Tranquility. From low lunar orbit (LLO), Space tugs moved the Cryo module to the reassembly point between two Marker beacons: The Inner Marker 1,900 nautical miles from Sidjartha Moon Base and the Outer Marker 43,000 nautical miles. Linking each sequential piece of Orbiter challenged complex machine technologies, pushed human endurance to the ultimate limit. A media statement alluded that the Orbiter was the first significant advance since completing the International Space Station 389 years earlier.

Working in space is vastly different today; there are thousands of specialized robotic fabricators servicing LOS. On the Moon and other resource-rich mining colonies throughout the Solar System, large physical networks are necessary for modern planetary bases to function, such as low-pressure Greenhouses and power plants. Despite the technological breakthroughs in robotic engineering and artificial intelligence, scientists and engineers frowned upon what they saw as direct competition with thinking machines. Regardless of the unwarranted disdain towards thinking machines, fabricators play pivotal roles in hostile work environments. They detect and report potential problems before expected damage levels to various types of critical equipment become dangerous to humans. Their most recent safety concern was the proximity of the new docking port to the bulkhead of Module 5, the living quarters on LOS. Gordon Winthrop was unlikely to resolve the safety concern anytime soon, even though he knew the steel bulkhead was too thin. Without more rigid support, the slightest damage could cause a hull rapture. Gordon had said to his team of twelve structural engineers that reinforcing the bulkhead was essential but not a priority. Gordon needed his engineers to focus their attention, energy, and time on the Endeavour spacecraft. Still, he was careful not to override any or all safety measures slowing them down.

***

Before the Endeavour and Phoenix spacecraft reached completion, LOS was the most advanced vessel in space, and its crew of 420 young men and women were the most admired. Ryan Chyloe and his talented team of cybernetic specialists were busy testing and commissioning Dyne Thrusters attached to Endeavour's Propulsion Module and running out of time; Gordon Winthrop was returning to LOS.

"Ryan, I have active red flags on the starboard bulkhead display. Three magnetic latches on the starboard Dyne Thruster are reporting major faults," Robert Jandamarra said, eyes following a rolling list of warning symbols on a diagnostic screen.

"Clear all alarms and reset the key interlocks. Delete the estimated repair time from the data logger and reboot the diagnostic tree," Ryan said.

"I did all that...three times! The same alarms keep popping up."

"I don't see any queries in the data cache. Did you recompile the data?"

"No. I meant to recompile the algebrizer, but it skipped my mind. I'm sorry, Ryan. I must be going senile."

"You are not going senile. Stop rushing. Focus on the job."

"Okay, I won't rush, and I won't worry about Gordon Winthrop's unachievable deadlines anymore," Robert said.

"It would be in everyone's best interest to stop worrying about Gordon's unachievable deadlines or what others think of me and you and Rachel. We are the best Sequanta coding team here, and that's a fact no cybernetic specialist will deny."

"Damn right, mate," snapped Robert.

Robert's frustration lessened when the love of his life 2IC Rachel Vaughn, returned to her workstation. "What are you two jabbering about now?"

"Hey, Rach, did you know we are the best Sequanta coders in this tin can?"

"There's no WE because I'm the best Sequanta coder that money can buy. Rob, what's wrong with the FDS unit? Real-time data projections are all over the place."

"It's okay. All fixed now. I found the problem."

"Sweetheart, the problem is you," Rachel whispered.

"I heard that!"

Ryan shook his head and smiled. He loved Robert like a brother, and Rachel was the little sister that he had always wanted to love and protect.

The Forward Diagnostic Simulator (FDS) flooded every pinyin display screen with the Sequanta Code, a computer language that is difficult to learn and understand; it's beyond the grasp of most cyber specialists. However, Robert was confident that he had successfully installed Endeavour's onboard FDS unit; the unit was now ready to inspect every critical piece of equipment before reaching its fatigue life. Unfortunately, the builders of Phoenix had no access to the FDS source code because of the high level of mistrust between the Freelanders and the developer of the FDS, Winthrop Space Technologies.

"According to the FDS, the latch fails sometime during our last course correction," Robert said, getting out of his chair.

"Ryan, if we lose the starboard Dyne Thruster accelerating around Neptune."

"Endeavour will overshoot the Liaoning Gateway. No need to remind me, Rachel. I know the risk."

"Do we replace the faulty starboard Dyne Thruster now, or do an EVA (Extravehicular activity) during the flight? I think we need a more detailed discussion of the thruster problem," Robert said, not sounding confident enough for Ryan to agree.

"Floating around in space during the fight is too fraught with possibilities that something could go wrong during the EVA," Ryan said.

"Okay, then it's settled. Who's suiting up and going out there? Or do you want to consult with Winthrop first?" Robert said, looking at Ryan.

"No, he doesn't need to know. I'm confident we can get the job done before Endeavour's departure window closes."

"I hope you don't get into trouble for not telling him. Winthrop will skin you alive if you delay Endeavour's departure."

"I couldn't care less, Rachel. I'm past caring," Ryan retorted.

"Ryan, you don't mean that."

Ryan looked away. Then after a moment, he said: "I'm in two minds whether to go back to Earth or continue on to Galraithia and start a new life there."

"Return to Earth and do what, spend your money entertaining glamorous whores?" Robert

said testily. "You shouldn't talk in your sleep, mate."

"LOS has very thin walls," Rachel said with a polite smile.

Ryan laughed, then his expression became serious. "I'm going to suit up and head down to the Pipe-12."

"Ryan, I'll have a fully prepped fabricator waiting for you at the EVA airlock," Rachel said.

"Copy that, thanks."

Once Ryan left, Rachel spoke to Robert about news the comm officer had shared: The death of Ryan's older brother and sister-in-law. "Did you tell Ryan?"

"No," Robert said, looking away.

"Ryan needs to know!"

"What?"

"You heard me, Robert."

"Ryan doesn't need to know that right now; he has an EVA to focus on."

"If you don't tell Ryan, I will," Rachel snapped. "Now, open Cargo Bay-5, please, I have work to do."

***

An Aegis-class transport from Earth shot out of the moon's far side. Henry Tolson applied full reverse thrust until the rocket engines slowed the vessel to a complete stop before entering the twenty-mile buffer zone between the Inner Marker beacon and the Lunar Orbital Station. This trip to LOS wasn't Henry's run-of-mill delivery to LOS; the Aegis transport carried two thousand people from selected gene pools around the United Allied Nations.

Beyond the flight-deck windows, the Inner Marker beacon was flashing red, and the Lunar Orbital Station was spinning in the distance. Henry set the angle of approach at 45 degrees and initiated ADP, the automated docking procedure. From the flashing Inner Marker beacon, Sequanta computers piloted the Aegis transport.

"Lunar Orbital Station, Aegis HT. I'm in the Docking Lane, final approach. Docking sequence is set on auto mode," Henry said over the radio. After a moment, Docking Officer Emma Wells replied, *"Aegis HT, Lunar Orbital Station. You are looking good on final approach Bay-12A is open. Welcome back, Henry,"*

"Thank you, Emma."

While Henry focused on the yellow docking lights flashing outside Bay-12A, another Aegis transport entered the Docking Lane (DL). Gordon Winthrop was sitting in the pilot seat, and he wasn't happy. Emma Wells had given him explicit instructions: Navigate the Aegis transport through the DL and loop around Endeavour and Phoenix, join the docking queue and wait for all outgoing shuttlecraft to clear the Bay-17 traffic area. Far to the right of Bay-17A moving fabricators swarmed like bees around Endeavour and Phoenix, finishing the last of the scheduled tasks before the two tethered vessels undocked from the docking ring and repositioned at the Outer Marker.

Staring out the cockpit window, Gordon thought back to the few days in Dome Fuji, Antarctica. Visiting the Freelander people living in Dome Fuji was little more than a public relations exercise, and his meeting with Professor William Briar did not go well. But there were instances when the interests of Gordon coincided with the professor's dream of colonizing Galraithia.

The dream was the same, but Gordon realized that securing Professor Briar's complete trust was unlikely. There was too much mistrust between the people of the United Allied Nations and the Freelanders.

The Aegis looped around Endeavour and Phoenix. Gordon was still in the pilot seat, looking doubtful. Gordon came back to LOS, thinking of Phoenix as inferior to Endeavour and its Far-star engines as being very unreliable. He had said these things openly and expressed more unfair criticism by saying Phoenix would break apart before reaching Galraithia. Like all Freelanders, Professor Briar was fiercely nationalistic and very vocal in denouncing the policies ratified by the United and Allied Nations.

The overall length of Endeavour was 1,434 feet, 400 feet wide, and 320 feet high. Its design characteristics and Shustak's time-proven Quantum propulsion system were common to all oversized Regolith carriers. These long-standing technologies made long-distance space travel efficient, affordable, and reliable. Phoenix was the smaller of the two vessels, measuring 947 feet in length, 275 feet in width, and 200 feet in height. But what set the Phoenix apart from other Starchasers was its bulbous bow and the scaly skin encasing a double hull; from a distance, Phoenix looked more like a long reptile than a Starchaser. Crucial to making Phoenix's innovative design stronger were five Far Star engines and a propulsion system that incorporated nanotrine reactor technology with an ElectroMagnetic drive (EmDrive). The combination of rocket boosters and an electromagnetic drive system (EmDrive) would shift the space around Phoenix's stretchable outer hull and propel the elongated Starchaser faster than the speed of light. Albert Einstein had said that traveling faster than the speed of light was an impossible dream. Joseph Arunui set out to disprove Albert Einstein's theory that light has a maximum speed limit. Gravitation waves in interstellar space are not slow-moving; Joseph's mathematical equations show how gravitation waves behave like deep ocean water currents, global weather patterns, and jet streams discovered in the 1920s by the Japanese meteorologist Wasaburo Ooishi.

***

Both ships had innovative and costly technologies: self-repairing Armadillo-like metal scales that moved on the outer hull, like the individual squares of a Rubik's cube, move up, down, left, and right. Nevertheless, the moveable interlocking scales had proved their effectiveness against the persistent bombardment of hypervelocity particles and small meteorites striking the outer skin of deep space Starchasers and Regolith carriers.

"Lunar Orbital Station, Aegis GW. You are on the final approach. Docking Bay-17 is open."

"Aegis GW, Lunar Orbital Station. The docking sequence is set on auto mode, and my docking lights are on. Thank you, Miss. Wells."

"You're welcome, Mr. Winthrop. Welcome home, sir."

Emma was expecting two more spacecraft from Earth today: RC-56B, a Parom Class regolith carrier converted into a passenger ship, and a Xiangshan-7 transport. Since the launch into Earth orbit from Evans Point Spaceport in Antarctica, RC-56B had been flying on automatic pilot for security reasons. It had arrived safely at the Inner Marker beacon, and its onboard navigation system was awaiting further instructions. Pilot Officer Anthony Vargas had the authority to remote pilot the ship to Docking Bay-12B. Bulk carriers like the Parom class delivered tons of lunar regolith to Earth each month then returned to LOS with food and water before continuing to Sidjartha Base and Ercial Penitentiary on the far side of the Moon. Vargas read the flight manifest on a computer screen. The validation code was defined as human cargo. The 4,000 Freelanders beginning a once-in-a-lifetime journey to Galraithia, an alien world with landscapes and vegetation no human eyes had yet seen.

***

Onboard RC-56B Joseph Arunui occupied the last four seats next to the rear cargo bay door and had been sleeping soundly inside his sleeping bag when the voice of Emma Wells is heard over the radio.

"Passengers on board RC-56B this is Docking Officer Emma Wells. Your vessel is under the direction of Pilot Officer Anthony Vargas, sit back and enjoy the ride to Docking Bay-12B, thank you."

"Brendon, wake him up."

"Yes, Captain."

Brendon prodded Joseph in the ribs to get his attention. "Joseph, wake up, man…we're here."

Joseph rubbed his eyes. "Okay, I'm awake, Brendon. Stop pushing."

"Joseph, I can see Phoenix and Endeavour," Satori said at the viewing window.

Joseph stood up, relaxed his body, and glided effortlessly across the cabin floor to the viewing window. Martin struggled; he floated towards the cabin ceiling without rational control of his body. Joseph had to reach up and grab Martin's feet. "I have you, Martin."

"Well, that's a sight you don't see every day," Bill Aldridge said.

"Commander Brindle failed zero-gravity training three times. Anyone else would have been kicked out of astronaut training school," Fredericks said in a mocking tone.

Satori glowered at Lesley. "I think Admiral Fletcher made a huge mistake. What could have possessed him to nominate a coward for astronaut training?"

Satori's remark angered Fredericks. "You are a bitch, aren't you? You never made a mistake in your privileged life?"

"I've made my share of mistakes," Satori said bluntly. "But I'm not a coward. I don't run away when there's a problem. I face it head-on."

Brendon moved away from the viewing window and put himself between Satori and Lesley. Fredericks wanted to push Brendon away, but he thought it best to take a step back from the tall, large-framed New Zealander.

"Get off my case, Aitama."

"Lieutenant Fredericks, you ran away and hid when Taimaha's galley burned. A smart man like you…hiding in the dark like a frightened child."

"I wasn't hiding!"

"Brendon, I've had enough of this nonsense!" Martin said.

"Yes, Captain."

"Regardless of your poor opinion of Mr. Fredericks, there will be no more personality clashes, no arguments," Martin said. "And that goes for everyone. Winthrop's people would love nothing better than to see Freelanders at each other's throats. I hope I have made myself clear."

"Very clear, sir," Satori said.

Father Antonio was the only person aboard RC-56B who was not a Freelander. However, he seriously entertained the possibility of becoming one. He felt confident that if Father Sandor nominated him as a candidate, Professor Briar would approve.

"The Endeavour spacecraft…she reminds me of the great ocean liners of the past," Father Antonio said in his lilting Italian accent.

Bill looked out the window. "You're not wrong. Endeavour is a beautiful ship."

During astronaut training, Bill and Antonio became good friends. They respected each other's strengths and weaknesses, shared their life experiences. William Aldridge grew up as the son of a steelworker. He fought to the top of professional boxing, then turned his boxing interests to psychology and obtained his degree. In contrast, Antonio Marsi, the eldest son of an Italian aristocrat, had the world at his feet growing up. But Antonio chose the priesthood as a vocation and entered the Rome Seminary. Pope Leo XIV, a man with a great desire for peace and equality for all, anointed Antonio with the oil of gladness. Father Antonio devoted his life to God's service in a world gripped by famine and war from that day forward. Six years of unceasing commitments to the world's most impoverished communities brought Father Antonio to the Pope's attention and granted a private audience. Father Antonio left the Freelands in the Arctic Circle and hastened to the Papal Basilica in Rome and found the aging pontiff confined to his bed through severe illness and near death. The dying Pope could not whisper even a few words to the God-loving, God-fearing priest. Instead, he scribbled a few words in pencil.

"Bring the word of God to Galraithia, my son." Then the longest-serving pontiff in history breathed his last breath.

When Pope Leo XIV died, a night of great sorrow turned to a night of great urgency for Father Antonio. The young priest had to leave Rome and travel to Dome Fuji, Antarctica. Cardinal Salvatore Bresciano, the Pope's younger brother, had also decided to go with Antonio to Dome Fuji. Cardinal Bresciano wanted to meet with Professor William Briar, the leader of the Freelander expedition to Galraithia. The discovery of this new world was regarded as the answer to human overpopulation on Earth and a foothold for religious refugees.

***

RC-56B entered Docking Bay-12A, hovered for a moment, then ever so gently set itself down on the grated steel floor. Two large doors closed, and noisy alarms repeated the *equalize pressure* warnings. Bay-12A was a busy place, a hive of activity, as passengers exited from one shuttle spacecraft to enter another, commuting Freelander colonists to Phoenix. Professor Briar and Father Sandor were drawn into one of the small conference rooms. Standing at the viewing window, William could see fabricators herding Freelander passengers like cattle. William looked troubled, and he noticed a deep frown on Father Sandor's brow. Leaders should be the ones greeting their people, but both men could hardly walk and move around without their chest hurting.

Doctor Miles Coverdale greeted the new arrivals from Earth and gave them an insider's guide to LOS, advice, and helpful hints. "Walking and working in LOS's environment will be challenging initially; moving around feels awkward due to the artificial gravity, but you will get used to it. Another noticeable difference when you first enter LOS is the uncomfortably cold temperature; I hate the artificial gravity and the damn cold. Many first-time visitors also suffer symptoms like asthma due to nanoscopic threads of therapeutic peptides pumped through air vents by nebulizer machines." Then Doctor Coverdale spoke to Martin and congratulated him on his Captain of the Phoenix spacecraft promotion. Martin had not mentioned the captaincy to Joseph or anyone else because Martin rarely discussed his career or his personal life.

"Captain Brindle!" Joseph proclaimed. "Why didn't you tell anyone?"

215

"I wanted to tell you, Joseph, but I thought it best to wait until we boarded Phoenix."

"I'm sorry, Captain," Doctor Coverdale said.

"Sorry?"

"For spoiling your surprise," Doctor Coverdale replied.

Martin smiled. "There's nothing to be sorry about. If you'll excuse us, Doctor, we have an important meeting with Professor Briar and don't want to be late."

"No. No, of course not. Professor Briar would not be too happy if you were late. Follow Funnel-2 until it ends; that's the quickest way to the small conference room and Professor Briar. Enter via the hatchway on your right."

"Thank you," Martin said, walking away.

"Captain, before you go, I have one last question for you and your crew."

Martin looked at his wristwatch and nodded yes; he had about twenty-five minutes before the meeting with Professor Briar started.

"Thank you, Captain. Is anyone experiencing respiratory distress, difficulty breathing, or experiencing any chest pain?"

"My lungs feel like they're on fire when I inhale," Joseph said with a concerned look.

"Painful respiration is not unusual on LOS; this a manufactured environment. The burning sensation lasts a few minutes to several hours but will pass."

"I hope so."

Tom Granger stepped out of a cargo elevator just as Joseph neared the hatchway leading to Funnel-2.

"Joseph, wait up!"

"Hey, Tom, when did you get here?"

"I arrived a week ago. Settling in and acclimatizing took a while. How do you feel?"

"Apart from my lungs feeling like they're on fire when I breathe in, I feel okay," Joseph said.

Tom shook his head. "I wish I could say the same."

"Why, what's the matter?"

"There's nothing wrong with me physically. It's the Far-Star engines. Too many problems," Tom said.

"Too many problems? What kind of problems? Make sense."

"The kind that blows up!" Tom said, handing Joseph graphs comparing heat profiles of five rocket engines manufactured by Far Star, a joint Chinese/Freelander company.

"Tom, the engine profiles are four weeks old."

"Look at the heating curve graph and the temperature ranges inside engine 5. Again, dangerous temperature levels during a static firing test."

Joseph looked at the four-week-old graph, noticing how engine five's engine management system had to shut down five minutes into the final static firing test, avoiding irreparable damage to the engine. That could have shattered the engine into a million pieces if temperatures exceeded thermal safety thresholds. "Sidjartha engineers had a hand designing Phoenix's advanced engine management systems. They were competent, meticulous, and accurate. I'm sure they would have investigated and solved the engine overheating problem by now," Joseph said, unconcerned with old thermal data.

"A work order for Engine-5 was never scheduled; the order does not exist anywhere on the Request a Repair (RAR) System."

"Someone may have deleted the entry," Joseph suggested.

"Joseph, you know very well that Sign Off Procedures cannot be deleted without Professor Briar's written approval."

"Yes, I know the Sign Off Procedures. But the heat profiles are old profiles, Tom. You are wasting your time on this batch."

"I'm not wasting my time."

"Tom, you have wasted your time and are now wasting my time! Phoenix has 24 robotic fabricators that are more than capable of correcting...the overheating or any other problem that may delay or endanger the accomplishment of our primary mission: touching down safely on Galraithia."

"Joseph, hear me out."

Joseph drew an impatient heavy breath. "No, Tom. I have heard enough. You've become an alarmist, a fearmonger."

"A fearmonger?"

"An alarmist fearmonger, yes. Sequanta computers are self-learning and self-repairing. So, if they make an error somehow, what of it? You and I know that even the most intelligent computers can make mistakes. They don't need people like you and me to prove anything or tell them what to do next. We have learned to rely on the computer's judgment; its logic control system and programming must operate error-free, and any functioning error immediately fixed."

Tom turned and was about to walk away, angry at Joseph's hardness.

"Six months ago an Asteroid Catcher carrying miners to Sidjartha Base exploded on power-up! The direct cause of the explosion was a faulty heat sensor manufactured by XTC (Xiangshan Trading Company). A Sequanta computer found the heat sensor fault but couldn't dispatch a fabricator to replace the faulty sensor in time to save the Asteroid Catcher!"

"I wasn't aware that there was an accident," Joseph said, thinking back to when Sequanta computers were officially endorsed by the best scientists worldwide.

"Well, you're aware of it now. You better act fast to prevent the same thing from happening to Phoenix; our Far Star engines use the same type of sensor to detect abnormal thermodynamic fluctuations inside the engine cowling."

"Tom, I understand your concern but don't understand why XTC hasn't recalled their heat sensors while rocket engines are exposed to possible thermodynamic imbalances. I will talk with Professor Briar. I don't think he knows about the faulty heat sensors. And Tom, I'm sorry for calling you an alarmist fearmonger. It was incorrect and uncalled for."

"It's all water under the bridge, Joseph."

"Good heavens, look at the time; we will be late for the mission briefing," Joseph said, looking at his wristwatch.

"Call me after you talk to Professor Briar. I'll be in Cryo," Tom said.

"You're not going in for a mission briefing with Professor Briar?"

"No. Several cryo beds onboard Phoenix are reporting faults. Father Sandor wants the beds fixed before we leave."

"Yes, of course," Joseph said, stiffening. "Phoenix is a new ship. There are bound to be annoying teething problems."

"XTC manufactured the cryo beds onboard Phoenix," Tom said, hoping to get a reaction from Joseph.

"The beds are Father Sandor's problem."

"Passing the problem to someone else is not the answer. If we find problems, let's work together and fix them now, Joseph. While we have time."

"I have enough to worry about," Joseph said.

Tom shook his head and said, "Fine, if that's how you want it. Just remember, one day you might regret this decision, Joseph."

***

Down in Cargo Bay-5, cybernetic specialist Rachel Vaughn opened a wooden crate containing all the parts to build an XL5 Fabricator and an arsenal of tools and materials: Plastics, ceramics, high-grade alloy steels, and different materials that could be used for 3D printing.

In addition, this new model XL5 came equipped with a state-of-the-art Van Wagner laser cutter and the best laser positioning system that money could buy as standard equipment. It was vastly different from the earlier models. Rachel was at her metal workbench when she heard the hatchway door open. She glanced over her right shoulder

220

and saw Robert enter Cargo Bay-5. "What are you doing here?" Rachel said, resuming her work.

"John Randal and the other visitors haven't left the Quarantine station."

"You came down here just to tell me that?" Rachel said mockingly.

Robert smiled, looked around the room, and walked to a wooden crate that Rachel had placed next to a freestanding jib crane with a 360-degree rotation. "No. I've come to help you with the XL5 unit."

"That's nice of you, but I can manage on my own."

With the help of a motor controller, Robert used the jib crane to lift the heavy torso of the XL5 unit out of the wooden crate and placed it carefully on Rachel's metal workbench. "The XL5 model is bigger than the L4 and much heavier."

"290 pounds according to the assembly instruction manual," Rachel said, prying open the back of the wooden crate. "Faith is bigger and has much more power. So, I don't think the increased weight will be a problem."

"Faith?"

"Yes, Faith. This XL5 has a real name," Rachel said, smiling.

"A real name?"

"Yes. I named this fabricator Faith, and Faith is 1000 times smarter than your Five-o-nine."

Robert drew Rachel close to him and kissed her. "I like the name, but don't let Five-o-nine hear you say Faith is 1000 times smarter. You might hurt his feelings."

"Fabricators don't have emotional intelligence, not yet anyway."

"Five-o-nine has feelings. You just have to learn how to interpret them," Robert whispered, holding Rachel close, kissing the nape of her neck.

"Stop fooling around, Rob, Camera 4 is watching us."

"No, it isn't. I switched off Camera 4 before I entered the cargo bay."

"Stop it, your nose is cold, and you're tickling me," Rachel said, trying to wriggle her way out of Robert's embrace. Rachel did not push him away as he stole a long-overdue kiss. She felt his right hand move further down her thigh, his fingers probing between her legs. Rachel bit hard on Robert's bottom lip. "We play by my rules, remember? No fooling around on duty and never in front of others."

"Holding you in my arms isn't fooling around."

"Rob, you don't know when to stop. We could lose our jobs if we get caught. Now be a good little boy and secure the jib crane back in its place on the other side of the room."

Robert reluctantly nodded affirmation, though his feelings for Rachel were no closely guarded secret.

Ryan suited up quickly and headed down to the aft EVA airlock. As he entered a narrow tubular passageway, he realized he had inadvertently donned a spacesuit with only two hours of air left in its primary life-support system. "You should have paid more attention during training," Ryan said softly. Then he looked at his wristwatch and did some quick math in his head; Endeavour's scheduled departure time was ticking away. "Not too much time left to turn back and find another spacesuit," he thought. "Fabricator Five-o-nine, can you hear me?"

"Yes, Mr. Chyloe. I can hear you, sir."

"Good. Prep the Eva airlock. Open the pressure equalizer panel."

"Yes, sir."

Five-o-nine followed Ryan's instructions, entered the Eva airlock, opened the pressure equalizer panel, and waited for three green lights to flash. Ryan arrived shortly after, closed the inner door behind him, and waited for the three green lights to stop flashing. That meant the pressure inside the airlock equaled the pressure outside, and the outer airlock door could open. Five-o-nine scanned Ryan's Spacesuit and gave an audible warning. "It's a breach of safety regulations, I know. But Calibrating the Dyne Thruster should not take too long," Ryan said.

As the outer airlock door opened, a fisheye camera mounted above Ryan's visor focused on Endeavour's spinning Habitat Module. "Okay, Five-o-nine, let's go," Ryan said, using steering thrusters connected to his spacesuit to maneuver down to the faulty Dyne Thruster assembly unit.

***

Working under Ryan's supervision, Five-o-nine installed a brand-new Dyne Thruster unit in record time. Ryan had 55 minutes of air left in his primary life-support system, more than enough time to calibrate the Dyne Thruster.

"Good job, Five-o-nine. Return to your Lockplate and power down."

"As you command, sir."

While Ryan finished calibrating the Dyne Thruster, Five-o-nine made its way to Pipe-12, the narrow passageway leading to the Maintenance Module. Two men, a Winthrop security guard and a hooded man clad in a long robe, were waiting at the Maintenance Module end of Pipe-12. Understanding that humans always have the right of way, Five-o-nine moved aside and waited for the two men to pass. The hooded man, well disguised, stared at Five-o-nine with complete suspicion. While the security guard made no effort to look away, he couldn't care less, or so it seemed. He said something to the hooded man before handing him a wad of money in exchange for a vial filled with blue liquid. The two men walked past Five-o-nine without saying a word to each other. Then the security guard took a backward step without conscious thought. Frowning deeply, he spat on Five-o-nine's optical visor display.

"I don't like Fabricators!"

The hooded man scowled at the security guard. "Vargas, you are a drunken fool. Fabricators record everything they see and hear."

Despite the hooded man's warning, Vargas opened the glass vial and gulped down the blue liquid. "Watered-down scura alcohol! You ripped me off! I want my money back."

"You got what you paid for, Vargas."

"I didn't pay for watered-down scura," Vargas said, poking a finger in the hooded man's chest.

The hooded man grabbed Vargas by the throat with one hand and squeezed.

"Rat-faced bastard! Don't ever touch me again, or I'll drop you where you stand."

"Okay, I'm sorry," Vargas said, stepping back, fearing the hooded man's anger.

The hooded man moved closer to Vargas. "You're afraid of me," the hooded man muttered. "You know your place. That's good. Now, take care of that thing over there! I don't want to see that mechanical abomination again."

Vargas was afraid; his mouth was dry, and his hands were shaking. The hooded man had made many enemies, though none lived long enough to threaten him. "I'll do what you ask, sir."

"When the machine powers down, that's the best time to strike. And delete the datastore from the hosts controlling the wall-mounted cameras," the hooded man said.

"Don't worry about a thing. I know what to do," Vargas said, thinking corborane acid would destroy every piece of circuitry inside Five-o-nine's headpiece.

The hooded man turned to Vargas and said, "I always worry when dealing with an amateur."

Watching the hooded man hurry away with the money angered Vargas; he thought about killing the man with the black hood and black clothes and taking over his smuggling business and assets. The opportunity would come, he thought, only if he was patient and clever; he just had to bide his time.

While Vargas considered what he would gain by the hooded man's death, he hurried to the Aft Battery room without being seen. He looked nervously around and found Five-o-nine powered down on the Lockplate charging station. Stealthily he began drawing near to Five-o-nine. Vargas had to work fast, and with cunning. Making sure no one was looking, Vargas turned towards Five-o-nine, and with a last disdainful look, he hurried to open Five-o-nine's headpiece. But Vargas was careless with the glass bottle holding the corborane acid. He poured it too quickly on every circuit board and gloated as the highly corrosive substance melted the circuitry into transparent plastic and steel globules.

Suddenly Vargas yelled in pain; acid fumes had touched his skin. Quickly pulling his right arm away, he dropped the empty bottle. He cursed his bad luck as the evidence rolled across the floor and into a metal grate covering a deep drain. Wincing with pain, he held his injured arm against his chest. Then the swishing of a cloak from behind startled him. "Oh, it's you! You came to check up on me?"

"You disappoint me, Vargas. You told me not to worry about a thing, and now you're hurt," the hooded man said.

"It's nothing, a little burn on my arm."

"Do you know what corborane acid will do to your arm, man? It will keep eating through flesh and bone until there's nothing left," the hooded man said.

Vargas started to feel light-headed and unsteady on his feet. "You'd better help me to sickbay," Vargas said, breathing heavily.

"I cannot help you."

"You must help me, please!" Vargas pleaded.

"You have corborane molecules coursing through your veins. There's no cure, nothing anyone can do. I'm sorry, Vargas."

"You're not sorry about anything," Vargas said, feeling his energy fading and his body shutting down. "Please help me! This pain is unbearable."

"I will help you, Vargas. Now, lie down. I'm going to get you some water."

"Thank you."

The hooded man stood quietly beside Vargas and waited for Vargas to close his eyes. Then he reached into his pocket and pulled out a loaded pistol.

***

After months of developing the software, Rachel put the final touches on a new motor drive system for Five-o-nine. Now it was ready to install. First, she tried contacting Five-o-nine, but on the diagnostic chart, Five-o-nine showed offline. For some reason, its visor camera was switched off.

"Ryan, where are you exactly?" Rachel said over the Vox speaker system.

Ryan touched his throat microphone, "Airlock 8, heading aft. Is anything wrong?"

"I'm not getting a response from Five-o-nine. It hasn't completed any of my commands."

"Five-o-nine is powering down," Ryan said.

"No. Five-o-nine's Lockplate isn't active, so I'm guessing the Lockplate transmitter/receiver unit isn't working."

"There could be a power drain somewhere inside the transmitter unit."

"The battery pack has four green lights, full charge," Rachel said with concern in her voice.

"Okay. I'll go to the Lockplate. Open hatchway B for me, please."

Ryan entered the open hatchway and climbed down a long vertical tunnel leading to the aft Battery room and Charging station.

"Rachel, close the air vents on this level. Five-o-nine is on the Lockplate and venting smoke."

"Venting smoke! From where?"

"From the openings around the headpiece. The drive track on Five-o-nine's collar is bent."

"Someone must have forced the outer casing open if the drive track is bent," Rachel said.

"Yeah. It certainly looks that way. Airlock 9 is open!"

"Airlock 9 is tagged as out of order at my end. It should be closed," Rachel said.

Rachel was curious to know what was going on. She toggled every camera view in the Maintenance Module, but the cameras were all offline. "Ryan, can you hear me?"

"Rachel, get a medical team down here!"

"What is going on down there?"

"Do it!"

Fifteen minutes later, three paramedics came bustling into the airlock, one of them wheeling a stretcher and medical equipment. As they knelt beside the body of a security guard, one of them asked Ryan, "Do you know this man?"

"No, I've never seen him before."

"There's nothing we can do for this guy. He's dead," one of the paramedics said, turning the right side of the dead man's head where blood and gray brain matter had coagulated around a small hole. "He has been stabbed by a sharp object, most likely a cross-tipped screwdriver."

A paramedic removed the name tag from around the man's neck. "Emilio Vargas, Winthrop security," the paramedic said, searching Emilio's pockets. The paramedics zipped Emilio Vargas into a body bag.

When two Winthrop security guards came onto the scene, they quickly unzipped the bag, looked at the body, and then commanded the paramedics to wheel the stretcher to the morgue. The security guards then sealed off the area around the EVA airlock and declared it a crime scene.

The Chief Security Officer assigned to LOS, Collin McAllister, spoke to Ryan later that day. McAllister had enough blood evidence to suggest that Emilio Vargas was killed a few feet away from Five-o-nine's Lockplate. Whoever killed Emilio had then carried the body to the EVA airlock, planning to dump it into space before Ryan arrived.

***

On the crowded Phoenix bridge, anxious eyes watched the countdown clock.

"T-minus 12 hours and counting," Tom said from behind the control desk.

Martin turned to Tom and Satori and put them under competition pressure as they checked the engine firing sequences and supplied new mission parameters to the Sequanta Control Computer (SCC). Professor Lin looked worried when Joseph reassured her that all five rocket engines worked correctly regardless of the failed static firing test. Joseph also said he was confident the engines would not overheat; they could cope with the punishing load of full thrust. While Peng trusted Joseph's opinion,

229

Tom shook his head and quietly continued watching the countdown.

"Well, Joseph, after two years of hard work and 12-trillion yuan, it all comes down to the press of one tiny button," Peng said.

"Captain, we are set and ready to leave the docking ring."

"Very well, Mr. Granger, open magnetic latches. Prepare to the leave the docking ring."

"Undocking procedure set to manual, Captain. All magnetic latches are fully open."

"Commander Thomas, remove the docking rail. Set artificial gravity and gyroscope gradient to the maximum."

"Gyroscope gradient is at 38% ... maximum setting, Captain."

"Very well. Aft thrusters ahead one-third."

"Ahead one-third, aye, aye, Captain."

Martin turned to Joseph, "You have control."

"I have control," Joseph replied. "Firing maneuvering thrusters, 0.2 feet per second."

Forward momentum pushed the ship away from the docking ring toward the outer marker beacon (OMB). Joseph's fingers glided on the command console and confirmed the engine firing order. "Switching Engine 5 to Idle Mode. Give me a five-second burn, please, Tom."

"Engine 5 has ignited," Tom replied. "The turbine outlet temperature is approaching normal operating limits. Wait! I see four green lights only. Engine 5 is flashing red on the diagnostic tree!" Tom turned to Joseph; he looked troubled. "Engine 5 is overheating!"

The temperature inside Engine 5 steadily increased, and so did Tom's anxiety. The bridge fell silent; Sequanta computers with neuromorphic processors quickly redesigned Engine 5's temperature profile. Narrowing the engine's magnetic nozzle diameter and adding more cooling liquid with extra viscosity to the thrust chamber wall lowered the temperature inside the engine cowling.

"Well, I'll be damned," Tom said.

Sitting back in his chair, seeming pleased with the computer running the engine management system, Joseph smiled at Tom and Martin. "I'm glad that you two were here to see the neuroevolution in Sequanta Algorithms working in real-time."

"I don't understand what just happened," Tom said. "One minute, Engine 5 is about to explode, then I see five green lights on the diagnostic tree, and everything goes quiet."

"Neuromorphic processors are self-learning!" Joseph said, showing his frustration. "They find ways to solve problems without making any mistakes along the way."

Martin turned to the only real friend he had aboard the Phoenix, "Joseph, placing complete trust in any computer is a concept many people are not comfortable with, and you know how I feel about the automation of complex tasks without any human intervention. But the thought that scares me the most is an undetectable computer error when Phoenix is traveling at the speed of light."

Professor Lin moved forward to the control console until she stood beside Martin.

"Rest assured, Captain. Our Sequanta computers can out-think the best minds on board this ship," Professor Lin said. "And their current level of intelligence will undoubtedly increase by the time we reach Galraithia. Without them, I'd say there's a 90 to 100% chance every human on board Phoenix and Endeavour will not survive the journey." She was looking at Martin with an enigmatic look on her face.

"Professor, I've been accused of being an alarmist fearmonger. Nothing can be further from the truth, but Sequanta computers do make mistakes," Tom said.

Professor Lin's gaze shifted toward Joseph; she expected him to counter her argument. But Joseph and Satori were busy monitoring the final flight test of the Aquarius Lander on the far side of the moon. "Phoenix has reached the OMB, Captain."

"Very well, Commander Thomas. Relay our new coordinates to Aquarius," Martin said, his voice deliberately calm.

"Aye, sir."

"Mr. Granger, report to Cryo. Doctor Coverdale wants to do some blood tests before you prep for deep sleep."

"Aye, Captain."

"Joseph, are you ready to set the Jump-point coordinates in the Auto-Nav computer?"

Joseph swiveled his chair slowly and met Martin's anxious gaze. "Yes, I'm ready and waiting for you to give the order to get underway."

"You can set the Jump-point coordinates and engage the Auto-Nav computer as soon as Aquarius returns to the ship."

"Okay."

Martin appreciated that a person's potential is a very individual thing determined primarily by human behavior, social environment, and those closest to you. So, when

Martin left the bridge, he had every confidence that Joseph was the right man for the job. He was an invaluable source of knowledge on every aspect of Celestial Navigation and Far Star engine technology. And Martin believed that Joseph would always do his best to fulfill mission goals and help Phoenix reach Galraithia no matter the circumstances. No matter how many problems may arise during the voyage.

***

Meanwhile, four men and two women, first-time visitors to LOS, were on an organized tour and making their way up to Deck-12 via Cargo Bay-6, where Robert Jandamarra was busy stacking colored-coded crates. One of the visitors, John Randal, an accountant on the Winthrop payroll, wanted to speak to Robert and the other members of the cybernetic team. But a fabricator returning to its Charging Station stopped at a green pedestrian walkway, and John was too scared to take another step. "Don't be scared, Mr. Randal. You have the right of way, sir," Robert said.

"Fabricators are so much bigger than I had imagined."

"Fabricators vary in size," Robert said. "But inside, they are the same, just like human anatomy."

A redheaded woman in blue visitor coveralls called out, "John, are you coming with us to the Observation deck?"

"Yes. I'll be there soon."

"Okay. But don't be too long. The Moon shuttle will leave in half an hour."

John waved at the woman as she entered the Observation deck airlock.

"Your wife?" Robert asked.

"Yes."

"Your wife isn't interested in robotics, is she?"

"No, Susan is a devoted astronomer. She loves telescopes, stars, and planets. That's where we differ; astronomy is tiresome and boring to me."

"I understand what you mean," Robert said. "I get bored looking at the stars after a while."

"Mr. Jandamarra, tell me more about these robotic fabricators. I am fascinated by the eyes. They have very human-like eyes."

"Fabricators vary in size," Robert declared. "This XL5 unit is a medical model fabricator. It has learned all the skills that only the best health professionals have."

John rubbed his fingers on XL5's metallic skin. "A medical model, you say. So how do you know where it fits in the workplace order of things?"

"Clothes can tell us a lot about a person's background, social status, etc. The painted color code on the outer skin of this XL5 medical unit, the white body color, and the red stripe down the right shoulder tell us a lot about job position and responsibilities," Robert said.

"I haven't seen too many working fabricators moving about LOS," John said.

Robert tapped on a computer screen and XL5 powered up. "The Orbital Station has 200 working fabricators, but most have little or no access to public areas. They follow restricted passageways to the internal and external sections of the Orbital Station."

John was hesitant to approach the active fabricator. "I may be a Winthrop accountant, but I have no idea how much each fabricator costs to manufacture or why we manufacture so many units."

"Maybe that's a question you should put to Mr. Winthrop."

"Duly noted," John said quickly. "Goodbye, Mr. Jandamarra. Thank you for that very lucid explanation. I'm leaving with a greater understanding and appreciation of our fabricators' work and their value."

"I hope you and your wife enjoy the rest of the tour, sir."

"I'm sure we'll enjoy it," John said with a grin.

Robert looked at his watch. *"Where is Ryan? He said he'd help me move these crates to Cargo Bay-5."* Ryan entered Cargo Bay-6 just as John Randal was leaving. Ryan gave the accountant a cold look, remembering that Randal had proposed to drastically cut funding for the planned Winthrop's Biocybernetics development program on Galraithia.

"Well, well, well! Mr. Jandamarra. Sucking up to a bean counter, what's going on?"

"Nothing is going on. Randal is a harmless old man going about his business," Robert said.

"Randal is the Chief Accountant of the Winthrop Finance Corporation. He wants to save money by abolishing the planned cybernetics factory on Galraithia and that makes him a dangerous man and our enemy."

"Gordon Winthrop will not allow that to happen," Robert said. "Setting up a viable future colony on Galraithia will depend on a modern cybernetics factory to manufacture and develop support for a resilient fabricator workforce that can work around the clock and in all environments."

"I hope you're right. Without that factory, we won't have a job," Ryan said.

Robert hesitated for a moment before saying, "What do you mean, we won't have a job? You told Rachel and me that you're not renewing your work contract with Winthrop Corporation. You said you'd be returning to Earth to spend your money on glamourous whores and drinking the best champagne while your friends roast and freeze on an alien planet."

"That dream is long gone. I've finally woken up and changed my mind about going to Galraithia with you and Rachel."

"I'm guessing that you would have received bad news from Rachel?"

"You guessed right, Rob. It's never easy to accept the death of a loved one. I'm finding it hard not to think back to the very last conversation I had with my brother Alex. He and his wife had hoped to join the expedition to Galraithia after the birth of their first child. I remember how proud Alex looked. He would have made a good father."

Robert couldn't help but feel deep sorrow and sympathy for his close friend. "I truly am sorry for your loss, mate."

"Life goes on regardless of the pain," Ryan said.

"Ryan, you don't have to be here. I'll secure the cargo crates."

"No. I said I would help you, and that's what I intend on doing."

"I can manage on my own just fine."

"It's faster with two people chaining," Ryan said, putting on his power-suit harness. "Every crate must be double-chained and magnetically tied to the bulkhead. So, we'd better start now, or we'll be late for dinner."

"I'm afraid dinner will have to wait," Robert countered. "Rachel has an urgent meeting with Collin McAllister, Security services."

"Security services?" Ryan said, looking surprised.

"I know what you're thinking; the security service provider on board LOS can't be trusted."

"You got that right," Ryan thought.

"I don't want to say this, but I don't think we have a choice," Robert said.

Ryan looked at Robert and gave him his full attention.

"Rachel managed to retrieve several voice recordings from Five-o-nine's head unit! The recordings may hold the key to Emilio Vargas's murder."

"Why is Rachel wasting her time with voice recordings?" Ryan asked. "Whoever murdered Emilio Vargas would be long gone by now."

***

The small Xiangshan-7 spacecraft raced toward the Lunar Orbital Station, carrying over 265 passengers who had departed in urgent haste from China's Wenchang Spaceflight Facility. As they reached maximum velocity just beyond Earth's orbit, the travelers murmured hopes for safe passage, but noticeably absent were handshakes, "good luck" wishes, or "see you soon" farewells.

They honored an unspoken rule born from the legacy of the legendary Chinese space explorer Captain Jian Zhao. Often compared to Captain James Cook, Zhao had met a similar fate to Cook; never did he see his homeland again.

Headlines worldwide had blared the tragic news about Star Chaser Liaoning: "Lost in space! All lives lost!"

Since that disaster, expressing "good luck" before missions became taboo—considered a harbinger of doom. Yet accidents struck randomly, with fortune playing no role in their occurrence. The true culprits behind most space catastrophes were knowledge gaps, inadequate preparation, and dangerous operational habits.

***

Captain Caterina Cymerman activated the Lindal gyroscope attached to the underbelly of the Xiangshan-7 spacecraft. As the Lindal gyroscope spun faster and faster at maximum revolutions per second, it generated artificial gravity. Caterina left her seat and the Xiangshan-7's cramped flight deck to walk out into the Forward cabin. She smiled at passengers lying back in their seats with their seatbelts fastened. Caterina sensed anxiety, which many, if not all, passengers experience on their first flight. But this flight was an unforgettable one for the Freelanders on board; they had chosen to leave their homes, family, and friends for just one chance to start a new life on Galraithia.

Michael Stoddard and Dani Li had settled down in their seats for the 5-hour flight to LOS. Dani looked out the window and quietly said goodbye to planet Earth. It was clear he could never return. Dani looked at his friend Michael sitting next to him. Michael always read a book whenever he felt anxious about something or wanted to relieve his boredom. Michael's eyes slid off the pages of the book he had previously read when Caterina entered the dimly lit cabin. As captain, she had to greet all passengers and wish them all a safe journey and good fortune in the years ahead.

"Mr. Stoddard, Mr. Li. Glad to have you aboard. Welcome, guys."

"Thank you, Captain," both men said courteously.

"Captain, why haven't you joined the Galraithian Expedition? We need good pilots," Michael said.

"Oh, I have given it a lot of thought, believe me. Stay safe, gentlemen."

"Stay safe, Captain."

"I always try my best to stay safe, Michael."

"Invoca pericol," Dani said.

Seeing Caterina's questioning look, Dani added, "Invoca pericol means: 'Stay safe' in Freilish."

Caterina didn't speak any Freilish, a language difficult to master. Finally, she returned Dani's smile and said, "Invoca pericol, Mr. Li." Then she walked up the aisle and found Rihanna and Lanfen wrapped in blankets and laughing gently. They were delighted that the journey to Galraithia, still regarded as a fancifully idle dream by many people on Earth, was fast becoming a tangible reality no one could ignore.

"Miss Wakeman and Miss Lanfen Li. Hello, ladies. Are you enjoying the flight?" Caterina asked.

"This is my first flight, and I'm enjoying it very much," Lanfen answered. "Lift Off was fun."

Rihanna looked at Lanfen, "Lift-Off was scary; the rumbling and vibrations nearly shook me out of my seat. I am enjoying the smooth flight now, though." Aware that other people were trying to sleep in the cabin, she quietly added, "I hope Michael and Dani didn't misbehave back there."

"Both were perfect gentlemen," Caterina said, smiling.

"Michael is courteous, polite, and respectful, a perfect gentleman when he wishes to impress someone, especially pretty young ladies," Rihanna said, revealing disappointment and jealousy.

Rihanna Wakeman is a beautiful woman, Caterina thought. *And she doesn't seem to be the jealous type.* "Lanfen, you should try and get some sleep," Caterina said.

"I'm too excited to sleep."

"Captain, how long before we reach LOS?" Rihanna asked.

"The flight takes 5 hours, 35 minutes. So, it will be 6 a.m. solar time when we reach LOS, enjoy the rest of the flight."

"Thank you, Captain."

Rihanna turned to Lanfen and zipped up Lanfen's sleeping bag. "Now, young lady, you'd better get some sleep."

"I'll try and get some sleep soon. Look out the window and tell me what you see."

"Looking out the window, Earth is a small blue marble. I see countless stars, but they don't twinkle in space," Rihanna replied.

"Do you see the Sun?"

"From this angle, I see only a small piece of the Sun's South pole," Rihanna said.

"Is the Sun yellow?"

"No, the Sun is boring white," Rihanna sighed.

"When I dream, the Sun is yellow and sometimes orange," Lanfen said. "There are brilliant blue-white stars in space and planets bigger than Jupiter. Cities sparkle like diamonds, and people wear colorful clothes and fine jewelry. There are dogs and cats, birds and wild ponies, and ships with painted sails glide on deep oceans rich with distinct species of marine life." Lanfen felt her eyes feeling heavy.

With a gentle kiss on Lanfen's head, Rihanna said, "I'm sure that somewhere out there in this vast universe, there is another little girl who dreams the same lucid dream."

***

Dani unbuckled his seatbelt and stood up. He thought about artificial gravity and how a rotating gyroscope produced the centrifugal force to hold his feet firmly on the floor. Then, Dani walked over to an empty seat across the aisle from Rihanna and Lanfen. Rihanna smiled and gave Dani a gentle nod while Lanfen peacefully slept. "Do you think we are doing the right thing bringing Lanfen with us?" Rihanna whispered.

"For a blind person, living in an overcrowded city is like living in a jungle; only the strong survive," Dani said.

"Yes, but Galraithia may not be the world we think it is."

"Lanfen is a knowledgeable young woman with non-vision senses that are finely tuned. She can sense things we cannot sense with our five senses."

"I guess it all boils down to trust and commitment to one another," Rihanna said.

"Yes. Trust and commitment," Dani said, as she looked over his shoulder at Michael urging him toward his seat. "Talk to you later. Michael is becoming restless."

Rihanna nodded yes and gave Michael a cold stare.

When Dani came to sit next to Michael, he said, "Lanfen is fast asleep."

"Yeah, okay, that's nice. How's Rihanna?"

"She's okay."

"I see quite clearly that you're besotted with Rihanna and all you can say is she's okay?"

"I don't know what you're talking about, Michael."

"Yes, you do."

Dani wanted to leave his seat and kept thinking about Michael's many shortcomings and how he was always there for Dani whenever Dani needed help.

"Hey, man, relax!" Michael said. "I'm speaking my mind, okay?"

"Michael, there's nothing wrong with speaking your mind. You just need to think twice before saying something you regret."

"Duly noted. Thank you, Mr. Perfect."

A few seats behind Rihanna and Lanfen, a middle-aged man was looking over his shoulder, annoyed by Michael's loud voice. Dani smiled at the man but only received a cold stare before the man looked away to complain to another middle-aged man beside him, who was resting feet up in a recliner, watching a movie on a holographic tv.

"In case you haven't noticed," the man remarked, "have you seen the sort of Freelander riff-raff we have on board?"

"No, John, I haven't, and I don't really care," said the other with his eyes on the holograph. "Now, be quiet and watch the movie."

Both men had boarded the Xiangshan-7 transport en route to LOS with their feisty spouses now sitting in opposite aisle seats.

"Do you know those people?" Dani asked Michael.

"The man seated next to the portside window is Professor Ben Stein, and man nearer to the aisle is Doctor John Steele," Michael replied. "Both are on the Winthrop payroll and rated amongst the best in the cryogenics business."

Dani looked at Michael. "Isn't that just typical of Winthrop to hire the best people for his beloved Endeavour?"

"If I had his kind of money, I, too, would hire the best cryo engineers that money can buy. But instead of hiring the best cryo engineers that money can buy for the Phoenix spacecraft, Professor Briar hired retrained Freelander farmers."

Dani did not understand the intricacies of cryogenics, nor did he like the idea of prolonged hyper-sleep; he had viewed countless movies and photographs from the earliest days of Deep space exploration. Images of Captain Jian Zhao and his nervous crew, the physical distress they had to endure prepping for deep sleep. Medical fabricators now carried out all the cryogenic prepping procedures and maintained life-support systems inside the Cryo module. However, it must be said that a Fabricator's prepping technique created fear and caused anxiety even among the best astronauts.

Dani seemed a bit surprised when Michael reached for a sick bag. "I feel a sudden urge to throw up inside this tin can," Michael said.

"But you did extremely well during zero-g training."

"Hey! Do not remind me of zero-g training. That was the worst week of my life," Michael said, positioning the sickness bag closer to his mouth.

"Even the best astronauts experience the effects of space motion sickness, Michael. Don't sell yourself short."

As Michael buried his face into the sickness bag, one of the passengers, a sandy-haired young man with round-rimmed glasses, entered the Forward cabin and sat down on the only single recliner next to the escape hatch on the starboard side of the vessel.

"Any idea who the guy is?" Dani asked.

Michael sealed the empty sickness bag and craned his neck to peer over the passenger headrest in front of him like a curious child. "Well, well, well. This little vessel has attracted some very wealthy people, my friend," Michael said. "That's Peter Winthrop, Gordon Winthrop's son and heir to the unpopular Winthrop dynasty. According to rumors, there are many mutual disagreements between father and son, particularly Peter's view on the direction of the Freelander Movement. Gordon has only contempt for our people." With that Michael turned away, wanting to sleep.

"Peter Winthrop has every right to have a different view. But wearing a UAN army field uniform among Freelander passengers is an insult to our people and wrong on many levels," Dani said.

"I don't know if young Winthrop is wearing that uniform to put up a brave front or to please his father," Michael said, switching off the reading light above his head.

***

244

Back on LOS, sixteen miners had completed the mandatory medical checks and had rushed into the dining area. Hungry after their long flight from Earth, the miners came together and looked forward to having a delicious meal before boarding the Space tug scheduled to take them down to the lunar surface. All sixteen had signed up for a nine-month mining stint extracting ice and Helium 3 from the lunar polar regions. Lunar mining jobs provided miners an adequate wage for a lavish lifestyle back on Earth. However, as with almost any work activity, there was a downside. And being a lunar miner was no different; the mine managers often ignored many safety concerns. Miners worked with machinery covered by abrasive lunar dust, damaging airlock seals, and electrical equipment components. For this reason, the Space tug service transporting people to and from Sidjartha Base, LOS, and Ercial Prison had ceased operations. At the same time, maintenance crews cleaned the solar cells producing electrical power.

The rowdy group of miners had seated themselves around two large tables in the front of the crowded dining room. Ryan acknowledged the hard work the miners endured to support families back home on Earth with a friendly smile and a warm greeting. Robert scanned the dining room. "There she is," he said, gesturing Ryan towards Rachel; she was waving at them and directing them to sit at her table. But ordering food was the last thing on Rachel's mind. She had brought audio recordings, graphs, a diagram of Pipe-12, and photographs of Five-o-nine powered down on its Lockplate. "I managed to save three minutes of Five-o-nine's real-time audio recordings. Scratchy sounds mostly, no images. The timestamp data equates to three minutes of dialogue between Emilio Vargas and a second unknown individual," Rachel was explaining, handing Ryan and Robert copies of digital sound recordings. Robert looked at the timestamp data, trying to guess which of the scarcely discernable data was correct. "There are broken lines of data, missing information at the beginning and the end of the voice recording. Did you verify that your timestamp data isn't corrupted?"

"The timestamp data and the vocal recordings match," Rachel said. "Now, listen to the voice recording and tell me whether the acoustic analysis is enough as admissible evidence."

"I know that look on her face, Ryan. Don't expect dinner anytime soon."

"She's onto something that's for certain."

"Will you two shut up for a moment and listen," Rachel said, playing back the voice recordings:

"Rat-faced bastard! Don't you ever touch me again, or I'll drop you where you stand."

"Okay, I'm sorry, calm down."

"You know your place, don't ever forget it when you're around me. Now, take care of that mechanical abomination. I don't want to see it again."

"I'll erase the fabricator's memory circuits after it powers down."

"And delete the datastore from the hosts controlling the wall-mounted cameras."

"Don't worry about a thing. I know what to do."

"I always worry when I'm dealing with an amateur."

Then there was muffled whispering and the sound of static.

"We know Vargas poured the corborane acid; he had acid burns on his right hand and inflammation inside his lungs," Ryan declared.

"That's correct. Hopefully, the recordings will help us pinpoint the person behind the second voice," Rachel said, but her voice got drowned out by an argument between tug pilot Malachy Sutcliffe and Emma Wells. Malachy was terribly angry, and Emma didn't seem to care. Both had differing opinions about the inconsistencies and inefficiencies within the Space Tug service, which relied on many internal and external variables independent of Emma's sphere of influence and control.

"Emma, I have 16 people just sitting around waiting for someone to take them to their assigned worksite. They risk losing their job if they don't report to work in the next two hours. Now, get a Space tug up here!"

"Malachy, you and your people must wait like everyone else traveling down to Sidjartha Moon Base today. I'll call you when the Space tug arrives."

"Why wait for a space tug when a transport shuttle sits idle inside Docking Bay 9?"

"The transport shuttle in Docking Bay 9 is reserved for Freelanders en route to the Phoenix spacecraft," Emma said, rechecking the flight schedule database.

"Freelanders be damned!" Malachy snapped. "We are not prepared to be kept waiting any longer."

"Okay, Malachy, go down to Docking Bay 9, but it won't do you any good."

"It's pointless to talk, Emma. You're just too incompetent to do your job properly."

"And you are a turd," Emma countered. "Someone should flush you down the toilet."

One miner called out, "Hey, Malachy! Don't worry, man, you don't pay our wages."

Malachy became even more annoyed. "I always worry when I'm dealing with an amateur."

Rachel looked at Robert and whispered, "I have to call Security!"

"Security? Why?"

"The man Malachy, I've heard his voice before. I'm positive his voice is what I heard on Five-o-nine's timestamp recordings," Rachel said.

"A partially corrupted voice profile that isn't distinguishable may not render the timestamp recordings admissible evidence or proof that Malachy was with Emilio Vargas," Ryan said.

"The voice recordings are all we have right now. Emilio Vargas was not alone before he died; the other voice on the recordings is certainly Malachy's, not someone else's," Rachel countered.

Robert turned to Ryan, "Rachel's acoustic analysis of Malachy's voice profile would raise questions."

"I'd like to think so," Ryan said.

"Rachel, you call Security," Robert said, getting out of his chair.

"Rob, come back," Rachel said in a whisper. "Where are you going?"

Robert brushed aside Rachel's question, and approached Malachy, who was snacking on dried apple slices comfortably in a chair. "Excuse me, sir. Is the Security Station on this level?" Robert asked.

Malachy looked up with calculating eyes. "The Security Station?"

"Yes, the Security Station," Robert said quickly. "I'm new here and was told to report to the Head Guard at the Security Station."

"The Security Station is on Level 3," Malachy said, looking at the hatchway leading to Level 3.

"No. I went to Level 3 and asked a communication officer to direct me to the Security Station," Robert said. "He told me to take the elevator and go to Level 5." Robert noticed Rachel talking on her phone.

"The comms officer lied to you. The Security Station is on Level 3."

"Lied to me? Why would he do that?" Robert asked.

"Listen here, mister! The Security Station is on Level 3. You got that?"

"I'm so sorry for interrupting your lunch, but I'm very anxious to meet my cousin. His name is Emilio Vargas. Do you know him?"

"No, I can't say that I do."

"How can that be?" Robert said, expecting a reaction from Malachy. "You were the last person to talk to him, weren't you?"

"Move away from me, man, leave me alone," Malachy said, getting out of his chair and frowning hard at Robert. "Mister, I don't know who you are, and I don't know your cousin. Now get out of my face or I'll...."

"Or I'll what? Drop me where I stand?" A suspicious scowl had overtaken Robert's face.

Malachy snatched the bread knife from the dinner table. Appearing ready to attack, he pointed the knife at Robert. "Who are you?"

"Put the knife down," Robert said calmly.

Malachy lunged and thrust the knife toward Robert's neck. Stepping back quickly, Robert blocked the bread knife with his right hand and forced the blade downward. Then, in an instant, Robert grabbed Malachy's arm and held it in a vice-like grip, twisting and bending the wrist back until Malachy fell to his knees. Malachy protested angrily, but Robert kept the pressure on the aching wrist until a security team arrived and arrested Malachy for the alleged murder of Emilio Vargas.

"Uncuff me!" Malachy cried. "You people don't know the risk you're taking. I will you kill you all, one at a time when I return."

"Return? There's no coming back from where you're going," Rachel said.

Rachel followed guards marching Malachy down to the security monitoring station on Level 3. Then she met with Collin McAllister and handed him Five-o-nine's timestamp recordings. Rachel's acoustic analysis of the timestamps was the hard evidence McAllister had been waiting for. It was proof that tug pilot Malachy Sutcliffe was with Emilio Vargas just minutes before Emilio was shot and killed.

Later that day, McAllister phoned Emma Wells while she was working at her desk and asked if she would be a character witness against defendant Malachy Sutcliffe. The man had a violent reputation. Emma looked at her computer screen, and the tug pilot named Malachy Sutcliffe was no longer on her work schedule. She quickly put her hand to her mouth to cover a girlish giggle. Emma then told McAllister she would gladly be a character witness against Malachy at trial. While talking to McAllister, Emma took her eyes off the computer screen. Instead, she watched Captain Cymerman maneuver the Xiangshan 7 transport inside Docking Bay 12. Ordinarily, space tugs from Sidjartha Base to LOS had Docking Bay 9 all to themselves. Outside forces, however, canceled the space tug service to carry out maintenance checks on electrical equipment, which meant miners en route to the Moon and Freelander passengers en route to Phoenix would have to wait until the Orbital Transportation Service resumed.

***

Freelander passengers disembarking from the Xiangshan 7 transport with their belongings lined up in front of a security station. Uniformed soldiers from Gordon Winthrop's elite guard had sealed off eight hatchways leading to the central hub of LOS's octagonal-shaped habitat module. There was one final security check before Freelander passengers boarded Shuttle-1157, which was the transport link to the Phoenix Spacecraft waiting at the Outer marker.

Michael, Rihanna, Lanfen, and Dani were making little headway. The long line of people was cautious moving forward when automated Pacher fork-lifts arrived and started loading 100 containers of fine Lunar Regolith and Helium-3 inside Xiangshan-7's cargo bay. But the most precious cargo came from deep below the lunar surface where rock samples held traces of dark matter. Also known as axion particles, this matter powered energy-efficient nanotrine/axion reactors.

Professor Robert McEwen from Edinburgh University had discovered the axion particles in 2056. Back then, distinguished geologists believed that the Earth's inner core and the Moon were made of solid iron. Professor McEwen proposed another theory: *"The Earth's inner core is a solid ball made mostly of iron. However, there is also a liquid layer in which liquefied axion particles exist. Comparable to solid dark matter particles, which cannot bind with ordinary matter, axion particles can dissolve in liquefied iron at extremely high temperatures and transform into an inert gas called Nanotrine gas. Under extreme heat and tremendously high pressure, small volumes of nanotrine gas are pushed outward, drawing ever closer to the Earth's crust. I am convinced that there are denser axion particles in basaltic lava and pockets of pure nanotrine gas trapped in the pore spaces of igneous rocks. My research in axion particles, undetectable with other conventional particles until recently, has also led me to a more manageable conclusion: Nanotrine gas can also dissolve in water ... the Earth's oceans which I recognize as a potential major source of pure nanotrine gas, particularly in waters from 4,000 to 11,000 meters."*

Professor Robert McEwen's scientific paper also said: *"The Earth's core is not likely to cool before the Sun approaches the end of its life. Thus, for the human race to survive and leave Earth long before the dying Sun expands and becomes a red giant star that will engulf the inner planets, Mercury, Venus, Earth, and Mars, humankind will depend on its unique ability to discover and colonize new habitable zones beyond the Oort Cloud and the Cassandra Major System. However, suppose humanity cannot live together in peace and harmony with all living things. In that case, the end of human existence in this universe is a predictable hypothesis."*

***

Sergeant Philip Sheridan was in charge of Winthrop security. He had set up a temporary security station at the front of the embarkation line and was scanning identity cards. He quickly checked Lanfen's, Michael's, and Rihanna's cards and verified their identity. Then, as Dani approached the front of the line, a tense and anxious Embarkation Coordinator pushed Dani aside to speak with Sergeant Sheridan. "There's enough room for two or three more people on 1157, and that's it. What should we do, Boss?"

"How many passengers have you on board?"

"Counting the Freelander passengers from the previous flight from Earth, 265 passengers, maximum capacity, Boss."

Sergeant Sheridan pointed at Rihanna, Lanfen and Michael a few feet away. "Okay. Those three are the last passengers." Then Sheridan turned to Dani, gave him and the identity card a cursory glance, told him there was no more room on shuttle 1157, and assured Dani a seat on the next shuttle. Sheridan was not sure when the next shuttle would arrive. Dani wasn't happy about it, but he just nodded an okay. As he moved aside and looked behind him, he saw the 50 people nearer to Docking Bay 12. Some were standing and chatting loudly while their noisy children playing games. Others sat beside their belongings on a cold steel floor, patiently waiting in line for their names to be called. Rihanna, Lanfen, and Michael were allowed to board shuttle 1157, but they stopped and waited for Dani. Dani said he would catch up to them later. He didn't want them to know how much he would miss them all so he simply told them to go ahead without him. "I need to tie up a few loose ends before boarding."

"Okay, Dani, we'll see you onboard the Phoenix," Michael said. He knew Dani's meticulous planning and extreme care would make it impossible for anyone to get close enough to harm Lanfen and Rihanna.

***

As Sergeant Sheridan started to close the security station, he saw a young man approaching from Docking Bay 12. As the young man came nearer, Sheridan recognized Peter Winthrop. He looked fitter and much stronger than the last time he'd seen him. Dani also recognized the young man who had been on the same shuttle flight from Earth. He still wore the disgusting and pathetic United Allied Nations field uniform. Dani remembered Martin talking casually about Peter Winthrop, who had been heir apparent to his father's vast fortune until Peter emigrated to Freeland, Antarctica.

"Welcome back, Mr. Winthrop. Good to see you, sir."

"Thank you, Sergeant. It's good to be back."

Having exchanged pleasantries, Peter Winthrop and Sergeant Sheridan spoke loudly enough for Dani to overhear. The Endeavour spacecraft would be rushed from LOS's docking ring and proceed to the Outer Marker, the rendezvous point. The Phoenix spacecraft was already at the rendezvous point and had been waiting for Endeavour for some time.

"Sergeant, our slow-speed security and embarkation procedures are unacceptable, to put it mildly. I need your help to speed things up. Slowing Endeavour's departure could jeopardize the entire mission."

"Our embarkation procedures are slow because most Freelanders don't have high-tech identity cards with all the built-in security. We don't know who these people are or where they came from. Most don't speak English, and our best translation software cannot understand Freilish."

"Look behind you, Sergeant. More than 50 people are waiting to embark!"

"There are no more shuttles available, sir. The Freelanders just have to wait for the next one available."

"Sergeant, I want you to get all these people aboard the Xiangshan-7 transport and advise them to stow their belongings securely."

"I don't have the authority to do that, sir."

"The clock is ticking, Sergeant. Follow orders."

"I am following orders, sir. The Xiangshan-7 transport shuttle is returning to Earth and loading with fresh food supplies and urgently needed life support equipment for the Orbital Station and Sidjartha moon base."

"Yes, I am well aware of that, Sergeant, and taking full responsibility for overriding those orders. Do I make myself clear?"

"Yes, sir, very clear," Sheridan said reluctantly.

"Now carry out my orders."

"Yes, sir!"

***

When Peter Winthrop announced that he was leaving the Lunar Orbital Station and emigrating to the Freeland territories of Antarctica, he created a serious rift within the mega-rich Winthrop family. Peter shrugged at the disappointment and anger on his father's face. Peter casually told his father that he had had enough of being cooped up in the family's most significant acquisition: a floating tin can in space. He said he was cutting ties with the family business. Unsure about his future, Peter always felt alienated when his father was around and needed his

own space. Emigrating to the wide-open spaces of
Antarctica seemed the logical answer.

Gordon just could not believe why his son was willing to
give up everything he had worked so hard to possess. Was
it the conflicting opinions regarding Antarctica and the
Freelander cause? Father and son did not and could not
agree entirely about the escalating social and political
conflicts between the often-oppressed Freelanders and the
Allied folk: the untouchable caste only the rich and mega-
rich belonged to. The biggest slap to the Winthrop name
came soon after Peter started earning a living working
alongside Freelander terraformers, learning their
philosophy, and understanding how and why Freelanders
triumphed over environments fraught with dangers.

The Freelanders of Antarctica, Freelanders everywhere,
loved to change things. They helped people change, helped
them develop, and adapted regardless of their station in life.
They taught Peter Freilish, helped heal his unhealthy body,
rebuilt his self-confidence, and instilled a deeper
understanding of Freelander values: selfless devotion to
duty, loyalty, bravery, sincerity, and respect for all living
things.

Gordon tried to phone Peter, wanting to ask him how he
was faring, only to find that Peter's cell phone account had
been disconnected. Despite the rejection, Gordon was
hopeful and passionately believed that his son would come
home one day wherever home was. The mistakes his son
had made in the past would stay in the past. Squandering
money, bedding whores, and boozing the last years of his
youth away were best left forgotten.

Peter mastered the social graces necessary to please his
father, Allied society's upper class, and the wealth-hungry
elite from an early age. However, his worldview, attitude,
and life changed dramatically after encountering the

Freelanders, who had suffered decades of oppression under Allied rule.

The Allied and Freelander lifestyles stood in stark contrast. Allied citizens dismissed the Freelander way as suitable only for lower classes. Yet this physically demanding lifestyle fostered the mental toughness, motivation, and resilience required to establish a permanent settlement on Galraithia and ensure human survival there.

Time was running short in the race to colonize Galraithia—widely viewed as humanity's salvation. Peter recognized this unique opportunity to witness history's second great human migration and wanted to participate.

So Gordon's once-rebellious son returned to the Lunar Orbital Station transformed. Some believed he came back humbled, ready to beg forgiveness and accept whatever position his father offered. What Gordon didn't realize was that Peter now harbored a new passion: the Freelander dream of colonizing Galraithia and preserving their traditions there.

***

"Hello, Father, I've arrived, finally."

"Welcome back to LOS, Peter. Welcome home, son. Come up to the bridge. Let me look at you, and I can update you on our slow embarkation situation."

"Your intelligence debriefing officer debriefed me en route to LOS via encrypted computer. He told me about the slow embarkation procedures, mission status, and enough information to familiarize myself with LOS. This place has certainly changed," Peter said, looking around the docking bay.

"My son, there's much to do and little time to do it."

"Father, I'm in Docking Bay 12. The entire loading area is crammed with people...Freelanders en route to Phoenix without transportation. I have taken the liberty to redirect the Freelanders to another shuttlecraft, the Xiangshan-7."

"The Xiangshan-7... Captain Cymerman's ship?"

"Yes. Is there are a problem?"

"A little while ago, one of our maintenance fabricators reported an anomaly in the Main FS engine, a leaking hydrogen valve. Stay on the line, Peter. Chief Engineer Higgins just walked in." There was a momentary silence before Gordon spoke again. *"Chief Higgins has given me an update. A technician has tightened the bolts and fixed the leak. The Xiangshan-7 is good to go."*

"Has Chief Higgins informed Captain Cymerman?"

"No. I want you to inform Caterina and the duty officer and take command of the bridge crew."

"Yes, Father."

Caterina entered the cockpit, knowing engineers had fixed the hydrogen leak while the cargo had been stowed away and properly secured. As she checked the Engine management system, her focus shifted to a radio transmission from Earth: *"Large pieces of flaming debris fell on Hainan City after a Xiangshan transport exploded in midair shortly after launch,"* the radio announcer said, his stoic voice murmuring over the hidden speaker in the ceiling. Meanwhile, Dani Li stood under the forward section of the Xiangshan-7's fuselage. Looking up the straight ladder leading to the cockpit, he called out to Captain Cymerman, "Hello, Captain? I request permission to come aboard. Hello, can anyone hear me?"

Caterina met Dani at the airlock between the cockpit and the passenger cabin.

"Permission granted. Hello, Dani. I'm sorry I didn't hear you call out. I was too preoccupied with news from Earth."

"No bad news, I hope."

"Bad enough," Caterina replied. "A Xiangshan transport not too dissimilar from this one exploded shortly after take-off this morning. But there's no need to worry about this vessel. Please make yourself comfortable. I have a few more engine checks to do before we can leave. And give Lanfen a big hug for me when you see her, okay?"

Dani nodded and smiled.

***

On the Phoenix Bridge, there were looks of surprise on everyone's faces when Gordon Winthrop's voice crackled over the loudspeaker. *"Captain Brindle! Are you there, Captain?"*

"Commander Thomas, clear the bridge of all non-essential personnel," Martin whispered.

"Aye, sir."

"Can you hear me, Captain?"

"Yes, Mr. Winthrop. I hear you, sir. What can I do for you?"

"Captain, I do apologize; there have been significant delays at our end, and we are doing all that's possible to prevent further delays. Rest assured; we have the last of your people aboard a transport shuttle ready for departure from the Orbital Station. Please accept my apologies for any inconvenience this has caused you."

"No need to apologize. There is plenty of time left on the countdown clock to do what we know best, eh, sir."

"Indeed, Captain, do what we know best. That is why I have appointed my son Peter as captain of the Endeavour."

Martin did not know Peter Winthrop; they hadn't met. Martin looked to Joseph for reassurance, but Joseph shrugged his shoulders; he hadn't met Peter Winthrop either.

"Mr. Winthrop, I'm sure your son is a capable man with all the necessary skills to be a good captain," Martin said.

"Yes, but Peter can be too headstrong and easily misled when I'm not around. But that's a different matter. Now, Captain, concerning the Aquarius and Icarus. Flight testing of the two Landers on the moon's far side has taken a considerable amount of time. How are things progressing?"

"All the tests and practices went well, sir. Both Landers have returned safely to the Phoenix."

"Mr. Winthrop, we understand that we cannot afford to take any risks or be complacent about safety," Joseph said.

"Being this close to our departure window, I do not expect anything less from you people," Winthrop said in a condescending tone. "Captain, I would like a word with Professor Briar. Is he about?"

"Professor Briar is prepping for cryosleep and cannot be disturbed, sir."

"That is understandable; prepping for cryosleep is never a pleasant experience, but having a conversation with a medical fabricator is the most common frustration I hear from colonists. Have a safe journey, Captain."

"Thank you, sir. You and your crew have a safe journey as well. See you at the rendezvous point."

"How much would you want to wager that Endeavour will get there first?"

"It is a forgone conclusion who will win this race, sir. Keep your money."

"Ha! I can see why Professor Briar thinks of you so highly. You are infuriatingly arrogant, Captain."

"Coming from you, Mr. Winthrop, I'll take that as a compliment."

"It certainly wasn't meant that way. In any case, Endeavour will reach the rendezvous point first."

"Not if I can help it," Martin whispered. He turned to Commander Satori Thomas. "Is Phoenix ready to get underway?"

"As ready as she'll ever be, Captain. We are just waiting for a group of passengers aboard the Xiangshan-7 to join us."

"No, Commander. The time has come to leave the nest," Martin said, frowning.

"Leave without them?" Joseph said.

"Joseph, you've been waiting for this moment your entire adult life. Do you want to miss the launch window for the sake of a few people?"

"There's still time left, Martin."

"No, Joseph, there is no time left for them. You are either up for the challenge, or you are not," Martin said flatly and coldly. "Are you up for the challenge, Joseph, or do you want to wait for our launch window to close?"

"I am ready for any challenge ahead of us, Martin. You know that."

"I'm ready, Captain. You can count on me," Satori said.

"Set course for the Liaoning Gateway. The best speed for rendezvous with Faxian."

"Aye, Captain. Setting course for the Liaoning Gateway and the best speed for rendezvous with Faxian," Joseph said confidently. "AutoNav, voice command. Set course trajectory. Alpha through to Epsilon - 5060564 Faxian, best speed."

Satori verified the trajectory coordinates. "Course is set and locked, Captain."

Martin turned to Satori. "Very well, Commander. Contact Eris Mining and give them our current and projected trajectory coordinates. Tell the officer in command. No, order the officer in command to ping the Faxian Telescope with their long-range scanners and clear any space rocks or space junk on our trajectory coordinates. Only clean space from the Liaoning Gateway to the Kuiper belt, please."

"Aye, sir."

"Long-range scanners are at their technical limits beyond the Kuiper belt," Joseph said.

"They are of little or no value, I know. But LRSs are all we have, Joseph."

"There's no point worrying about it, Martin. If Phoenix sustains a collision with a large rock or meteor, it's game over for everyone."

***

On board the Xiangshan-7, Anders Kruger's eyes were locked on the thruster controls. Anders was a skillful copilot, providing Captain Caterina Cymerman with backup and technical knowledge. But Caterina looked worried; the Xiangshan-7 was an old ship retrofitted with Far Star engine technology and five big, powerful rocket engines that often overheated after powering up to maximum thrust. "Not too much reverse thrust, Mr. Kruger."

"I'm doing the best I can, Captain."

"Okay, go for main engine power up, but stay on slow idle mode until we reach a safe distance from LOS."

"Aye, Captain, powering up to slow idle mode."

Suddenly, an engine exploded without warning, rocking the ship violently to one side and sending shrapnel into the four smaller FS engines. The engine cowlings stripped away, rocket fuel ignited, and exploded. The force of the blast buckled the inner bulkhead and ruptured the outer hull. Broken pieces of steel and ceramic slammed into Endeavour's pressurized rubber/carbon fiber mating adaptor. The life-sustaining atmosphere inside Endeavour escaped. People, chairs, and anything not tied down were blown into space. The rear cargo bay of Xiangshan-7 was also gone, torn off by the force of the blast that ripped through Docking Bay 12. Caterina lurched against buckled bulkhead plating, almost splitting the back of her head open. She grabbed a handrail and sounded the evacuation alarm as precious air escaped rapidly out of the ruptured hull.

Passengers followed the evacuation procedure and scrambled to the nearest life pod, unaware that inside the Xiangshan-7's Battery Room, the temperature was rising to dangerous levels; Nanotrine-ion power coils were heating up and beginning to melt. Seconds later, the first of twelve power coils mounted at the front of a battery rack exploded into lethal shards of searing steel, killing a passenger scrambling to get to the life pod.

***

Life pod-11 launched into space with a shudder. Behind it, the Xiangshan-7 disintegrated into a wide debris field that moved at velocities almost impossible for Life pod-11 to avoid. Shards of steel and plastic slammed into Life pod-11, pierced its thin inner bulkhead, injured several passengers. Caterina and Anders could hear people groaning and screaming in pain. "Captain, we have to move away from the debris field."

"The collision avoidance system isn't working," Caterina said, struggling with the flight controls. "Stay calm, everyone. We will get through this," Caterina said into her helmet microphone. As Caterina's voice came through the loudspeaker, seven passengers lay critically injured in their seats. Some passengers helped the wounded, while others did not attempt to help unless they were members of their own family or belonged to the same political ideologies. Allied Folk versus Freelander people.

One man covered his head with both arms. "I don't want to die," he sobbed.

Dani looked at the man beside him and said stubbornly, "No one is going to die! Captain Cymerman is an experienced pilot. Now stop moaning and find a first aid kit."

Caterina's blue eyes darted side to side, tracking the debris, as though she was watching a tennis match.

"I can do this," she said. She trusted the long hours of pilot training she had done to understand the catastrophic impact of debris fields on spacecraft. But that was when she had completed the exercise and safely locked herself inside a flight simulator. This situation did not come with a respawn option if she failed and died. This was not a game. She was facing her first real-life struggle.

***

With only one window and no other external visual references, the passengers inside life pod-11 felt trapped. The explosion had set everyone's nerves on edge. Then, a nurse from Sidjartha Moon Base cried out, "Look, we are out of the debris field!"

The senior engineer, Dale Neiman, looked at his friend Ferris, who had been sobbing about not wanting to die. "Are you okay?" Dale said.

"Yes, Dale, I'm okay. I don't know what came over me. I was scared! I thought I was going to die!"

"It's okay, Ferris. No one here will judge you for being scared," Dale said.

The youngest Freelander engineer appointed to Phoenix was Karl Weiss. He looked up to Dale and old Ferris. He respected them, and he was thankful they were with him. "I'm not ashamed to say that I was scared. It's been one fuck-up after another ever since Gordon Winthrop designed the new docking port."

"Winthrop didn't design the new docking port. It's too close to Endeavour's mating adaptor," Dale said.

"I agree with Dale," Ferris put in. "The new docking port is dangerously close to the mating adaptor. Winthrop would never endanger the lives of his people or his beloved Endeavour."

"If Gordon didn't design the new docking port, who did?" Karl asked.

"It was a design flaw created by a Sequanta computer," Dale said with profound conviction.

"Sequanta computers don't make mistakes," Karl countered.

"Well, that's not necessarily true," Ferris declared. "I'm sorry to disagree with you, Karl, but I have hard evidence that backs up Dale's claims."

"Sequanta computers do make mistakes. The debris field out there proves it," Dale said.

Then Caterina's voice came through the loudspeaker, *"I can see the Phoenix spacecraft!"*

From inside the flight cabin, Phoenix appeared to be extremely far away. Caterina could not confirm visually whether Phoenix was stationary, getting closer, or heading away from her current position. She looked at the radar screen only to confirm her worst fear. Phoenix was heading away from Life pod-11.

"Comms are down. There's only static on the radio," Caterina said.

Karl looked at the camera mounted on the roof of the life pod. "The transmitting antenna is damaged. I'll suit up and fix it."

"No. Stay where you are," Caterina commanded. "I'm heading back to LOS before we run out of fuel."

Dani unbuckled his seat belt and rushed to the viewing window. Peering out, he saw the Phoenix spacecraft leaving the Outer Marker, the blue glow of its Far Star rocket engines slowly disappearing into the blackness of space. Hope now rested only on the Endeavour spacecraft: sufficient passenger quarters, empty cryo beds, and Gordon

Winthrop's relentless determination to win the race to Galraithia.

***

When Professor Briar heard about the explosions and hull breaches on LOS and the Endeavour, he was shocked by the terrible news. He thought of flawed engineering or poor decision-making as the underlying cause of the accident. He could only guess at how many might be injured or may die as the Phoenix spacecraft headed through the Liaoning Gateway and the Kuiper belt towards a rendezvous with the Faxian telescope.

The professor stopped prepping for cryosleep and began weighing his options: return to the Outer Marker and wait for the Endeavour spacecraft. Both ships would then head out to the Faxian telescope together. Or he could increase Phoenix's speed and stay on its set course. Phoenix would rendezvous and dock with the Faxian telescope alone.

"There are critical time constraints in any mission. Operational requirements that cannot be ignored. I also know I'm responsible for leaving many of our best people behind," Martin said.

"If we go back for our people or wait for engineers and fabricators to repair Endeavour's hull, we risk missing the rendezvous window with the Faxian telescope," Tom Granger countered.

Martin glared at Tom, his anger leaking through his eyes. "I wasn't addressing you, Mr. Granger."

"Everyone's input is important, Martin. Don't forget that."

"I won't forget, Professor. But good people were left behind. I cannot ignore that fact."

267

"We can alter the mission parameters and accept the delay or travel faster to make up for the lost time," Joseph declared.

"We can," Professor Briar put in. He was looking at a predefined mission model displayed on a computer screen. "But I'm not prepared to do that, Joseph. However, the essence of our mission has not changed: the first Freelander colony on Galraithia."

"Joseph, this first mission to Galraithia is of incredible importance to our Freelander brethren, to humanity. But Winthrop's negative evaluation of our technical and leadership skills may jeopardize the entire mission and more," Father Sandor said.

"Endeavour is loaded with vital terraforming equipment," Joseph said in a stern tone. "Oxygen makers, all-weather communications systems, the bulk of our food supply."

"What's done is done, Joseph," the professor countered with a frown. "There's no turning back from this moment on."

Professor Briar, often easygoing when making decisions, acted quickly. He stopped the negative and unproductive conversations, increased the distance between Endeavour and Phoenix, and headed toward solo rendezvous with the Faxian telescope and orbital insertion around Galraithia. "Joseph, don't look so grim. Professor Briar made the correct decision," Father Sandor said.

"That's right!" Professor Briar snapped. "Winthrop would have done the same if the explosion had crippled Phoenix instead of Endeavour."

While Martin pondered over Professor Briar's actions, he remained in the Cryo chamber until Professor Briar and Father Sandor entered the REM (rapid eye movement) phase before cryosleep. Then, Martin and his staff officers returned to the Bridge of Phoenix.

"Commander Thomas!"

"Sir!"

"Note the time in the Phoenix log, please."

"Aye, sir."

"Doctor Mason wants to see you before she preps for hypersleep, Captain."

Martin looked at the chronometer on the wall and then his wristwatch. "Thank you, Mr. Granger. I am unaccountably late for the good doctor. Tell her I'm on my way."

***

With LOS safe in a higher orbit, Gordon Winthrop had another problem. He must deal with a communication link failure between Endeavour and the Deep Space Network (DSN).

"I'm sorry, Mr. Winthrop, there's not much we can do. We have to wait until the DSN returns online," the communication officer said.

"Damn it, man! I want to know exactly how much longer we have to wait!"

"That depends on how intense the gamma rays and neutron emissions are, sir. Strong solar flares will often last from several hours to several days."

Peter knew exactly what would happen when his father was unhappy with a Winthrop staff member. He fired Senior Staff Officer Ray Spencer and blamed Spencer for his lack of initiative and too many preventable delays.

Gordon then turned to the next senior staff member present, Chief Engineer Dallas Fitch, "Congratulations, Mr. Fitch. You are also the senior staff officer" — Gordon was reading a computer screen displaying the delay time — "fix this mess, Dallas."

"Thank you for the opportunity, Mr. Winthrop, sir. I'll try my best," Dallas said, though he hardly sounded convincing, even to himself.

"That's all I can ask and want, Chief."

Peter approached Dallas with a stern, steely-eyed look and said, "I want the communication link between Endeavour and the Deep Space Network restored ASAP."

"I said I'll try my best, but I cannot do it alone, Captain."

"Then, get the best people around you," Peter said, getting annoyed. "Call out Ryan Chyloe, Robert Jandamarra, and Rachel Vaughn."

"Yes, Captain."

Peter approached his father, saying, "Mr. Fitch needs help and assistance. He cannot do everything on his own. Ryan Chyloe, Robert Jandamarra, and Rachel Vaughn are more than capable. Or do you have someone else in mind who could help?"

Gordon did not answer immediately; he seemed distant and worried. Unscheduled delays had increased, adding more days to Endeavour's planned course trajectory. If the delays continued, the Endeavour would arrive late for a rendezvous with the Faxian Telescope. Docking with the telescope would not be possible, failing phase one of the mission, which was to repair and refuel the Faxian Telescope, upgrade its computer systems, and install new primary and secondary mirrors. Arriving late for phase one could also affect phase two: the aerobraking maneuver, which was supposed to reduce Endeavour's speed for a safe and stable orbital insertion around Galraithia. Mistiming the spacecraft's aerobraking speed for orbital insertion would overheat and critically damage the spaceship. That meant endangering the lives of everyone onboard. The endgame scenario Gordon must avoid at all costs.

"I'm sorry, Peter. I wasn't listening," Gordon said.

"I said Mr. Fitch needs help and assistance. I think Ryan Chyloe, Robert Jandamarra, and Rachel Vaughn are more than capable. Or do you have someone else in mind who could help?"

"All three are exceptionally talented and loyal. You choose."

"Mr. Fitch!"

"Yes, Captain."

"Find Jandamarra and tell him to report to me on the bridge deck as soon as possible."

"Aye, sir."

"Mr. Fitch, also see to it that my men have everything they need," Gordon said, thinking he had spent little time with his personal bodyguard unit.

"Yes, Mr. Winthrop."

"Your men?" Peter said. "Father, have you forgotten the promise that you made? You clarified to Professor Briar that you would not bring your bodyguard unit or service people with weapons on the expedition."

"And Briar said he'd wait for Endeavour at the Outer Marker!" Gordon said, feeling his muscles tense but not realizing he was getting angry. "Our so-called friendship

271

was a pretentious fraud from the outset. William Briar cannot be trusted."

"Why can't he be trusted? Professor Briar is an honest, intelligent man who genuinely cares about the Freelander people. And every Freelander genuinely cares about him despite being persecuted and despised by the Allied world you helped create. Give the Freelanders more to hope for and less to fear, Father. We will need their help, and they will need our help to get Galraithia colonized."

"Are you telling me that you want Briar and his Freelander scum to succeed on Galraithia?"

"No, Father, I am pleading with you to forget the past. The conflicts between the Allied folk and the Freelanders cannot continue on Galraithia."

"Stepping backward is not the Winthrop way. You, of all people, should know that. And I will not be overshadowed by any man, let alone William Briar, a Freelander who cannot be trusted; Freelanders are untrustworthy people. Now, get the docking collars off and get Endeavour underway! I'm sick and tired of waiting here tethered to LOS while the Phoenix adds more miles and time between us."

"As you command, Father."

"Exactly as I command!" Gordon yelled. "The race to Galraithia has begun, and we are still on the starting block!"

***

Beyond the Kuiper Belt

Over the last 200 years, mining companies had restructured their core business activities and sustainable management systems as precious metals and raw materials dwindled to almost nothing on Earth. Millions of miners worldwide were involuntarily out of work, and millions of families could not afford the bare essentials. In contrast, Eris Asteroid Mining (EAM) bought convicted felons serving sentences longer than five years and hired tens of thousands of job seekers wanting mining work inside near-Earth metallic asteroids. Eris extracted raw materials essential for Earth's manufacturing industries: iron, nickel, and high rhodium concentrations. Metallic asteroids also contained rare metals: gold, platinum, and new chemical elements: Axion/nanotrine, the energy source powering the Phoenix spaceship.

***

Satori and Joseph reopened communication channels with Eris Mining. An unmanned Titan IV transport from Eris had delivered to the Phoenix containers full of electrical supplies, essential equipment that Robert Finnegan had donated to the expedition prior to leaving Earth. The unmanned Titan IV also scanned the Oort cloud for dangerous floating debris along the planned trajectory path to the Faxian Telescope. "Goodbye, Eris, and thank you."

"Goodbye, Satori. Goodbye, Joseph. We all wish you well," the Eris comms officer said.

Joseph sighed deeply and smiled, "Many thanks, Eris."

"There's no turning back now," Satori said.

Joseph and Satori left Comms and walked over to the NavStation chart table, joining Martin and Tom, monitoring Quadrant-7.

"All containers chained and secured?"

"Yes, Captain. All containers chained and secured," Satori replied.

Martin nodded. "Good job."

"Fabricators did all the work. You should be thanking them," Joseph said.

Martin just shook his head, but Tom seized the opportunity to embarrass Joseph.

"This vessel is interspersed with all manner of working contraptions. Do I thank them one by one for making my work life easier? I don't think so!"

Joseph murmured an inaudible reply under his breath; he called Tom a jackass.

***

On a radar viewing screen, NavStation officer Steven Jerrard focused on planet Neptune crossing in front of the Sun. The Endeavour spacecraft was accelerating and nearing Neptune, gaining more speed as it prepared to leave the Solar System. Meanwhile, Phoenix was traversing the cosmos slowly and for a good reason: the Oort Cloud, the natality of comets and other icy debris. "Endeavour has completed the slingshot maneuver around Neptune, Captain."

"Very well, Mr. Jerrard. Thank you for the update." Martin focused on a single green dot denoting Endeavour's coordinate on the digital Chart table. "Endeavour is the closest vessel...two solar days from our current position. Gordon Winthrop is trying hard to catch up with Phoenix."

"Gordon is a fool!" Joseph snapped. "If he doesn't reduce Endeavour's speed traversing the Oort Cloud, he endangers the ship and the lives of everyone onboard."

"Yeah, well, there's nothing anyone here can do about that, right?" Martin said, walking over to the nav station. "Mr. Jerrard!"

"Sir!"

"Enter Endeavour's transponder code into the AutoNav computer."

"Yes, Captain."

Martin sensed the young man's uneasiness. Stephen Jerrard had recently graduated from navigation school with little flying experience. "Distance to Endeavour from our current position, Mr. Jerrard."

"Distance to Endeavour from our current position … 20 thousand space miles, Captain."

"Maintain heading and distance until we rendezvous with Faxian."

"Aye, aye, Captain."

***

Satori Thomas struggled to fit in when she was a young schoolgirl. Making friends at university and attending social events was also never easy for her. After graduating from university, she joined the Navy and had little time for interpersonal relationships. They never worked well because her available energies were committed to the Freelander Navy and her ship, FS *Taimaha*, where she

275

turned negative character flaws into positive ones through her resilience and hard work.

Satori liked Joseph when she first met him onboard FS *Taimaha.* He was four years younger, boyishly handsome, and with the right blend of wit and charm. His maturity of judgment and selflessness, she considered his strongest suits. She went on liking Joseph and felt comfortable enough to spend much of her free time with him. During their lunch break, they often met in the Observation Bubble (OB) to discuss the mission and exchange ideas. From the OB, they often wandered down to Professor Briar's private library to read and enjoy old leather-bound books: *Shustak's Odyssey* and Rachel Sibley's *Sins of the Past* were the most enjoyable but also terrifying. Sometimes, Satori wanted to close those old books with terrifying stories and musty-smelling paper. She wished her free time with Joseph would turn into something more. But Joseph had never attempted to establish a relationship with a woman before he met Satori. He confided his deep love for her only to the pages of his diary.

***

After reading *Shustak's Odyssey* and *Sins of the Past*, Joseph and Satori finally understood how the Freelanders of Antarctica had managed to thrive in such a hostile environment. The secret lay in their large, genetically diverse population — an advantage that would serve them equally well during the brutal Galraithian winters. Their prosperity also stemmed from a sacred bonding ritual called Ròlegur, or "the Quiet Time," which occurred at the end of each harvest season in late December. During Ròlegur, the Council of Elders paired compatible couples for life-bonding, carefully selecting from diverse gene pools to strengthen future generations. This tradition had given the Freelanders remarkable resilience on an overpopulated

Earth, where many would gladly see them eliminated. After all, the Freelanders had made powerful enemies by converting city lands that once housed millions into agricultural terrain for livestock and crops, reclaiming a quarter of Earth's urban sprawl for farming.

Humanity had a future in Galraithia. It was a new world with endless opportunities and possibilities, a faraway dream for the Freelanders onboard the Phoenix. They looked forward to the first seeding season, harvest time in a new world. However, colonizing a new world without sustainable food supply chains could also be a struggle for any fledgling colony with a population projection of approximately 14,000 people and 40 births in the first year.

"I want a simple life without wars or the threatening shadows of war." — Rachel Sibley: Sins of the Past.

"Harmony with all living things is the intent of all freedom-loving people." — Jeremiah Shustak: Odyssey.

***

The stars Betelgeuse, Procyon, and Sirius formed a triangular portal known as the Liaoning Gateway—named after the SC Liaoning, the first Starchaser class vessel to pass through it 250 years ago. The Liaoning had been a marvel of engineering: the first Starchaser built in space, nearly two miles long and a quarter-mile wide at its broadest point. When she departed her high-orbit docking platform, she was celebrated as the fastest spaceship ever constructed, a triumph of cutting-edge rocket propulsion and ambitious aeronautical design. But the Liaoning's journey ended in tragedy. Shortly after entering the triangular gateway, the massive vessel vanished from deep-space radar tracking and was never seen again. In the aftermath, insurance companies refused to honor claims, citing fraudulent engineering cost overruns, unreasonable project deadlines, and critical design flaws they claimed went undetected during construction—disputes that would have resulted in bankrupting payouts.

After celebratory drinks, everyone on the bridge enjoyed a well-earned rest period. Martin woke up refreshed and slowly made his way to the Bridge deck elevator. Ahead was a broad staircase leading up to the Observation Bubble. Familiar voices floated down the stairs and broke the silence. Martin smiled; he was sure Joseph and Satori were embarrassed when he showed up.

"Hello, Captain."

Martin nodded politely, "I had a feeling you two would be up here."

"If you're looking for the bridge, it's that way," Joseph said, pointing to an exit door.

"I know where the bridge is!" Martin snapped.

"What's the matter, Martin. What are you upset about?"

"Joseph, a passenger came by the bridge earlier today?"

"Let me guess. Father Antonio?"

"You're damn right! Father Antonio."

"Father Antonio told me he wanted to discuss his idea with you before reporting to Cryo. I told him it was okay and that you wouldn't object."

Martin shook his head. "Keep your priestly friends away from the Bridge deck. I'm not asking for much, am I, Joseph?"

"Should have told you, I know, but it slipped my mind. I'm sorry, Martin."

"I had to call a security team to escort Father Antonio off the bridge after he entered the bridge unannounced, babbling about his idea. I politely told him to leave the bridge; Doctor Mason had ordered all passengers to their cabins until it was time to report to Cryo. That's when he began arguing, telling me his idea was too important for me to ignore. I still don't know what idea he was babbling about."

Joseph never talked much about feelings or anything like that. And he'd never been good at making small talk, but Martin expected a full explanation.

"Father Antonio has an idea that he believes is important," Joseph said.

"What idea? Make sense, Joseph."

"Strategically placed pulse radar beacons. The beacons act like lighthouses in space."

"Lighthouses in space. I've never heard of anything more ridiculous," Martin said bluntly.

"Don't be so judgmental. Father Antonio's idea has merit," Joseph countered. "The intensity of the Sun's magnetic field is increasing alarmingly. Solar flares often render vital telecommunication satellites and deep space radar stations inoperable, posing a major risk to all spacecraft entering Quadrant -7. The beacons will provide the navigation computer with the information to steer Phoenix safely through the Kuiper Belt and the Oort Cloud in Quadrant-7, avoiding asteroids, rocks, ice, and other planetary fragments directly in Phoenix's flight path."

"I'll be honest with you, Joseph. I'm not convinced," Martin said, rubbing his chin nervously.

"The idea is not a difficult concept to understand," Joseph said. "Krill harvesters back home use fixed and freestanding pulse radar beacons to warn other harvesters of approaching icebergs."

"Yeah, well, I'm still not convinced," Martin said, turning to Satori. "Commander, Thomas...your thoughts." Satori was under pressure but understood all the information the navigation charts contained. She had memorized every celestial object considered a threat to the Galraithian mission. "Since our long-range radio transmitters cannot communicate with Endeavour. Deploying an optical warning device would buy Captain Winthrop time to replan Endeavour's trajectory and steer his ship from approaching danger. Certainly, he could increase speed, maneuver past Phoenix to reach Galraithia first, provided that Endeavour is unlikely to encounter dangerous space hazards along its interplanetary trajectory and beyond."

"If we don't help each other, we risk losing everything; the first human settlement on Galraithia will remain a dream," Joseph said.

"Well, we cannot allow that to happen, can we, Joseph?"

"No, Martin, we cannot. The long-term survival of a colony on Galraithia, be it Freelander or Allied one, depends very heavily on human resource management and terraforming equipment onboard the Endeavour and the Phoenix."

"Have you anything more to add, Commander Thomas?"

"Phoenix is a Star Chaser class spaceship, one-quarter of Endeavour's size. There's enough food, water, and equipment onboard Phoenix to last three to five years, Captain."

"Okay, you sold me, Commander Thomas. Deploy Father Antonio's warning beacons. Comms will work closely with you and Joseph. I want to re-establish radio contact with the Endeavour."

"You won't regret your decision, Martin."

"I have never regretted anything that I did or did not do. So, I'm not starting now. Relative distance to Endeavour, please, Joseph."

"Endeavour is one day behind and increasing speed," Joseph said with a serious look.

"Increasing speed to maneuver past Phoenix, as Commander Thomas pointed out earlier?"

"Increasing speed is a standard operating procedure, sir. Endeavour's engines cannot sustain velocities below the minimum acceleration threshold without overheating."

"Commander Thomas has been studying Endeavour's overheating problem for some time, Martin."

"Initiative is a high premium, Commander Thomas. Well done."

"Thank you, Captain"

"Well, I'll see you both later," Joseph said, standing up from his chair. "I must show Father Antonio's schematic diagram to Fabricator-1107 before I suit up."

"Suit up? I hope you're not seriously considering deploying the beacon on your own," Martin said with concern.

"What do you mean?"

"I mean, you are too inexperienced, Joseph."

"Martin, I know what work needs to be done."

"Joseph, you haven't logged enough EVA time to work outside alone," Satori said.

"Commander Thomas is right. It's too risky. I'm not sending you out there without a robotic fabricator."

"I'm not a child!" Joseph countered. "I don't need a fabricator to hold my hand."

"Let the fabricator deploy the beacon, Joseph. The robot is expendable, you're not," Satori said.

Joseph shook his head in frustration. As he began to walk away, he said, "How can I ever gain more EVA time if no one gives me a chance?"

***

Fabricator-1107 deployed its warning beacon just in time. The signal reached Endeavour's navigation computer, which immediately altered course to avoid the C-type asteroid Neo-57.

Martin watched from the navigation table as their ship steered clear of both the asteroid and the treacherous Oort Cloud—that distant realm where gravitational forces constantly knocked asteroids loose, sending them careening toward the inner solar system like cosmic bullets.

As Endeavour pulled away from danger, Martin's thoughts turned to Gordon Winthrop's ambitious plan: one ship, one chance to reach the distant world of Galraithia. But Martin wasn't fooled by such romantic notions. Professor Briar had been blunt about it, calling Winthrop's single-ship strategy "stupid and irresponsible."

The professor was right. Without both the Endeavour and the Phoenix working together—along with all their crews and advanced equipment—their mission to colonize Galraithia would likely end in disaster.

***

Rendezvous with the Faxian

Phoenix sliced through the Heliopause. It was the invisible boundary where their solar system ended and the vast emptiness of interstellar space began. What had been mere computer simulations for months was now happening: both Phoenix and Endeavour flew in parallel formation, approaching the massive bulk of the Faxian 1-9D Interstellar Telescope.

On Phoenix's bridge, Martin supervised the delicate docking procedure while photographers captured this historic moment. The bridge hummed with tempered energy as his crew worked to achieve hard dock with the telescope.

Meanwhile, in his cramped cabin, Joseph sat alone with his diary, still fuming about Martin's refusal to let him spacewalk solo. He wrote with careful precision about what he witnessed:

Endeavour holds position ten miles off our starboard side as we close in on Faxian-1-9D. The telescope is a wreck— her starboard hull torn open, fabricator modules mangled, radar and communication arrays twisted into scrap metal.

Yet somehow, despite her wounds, Endeavour had limped through both the Kuiper Belt and Oort Cloud without breaking apart completely. At least our communication link is stable now.

The radio chatter between Martin and Gordon Winthrop tells its own story through brief, polite exchanges that barely mask the tension. Winthrop's responses are always curt, dismissive. It's obvious to both Martin and me that the

*man couldn't care less about the Freelander colonists
under our protection.*

***

"Chief Engineer," Martin said on his collar mic. "Are you there, Mr. Fredericks?"

"Yes, Captain."

"Reduce the reactor load to ten percent."

"Ten percent, aye, aye, Captain."

"Mr. Aitama, set docking thrusters."

"Docking thrusters are ready to fire, Captain."

***

Professor Lin accessed a hatchway leading to the bridge deck and another hatchway leading into the bridge. "Request permission to come on the bridge," she said.

"Permission granted."

"Thank you, Captain."

Professor Briar turned around as Professor Lin walked onto the bridge. "Ah, you're here finally. We are about to hard dock with Faxian."

"I cannot believe I am actually here."

"This day should be celebrated and never forgotten," Professor Briar said.

"Do you think Winthrop is celebrating?" Professor Lin asked.

"I doubt it," Martin said with a change of tone. "Gordon Winthrop has an unhealthy suspicion of Freelanders and has long derided our achievements."

"Whether he likes it or not doesn't make any difference because Freelanders arrived here first. A Freelander-built spacecraft has reached the farthest human-made object from Earth!"

There was a slight shudder as Professor Briar finished talking. "Contact! We have completed the docking maneuver," Martin said.

"We just witnessed history, gentlemen. The first successful rendezvous with the Faxian Interstellar Telescope is the most outstanding achievement since Rachel Sibley's Freelander integration campaign. If Rachel were here, she'd be immensely proud of her Freelander brothers and sisters," Professor Lin said.

***

For two solar days, the ancient telescope became a hive of activity. Engineering teams swarmed over Faxian's damaged hull while specialist fabricators worked around the clock. They installed cutting-edge Sequanta computers, enhanced the telescope's observation arrays, and fitted a brand new Far Star engine. Most importantly, they loaded enough axion-nanotrine fuel cells to power the telescope for the next 250 years.

Joseph barely surfaced from his work during those frantic days. He wrote in his diary:

I missed the docking spectacle, but I've been buried in technical work ever since. Haven't seen much of Satori or Martin—too busy programming the most advanced Sequanta computer ever built in space.

Then came the moment we'd all been waiting for. Faxian's new Far Star engines roared to life, flooding Phoenix's bridge with brilliant blue light. We had to shield our eyes as the massive telescope slowly pulled away from us, following the navigation instructions I'd carefully stored in her computer brain.

Professor Lin found me afterward, practically glowing with pride. When I asked about Faxian's chances, she didn't sugarcoat the challenges ahead. "Our communication equipment has its limits," she admitted, "but my team and I believe Faxian can reach the edge of known space. If we're right, humanity might finally get answers to the biggest questions of all: how our universe began, and what lies beyond the boundaries of everything we know?"

Later that day, there was much discussion about Faxian's ultimate goal on the Phoenix Bridge. "Professor Lin believes Faxian will provide humanity with answers to questions about the origin of our universe and what lies beyond," Joseph said.

"You really think so?" Tom said, leaving the NavStation. "Humanity on Earth is torn apart by conflicting social issues and political views. Another global war is inevitable. That is why I doubt anyone will be around to process Faxian's data in the future."

Martin was becoming increasingly impatient with Tom. There were lengthy isolation procedures to consider, and Tom was wasting valuable time. "Commander Granger, your undivided attention is needed in the Engine Room."

"Yes, sir!"

Professor Lin followed Tom out of the bridge. "Commander, I'll give you a hand with the isolation procedures."

Tom looked at Professor Lin from the corner of his eye. "I don't need your help. I can manage on my own."

Professor Lin wasn't surprised by Tom's attitude. She considered his personality style arrogant, brash, overly confident, and brutally cynical. "Granger, do you know what I like about you?"

Tom looked over at Professor Lin with a smugly expectant look on his face.

"Nothing!" Professor Lin said.

***

With Faxian now gone, Martin and Peter Winthrop turned their attention to the mission's most dangerous phase: orbital insertion around Galraithia. They ran simulation after simulation, knowing there was zero margin for error. The odds of both ships bouncing off Galraithia's thin atmosphere and careening into deep space were low, but not impossible.

The real worry wasn't the physics. It was the software. Even the most brilliant programmers working with cutting-edge computers made mistakes, and those mistakes had a way of surfacing at the worst possible moments. The ghost of the Liaoning haunted every calculation.

The Chinese vessel's final voyage remained shrouded in mystery, but science journals agreed on one chilling detail: her navigation system had malfunctioned during flight. While Captain Zhou and his entire crew lay helpless in hypersleep, the ship spun wildly out of control. Had anyone been awake to recalibrate the central computer, they might have saved themselves. Instead, the Liaoning's radio signals simply faded from deep space tracking systems. The ship and everyone aboard vanished without a trace.

This nightmare scenario kept both Martin and Joseph awake at night. Despite having specialized fabricators monitoring their life-support and engine systems around the

287

clock, the risk of system failure during hypersleep gnawed at them both.

Joseph had done the math, and the numbers were sobering. On short interstellar voyages under five years, three percent of passengers never woke up from hypersleep. For journeys over ten years, the death rate climbed to a terrifying 35 to 40 percent. Those weren't odds, they were a coin flip with eternity.

***

Tom looked nervous as he lay inside his cryo bed with a medical fabricator called Tin Man hovering over him. "Hey, Tin Man. You'd better care for my sleeping body, or I'll sell you for parts and scrap metal when I wake up."

"Mr. Granger, rest assured that I will do my best for you, sir."

"Do me another favor, Tin Man. Wait till I'm fast asleep before you insert plastic tubing up my nose."

"Mr. Granger, I cannot do what you ask," Tin Man said, holding a pair of sterile opaque lenses. "The patient is awake and responsive for most cryo-prepping procedures. Now, please, keep your eyes wide open, sir."

"No. You can wait," Tom said, hearing the noise of an elevator door open. Joseph exited the elevator and approached Tom and the fabricator Tin Man, preparing the cryo solution and inserting catheters and tubing into select areas of Tom's body.

"Too late for goodbyes, Joseph. Captain Brindle and Commander Thomas fell fast asleep ten minutes ago," Tom said, wincing as Tin Man inserted a narrow, flexible tube into his nostrils.

"Once you are completely asleep, I will insert the last tube, sir."

"Cut the chatter and get on with it," Tom said.

The final piece of tubing filled Tom with deep dread, making him question the highly discomforting procedure. "Tin Man, you are definitely being a pain in the ass."

"Almost done, sir."

Tin Man carefully placed a pair of opaque lenses over Tom's eyes, obscuring his vision. Joseph stood nearby, captivated by the scene unfolding before him.

"Good night, Joseph," Tin Man said, his voice filled with hope and optimism.

"Sleep well, Tom."

"See you in 36.9 years," Tom said as the lid of his cryo bed sealed shut.

***

A staggering 36.9 years in was considered an astonishingly long period for the human body to endure! It raised the question: can humans truly comprehend the toll of such an extended duration of hypersleep? The cocktail of cryogenic drugs, voluntary starvation, and the science behind cryo-sleep didn't bother Joseph. Rewarming and reviving human miners traveling to and from distant asteroids, planets, and moons had become standard cryogenic procedures. Additionally, the likelihood of permanent brain injuries and deaths was significantly lower on fast interstellar transports like the Phoenix and Endeavour. Both vessels were equipped with medical fabricators that could effectively manage life support and cryogenic systems. Nonetheless, Joseph's genuine concern was not dying during hypersleep but waking up and walking away from the cryo module sane.

"No matter what happens, I'll be here when you wake up," Joseph said, looking at Satori and Martin, who were secure in their cryo beds, soundly asleep.

The long sleep

The day Endeavour started its journey from the Lunar Orbital Station, she was the biggest and the most extravagant space-faring vessel ever built in space. The Endeavour's multi-deck Sleeper ship configuration, clever engineering, elegant interiors, and comfortable cryo beds supplied maximum passenger safety and satisfaction. The Endeavour surpassed other mega-ships in terms of engineering design. It had two detachable barrel-shaped modules mounted along the outer hull and attached to the lower port and starboard sides. Additionally, Gordon Winthrop set a cap on the number of passengers at 10,000, which corresponded to the maximum capacity of the onboard cryo beds.

Thousands of people on Earth watched the live broadcast beamed directly from LOS to home TV sets and outdoor display screens worldwide. They celebrated the vessel's departure and cheered the Allied colonists who had embarked on the farthest voyage in human history with contagious confidence and hope. In contrast, the Phoenix's departure raised eyebrows. The Star-chaser-class spacecraft left the Outer marker without Gordon's permission. Gordon argued that Freelanders relied heavily on Professor Briar and blindly followed his every command. So, Gordon laid the blame squarely at the Freelanders' door, insisting that the source of the explosion and the degree of damage that Endeavour sustained were from acts of sabotage.

***

Joseph left the Cryo module, a honeycombed chamber containing 4000 cryo beds. There was a sudden awareness that the number of cryo beds was also the maximum

passenger limit the Council of Freelander Elders and
Professor Briar had set for the Phoenix spacecraft. He
broke into a cold sweat, thinking Briar, the Council of
Elders, and the design engineers had made a mistake. With
only one Cryo module attached to Phoenix's hull, human
survival would be significantly affected should an
unexpected emergency arise during the journey to
Galraithia. Joseph believed Professor Briar and Gordon
Winthrop would play cards close to their chest in the
unlikely event of an emergency evacuation of passengers.
Both men were shrewd; they could mount a rescue mission
or prevent rescue drones from leaving their hangar bays,
overriding the onboard rescue systems. The latter would be
a valid excuse for not mounting a rescue mission; neither
ship could accommodate evacuees; there were not enough
onboard cryo beds. Could Joseph ever forgive Professor
Briar for not mounting a rescue mission? That was the
troubling question he wrote in his diary: *Is the Galraithian
expedition more important than people? Or will the journey
to Galraithia remain the principal reason for Gordon
Winthrop and Professor Briar repeatedly looking the other
way, ignoring requests for help and support, and
disregarding the peace agreement between the Allied and
Freelander people?*

***

The speed differential between Phoenix and Endeavour was
another concern in Joseph's diary: *Phoenix has fast and
efficient engines, which is the best assurance that it would
reach Galraithia first. The Endeavour has significantly
weaker rocket engines. Her five highly rated Davis-Molby
engines cannot supply the maximum rated thrust to
maintain 86% of light speed without overheating the
coolant in Endeavour's engine management system, not to
mention exceeding stress constraints design engineers have
imposed on her hull.*

292

In comparison, Phoenix's Far-Star rocket engines supply all the necessary power and rapid speed increase to exceed the light speed barrier by a factor of 10. Traveling at the speed of light was considered an overwhelming improbability before Professor Jonas Ryko developed and presented the three laws of Sequanta Mechanics to the world in 2375 AGU (after global unification).

By 2400, Sequanta computers were designing rocket engines and energy-efficient spacecraft that collected invisible nanotrine particles while traveling through the blackness between stars and planets. Onboard nanotrine reactors process the nanotrine particles and produce tremendous amounts of nanotrine energy with mind-blowing thrust and the rapid speed increase that propelled the first interstellar spaceships beyond the speed of light barrier: 186,000 miles per second.

Gordon Winthrop was aware of Phoenix's speed potential and didn't like it. Word got out that he had impelled his engineers and sequanta coders to set the optimal velocity for the journey to Galraithia at 80% of light speed for both vessels, even though Phoenix could travel much faster than Endeavour.

Mission planners aboard the Endeavour warned Winthrop that slowing down to 80% of light speed would add ten more years to the journey. Gordon responded quickly and firmly.

"If you think I will take a secondary role to Professor Briar or any other Freelander, you are mistaken. Contact Briar and inform him that we will land both ships simultaneously on Galraithia, or this mission will end now!"

Endeavour's mission planners tried to establish radio contact with Phoenix but failed. With the exception of two senior officers, all crew members aboard the Phoenix had undergone cryopreservation. Joseph Arunui and the acting chief engineer Lesley Fredericks were busy preparing the ship for the scheduled handover of the navigation, life support, and engine management systems to sequanta computers and highly skilled fabricators.

***

As Phoenix approached light speed, her electromagnetic shielding kicked in, blocking all radio frequencies and radiation hazards. But something remarkable began to happen. Negatively charged nanotrine particles started clinging to Phoenix's neutral hull, creating a swirling effect that gradually shifted the entire outer surface to a positive charge.

This transformation triggered Phoenix's most extraordinary feature. Her engineering systems engaged, stretching the hull from 1,250 feet to a massive 1,800 feet in length. The extension sent violent shudders through the spacecraft, rattling every bolt and rivet. But as Phoenix gained speed and more nanotrine particles locked onto her hull, the ride smoothed out completely.

Endeavour wasn't so fortunate. Her older Davis-Molby engines made her vibrate violently at high velocities, especially near light speed.

Phoenix belonged to the elite Starchaser class—ships that could adjust their dimensions along all three axes, stretching into pencil-thin profiles when necessary. This flexibility was crucial for any vessel designed to reach or exceed light speed. Both Starchasers and massive sleeper ships like Endeavour shared one critical technology: computer systems that could flip a hull's charge from neutral to positive, creating a magnetic field that drew in nanotrine particles.

Giant compressors housed in room-sized engines sucked these particles through intake ducts at both ends of the ship.

294

The onboard nanotrine reactors then processed them into nanotrine plasma—the primary power source for modern space travel and the most vital energy in the universe after the sun itself.

Astrophysicists had once dismissed nanotrine particle waves as optical illusions. Then Joseph Arunui developed his Dark Matter theory, proving these particles were real and everywhere. Even so, navigating the narrow funnels of swirling nanotrine streams that raced across space at mind-bending speeds remained beyond human understanding.

The universe guarded its secrets jealously, even from humanity's brightest minds. Until the next breakthrough in astrophysics arrived, modern starships had to rely on the advanced computing power of Sequanta computers to thread these cosmic needles safely.

****

The Sol-gel (radiation-absorbing bacteria) between Phoenix's inner and outer hull liquefied to absorb any cosmic rays leeching through the double hull. Heating coils inside atomizers and radiation separators filtered the cloudy orange liquid to remove undesirable by-products. The filtered liquid was clear, colorless, and stored under pressure in tungsten/titanium cylinders. A secondary network of interconnected pipes carried the pressurized fluid to the Lorentzian manifolds, feeding the main nanotrine reactor and Phoenix's hydraulic power supply.

Lesley Fredericks turned his chair and his attention to Joseph. "Hull extension is 90% and holding, sir."

"The vibrations coursing through the ship are a minor annoyance at this maximum hull extension. Can you take a moment to check the dosimeter?"

"Dosimeter is at zero, sir. No ionizing radiation detected inside the inner hull."

"Then we're done here, Chief. Report to Cryo."

"Aye, sir."

***

Fredericks reported to the Cryo module. A medical fabricator prepped him for hypersleep. Then, a hibernation capsule with the cryo bed retracted from a honeycombed cell. The hibernation capsule opened, and Fredericks slipped into a sterile cryo bed. Fredericks looked at the medical fabricator. The robot was small with a lightweight upper and lower torso, strong limbs, and subsystems made of titanium alloys, not too dissimilar in shape and engineering complexity to the robotic fabricators working in the engineering module of Phoenix. However, the medical fabricator had fourth-tier medical programming and dexterous limb movements.

"I hope you're more intelligent than the fabricators in engineering," Fredericks said.

"I completed my medical studies 12 years ago, sir."

"I trust you, robot," Fredericks said as the medical fabricator injected a solution into Frederick's blood through a catheter in his left wrist and placed a pair of double-lensed goggles over Frederick's eyes. "This is home for the next 36.9 years. Dream only happy dreams." With that Fredericks surrendered to the sleeping solution, the first line of defense against the effects of cryopreservation. Under the watchful eye of the medical fabricator, supercooled orange fluid entered the hibernation capsule and the cryo bed. After several seconds, the fluid filled the capsule and covered Fredericks, who was sound asleep and unaware of his surroundings.

***

While the human population aboard Endeavour slept, fabricators moved freely around all areas of the ship, particularly inside the engine room and the nanotrine reactor. These areas had extremely high levels of noise. On the Bridge deck, chirping Sequanta computers sent data to all critical operational areas of the vessel. Inside the Greenhouse, humidity sensors flashed and running water rich in nutrients preserved precious moisture locked in the leaves and roots of plants. Inside Endeavour's 12 cargo holds, hundreds of containers stored food, machinery, and all the necessary equipment and infrastructure to colonize a new world.

***

Aboard the Phoenix, Joseph had decided to stay awake; he wasn't ready for hypersleep. Inherent problems with the regenerative engine cooling systems had kept a small army of fabricators busy in Phoenix's engine room. Joseph trusted them implicitly with the maintenance of the nanotrine reactors. They understood the intricacies of reactor control systems and were well-organized in analyzing and resolving problems. Joseph didn't have much work to do in the engine room, so he sat in his comfortable chair, playing around with display screens and cameras on different decks. Switching camera angles inside the Greenhouse, he followed three fabricators tending a thriving vegetable garden. Another group of fabricators controlled the air pressure inside sealed, air-tight containers brimming with clean seeds, rice, honey, cotton bales, and wool. The Endeavour, bigger than conventional interstellar spaceships, carried more fabricators and a wider variety of construction machinery and equipment needed for a successful human settlement on Galraithia.

After leaving the engine room, Joseph hit the gym and trained with heavy, manageable weights. Then, he went to the Cryo module; he visited Martin and Satori daily. He spoke to them, believing they could hear his voice. Joseph checked Martin's cryogenic health settings before peering inside Satori's hibernation capsule. Her cryogenic health settings were also in the normal range. Joseph sat in a chair beside the hibernation capsule and spoke to Satori until it was time to leave. "I have to go. I'm doing my first solo EVA today. Don't worry. It's just a training exercise in the simulator. Tell you more next visit. Pleasant dreams, Satori."

***

The next four months flew by in a blur of activity for Joseph. Every day brought fresh data from the Faxian telescope—stunning long-exposure images of Galraithia that revealed the planet's major surface features in breathtaking detail.

Joseph threw himself into his most critical project yet: designing eight spherical reconnaissance drones. Working alongside fabricators and banks of Sequanta computers, he crafted each drone from titanium and tungsten, then loaded them with the finest AI technology and high-resolution cameras available.

His programming was meticulous. The drones would orbit Galraithia three times, mapping the planet from a safe distance, before swooping in for detailed flybys over both the Northern and Southern continents. Their cameras and sensors would survey everything—the vast Tezarian Ocean, the turbulent Ithinian Sea, and every crucial geographic feature that could affect their landing.

With so much riding on these machines, Joseph became obsessive about testing. He ran simulation after simulation, checking and double-checking for any possible defects. He personally monitored every computer model of Phoenix's approach and landing sequence on the Southern Continent.

The weight of responsibility never left him. The fate of Phoenix, the lives of everyone aboard, and the centuries-old dream of bringing the Freelander people to their new home—it all depended on getting this landing right.

***

Joseph stepped away from the navigation console and the landing trainer, nerves pulled taut. One slip during the descent could mean disaster. Learning Sequanta hadn't helped his stress levels either. It wasn't just a language, it was a code system built on fourth-tier encryption, with layers of syntax that had to be decrypted and translated into Sequanta, English, and Chinese. Most programming languages stuck to English or Chinese. Sequanta was different: a universal tongue, like math or music, drawn from over 7,000 spoken languages. Still, Joseph stuck with it. Every day, he pushed through lines of code until he could work fluently with any Sequanta system, especially the adaptable Fabricator Five/O units aboard the Phoenix and Endeavour. He remembered writing once in his diary how the fabricators on Phoenix had sounded irritated when he didn't understand them. At the time, he hadn't known machines could sound that way.

***

Joseph missed Satori and missed spending time in the Observation bubble where he could relax, read, or just stare into space and think of Satori, Martin, Professor Briar, and Father Sandor. He missed their company: missed Father Sandor's dry humor, Professor Briar's unwavering trust, Martin's cryptic logic, Satori's intelligence and wit; her elegance and charm. Joseph sighed and thought, until they woke from cryosleep, he would make new friends: robotic fabricators and computers that could respond to human emotions.

"Computer, set hyperspectral imager at 180 degrees. Time delay, long-duration shutter speed. Adjust for angle shift," Joseph said.

A blurry image appeared on the spectral imager screen: a blue dot surrounded by blackness. Then, a soft female computer voice responded, "Angle shift complete, sir."

"Sharpen luminance or change filters? Your call, computer."

"Changing filters, sir."

"Enlarge pixels and enhance the image."

"Yes, sir."

"The blue dot on the spectral imager screen was once our home. Now, it is simply the third planet from the sun—a unique, watery world within the Solar System, teeming with life and rich in diverse ecosystems. Unfortunately, its richness has often been taken for granted and harmed by careless individuals. The day will come when the Earth is no longer visible in the vast darkness of space."

"I don't understand your statement, sir. Would you repeat it, please?"

"Never mind!" Joseph said, "Switch to camera 6, wide-field view."

"Wide-field view on the screen, sir."

Camera-6 zoomed in until planet Earth filled the screen.

"Capture image… save the image."

"Image captured and saved, sir."

***

300

Joseph left the Observation bubble, walked to the midship hatch, and entered the Habitat ring, a spinning collar or rotating wheel attached to the middle section of Phoenix's double hull shell. The Habitat ring and the midship area, where the living area was located, consisted of large luxurious cabins for families, and small austere cabins for singles.

Having washed his face and hands, Joseph slipped into bed, fully clothed.

Diary-writing was a ritual before bedtime. *"Looking through my cabin window, the last binary asteroid is far behind us. Gamma Centauri is the brightest star, but there's a long way to go before the light rays of a different star shine through my small window. I can honestly say that I have confidence and a deep sense of pride in the fabricators operating and maintaining Phoenix's onboard management systems. With their help, I have redesigned the Lorentzian manifolds and the collector combs attached to the bow and stern of the spaceship. Both combs are now coupled to solar generators that run parallel to generators powering the Lorentzian manifolds feeding the main nanotrine reactor. The redesigned Lorentzian manifold injection system is now more efficient; compressing more nanotrine particles creates an immensely powerful propulsor, the required energy to propel Phoenix towards the distant star, Dimos, the gateway to Galraithia."*

***

Joseph had curled up in bed, awaiting blissful sleep, when the navigation control computer (NCC) activated the emergency alarm. As the audible alarm sounded throughout the spaceship, warnings flashed red on the NCC display screen; Phoenix and Endeavour had inadvertently entered the outer boundary of a collapsed star. Joseph jumped out of bed and hurried to the bridge, entering from the upper deck. He found the bridge abuzz with noisy sequanta computers, and audible warnings flashed brightly on every screen. The NCC quickly scanned Joseph's face as he approached the central control desk. Then Sequanta algorithms matched Joseph's intense facial expression to the values and attributes of a young man troubled and concerned. "The Arubra radar unit has detected gravitational radiation, sir."

"Description and size?" Joseph said calmly.

"The funnel-shaped anomaly is gravitational singularity attributable to a collapsed star, sir."

"A Gravity-well?"

"Yes, sir. XYZ measurements are unknown at this time."

Then, a fabricator added, "The entry point of the gravitational singularity leads to the inner boundary of a collapsed star through a spiraling left-to-right vortex attributable to faster-than-light Arubra electrons colliding with denser nanotrine matter particles."

"If there's an entry point for particles," Joseph said, thinking aloud, "there must be an exit point."

"Shall I initiate the level one emergency contingency plan, sir?" the Fabricator said.

"Yes. The safety of the ship and the lives of everyone aboard is the primary objective."

The fabricator initiated a level one emergency contingency plan, locking down the ship and preparing for an emergency.

"Endeavour's course and speed?" Joseph asked.

"Endeavour is maintaining course at full speed. However, the rate of acceleration is increasing," the NCC said.

"If the rate of acceleration is increasing," Joseph said. "Endeavour's navigation computer may attempt to slingshot the spaceship away from the Gravity-well."

"Negative! Endeavour is following a preset flight path, sir."

"Mission planners preset the flight path for both ships. Beyond Faxian, orbital insertion around Galraithia."

"Correct. The center of the gravitational singularity is on the same flight path. Steering Phoenix away is the only option open to you, sir."

"Portside camera view on!"

"Portside camera view on, sir."

Joseph moved closer to the navigation and helm control station display screen. From the portside camera view angle, Endeavour seemed motionless. Joseph was unsure whether Endeavour was advancing toward the Gravity-well or attempting to turn away from danger.

He said, "Endeavour's tracking antenna, is it maintaining a lock on Phoenix?"

"Endeavour's scanners report an active antenna lock to Phoenix, sir. However, there is a security protocol preventing any course correction."

"A security protocol preventing a course correction?"

"Correct. The Endeavour spacecraft is still on its preselected course, the center of the gravitational singularity," the NCC said.

Joseph adjusted the portside camera angle and zoomed in on Endeavour's rotating tracking antenna, sending data to Phoenix's computer systems. With the Davis-Molby engines overpowered by gravitational shear,

Endeavour was no longer maneuvering but being consumed by the singularity's center.

Joseph narrowed his eyes and inquired, "Can we override the security protocol from here?"

"Negative! Endeavour's navigation system is locked out to us. Do you wish to access another computer function, sir?"

"The security protocol is endangering the Endeavour and everyone aboard. There has to be a way to override the security."

"While Close Out mode is active Endeavour's navigation system is locked to prevent access by unauthorized personnel. Only Endeavour's captain and personnel holding Access One security clearance codes can remove any or all security restrictions imposed on the navigation computer.

Do you wish to access another computer function, sir?"

"No. There's no time to help the Endeavour. The distance between Phoenix and the Gravity-well is still too close for comfort."

"Sir!" the navigation computer said. "Long-range scanners also report pressure waves stressing Endeavour's hull."

"Distance from Endeavour."

"New relative distance to Endeavour…100 miles…200 miles. 400 hundred space miles and increasing, sir."

"Record the time in the log. Bow camera view on!"

"Yes, sir."

"Endeavour is oscillating badly," Joseph declared. Then, another image appeared on a viewing monitor nearby, Endeavour's bow and stern Collector combs set in the wrong position, raised, and locked, set that way for maximum speed, stressing the outer hull.

"Hello, Endeavour! Hello, can anyone hear me? Please respond," Joseph shouted into the radio handset. "Can anyone hear me? My name is Joseph Arunui, and I am aboard the Phoenix. Lower Collector combs. This is Joseph Arunui aboard the Phoenix. Lower your Collector combs!" Frustrated at having to wait for a reply, Joseph climbed into the navigation chair and shook the computer screen. Endeavour's Collector combs were still up and locked.

"The next pressure wave could break Endeavour apart. Lower all Collector combs. Please respond!" Joseph looked at a loudspeaker on a bulkhead and hoped someone on board Endeavour would respond quickly, but he heard only static. The fabricators aboard the Endeavour and the central control computer could not communicate with Phoenix. The gravitational singularity jammed all radio frequencies. Making matters worse, the necessary commands to disengage or override the security restrictions imposed on navigation control systems were unavailable in the mission database. Gordon Winthrop had locked the course coordinates to Galraithia when he activated Closeout Mode. This computer function denied all authorized access to Endeavour's onboard navigation control computer and, more importantly, prevented unauthorized access to Endeavour's mission abort codes.

Endeavour's Davis-Molby engines heated up and exceeded the permissible temperature limit. The Engine room's monitoring computer had shut down the main nanotrine reactor when it began overheating to explosive temperatures. The shutting down of the engine room computer was a programmed interlock that protected the main nanotrine reactor. However, by doing so, the Endeavour's fate was sealed. Lacking sufficient thrust to escape the gravitational forces, the Endeavour rushed inexorably closer to the center of the singularity.

Desperate to help but forced into inaction, Joseph observed from a safe distance and recorded the fate of the most technologically advanced interstellar spaceship as it spiraled down into a spherical spiraling vortex created by longitudinal gravitational waves. Joseph had to look away, or he'd vomit.

"Get us out of here! Initiate course correction. Steer Phoenix away from the Gravity-well."

"Initiating course correction, sir. Steering Phoenix away from the gravitational singularity."

Then, with a sudden jolt, Phoenix tilted violently to its portside as the navigation control computer struggled against the gravitational forces rushing Phoenix toward Endeavour and the center of the spiraling Gravity-well. Phoenix's outer hull twisted violently, like a corkscrew. Spiraling down a bottomless void. Warnings sounded throughout the vessel, directing fabricators to close all hatchways leading to the living quarters on the Habitat ring and the Cryo module. Maintenance fabricators switched to Survival Mode and prepared for the worst-case scenario, outer hull breaches and catastrophic blowouts. Unendurable outcomes that would destroy the Phoenix and all human life on board. Joseph turned to the Navigation computer and said, "Regardless of the emergency flight protocols, control this ship! Disregard the alarms telling you to raise the collector combs. Keep the collector combs lowered and locked until I say otherwise. Is that understood?"

"Yes, sir."

"We must avoid picking up too much speed."

"I understand, sir."

"Good! Now, on my count, vent all gas capsules forward of midships and empty the auxiliary cryo tanks."

"Yes, sir."

"Three, two, one. Vent!" Joseph commanded. All five gas capsules vented simultaneously, ejecting pressurized nanotrine and axion gas into the blackness of outer space. The two gases mixed with hydrogen gas, the most abundant element in the universe, supplied the power propelling Phoenix. A bright blue/green flame shot out the front thruster assembly, slowing Phoenix's forward momentum. The hull stress monitoring system (IISMS) activated anti-vibration mounts inside Phoenix's hull, absorbing those hull oscillations that impacted design values and limits. Nonetheless, the seriousness of the situation seemed uncertain. "Damage report!" Joseph shouted.

"Fabricators on all decks report no serious hull damage, sir."

"What is Endeavour's distance from our current position?"

"30,000 astronomical units, sir. 2.8 billion space miles," the Navigation computer replied.

"Recalculate Endveaour's rate of speed and distance."

"Endveaour's rate of speed and distance is increasing, sir."

Joseph focused on the long-range infra-red scanner. The Navigation computer had calculated correctly. Endeavour and Phoenix were constantly diverging, rapidly increasing the distance between them. "We're losing both ships!" Joseph shouted.

***

As Phoenix descended into the Gravity-well, pressure waves battered its scale-covered outer hull. The gyroscopes within Phoenix's sturdier inner hull quickly countered the violent twisting and lateral rolling. Joseph wondered how much structural stress the outer hull could endure before a fracture opened it up. He wasn't certain, but he could feel short yet noticeable vibrations on the bridge deck floor and hear unwanted noise emanating from the bulkhead walls and ceiling panels.

Suddenly, zero gravity triggered a continuous blaring alarm. Joseph was weightless, floating up to the ceiling. Phoenix was also weightless, freefalling down the Gravity-well. To Joseph's surprise, the navigation computer reported weakening gravitational forces inside the Gravity-well. Systemic in-flight countermeasures prioritized the main mission parameter: *Save the Phoenix*. Countless hours of computer programming and simulator training enabled the navigation computer to stop Phoenix's free fall and restore artificial gravity throughout the vessel. Joseph's eyes widened as he fell to the floor with a thud. His left shoulder took the brunt of the fall, which made Joseph wince. Joseph rubbed his aching shoulder and hurried to the navigation control console, grateful that the navigation control computer had followed its programming and pushed Phoenix's main nanotrine reactor and engines beyond their design limits to break free of the gravitational forces.

Joseph opened a star chart and circled Phoenix and Endeavour's last known coordinates. He opened another chart and circled Phoenix's new position.

Some star patterns appeared familiar; Joseph could identify those he had studied and come to know. However, Phoenix's long-range spectral scanners called the oscillating waves of light coming from those identifiable constellations' redshifts because the light from those stars is moving away from Phoenix.

Joseph measured the difference between Endeavour's last known coordinates and Phoenix's new position. Then, he recalibrated the long-range spectral scanners and confirmed Phoenix's revised coordinates. Gravitational waves inside the Gravity-well had somehow accelerated Phoenix at twice the speed of light to another quadrant of the Milky Way galaxy, almost 10 light years from Endeavour's last known position.

***

Fabricators replaced burned-out cameras, computers, and display screens with functional consoles. Joseph was grateful that Professor Briar had spent much Freelander money on the best fabricator technology that money could buy. Fabricators repaired the outside hot water storage tanks quickly and efficiently. Then, they refilled and secured the spare nanotrine gas cylinders stored inside the cargo bay.

"All repairs are complete, sir. Navigation settings have been reset, and all cameras are operational," a fabricator reported over the radio.

"Thank you, fabricators. To everyone, I appreciate your hard work," Joseph said. Turning to the navigation control computer, he added in Freilish, *"Tak orgo, Fabrimenses. Uto tak sequanta orgo!* We owe a debt of gratitude to every sequanta computer for saving Phoenix and the lives of everyone on board." There was an awkward silence; fabricators and sequanta computers could not comprehend the concepts of oneness and gratitude.

"Long-range scan of this quadrant, please. Infrared view," Joseph commanded.

"Yes, sir."

The amount of gravitational radiation in this quadrant of the Milky Way galaxy astounded Joseph. In his diary, he wrote that the Gravity-well can be likened to jet stream winds moving across Earth's hemispheres in wave-like patterns. He also noted that he was saddened by the fact that long-range thermal scanners could not find the Endeavour without her Davis-Molby engines emitting infrared radiation. "Where did the Endeavour go? Did it break apart inside the Gravity-well?"

Joseph observed that Phoenix's long-range scanners revealed no debris field or evacuation pods in this quadrant, only stars and clouds of interstellar dust and gas.

"Relative distance to Endeavour?" Joseph asked, tensing up like a patient about to receive disturbing news from his treating physician.

"Relative distance is unknown at this time, sir."

"She's out there somewhere," Joseph said, resting his hands on the table covered with old star charts. "The gravitational forces within the Gravity-well should have torn the Phoenix apart. But the Phoenix continued its journey without human input, traveling over 10 light-years from our last known location."

The main sequanta computer opened the chart table, displaying the deck plans of the Endeavour along with intermittent engineering faults and design flaws. Joseph was understandably curious, as the learning mechanisms within artificial intelligence did not intentionally favor one spacecraft part over another. Joseph observed that certain assets on board the Phoenix, specifically the fabricator and sequanta intelligent computers, were rapid learners compared to those on the Endeavour. Joseph needed additional time to conduct thorough research and rest until the Phoenix spacecraft reached Galraithia's deceleration threshold and achieved orbital insertion. Joseph resolved to rouse Martin and Chief Fredricks, believing that their combined efforts would be vital in locating the Endeavour. The time for collaboration had come, and he was determined to rally his companions for the challenging journey ahead.

***

Joseph entered the Cryo module and approached the nearest row of hibernation pods. As he glanced at his friends, who were sound asleep, he felt a sense of unease. His mind was filled with intrusive thoughts about cold cryogenic fluid flowing through the human body and the inherent dangers: rupturing blood vessels, brain damage, organ failure, irreversible blindness, and the inevitable, death.

"I'm closing all open valves to pods 1 and 9. Stand by!" Joseph instructed the medical fabricator.

"Cryo systems are normal. Awaiting your command, sir."

"On my mark, initiate liquefying procedure…three, two, one, mark!"

Cryostatic jelly glowed orange when confined to its coldest threshold, minus 500 degrees. However, cryogenic beds were not deep freezers. On the contrary, a cryogenic bed was an enclosed healthy ecosystem regulating and balancing the human body's workings. Purified seawater combined with cytostatic gelatins that rid the body of dead skin and body hair. Human blood was infused with Malusol, a derivative of antifreeze proteins discovered in micro-organisms living deep beneath dwarf planet Ceres and found in the north and south polar regions. Malusol was essential in preventing ice crystals from forming in protein molecules in red blood cells. Malusol also expanded veins and arteries and stimulated the heart and other muscles and tendons. It was a potent antibiotic infused with chemical compounds that killed and inhibited harmful bacteria coursing through the body.

***

A shorter than unexpected deep sleep period drained the liquefied Cryo-gel away from Martin's and Chief Fredericks's hibernation pod. Then, a rectangular medical panel dropped from the ceiling and stopped just above the two hibernation pods. An electrical motor whirred and opened both hibernation pods. A pair of tiny robotic hands quickly lowered from the medical panel like two metallic spiders riding on a dragline made of spider silk. While one robotic hand removed several lines of flexible glass tubing from the body, the other pulled spoon-like eye lenses edged with tiny holes from which streams of medicated air stimulated the lacrimal system to flush away harmful bacterial infections.

The waking procedure continued, and a thin tube inserted in Martin's throat was removed too quickly. This triggered a strong gag reflex and heightened pain; his joints ached as he stood up. Martin felt extremely cold, causing his naked body to shiver, and he also felt hungry and thirsty. "Bring a warm robe to Captain Brindle and wake Chief Fredericks from his deep sleep," Joseph instructed the medical fabricator known as Tinman.

"Yes, sir."

"How do you feel, Martin?" Joseph asked

"Dizzy and nauseous. Next stupid question," Martin said, squinting as he adjusted to the bright ceiling lights.

"Here, drink this," Joseph said, handing Martin a cup of green tea. "It will warm you up."

312

Chief Fredericks woke up feeling dizzy and nauseous. Still, he made a point of doing everything himself and pushed Tinman away with a dismissive hand.

"Do not stand up too quickly, sir." Tinman said.

"Stay away from me! I don't need your help, Tinman."

"Take your time, Chief." Joseph said.

"Are you feeling okay, Fredericks? Are your feet feeling numb or experiencing any unusual sensations?"

"I'm doing just fine, Captain. My feet might be cold, but they're not numb!"

"Here you go, Chief," Joseph said. "Careful, the cup is hot."

"What's in it?"

"Green tea."

Chief Fredericks took a slow sip of his tea, enjoying the flavor and the warmth. He paused when he noticed the electric clock above Martin's open hibernation pod, which indicated that 129 days had passed since Martin's hypersleep procedure began.

"That's odd!" Chief Fredericks exclaimed, pointing to the time counter.

Martin glanced at the time counter. "129 days? That can't be right! Could it be a faulty processor?"

"Yes, I'd say so," Chief Fredericks remarked, his tone firm and assured.

"There is nothing wrong with the counting processor," Joseph countered.

Joseph vividly recounted to Martin the dramatic events that had unfolded while he slept, painting a picture of the Gravity-well, the severe damage the Phoenix had endured, and the fate that ultimately befell the Endeavour. He described the Gravity-well as an immense cosmic phenomenon, akin to a powerful jet stream or a winding river, swirling and carrying sediment and small stones before discharging them into the sea. This powerful force had pushed the Phoenix deeper into the vast expanse of interstellar space, a realm filled with unknown dangers.

"Are you saying that the Gravity-well accelerated Phoenix to another quadrant of the Milky Way galaxy at twice the speed of light?" Martin exclaimed.

"Yes, Martin, I am saying exactly that. We were extremely fortunate; I'm surprised we are having this conversation because Phoenix should have broken apart and shattered into a million pieces. We should all be dead," Joseph said.

"The Endeavour was a marvel of engineering, a beautifully crafted interstellar spaceship designed to explore the cosmos. I find it hard to believe that it could have broken apart under any circumstances," Martin declared, his voice brimming with conviction.

"I don't believe the Endeavour broke apart, but there's no sign of it anywhere. Our long-range scanners are searching at their maximum capabilities."

"Our long-range scanners should have detected Endeavour's infrared signature by now," Martin said, concerned. "Do you think the scanners might be damaged, Chief?"

"Captain, our long-range and short-range scanners operate perfectly," Chief Fredericks reported. "The Endeavour may have suffered critical structural damage within the Gravity-well. Her Davis-Molby engines could not produce the thrust to escape the gravitational vortex. She would likely have broken apart."

"I disagree!" Joseph countered. "Endeavour's navigation computer would have taken the correct measures to save the ship. Sequanta computers are smarter than you think, Chief."

"Then, ask them to find Endeavour," Chief Fredericks said cynically.

Joseph answered with frustration in his voice, "Our sequanta computers do not know where Endeavour is! Both ships branched out in two directions, but she did not break apart. Our long-range scanners report no debris field anywhere in this quadrant."

There was a brief silence. "Captain, if Endeavour is still in one piece as Joseph says..."

Martin cut him off. "I'm sure someone will find Endeavour if they search in the right place, Chief."

"Yes, Captain."

"Maybe we don't need to find Endeavour," Joseph said, speaking his thoughts aloud.

"How do you mean?" Martin asked.

Joseph raised his eyebrows and smiled. "Endeavour will find us with Faxian's help. We know Faxian's detector array and imaging system can see stars at the edge of the universe. So, we recalibrate the infrared sensors and point them directly at Quadrant-10. The infrared sensors should detect Endeavour's thermal heat signature."

"Joseph, I have never doubted your mathematical prowess, but how can you be so sure Endeavour is heading to Quadrant-10?" Martin asked.

"The gravitational waves that pummeled Phoenix traveled in a straight line. Therefore, while we traveled along one straight line with our collector combs lowered for maximum speed, Endeavour may have followed another straight line."

"Joseph, I'm sorry to interrupt, but Endeavour's collector combs were raised and locked, correct?" Chief Fredericks said.

"Yes, raised and locked."

"The bow collector combs functioned like a shield. Deflecting the gravitational forces on the hull and reducing Endeavour's speed also reduced hull stress and saved the ship," Chief Fredericks said.

"I disagree, Chief. The Endeavour has weak pivot joints, a design flaw," Joseph said.

"Do you two ever agree on something?" Martin said, frowning.

"Martin! The main sequanta computer pointed out Endeavour's engineering design flaws. The bow and stern collector comb pivot joints were a concern before the Endeavour left the Lunar orbital station. If you don't believe me, open the chart table, and see for yourself."

"Let's put aside that fact," Martin said. "We need to focus on a damaged Endeavour. Structurally, Endeavour is weaker than Phoenix and has weaker engines. She would have sustained some damage from gravitational forces inside the Gravity-well and traveling slowly, hypothetically speaking, of course."

Joseph rubbed his neck and smiled, trying to hide his anxiety.

"So, Joseph. Do you honestly believe Faxian can locate the Endeavour's exact position?"

"Given time, yes."

"Faxian can see through clouds of gas and dust blocking our long-range viewing scanners?" Martin said.

"Faxian has the technology to find Endeavour's infrared signature and more," Joseph said. "My best guess puts the Endeavour 15 light-years behind us."

"Your best guess?" Martin retorted. "Joseph is raising his eyebrows at me, Chief."

"Martin, mathematics is not a perfect science in interstellar space. However, I am confident that Endeavour's auto-nav computer calculations will pinpoint our homing beacon and use its relative position to determine our interstellar trajectory to Galraithia."

"And if Endeavour's Auto-nav computer doesn't find our homing beacon, then what?" Martin asked.

"Then Freelanders will be the first people from Earth to set foot on Galraithian soil," Joseph declared.

"That moment will define who we are," Chief Fredericks said.

"Dreams cost nothing, Chief. Come on, Joseph, you're late for your sleep rotation," Martin said, knowing that Joseph had worked feverishly over the past four months without human interaction. Still, he wasn't ready to spend several years in hypersleep.

"Go and prep for hypersleep. The Chief and I have a few details to sort through before we head back to the freezer."

"Martin, wake me when Phoenix approaches Galraithia."

"Okay."

"Joseph, I'm glad you were awake when Phoenix entered the Gravity-well," Chief Fredericks said. "You saved the Phoenix and everyone aboard."

"Sequanta computers and fabricators saved Phoenix, not me," Joseph said as he left room.

"Engine room computers worry me during major breakdowns, but that guy worries me more," Chief Fredericks said.

"For what it's worth, I don't think I've ever heard Joseph say anything bad about you, Chief."

Chief Fredericks nodded approvingly.

"Joseph is the only person aboard who understands the Sequanta language. You don't acquire that kind of knowledge if you don't love machines," Martin said.

"Well, we have something in common. I love machines," Chief Fredericks said.

"When we trekked to Shanawi Station, I asked Joseph, which is harder, dealing with intelligent machines or dealing with people? Joseph said people because they are demanding and vain and prone to making mistakes."

***

Approaching Galraithia

The shrill wail of alarms echoed through the Phoenix, jolting the silent ship from its long slumber. Pulsing white lights bathed the Cryo module in an eerie glow, stirring the Freelanders from their deep hibernation pods. After years adrift in the void, the endless journey to Galraithia had finally come to an end.

Medical fabricators whirred to life, dispensing adrenaline autoinjectors—tiny lifelines designed to reignite the colonists' weakened bodies. The shots promised relief from the stiffness and aching joints that plagued those waking from prolonged stasis, and helped drain the fluid swelling their hands and feet.

A medical fabricator handed Joseph a bottle of vitamin water and a handful of herbal tablets, soothing the throbbing in his swollen ankles. Feeling the familiar mix of fatigue and resolve, he rose and made his way to the bridge deck.

There, Martin sat hunched over the navigation console, flanked by officers Brendon Aitama and Bill Aldridge. Their eyes scanned star charts with intense focus. Joseph approached, his steps quickening with a determined urgency.

"Where is Commander Thomas?" Joseph asked, his eyes scanning the bridge deck.

Martin said she had gone to her cabin to shower and change her clothes.

"And the others?" Joseph asked.

"Tom Granger, Doctor Margaret Mason, and Professor Lin are still in Cryo," Bill Aldridge replied.

"Mr. Aitama, are intercom loudspeakers working in the Cryo module?" Martin enquired.

"Negative, Captain. We have no communications with the Cryo module. Other outside modules, the Navigation antenna, Habitat ring, and Observation bubble, have a secondary communication system online for fabricators and handheld radios."

"Fabricators are working at top speed on every deck. Three days is the estimated time for repairs to be completed," Joseph said.

"I want all necessary repairs completed before orbital insertion around Galraithia," Martin instructed as he moved from the navigation console to the command chair. "Mr. Aitama, call Chief Fredericks in the engine room."

"Yes, Captain."

"Hello, Bridge! Fredericks, here."

"Communications are still offline in Cryo, Chief. Please find Doctor Mason and Professor Lin and inform them to report to the bridge. I need every staff officer updated on our current situation and emergency landing procedures. The only exception is Commander Granger, who is occupied in the Cargo Bay. It shouldn't take long to brief him once he finishes his assigned duties."

"Aye, Captain."

***

After showering, Satori sat on her bed, drying her short-cropped hair with a towel as she considered which clothes to wear: her navy uniform or a more casual outfit consisting of a standard-issue dark blue coverall, a black officer's cap and black leather boots. Ultimately, she chose the more casual look and left her cabin.

She made her way to the bridge deck elevator, walking down a narrow corridor toward the bow section of the Phoenix. She noticed electrical fabricators installing new optic fiber cables through the wall paneling and bulkheads.

Upon exiting the elevator, Satori approached the captain, seated in the command chair. Martin glanced up at her and smiled. Joseph quickly noticed Satori when she entered the bridge; he concentrated on concerning damage reports. After completing his damage assessments, Joseph couldn't help but gaze at Satori. She looked even more beautiful than the last time he had seen her, peacefully sleeping inside her hibernation pod.

"Commander Thomas, do you feel better after a hot shower and changing into clean, comfortable clothes?"

"Yes, Captain. I feel much better," Satori said.

"Good. We will need you on the bridge until orbital insertion around Galraithia."

"Yes, Captain."

"Joseph, you can help Commander Thomas and Doctor Mason prioritize our transport logistics before orbital insertion."

"Okay."

"Hello, Joseph. It's good to see you," Satori said.

"It's good to see you, too, Commander Thomas."

Satori gave Joseph a curious look. She smiled and thought Joseph was being too formal. She could play the game, be stiff, and official, like the little socialite her parents always portrayed her to be. There were times when she liked to embarrass her parents in front of company.

"Mr. Arunui, your time in the gym has certainly paid off. Your strong and muscular body has helped you through the long years of hibernation," Satori said.

"How do you know Joseph spent time in the gym?" Martin teased, "you were asleep the whole time."

"I remember hearing his soft voice as he shared stories with me. He talked about the long hours of training, the simulated landings on Galraithia, and his workouts at the gym. He spoke about his family, New Zealand, and Antarctica. He also mentioned how Shanawi Station frightened you, Captain. Joseph relayed everything I needed to know…and much more."

Satori and Joseph kept their relationship a secret, sharing the news only with Martin. They planned to start a new life together on Galraithia, building a home and raising a family. While Joseph was excited about this new chapter with Satori, he kept his growing love for her hidden from the rest of the crew. He dedicated most of his time to working with the fabricators, pushing their programming closer to the point where they could understand and judge every human frailty.

"I don't remember a thing after I closed my eyes," Joseph declared.

"Consider yourselves lucky," Dr. Margaret Mason said, her tone despondent as she attempted to wipe the smiles off everyone's faces. "A faulty hibernation pod has claimed the life of a young woman named Martha Allen." As Dr. Mason handed Martin the death certificate for co-signature, Chief Fredericks entered the bridge alongside Commander Granger.

"Let me do the talking," Chief Fredericks instructed.

"Alright, Chief, you talk to the captain. But make it quick. I have to get back to the Cargo Bay. Orbital insertion isn't too far away."

Commander Granger walked over to Joseph as Chief Fredericks approached the captain seated in the command chair.

"Have you told the captain?" Granger whispered.

Joseph shook his head. "No, not yet."

"Why not?" Granger whispered.

Martin glanced at Granger, irritated. His annoyance grew when Chief Fredericks approached the command chair. He wasn't prepared for another report on damaged equipment.

"Whenever I see you, Chief," Martin said, "it only means trouble and more work for everyone."

"Carrying out the necessary tasks to complete the mission is at the top of everyone's priority list, Captain."

"I'm not complaining about your work, Chief," Martin said. "Both you and your team of fabricators are doing a marvelous job. How is rectification work on reactor containment systems progressing?"

"Completed, Captain. The nanotrine reactor is running at 40 percent. Further reductions will be necessary approaching negative acceleration and orbital insertion."

"A very satisfactory report, Chief."

"Thank you, Captain."

"Commander Granger!" Martin called.

"Yes, Captain!"

"Whispering on the bridge is a weakness in my book. I do not tolerate that kind of behavior. If you have something constructive to say, let everyone hear what you say, or keep your mouth shut unless you're spoken to. Let me be sure you understand what I am telling you."

"I understand, Captain."

"Good, Granger. Then tell me and everyone here, in a loud voice, why are you here on my bridge instead of the cargo bay assembling the Icarus Lander, calibrating lasers, and prepping the drilling equipment?"

"I came here to report Comms are still offline below D deck, Captain."

"You came up here just to tell me that?"

"No, sir, I have more to add. Communications systems inside the Cargo Bay will be repaired before orbital insertion," Granger said.

"Commander Granger. I can always depend on fabricators doing the right things. Unlike your broken work ethic and lack of leadership qualities."

"For mercy's sake, Joseph. Tell the captain," Granger pleaded.

Martin turned his face and looked at Joseph; he seemed edgy about something.

"Joseph, tell the captain what you told me," Chief Fredericks said.

Martin looked at his wristwatch. "This had better be important."

Joseph hesitated momentarily before taking small and slow steps toward Martin, who knew his hypervigilance behavior better than anyone. Joseph's breathing would grow ragged when anxiety took hold, but Martin never failed to notice. He steadied his friend with calm words and gentle reassurance, reminding him that the storm would pass, that everything was okay.

"Go on, Joseph, there's no need to worry. I'm listening," Martin said calmly.

"We all know that Sequanta computers are self-learning machines…incredible thinking machines, and with their help and with their help…"

"Speak louder," Granger said. "We can't hear you, Joseph."

"Granger! Let him speak," Chief Fredericks said, frowning.

Martin shook his head. "Granger, you are making my head spin. I don't want to hear another word come from your mouth. Mr. Aitama and Mr. Aldridge report to the Cargo Bay and prep the Icarus Lander. I need two good pilots to operate the lander. Commander Granger will be there to help if you require assistance with anything."

"What if Commander Granger stops working without a valid excuse?" Bill Aldridge asked.

"In that case, Mr. Aldridge, you have my permission to place him in the brig for dereliction of duty!"

Bill Aldridge gave Granger a cynical smile. "Aye, Captain. It will be my pleasure."

Granger said, "Captain, may I speak, sir?"

"Yes, Granger, you may speak. I am listening."

"Captain, I would like to formally protest against the unfair judgment by you and Mr. Aldridge. I wish to record in the ship's log that I strongly object to this treatment, sir."

"Understood, Commander Granger. Now, leave my bridge!"

"Yes, Captain."

"Good! Now, there will be no more distractions," Martin said as the three men made their way to the cargo bay via the bridge deck elevator. Second Lieutenant Lesley Bracewell stepped out of the elevator and walked over to Martin.

"Lieutenant Bracewell reporting for duty, Captain."

"Good to see you back on your feet again, Lesley."

"Thank you, Captain. Medical fabricators took good care of me, sir."

"You may continue with your duties, Lieutenant."

"Thank you, Captain."

"Go on, Joseph, continue what you were saying," Martin said.

"Captain, I have good news to share with you and the bridge crew."

"I'm open to hearing any good news, Joseph."

"Our long-range infrared scanners have detected an infrared radiation signature close to the right corner of Quadrant-10," Joseph said, pointing to Cartesian coordinates on the electronic star chart. He said he believed that the infrared radiation signature could be from Endeavour's rocket engines.

Martin hurried to the navigation console, paying attention to Quadrant-10's star chart. "Lieutenant Bracewell!"

"Sir!"

"Do we have Endeavour's infrared radiation signature on file?"

"Yes, Captain, we do have a recording. The radar profile generator captured the image shortly after rendezvous with the Faxian telescope."

"Quadrant-10 is a vast area measuring ten light years diagonally. Too far away from our present position. Please display the image of the port-side viewing screen, Lieutenant."

"Aye, sir." Lieutenant Bracewell spun his chair around and selected an image file that he had stored in the radar data and tracking control console. Lesley had a master's in astrophysics, a ton of space pics saved up, and an extensive collection of jaw-dropping shots from that powerful Faxian telescope.

"Lieutenant, I need you to pull up the infrared radiation signature from Quadrant-10 on the port- side viewing screen."

"Yes, Captain."

"I'm convinced that's the Endeavour," Joseph exclaimed, excitement lighting up his face as he pointed to a vibrant red dot glimmering on the port-side viewing screen.

"Joseph," Martin said, "the infrared radar profile on the port side doesn't match Endeavour's recorded signature."

"Yes, there is a noticeable difference. I believe Endeavour's five rocket engines were glowing hot as it accelerated at high speed away from the Faxian telescope."

Martin sighed. "We are wasting valuable time, Joseph."

"I tell you; the Endeavour is halfway across Quadrant-10 and moving slowly," Joseph declared.

"Captain, I've analyzed the infrared radiation signature in Quadrant-10, and it suggests that two rocket engines are currently burning nanotrine plasma," Lieutenant Bracewell reported, his voice steady yet urgent. "The Endeavour is equipped with five Davis-Molby engines in total. However, suppose it's a damaged vessel with only two operational engines. In that case, the data from Quadrant 10 is likely correct."

"Alright, let's assume we're talking about the Endeavour. Why haven't we received any radio contact?" Martin asked

"I've been trying to establish communication with Endeavour for quite some time now," Joseph explained, a hint of frustration in his voice. "Unfortunately, I haven't received any response from its central sequanta computer or communication systems. It's as if the ship has completely disconnected from all networks, leaving us in the dark about its status."

"We're not getting any response from her, and at this point, we've already wasted too much time," Martin said, his frustration evident. "Even if the ship is the Endeavour, we're still too far away from her current position to make any meaningful progress." He looked at the navigation screen, which showed empty, unyielding space. The crushing weight of responsibility pressed down on him. Martin couldn't shake the feeling that every decision he made could have profound consequences, not just for himself but also for the future of Phoenix and its passengers and crew.

"Endeavour is moving too slowly to come to us, but her power coils are still active, Martin. Our long-range infrared scanners can easily track Endeavour's infrared radiation signature."

"Quadrant-10, located in the Cygnus-7 region, is engulfed by thick gas clouds and expansive swathes of cosmic dust, creating an almost impenetrable veil across the stars. The intense obscurity these particles render poses a significant challenge for our infrared scanners, leaving them ineffective for any meaningful detection or analysis. Regrettably, this means we cannot assist or support the Endeavour. Phoenix will be at risk, Joseph. I won't endanger the Phoenix, passengers, or crew."

"All those people will die! I can't bear the thought of their deaths weighing on my conscience," Joseph said, his voice heavy with sadness.

"Changing Phoenix's course to help Endeavour is an invitation to mission failure. A risk I am not willing to take."

"What happened to you, Martin? Have you given up on what every Freelander believes matters the most: helping others?" Joseph said, turning his back to walk away from Martin and leave the Phoenix bridge with a worried look.

"Joseph, you are listening without understanding. The Endeavour is too far from our current position, and is not my responsibility!" Martin yelled. "I am duty-bound to ensure your safety and the safety of every Freelander aboard the Phoenix!"

"I don't want to hear excuses, Martin! You have no empathy for the needs of others," Joseph said as he walked to the bridge deck elevator, not bothering to look back. Deep down, he understood that Martin's indifference and lack of compassion stemmed from his inability to accept statistical certainties: the risks associated with cryopreservation biotechnology, the extended travel time to Galraithia, and the increased potential for equipment malfunction and death.

Martin believed, whether accurately or not, that their journey through the Gravity-well was a matter of sheer luck rather than the result of skilled navigation. The spaceship Phoenix had surpassed the light-speed barrier by a factor of two, reducing the expedition time to Galraithia by 18 years. This fortunate outcome, stemming from uncertain luck, was a gift Martin had no intention of squandering. As a result, he placed his trust in the AutoNav computer; human error typically occurred when rules were not adhered to, and there was zero tolerance for mistakes in this situation.

****

Joseph programmed the AutoNav computer to deploy Phoenix's braking sails at significantly below light speed, slowing the ship as it approached Galraithia. The approach had to be perfect—a shallow entry angle or excessive speed would send Phoenix bouncing off the planet's atmosphere, spiraling helplessly toward the alien sun, Dimos.

The AutoNav computer plotted their safe orbital trajectory, and the final row of hibernation pods hissed open. Level-1 Freelander colonists stirred from their long cryosleep.

In the far corner of the Cryo chamber, Lanfen's heart filled with joy as bright lights flooded her vision. The medical fabricators had restored her sight during the journey, repairing the damaged optic nerve connections that had blinded both eyes. Such delicate work would have cost a fortune on Earth, but it was a gift from Walter Briar—the generous benefactor who, alongside Dani Li, held a special place in her heart.

As her eyes adjusted, Lanfen noticed the ominous stillness of other pods. Walking carefully to her cabin, she wondered how many had survived the long sleep. After showering and changing, she sat at her computer console and searched for Dani Li. His name should have appeared with the other level-1 Freelanders assigned to her deck, but many cabins remained empty. His name was nowhere—not in the passenger manifest, not in the death records.

Father Sandor delivered the crushing news: Dani Li and fifty other Freelanders had been left behind when Phoenix departed from the Lunar Orbital Station. The revelation devastated Lanfen. She had dreamed of transforming their friendship into love, but now that chance was lost forever. Overwhelmed by depression and fatigue, she retreated to the medicine cabinet and then to her bed, seeking the comfort of natural sleep.

While Lanfen slept, Doctor Mason declared a medical emergency. She met urgently with Professor Briar, Father Sandor, and Martin to discuss the crisis: one hundred and fifty colonists had died in hypersleep from toxic shock syndrome, an inherent risk of deep space travel. Without constant medical fabricator supervision, the toll would have been even higher.

The culprit was simple but deadly—cheaply made control valves had failed to prevent human waste from bypassing the filtration systems in each pod's dialysis unit. Professor Briar ordered Doctor Mason to solve the problem immediately, using whatever resources necessary. A maintenance team of fabricators arrived quickly, replacing the faulty control valves and screen meshes while upgrading each cryobed's dialysis unit with better-quality components.

The deaths stopped, but the damage was done. Despite the repairs, most colonists still considered the Cryo chamber Death Row.

"Doctor, I'll admit I was afraid and nervous the first time I stepped inside the cryo chamber. However, I have gained newfound confidence in cryogenics and fabricator technology," Chief Fredericks said as he replaced a cryogenic control valve under Professor Briar's hibernation pod.

"Many people fear hypersleep," Doctor Mason interjected. "However, I find it unfair that some passengers and crew hold William and me personally responsible for the deaths of 150 individuals."

"Why do you say that?" Chief Fredericks asked.

Doctor Mason explained that she and William sourced the components for the cryo bed from Winthrop Holdings. She clarified that neither she nor William Briar held any unjust suspicions against the Winthrop family. She aimed to make this clear to every member of the Freelander community aboard the Phoenix.

***

Before orbital insertion around Galraithia, terraforming teams from every deck vigorously checked their equipment. They made copies of maps and plans of Camp Alpha, the first human settlement on Galraithia. Martin was the target of their ire when he missed several essential meetings with them, preferring to help medical fabricators strip down faulty hibernation pods and cryogenic components.

Galraithia

The starboard side airlock door opened as the navigation computer started the last deceleration burn. Eight shiny metallic orbs and a Telemachus probe darted into space from a pod bay attached to Phoenix's underbelly. The ten-foot-long boomerang-shaped Telemachus probe settled into orbit around Galraithia, collecting atmospheric data. Meanwhile, the eight plate-sized orbs streaked silently across Galraithia's thin atmosphere. Heating up and glowing red hot from friction, the spheres left behind a two-mile-long orange vapor trail as they flew lower and lower toward the surface.

The spheres photographed two continents and thousands of smaller islands. They also mapped the ocean floor and measured high and low barometric pressures and altitude data ahead of Phoenix's scheduled landing on the surface of Galraithia. After sixteen hours and data banks full of stored knowledge, the orbs returned safely to Phoenix.

A fabricator stood silently, equipped with decontamination gear. It looked up at the eight orbs hovering above a narrow entryway. The outer protective skin of the orbs glowed with a fluorescent green and pale blue light, radiating intense heat that was too extreme for human hands to touch. The fabricator carefully scanned each orb for microbial contaminants and found none. However, Orb 3 had multiple scrapes and dents on its outer copper casing. After the inspection, the fabricator placed all eight orbs on a cooling rack and transported them to the lab module on Deck 5.

***

A powerful interferometer analyzed billions of bits of planetary data. It found verifiable evidence of abundant sources of drinkable water and a high pollen count in the air. There were signs that early-stage life forms existed in the equatorial regions, such as insects and small reptiles, birds, and plants. The Tezarian Ocean, which held the most water on Galraithia, had an abundance of marine organisms and evolving fish species. Early radar data recorded by the orbs suggested that the depth of the Ithinian Sea and the Tezarian Ocean was five times deeper than the Mariana Trench in the western Pacific Ocean on Earth.

Aboard the Phoenix, scientists stressed the value of these early discoveries. They sent out more drones and orbs, but the crushing water pressure and perpetual darkness shortened Orb 3's reconnaissance mission, leaving unanswered questions about the life forms flourishing on the seafloor.

***

A short retrograde burn positioned Phoenix in a safe geosynchronous orbit 22,300 miles above Galraithia. News of the historic event would not reach Earth for another five years.

"Our journey to Galraithia is a triumph of human ingenuity and determination. The team of people who worked extremely hard to get us here is enormous. There are many people to thank," Professor Briar said over the ship's radio, thinking back to when astronomers dismissed the notion of an earthlike planet with an extended elliptical orbit and seasons that change on an 86,000-year cycle. There was a somber tone in William's voice and total silence on every deck when he spoke about the missing Endeavour.

"Without any human intervention, the probability of Endeavour's navigation control computer overriding all

334

previous navigation data and plotting a new trajectory heading to Galraithia is improbable, to say the least. However, there is always hope while the communication link between Faxian and the Deep Space Network is open and active. Therefore, we must face the stark fact that we are far from Earth and on our own. I know it is a terrifying thought for many of you. Still, here we are orbiting Galraithia, and we should all be proud of who we are and what we have achieved as Freelanders."

As Professor Briar concluded his speech, the Freelanders erupted in cheers, their joy evident as they celebrated the momentous occasion of Phoenix successfully entering orbit around Galraithia, marking a new chapter in their journey among the stars.

Joseph and Satori enjoyed a glass of sasquala berry wine together, and Chief Fredericks and Bill Aldridge downed whiskey shots. Before long, the four friends seated in the Habitat Ring's lounge area were inundated by people who had rushed to the starboard viewing windows.

The rotational axis of Galraithia tilted away from Dimos, and profound darkness enveloped the planet, plunging it into an eerie abyss. The vibrant colors of its landscapes faded as shadows crept over the land, transforming awe-inspiring vistas into haunting silhouettes.

***

Preparations for the first landing on the surface of Galraithia were ahead of schedule. People pushed and shoved, pressing their faces against the viewing windows to see the first Galraithian dawn from space.

"We have long waited for this day to arrive," Chief Fredericks declared.

"Yes, we have, Chief. Our travel time was shorter than we had planned," Joseph said.

"We survived the Gravity-well, but arriving here without the Endeavour feels like a hollow victory," Bill said.

Satori told Bill, "The Endeavour's communication and sensor systems are well-designed and reliable. Sequanta computers might be listening to us right now."

"Then why don't they respond to our calls?" Bill asked.

"Our long-range scanners haven't received mayday calls, only faint intermittent chatter between Endeavour's sequanta computers and Faxian. However, there has been nothing since orbital insertion, just background noise from space," Satori explained.

Chief Fredericks downed a shot of whiskey and slammed the lid of his laptop shut.

"What's wrong, Chief?" Bill asked.

"A second Telemachus probe has just returned with the answer to your question," Chief Fredericks replied.

"How is it the answer to my question?" Bill inquired.

"Galraithia has a powerful magnetic field, and its ionosphere displays unusual disturbances. This means we might not communicate with Faxian, Earth's deep-space network, or each other once we land on the planet's surface."

"Chief, this is not the time to show a negative attitude," Bill said. "When things don't go our way, we must work harder to accomplish our goals."

"I don't believe any of us would have made it this far with a negative attitude," Satori said.

Joseph emphasized the confidence of the Freelanders by stating, "There is no problem that Freelanders cannot solve."

***

Airlocks and hatchways opened as Freelander colonists from every deck hurried to their muster stations. Professor Briar and Martin met on the bridge to review the mission briefing with their staff officers and assess their preparedness levels.

"As you can see from these digital images, Galraithia has three distinct regions: the Northern Continent of Ashyr, the Equatorial Zone, and the Southern Continent, also known as Southland. Phoenix will touch down on the continental region of Ashyr," Professor Briar explained, pointing to the landing zone on the display screen. "Two-thirds of Ashyr consists of the Northern Plateau, the Interior Highlands, and the Ashyr Basin, our preferred landing zone."

"The Interior Highlands are higher than Mount Everest. The entrance to the landing zone south of the proposed settlement will test my navigation skills," Satori said.

Joseph leaned over and whispered, "You are an excellent navigator. You won't face any difficult challenges while navigating the Keyway Valley."

"Thank you, Joseph. I appreciate your faith in me."

"There is a safer flight path available. Nevertheless, the data gathered by orbs during reconnaissance over the Tezarian Ocean yielded concerning results."

Professor Briar emphasized that navigating the planet's deepest waters or attempting a water landing would pose significant dangers, jeopardizing both the Phoenix spacecraft and the lives of everyone onboard.

"I believe the Equatorial Zone is the best choice for the first landing, sir. This bioregion has freshwater ecosystems rich in plant life," Tom Granger said.

"Thank you, Mr. Granger, for your input. However, the last thing we want is to increase the risk of human DNA contaminating the cells of lifeforms developing in those wetlands. Tom, let me be clear without going into too much detail: I am not suggesting that the Equatorial Zone will always be off-limits. Are there any more questions?" Professor Briar said as he gathered his briefing papers and scanned the room.

"No, sir," Martin said, eager to begin his mission to the southern continent, which was the ice-covered landmass surrounded by the Ithinian Sea and Tezarian Ocean.

"If there are no more questions, this concludes the mission briefing."

Satori walked up to Joseph and held out her hand, "I must say goodbye for now."

"You don't have to say goodbye if you join Martin's first team."

"Joseph, I can't join Martin's first team. Professor Briar selected me to navigate the Phoenix to landing zone Alpha." She looked deeply into his eyes while holding his hand. "It's a tremendous honor to be the navigator of the lead ship, but it also comes with great responsibility."

"Am I worrying too much?" Joseph asked.

"You don't need to worry, Joseph. I'll be at the Alpha settlement, ready and waiting for you," Satori's words enveloped Joseph like a warm embrace. "Trust that I'll be there, just as I promised."

"Team Icarus, report to Pod Bay 7, please," Martin announced over the ship's radio.

"I have to go," Joseph said, taking Satori's hand. "Will you walk with me to the Icarus Lander?" The more Joseph looked into Satori's eyes, the more she wished he would stay by her side.

***

As the Freelander colonists gathered on the lower decks to conduct final equipment checks. The computer navigation system followed Satori's instructions to verify the landing coordinates for Ashyr and Southland, and launched the twin-engine Icarus Lander. Viewing the launch from the bridge deck, Satori wanted to remotely record the landings on the southern and northern continents. However, computer and radio contact with both flights was lost soon after the Icarus lander and the Phoenix entered Galraithia's thin atmosphere. Icarus began to vibrate violently, but there was little frictional heating. Both pilots, Brendon Aitama and Bill Aldridge, relied on their well-rehearsed landing approaches and proven control strategies for a safe landing. Looking north, the majestic Cradle Mountains, the highest peaks on the northern continent of Ashyr, filled the cockpit window.

"I could never have imagined such unbelievable beauty," Brendon said, banking Icarus hard to the right, heading towards Southland's frozen interior.

Above was a sky filled with fast-rippling clouds, and Ithinia, the largest of the Galraithian moons, moved across its smaller counterpart, Galrah. As Ithinia passed, it blocked the sun, casting a soft blue-green light over Southland and the Fortress Mountains, which naturally divided the southern continent into eastern and western regions.

"Brendon, check the weather scanner," Joseph said.

"The scanner is indicating high wind pressure. Katabatic winds sweeping down the mountains, sir."

"Frigid air is being pushed higher and higher up into the atmosphere, causing the rippling effect. Set the mode switch to manual flight," Joseph said.

"Switching to manual flight, sir."

The single-deck Icarus lander tilted violently from side to side. "Stop sightseeing and focus on your job, Mr. Aitama. Fly this tin can properly," Tom Granger said, sitting rigidly in his seat. Overcome by fear, he tightened his grip on the shoulder harness straps.

Bill looked over his shoulder and saw that Tom Granger's knuckles were turning white with tension. "Hey, Granger, don't be afraid. How's your stomach holding up?"

"That's none of your business!"

"Well, I'm making it my business. I don't want you to throw up in front of everyone," Bill teased.

Tom raised his middle finger at Bill, believing he had just insulted him. However, the loud, contemptuous laughter from the cockpit caught him off guard.

"Brendon, show Mr. Granger how good a pilot you are," Bill exclaimed confidently. "Shut down both engines. We'll glide down to the surface." Bill knew Brendon was fighting the control stick, struggling to keep Icarus flying level.

"Don't panic, Commander Granger, sir. This turbulence will subside once we level off," Brendon said, looking at Martin, waiting for the thumbs up for the glide down to the surface. "Okay, do it, Mr. Aitama. Hold onto your shoulder straps, gentlemen!" Martin shouted.

Tom and Joseph leaned back in their seats, pressing back as far as they would go as Icarus descended like a hurtling meteor and the fast-approaching Fortress Mountains filled their viewing windows.

Meanwhile, far to the north, Phoenix gently landed on the vibrant Ashyr Plain. This sprawling landscape featured tall, golden grass and low-lying yellow shrub, adding splashes of color to an otherwise sandy, semi-arid region. The majestic, snow-capped Cradle Mountains rose high above the horizon to the north. At the southernmost edge of the Ashyr Plain, heavily forested lowlands transitioned into a jagged, rocky coastline battered by the crashing waves of the turbulent Ithinian Sea.

***

A wide loading ramp from Phoenix's cargo hold had lowered and touched the ground in soft morning light at 8.35 a.m., local solar time (LST). However, the actual arrival date on the Galraithian calendar had been set to zero. The year zero was to begin a new life for 3849 Freelander colonists. Sixteen-year-old Veronica Morgan and Lanfen, the youngest Freelander colonists, held hands while walking down the loading ramp. Both girls happily smiled at each other and giggled, thankful for the honor of being the first Freelanders to set foot on Galraithia. Lanfen suddenly went quiet, listening to her own thoughts.

"Lanfen, what's wrong?" Veronica asked, gently wiping the tears from Lanfen's face.

"Nothing is wrong," Lanfen replied.

"Then why are you crying?"

341

"Tears of both sadness and joy for two special people I will never forget," Lanfen said softly.

"Your parents?"

"No, my grandmother and my good friend Walter made this new beginning possible for me. I miss them both very much."

***

The journey to Galraithia marked a monumental leap for humankind. Settling a new world beyond the Solar System was widely seen as the next stage in human evolution. For the Freelander people, it also represented a crucial step in their social development. They had wisely appointed Professor William Briar as Galraithia's first Administrator, alongside twelve elected legislators. Together, they tackled social grievances and upheld human rights under Freelander laws covering science, research, construction, education, technology, communication, recreation, exploration, cohabitation, and even funeral rites.

For the first colonists, the vast unknown of Galraithia's northern and southern continents loomed dauntingly. The equatorial region, lush and teeming with life under heavy rainfall, was off-limits—Professor Briar declared it a No-Go Zone, citing insufficient weather data to ensure safety.

By popular vote, the initial settlement was named Alpha. Mechanical fabricators and engineers worked side by side, assembling building panels filled with liquid regolith. Once cooled and hardened, these panels proved ten times stronger than steel. Yet progress was slow. Premade containment tanks fell short of standards and had to be recast in regolith concrete. This setback delayed completion of the underground pipeline that carried water from the Ashyr River to Alpha by twelve hours. The domed roofs of the in-ground tanks stored human waste and purified water, crucial for preventing respiratory diseases caused by contaminated soil and water—threats that could jeopardize the entire colony's health if left unchecked.

Meanwhile, the adaptable modules attached to the Phoenix spacecraft were being dismantled with care. The Cryo module was the first to be removed from the ship's hull. Once standing upright, it would become the tallest engineered structure on Ashyr's northern continent. The Habitat ring followed—cut in two halves, laid flat, then bolted and welded around the base of the towering Cryo module. Three Y-shaped radials, tubular passageways, connected the Cryo module to the Habitat ring, forming a sturdy network.

Stripped from flight deck to power core, the Phoenix— some 1,200 feet long, excluding five engine bays— resembled the skeletal remains of a fish picked clean from head to tail. Yet, through expert logistical planning and engineering foresight, adaptable superchargers and electrical generators harnessed the immense power of three Far Star engines. The other two engines were mothballed and stored perfectly inside a newly built warehouse, ready for future use.

***

While fabricators busily constructed the vital infrastructure needed for the colony to function, the first teams ventured beyond the Keyway—a narrow valley just five miles from the landing site. Ten people split into three groups: two led by seeders from Australia, who set off on foot heading north and south, and a third group of geologists and fabricators riding comfortably in heavy-tracked vehicles bound for the western edge of the Diamantina Plateau.

They reached the plateau's summit just before sunset, where they began setting up Base Camp Hector. Shelters were dug into the earth, and supplies and equipment were carefully laid out, all in preparation for future missions. Each group found sources of water and patches of vegetation, but the news was sobering. The water, while present, was insufficient to support a thriving, long-term Freelander settlement. Even more troubling was the native plant life—highly toxic to humans, with no edible fruit trees or wild grains in sight. The absence of any native animal life dealt another blow to the struggling Alpha colony.

That evening, whispers of discontent rippled through the dining hall. Yet, the expedition beyond the Keyway was far from fruitless. The geologists returned with a diverse collection of rock and soil samples, while the pollinators reported discovering a deep sandstone gorge and thirty-two species of native plants thriving in dry, odorless soil. They also found living stromatolites clinging to the rocky eastern coastline and several volcanic fissures where molten lava poured into the Tezarian Ocean.

But amid the cautious optimism, tragedy struck. Botanist Doctor Michael Zhamosa became the first casualty of the excursion south when he accidentally brushed his right forearm against the thorny Zhamosa bush—a berry-producing native plant he had discovered and named after himself.

With his right forearm ravaged by a relentless infection—and Earth's antibiotics powerless against the alien bacteria—Doctor Zhamosa made the grim decision to amputate. The surgery itself was a success, but just two days later, he succumbed to toxemia, overwhelmed by postoperative septic complications. Professor Briar warned the regrettable incident had resulted from careless and irresponsible behavior: "We are not strolling through central London. We are living in an alien world we know little about. Life is tenuous and uncertain, and there is no doubt in my mind that more deaths will follow if we rush to get things done. Therefore, great care must be taken to avoid accidents."

Meanwhile, Martin and his Southland team huddled together, their faces tight with worry. From the moment they landed, they had been battered by brutal conditions— temperatures plummeting to a staggering 110 degrees below zero, blinding blizzards that erased all sight, and savage winds roaring at over 250 miles per hour, powerful enough to strip the paint clean off the Icarus Lander. The weather showed no mercy, with the fierce gusts only growing stronger, dashing any hope of relief.

***

Freelander scientists said Galraithia formed 3.2 billion years ago. However, the origin of life on the planet was still unknown. Furthermore, supplementary models that dealt with the atmospheric composition were incomplete, thwarting meteorologists' desire to understand Galraithia's unusual atmospheric components. Regardless of the missing data, clear and convincing evidence suggested that Galraithia was heading towards the next planetary evolution phase. Freelander scientists incited the hope of many colonists, including Professor Briar, by issuing a statement: *"Humankind can likely survive Galraithia's evolutionary destiny into the future, perhaps with intelligent planning rather than blind luck."*

This was the response that Professor Briar had hoped for. He sent out more expeditions, which only discovered reliable water sources. However, sending teams farther away to search for food was unsettling for the Seeders, who were busy planting agricultural seeds by hand. Despite their repeated efforts, they could not produce any millable flour from wheat. The healthy grains and seeds from Earth did

345

not germinate in Galraithia's odorless soil. With no viable options left, Professor Briar felt he had no choice but to hold a meeting with his staff in the conference room.

"As you all know, our supply of fresh food is relatively small, and our first priority is finding a sustainable supply of food and water that is not too far away from Alpha. Building reliable weather stations and communication networks is also high on our priority list. Therefore, I have appointed Lieutenant Commander Alistair Tyler as the leader of Group-1-North. My intent primarily for this group is to erect strategically placed automatic weather stations and communication towers on the Diamantina Plateau."

Alistair Tyler was a man of average height and looks other than his bony face, which made him look older than his actual age. Alistair looked over his shoulder and smiled confidently at his team. Then Professor Briar turned to Satori. "Commander Thomas, you are in command of Group-2 South. You have a very knowledgeable team: Professor Lin, Major Nikolayev, Margaret Gray, and Veronica Blainey are the best in their field."

"We try to be," Veronica Blainey said, smiling.

"Ladies, I'm counting on you not to repeat the mistakes of the Zhamosa expedition to the woodlands on the southern coast."

"You can count on us," Margaret said.

"We didn't come all this way to fail at the first hurdle," Veronica added.

"I have never failed at anything in my life," Major Nikolayev said in her heavy Russian accent.

Suddenly, Professor Briar's mood changed; his eyes had gone cold. "Well, if that's the case, Major, I give you the keys to Vehicle-2."

"Commander Thomas!"

"Sir!"

"Major Nikolayev is your driver/navigator. Father Sandor will issue your orders with the appropriate maps before you leave."

"Thank you, sir."

Professor Jason Tohvian looked down at his map and wished the ladies the best of luck. "The two-thousand-foot-high Diamantina Plateau is 53.6 miles from Alpha. The entire area beyond the Keyway Valley is strewn with shards of volcanic shale."

"A full-track Rover should get us there in under an hour," Commander Tyler countered. "Get your gear together; you're in the driver's seat."

"That's okay," Jason said, nodding thoughtfully. "I don't mind driving."

"Professor Briar, when do we leave?" Tyler said.

"As soon as possible, Alistair."

Robert Finnegan was the last name on Professor Briar's list. He knew Finnegan would not be happy; the Australian billionaire preferred to work alone rather than suffer the annoying company of the other team members. "RJ, you'll be joining Alistair's team," Briar said.

"Okay, William."

"Welcome to the team, RJ," Tyler said.

Finnegan gave Alistair a cold stare. "It's Mr. Finnegan to you."

The other members of Alistair's team included Russian-born physician Andre Zarovski and journalist Rihanna Wakeman, who quickly stepped forward to welcome the brash Australian billionaire. Andre remained seated with Professor Briar who was looking for vehicle keys but also paying attention to Zarovski's body language.

"You have been unusually quiet today, Andre."

"Maybe," Andre said bluntly.

"Go and say hello to RJ, make him feel welcome," Professor Briar said.

Andre nodded yes and walked over to Finnegan, who was about to walk out of the stuffy conference room. "Mr. Finnegan! I am happy that you are joining us."

"Why?"

"Because I'm not the oldest man in the team, that's why. And it makes me happy."

***

After the conference room was emptied of people, Finnegan stepped in close beside Andre and walked along a narrow corridor to the repository. Finnegan appreciated Andre's humor; his outwardly calm, good nature and being a Freelander from Russia (the last country to join the Freelander movement) put him in good stead with the cantankerous Finnegan, who really didn't know much about the people in his team. But everyone knew his social standing: the fifth richest man on Earth, his two sons dying in a car accident, his daughter Amiria overdosing on sleeping pills. Shortly after, R. J. Finnegan had diverged from his social standing; he gave away all his possessions

348

and business empire. The fledgling Freelander colony had solar panels spread over 35 acres of land, thanks to Finnegan's generosity.

Later that evening, Professor Briar visited Father Sandor and asked, "How is everything progressing in the Keyway Valley? Have you found more edible plants?" Father Sandor replied that he planned to return to the Keyway Valley in the morning with Michael Stoddard and Lanfen. He assured Professor Briar that they would return to the Alpha settlement with food samples for testing within the allotted time.

***

The next morning, after breakfast, Lanfen met up with Father Sandor and Michael. They loaded their gear into Rover-1 and headed toward the Keyway Valley. They stopped beside a winding stream bordered by towering trees and a riot of brightly colored flowers and fruit-laden shrubs. Father Sandor had dubbed this place Eden on his first visit—everywhere he looked, nature seemed flawless. Yet his instincts urged caution as they carefully navigated through thorny vines dripping with potent toxins.

Then a tree heavy with yellow fruit caught his eye. At first glance, the fruit looked like Earth's Seckel pear—similar in shape and texture—but the seeds were oddly different in size and shape. Its skin was thicker, and the pulp contained a clear, glistening juice. Despite the familiar appearance, the priest recoiled at the scent: a sharp, decaying onion odor. While Father Sandor collected samples of the skin, pulp, and juice, Lanfen bent down to gather fallen purple berries from a glossy plant nearby. She crushed one between her fingers and inhaled its sweet, trapped juice— her heightened sense of smell as keen as ever, even now that she could see.

"Father Sandor, look! These tiny purple berries are good to eat."

The priest trusted Lanfen's reputation as a psychic medium. However, he couldn't hide his concern when she popped another purple berry into her mouth. Father Sandor shook his head and said, "Those berries haven't been tested and could potentially harm your health."

"I should know better. I am sorry, Father Sandor."

The priest nodded, put a few fruit samples inside his leather satchel, and moved to the fast-moving stream. Michael had made his way up a steep and rocky hill. A few more steps led him to a grassy plateau overlooking the valley.

He sat down for a while, admiring the view to the northwest, enjoying the icy breeze blowing on his face. He could see the priest far below, busily collecting water samples. At the same time, Lanfen took cuttings from knee-high yellow shrubs growing near the water's edge. Michael's shouts of Coo-ee echoed all around the valley. Lanfen looked up, waved, and smiled at him, but Father Sandor paid Michael no attention.

Like many successful photographers, Michael Stoddard's patience was legendary. He would wait hours for the right picture moment. He looked through the camera lens. The light color and composition were perfect. He snapped photograph after photograph of Galraithia's two suns rising over the Cradle Mountains. Without a second thought, Michael decided to set up a temporary campsite on the Plateau and fired a whistling flare into the sky.

During breakfast, Michael informed Father Sandor that a whistling orange flare would signal them to return to the Freelander settlement without him.

The loud, drawn-out whistle of the flare had Father Sandor and Lanfen looking up at the sky. A burst of orange light was arching skywards, before it faded in the direction of Alpha. Finally, it was time to pack the gear and leave.

"That's all for today," Father Sandor said, starting the engines. "There's a greater variety of plant life on the other side of the valley. We'll go there tomorrow."

"Do you think we'll find purple berries?" Lanfen asked

"Possibly."

Father Sandor pushed the throttle lever forward. The engines whirred louder as Rover-1 picked up speed, heading towards Alpha, leaving behind a cloud of dust. "How many purple berries did you collect, Lanfen?"

"Not enough to fill a coffee cup. I did find a huge bunch growing on a low yellow shrub, but the berries were green, not yet ripe for picking."

"Never mind, my dear, we'll find more purple berries tomorrow. I'm sure of it."

***

Father Sandor parked Rover-1 near the hangar, said a quiet goodbye to Lanfen, and began the walk home. He lifted his eyes to the pale green evening sky, the twin suns casting a strange glow over Galraithia, and whispered a prayer to his God. As a scientist, he understood how the light and heat from these suns fueled every living thing on the planet. Yet his early Christian faith reminded him that God—the creator of all things—was the true force behind the universe. *My God, my God, creator of the universe, I shall worship you forever, hear my prayer. My God, my God, walk beside me, give me strength.*

351

The prayer echoed in his mind as he walked. Everything here was beautiful, yes—but dangerous. Vibrant plants heavy with fruit hid deadly toxins. Beneath the vast seas, strange microbial life thrived in toxic brine pools, while hundreds of hyper-thermal vents spewed ammonia in thick clouds.

Back at the quarters he shared with Father Antonio, Sandor closed the outer airlock door behind him, wrapped a blanket tighter around his bony shoulders, and headed straight to his room. Father Antonio was still awake, waiting. The younger priest's face was drawn with fatigue and worry; he needed to speak about what had happened in the dining hall that evening—an incident that defied all reason and decency.

A rowdy group of Freelanders had cornered Father Antonio while he dined alone, delivering a chilling warning: the small Church planned near the Keyway Valley entrance was not welcome. They threatened to burn it down—and to burn the priests with it. The tension had only worsened after Professor Briar refused to grant a building permit, fanning the flames of hostility.

The next day, the two priests faced Professor Briar beneath a sky as wild and ominous as the grim faces watching them. No solutions were reached, no protections offered. The threat hung heavy in the air, unresolved and dangerous.

"Resubmit the building application, and the Council of Elders will take any action it deems appropriate," Professor Briar said.

The first Ithinian Cycle

On day 27, a spiraling mass of purple-gray clouds and a black haze covered the southern horizon. As the ominous clouds moved steadily east, Alistair Tyler stepped precariously close to the chilly south edge of the Diamantina Plateau. Alistair looked through his binoculars at Cool Ridge, a narrow ridge of gravely rocks leading up to the summit of Mount Skrean, a pyramid-shaped mountain rising 7,575 feet above sea level. At the same time, Rihanna Wakeman attached a multi-angle solar reflector to a six-foot-high pyramid made of medium-sized stones that would be visible from Keyway Valley and the Alpha settlement.

Rihanna left the stone pyramid and was pushed by strong katabatic winds as she ascended the steep slope toward the edge of the plateau. She saw Alistair and greeted him, but he had no warm response or toothy smile.

"Okay, be that way, and don't say hello. Stuck-up snob," Rihanna said.

"You think I'm a snob?" Alistair said.

Rihanna opened her folding camera to take a few photographs. "You didn't say hello. That makes you snobby."

"Rihanna, there's a storm front brewing, and the wind is getting stronger. I didn't hear you say hello with this wind roaring in my ears." Rihanna approached the plateau's edge with tentative, cautious steps and glanced over the precipice. Beyond the profound depths and jagged rocks below lay a spectacular vista.

"Don't get too close to the edge!" Alistair shouted.

"This is a stunning location," Rihanna remarked as she thought of Michael Stoddard, the first man from Earth to camp near the edge of the Diamantina Plateau and photograph the twin moons of Galraithia rising.

"The two-hour walk was definitely worth the effort," Alistair replied.

Rihanna snapped picture after picture, exclaiming, "The eastern view reminds me of Gulha Kangri Mountain in Tibet."

***

As the shadows lengthened, the temperature dropped to just above freezing. Heat sensors stitched to Rihanna's orange-colored environsuit flashed blue, activating a pressure switch. The thermal layers of the environsuit compressed, drawing in warming sodium acetate closer to the skin. A matching face scarf protected Rihanna's pale face from a biting cold wind, and black wraparound glasses shielded her blue eyes. Feeling comfortable inside her environsuit, Rihanna wanted to explore and photograph more. However, Alistair was the expedition leader, and Rihanna knew exactly what Alistair would do: leave the Diamantina Plateau before the storm hit.

Alistair adjusted the temperature inside his red environsuit. He then removed the scarf wrapped around his bearded face because it made his skin itchy.

"Gather your equipment! We are leaving!" Alistair declared.

So, they both pressed on toward the easiest and safest descent route off the plateau's northern edge.

In the meantime, at Beacon Hill, Jason Tohvian and Andre Zarovski were finishing work on the early warning weather warning station; its titanium pole and wires were erected quickly in solid rock. They cared to ensure that the laser beacon attached to the weather station was calibrated correctly.

"Andre, the radio battery is good, and the antenna is functioning properly, but only on a single frequency," Jason said, looking at the antenna on the titanium pole.

"Okay, I will do another signal check," Andre replied.

Andre climbed to the crest of Beacon Hill and tapped hard on the heat sensor attached to his environment suit. "It's getting colder by the minute, Jason. The sooner we leave here, the better."

"Yes, the sooner, the better," Jason said, setting the only radio channel without static for maximum volume.

"I have a stronger and much clearer radio signal now!" Andre declared. "Call Tyler."

"Okay. Bravo Team calling Commander Tyler. Radio check. Over."

"Jason, I hear you loud and clear. Skip the radio protocol. There's no need for it here. Now, tell me, how are you two progressing?"

"Well, the warning beacon is operational, but there is one final calibration to do before we are done here, sir."

"Excellent job. Meet up at Marion's crater as planned."

"Marion's crater, yes. I understand, sir, team Bravo out."

"Jason, the weather radar map is showing a massive storm front moving south and fast," Andre said. "Marion's crater is on the south coast."

"Marion's crater?" Jason said, opening his map. "Tyler is a fool! There is nothing of importance or value there and surrounding areas."

"Forget Tyler!" Andre said. "He is a big man of little substance."

A surge of rage welled in Jason. "More honor to the Tyler name. That's what Alistair and his sickly-looking sister Marion came here for. Pompous Antarctic Freelanders. I can't stand the sight of any of them."

"Your parents and grandparents were Freelanders," Andre said. "You were born and raised in Antarctica, yes?"

"And!" Jason snapped.

"The Tohvian family ranks high among the Freelanders of Antarctica," Andre said, tugging at Jason's shoulder sleeve insignia, the Tohvian family coat of arms (*two fists clashing against a lightning bolt*).

"Why does that matter to you or anyone else? I didn't come here to bring honor to my family; I came here for myself, to escape my father and his political nonsense. Now, I have to deal with another judgmental, pompous jerk, and I can't seem to shake him off," Jason said in a sulky tone.

"Focus on the storm. Give me the distance and heading. I don't want to get caught out here when it hits."

"Okay, okay, there's no need to shout," Jason said. "I'm not deaf."

An intense pulse of blue light shot out of the warning beacon. "The storm front is one-hundred and twenty miles… moving south-southeast at 50 knots… maximum distance for the warning beacon."

Andre nodded, verifying that the data on a small computer screen is correct. "I want to recompile the computer data one more time."

"Okay, but make it fast," Jason said.

A small pressure valve hissed as the rotating beacon turned. Andre re-aligned the laser and calibrated the coordinates, sending a blue light pulse to the south edge of Diamantina Plateau, bouncing it off the multi-angle reflector on top of Rihanna's pyramid and returning the light to the receiver on Beacon Hill and Andre's light meter.

"Okay. Give me the distance reading to multi-angle reflector, please."

Looking through a pair of orange lenses, Jason found the triangular symbol representing the multi-angle reflector on a computer screen. "Eight miles!"

"Eight miles? No, wait! That is not correct! What is the current temperature?"

"18 degrees Fahrenheit," Jason replied. "Do you want me to do another sweep?"

"Yes, another sweep."

"Okay."

"Are you ready, Jason?"

"Yes, I'm ready."

"On my mark…3, 2, 1…mark!"

When the laser displayed the reading on the control panel, the actual distance to the south edge of the Diamantina Plateau in relation to Beacon Hill was correctly measured: Five miles, and the temperature reading on the thermometer was 11 degrees Fahrenheit and falling.

"Everyone working outside had better get inside Alpha, and that includes us."

"I'll set off a flare to get their attention," Jason said. "One illumination flare should be enough."

"No. I'll set off the flare. You seal the outer panel," Andre said.

"Okay."

***

The wind picked up and blew hard against Andre as he set off the flare: Professor Briar's severe weather warning system, a temporary measure until more advanced automated weather stations come online. Andre watched the flare slowly fade in the distance while Jason tightened four screws to seal the beacon's outer panel.

"Here, you keep the hex key. I'm done," Jason said, brushing dirt off his gloves and trousers.

"And where do you think you are going?" Andre asked.

"Marion's Crater," Jason snapped. "We assembled the weather warning station and calibrated the laser beacon." With that Jason started walking away.

"Wait! What is wrong with you, Jason? Did the cold freeze your brain?"

"There is nothing wrong with me," Jason said.

"No? Then tell me why you are acting like an idiot."

"I'm following Tyler's orders!"

"Following Tyler's orders is the right thing to do, Jason. But before we follow his orders willingly, we first must go to Marion's Crater and find Finnegan."

“Finnegan can find his way home without us,” Jason said.

“Stop your childish whining! Finnegan is a good man.”

“Okay, okay, we’ll go and look for Finnegan if it makes you happy. But that guy is a lost cause, and I don’t want to worry about a lost cause. I’m just worrying about myself.”

“Why do you say that?”

“Because Finnegan is a living paradox,” Jason replied. “He had said openly in the press that he no longer wanted to be involved in politics, nor would he have any business dealings with Freelanders, Allied folk, or anyone else. So, he gave away an unfathomable amount of cash to feed the poor, $400 billion and came to Galraithia without a penny. Finnegan can be likened to a condemned man who reflects on all the mistakes he had made during his life and feels sorry for himself only moments before the hangman’s noose ends it.”

“You have Finnegan figured all wrong if you think coming here to Galraithia was a publicity stunt,” Andre said. “Money has no value here and has never been more complimentary to public scrutiny or opinion; he can do whatever he pleases without having a penny in his pocket.”

“I tell you, Andre, something is very wrong with Finnegan. Even rich pricks, like Professor Briar and that self-important Gordon Winthrop, are made from the same mold as Finnegan.”

“The wrong is inside your head, Jason, and I can tell you why,” Andre said, skirting carefully around a sulfur spring. “You have a paranoid personality. Everyone is underserving of your respect; they are out to get you.”

“Really!”

"Yes, really," Andre said. "I think you need to be more like me."

"More like you? Overweight and out of breath."

"Ha, ha, very funny. Seriously, Jason. I am worried about the Allied folk aboard the Endeavour."

"Why? The Winthrop's and the Allied folk didn't waste a single thought on you or any other Russian during the famine of 98."

"I was a toddler when the Russian famine wiped out my entire family. I want to forget that past. I know they are resting in their eternal holy places," Andre said softly.

"I didn't know you were religious, Andre."

"Religious, no. Moralistic, yes."

"Well, these days will also pass away," Jason said quietly. "Resting in an eternal holy place is an excellent thought to cling to. But until then, we look to the future without the Endeavour; it's gone, and everyone aboard must be assumed dead."

***

The area surrounding the hot spring had several active volcanic vents and gigantic fissures filled with incandescent lava. Finnegan was nearer to the largest and most active vent, a fumarole emitting steam and sulfur compounds. The smell of rotten eggs quickly overwhelmed Andre and Jason's sense of smell as they approached Finnegan, who was busy collecting plant samples and filling his backpack with scentless rose-like flowers and cuttings of an odd-looking, low-growing yellow shrub, overburdened with tiny purple berries.

"Hey, Finnegan! How much longer in this stink hole?" Jason asked.

"I need ten more minutes," Finnegan replied after filling his mouth with a handful of purple berries. After eating the handful of purple berries, Finnegan felt a sudden surge of strength inside his body. "These purple berries are delicious," Finnegan said, offering Jason and Andre another handful.

"Hey, we didn't come all this way to see you stuffing your face with berries. There's a storm heading our way. The sooner we get back to Alpha, the better."

"You two can head back now if you want. Don't wait for me."

"You don't have to tell me twice. Are you coming, Andre?"

"No. I'm not leaving, not without Finnegan."

"Andre, it's okay, mate," Finnegan said. "Go with Jason. I left some seismic monitoring equipment, which I need, inside a cave near here."

"Okay, but don't take too long. A bad storm is closing in behind us."

"The cave is along a ridgeline just east of here. I won't be far behind you," Finnegan said, remembering hauling the heavy monitoring equipment along the ridgeline. However, after eating the purple berries, he felt strong enough to believe he could easily carry twice the weight.

Southland

Morning broke in Southland. The sky over Base Camp South was clear, and the Galraithian sun shone above the snow-capped mountains after 59 days of continuous storms and blinding blizzards. It was freezing cold but endurable with appropriate clothing and equipment.

With a joyful smile, Martin turned his bearded face to the sun, put on his goggles, rubbed his gloved hands together, and set the thermostat on his environsuit to a warmer, comfortable setting. When the other team members stepped outside, they were grateful the relentless, powerful winds had petered out during the night. Every team member had experienced freezing temperatures and blizzard conditions before in Antarctica, but nothing like the extreme cold of Southland, particularly the past 59 days and nights.

Joseph had written in his diary all the particulars of the landing on the southern continent. How extreme headwinds during the descent stage caused Icarus to plow belly-first into a deep snowdrift. Still, they had to drive titanium spikes one meter into the permafrost to prevent Icarus from being blown away like a tumbleweed: *"Thankfully, no one was injured when the Icarus lander plowed belly-first into the snowdrift. However, Icarus cannot fly after sustaining critical damage to its engine management system. Regardless of the damage, our power cells are all functional; we have light, warmth, and enough food for three months. Martin, however, is more concerned about the severe weather. He sits by the radar unit all day long, expecting the relentless storm front to begin to weaken, turn northeast, and head out to sea. We are all perplexed about the fact that if we don't reach the north coast in two weeks, we never will."*

Day 10 on Southland: "Strong swirling winds pile up more snow around the portside outer hull of the Icarus lander, covering the two portside viewing windows. The triangular windows let in the only natural light source, so someone must go outside and shovel the snow away. That person is usually me since I draw the shortest straw more often than anyone else."

Day 20 on Southland: "Fierce blizzards and temperatures touching minus 190 degrees Fahrenheit continue unabated, depriving us of much-needed sunlight. We are all ghostly pale and shuffle about the Lander (which is not much bigger than a city bus), counting days and longer nights. But the group has a collective understanding; I don't hear anyone gripe about the cold or cramped living conditions. That said, we all battle with boredom, anxiety, and stress. Taking turns shoveling snow breaks the monotony. It also keeps everyone reasonably fit. I have spent more time outside than I want to remember, tethered securely to the Lander, shoveling endless snow in gale-force winds.

Day 30 on Southland: "The level of wind intensity has not lessened, and my nerves are fraying. How much longer can this storm last?"

Day 40 on Southland: "This morning, the long-range scanner received a clear signal and valuable data from two north coast reconnaissance drones. With the benefit of hindsight, launching those two drones from the edge of space was the best decision Martin could have made. Regardless of the valuable drone data, Martin is furious and openly said that he wanted to kill the person responsible for leaving behind the core sampling unit and the laser drill. Tom Granger did admit to Martin that he had inadvertently loaded the drilling equipment inside the Aquarius, the wrong Lander, and was visibly upset."

Day 50 on Southland: "Leaving behind our primary drilling equipment will be remembered as Tom Granger's unforgivable mistake; Martin cannot trust him to do the right thing. However, mistakes often present an opportunity to turn failure into success. I say this because the two drones that went north have renewed our enthusiasm to continue the mission. Reconnaissance data suggests the landscape of Southland's northern coastline is densely forested, with trees rising higher than 120 feet above fertile soil free of ice and snow. The drones say that the melting is due to heat rising from an underground volcano. Recent volcanic activity has opened deep fissures on the surface of the ice flow. Therefore, on the journey north, great care must be taken traversing what is likely to be a treacherous expanse of ice."

Day 60 on Southland: "A cold and gentle breeze from the south has lifted our spirits this morning; we are heading north on foot."

***

Martin thrived on the thrill of adventure; he was not one to play it too safe. He knew he must embrace calculated risks and step out of his comfort zone to successfully carry out his mission.

His team covered 336 miles in 14 days, navigating thin sheets of young ice, bottomless crevasses, knee-deep snow, and tall ice spires that sparkled like diamonds.

Martin praised his team's hard work establishing weather stations, a communication tower, and arrays that measured magnetic field variations and record seismic activity. Despite their accomplishments, Martin and his team remain isolated; there was a lack of two-way communication between Alpha, the newly named Freelander settlement in

Ashyr, and Martin's team in Southland, advancing north toward the coastline.

***

Joseph had persuaded Martin to give Tom Granger another chance. Against his better judgment, Martin assigned Tom to set explosive charges at specific spots in the rocky debris embedded in an ice stream. "Fire in the hole!" The underground explosion immediately activated geophones and other seismic instruments. "Over here, Joseph. I think I got something," Tom said, showing Joseph the seismic survey results on a display scanner.

"The outline of geological features in this sector is the same as the landing site."

"The geological data is identical. The top layer of ice is two feet thick. But the layer of alluvial soil is only 10 inches deep," Joseph said, looking at the seismographic recordings with Tom. That is when Bill Aldridge approached to say that he had stowed the detonator charges safely away.

"We may need more blasting, do a more thorough job," Tom said.

"Did we dig and blast the wrong test site or something?" Bill asked.

"No. This is the test site Professor Tohvian selected," Joseph said, showing Bill the sector map.

"I have seen aerial survey data for this sector before. I'm sure of it," Bill Aldridge said. "And I remember seeing colored radar profiles of ice layers 200 feet thick."

"This ice is new ice!" Professor Ezra Tohvian declared. "But are we experiencing the beginning of a mini-ice age or the end of one?"

365

"What do you mean?" Bill Aldridge asked.

"We all know our Freelander history; we all remember our first Freelander astronomers and physicists, notably Amanda Klyst and Giovanni Alfiero, and their published journals detailing the discovery of the GY star cluster and Galraithia's galactic location between two stars Dimos and Daedalus. Later, Klyst and Alfiero added the black hole Cygnus Cy7. Galraithia's distance from the black hole worried Klyst and Alfiero until data from the Faxian telescope suggested Galraithia as being far enough away to escape its tidal forces and angular momentum. In other words, Galraithia is influenced by three gravities, which significantly slow down its orbital velocity. Now, with the aid of my ski pole, I shall endeavor to illustrate on the ice that Galraithia has an elongated orbit around Dimos, a G-type sun, and the closest to us, closest to Galraithia, and at the end of the elongated orbit, I shall add the red dwarf sun Daedalus, a dying star at the center of the Canis Solar System. At this particular time, relative to Galraithia's elongated orbital alignment, Galraithia is moving away from its home sun, Dimos, towards faraway Daedalus. Needless to say, we are experiencing the beginning of Galraithia's winter, which could last 90 years, calculating the distance and time traveled to reach the halfway point between Dimos and Daedalus."

Professor Tohvian removed his goggles, wiped his reading glasses with an anti-fogging solution put them on. "The planet's surface will almost be entirely frozen," he continued, "from the poles to the equatorial regions, due to Galraithia's 30 degrees of axial tilt."

Bill Aldridge moved closer to Professor Tohvian. This was a new learning phase for Bill, who proudly carried the wounds and scars of a world-champion rotor fighter. He wasn't born into a Freelander family. He didn't fully understand astronomy, let alone knowledge of Klyst and Alfiero or Galraithia's galactic position in the Canis Solar System. Still, he was a proud Freelander and proudly wore the insignia of Freelander Pilot/ Officer.

"Professor, does Galraithia have a summer phase?" Bill Aldridge asked.

"That is a good question, Mr. Aldridge. Yes, Galraithia has a summer phase. When the planet transitions to and around Daedalus and begins its return journey to Dimos. The summer phase could last 90 years, perhaps longer. According to my rough calculations, Galraithia's elliptical trajectory distance measured in time is approximately 186.8 years," Professor Tohvian said, moving his ski pole up along a line scratched into the ice.

"90 years of winter, 90 years of summer," Joseph said, understanding the complications of long seasonal changes on an evolving Galraithian ecology.

"If you do the math, Joseph, all this snow and the ice will be considerably thicker before the next melting phase begins," Tohvian said. "But don't get distracted by worrying about the future. Freelanders have adapted to the harshest climates on Earth by planning one day at a time and accepting any of Mother Nature's challenges. This is how we shall adapt to this life change regardless of what kind of life we live. Besides, we came all this way to challenge ourselves, did we not?"

"We strive not to fail, Professor. We strive to learn," Martin said, shouldering his backpack just as Marion Tyler rushed out from behind the newly erected radio antennas, her eyes alert and her heart racing. She brushed past Ezra and glanced back at him, saying, "Sorry for interrupting, Professor, but I must talk to the captain."

"It's quite all right, my dear," Ezra said, knowing that Marion was usually quiet. Still, when she had something important to say, she was determined to get her point across.

"What is it, Commander?"

"Captain, still no response from Alpha. Just a lot of static on every frequency, sir."

"Thank you, Marion. Keep trying," Martin said, looking up at a sky clear of atmospheric disturbances to the south and scattered clouds low on the distant northern horizon.

"Yes, sir."

"Brendon, anything on the hand-held radio?"

"Nothing but static, Captain."

"Well, I'm not prepared to sit and wait out here in the middle of nowhere any longer. Brendon, I'm giving you, Aldridge, and Granger the order to return to our little makeshift camp and start packing. We are leaving this sector today and still have work to do. Put the light gear in the small sled and leave everything else behind. And let Joseph know when you see him. Tell him there's a weight limit on every piece of equipment."

"Where is Joseph?"

"He had to go back to the communication tower and recalibrate the tower transmitter; it's not sending a strong enough signal," Martin said.

"The Winthrop Corporation manufactures poor-quality antenna cables, Captain."

"We can't blame Winthrop. Finn Corp supplied all the electrical equipment."

"Aye, sir."

***

Without daily cloud cover, Galraithia's ionosphere disrupted high-frequency radio waves. Looking through her binoculars, Marion saw thin, wispy clouds slowly drifting along the northern horizon. She turned the radio tuner on, flipped the tuner switch on and off, and bounced radio waves off the stringy clouds until four green bars appeared on the transmitter console. "Alpha, do you read me? Alpha, come in, over. Hello, can anyone hear me?"

"I can barely hear you. Hello, this is Roberta Tully speaking...Camp Victor. To whom am I speaking? Your name, please!"

Marion glanced back at Martin, who was running electrical cables for Ezra.

"You are speaking to Commander Marion Tyler. Do you read me?"

"I can barely hear you."

"Captain! I have a weak signal from Camp Victor. It's Roberta Tully, sir."

Martin dropped the data cable and hurried over to Marion. "Good work, Commander," he said as he grabbed the radio microphone, brought it to his lips, and pressed the transmit button. "Roberta, this is Captain Brindle. Do you read me?"

"Hello, Captain. There is too much static interference. I can barely hear you, sir."

"Is there another active frequency?" Martin asked.

Marion jiggled a corroded coaxial cable connected to the radio transmitter.

"Changing frequencies won't fix the radio static," she said, unplugging the cable and handing it to Martin. "This cable was in a sealed package just 30 minutes ago. It's frustrating not knowing how it got corroded so quickly."

"The insulating metallic braid has failed somehow," Martin said. He twisted the cable between his fingers and exposed more shiny copper and steel wire to the Galraithian air. The wire almost instantly began to corrode before his eyes, and soon turned into a blueish green powder.

Marion plugged another cable into the back of the radio transmitter. "This coaxial cable is stranded silver encased in braided aluminum shielding."

"How long will the shielding last?" Martin asked.

"I'm not entirely certain, sir," Marion replied, feeling her frustration ease as Martin held the microphone.

"Roberta, if you can hear me, we are 80 miles from the north coast. Support...no endpoint! Do you copy?" Martin shouted into the microphone.

"Support no endpoint! I don't know that code, sir," Marion said.

"Support no endpoint is a Freelander Navy rescue code, meaning: There is no way to get home without your help! Please come quickly," Martin said.

"Support no endpoint! Understood," Roberta Tully said.

"Selenographic coordinates: 19S 21N... ETA 18 hours. Do you read me? 19S 21N, ETA 18 hours, copy?"

"19S 21N..." Roberta Tully's voice sounded very faint over the static before the radio signal faded and her voice cut out.

Marion's head dropped as she removed her headset. "We lost the radio signal, sir."

"Well, that's that!" Martin's face showed frustration to the point of anger.

"You did the best you could, Commander. Thank you." Then Martin turned to Ezra, "Professor Tohvian! Our coaxial cables, connectors, and attenuators are corroding at an alarming rate. Any ideas on how to stop the corrosion?"

"My atmospheric research has not enlightened me on that score, Captain."

"Is there a better insulator to stop the air attacking the steel and copper strands?" Martin asked.

"Let me see what I can do to fix the problem when we return to camp."

"Okay. Start packing your gear; we'll leave soon."

Ezra removed his balaclava and bowed his bald head, feeling the bitterly cold northerly wind blowing hard at him. "I am at your command, Captain."

Ezra quickly adjusted the focal length of a zoom lens attached to the deployable time-lapse camera; he had decided to leave the time-lapse camera behind to observe the speed and motion of glacial ice. At the same time, Joseph scrambled over moguls of crusted snow and returned to the makeshift camp on the other side of the canyon where Brendon and Bill were busy loading the gear sled and preparing to leave.

"Hey, Brendon! Did the fabricator power up okay this morning?" Bill asked.

"No. The batteries didn't produce enough power, and the connectors were corroded. It's bizarre."

"We have spare connectors and batteries," Joseph said, removing his skis.

"No, sir, we don't. There's corrosion inside the battery box assembly and the cable terminals," Brendon said.

"We have to leave the fabricator behind, Joseph."

"The fabricator is essential equipment, Bill. We'll get it repaired when we get to Alpha."

"The captain wants the light gear in the small sled and everything else left behind. There's also a weight limit on every other piece of equipment," Brendon said.

"The captain knows what's best; he knows our strengths and weaknesses, but let's hope we don't live to regret his decision," Joseph said ruefully.

"The captain has made the correct decision; only short rations are left in the food container. We either move fast or starve out here on the ice," Bill said.

"You should know the captain by now, Bill. Martin does not tolerate failure."

"I'm sure the captain's thoughts are pushing us away from that unacceptable conclusion," Bill said.

Joseph nodded. "Now, I came here to lend a hand packing. Do you want me to help?"

"Thank you, Joseph. I can use a hand to move the fabricator," Bill said.

"Okay. I'll help you move the fabricator. That high rocky outcrop and ice wall offer protection from the elements."

"I'll throw a weatherproof cover over the fabricator. I'm sure someone will return here someday," Bill said.

***

When Martin returned to camp, he entered the day's events into his daily journal. In the journal, he wrote he felt like a failure for having to call for help; Roberta Tully would rally Group 2 South to mount a rescue mission. Martin and his team had 18 hours to reach the northern coastline and had to move fast. Martin exited his tent and called out to Brendon. "We're leaving the small sled behind! Unpack it, distribute the water bottles and the food satchels. And Brendon, bury the sanitation containers."

"Aye, sir."

"Brendon can help Ezra. Bill and I will bury the sanitation containers," Joseph said.

"I don't care who does the work. Just get it done before we leave," Martin commanded.

Joseph quickly removed his jacket and woolen undershirt, showing off his six-pack stomach.

Brendon shook his head in disbelief. "Mr. Arunui, please don't remove your clothing, sir. The temperature with wind chill is minus ten degrees Fahrenheit."

Tom Granger strolled by with a smirk on his face. He could never be accused of being overly enthusiastic about his duties, and avoiding physical activity was his specialty.

"I can't believe what I'm seeing. The great Joseph Arunui is digging a hole," he scoffed.

Waist deep in a hole in the ice, Joseph leaned on his shovel and looked up at Tom.

"Have you come to help?"

Tom shook his head, still wearing his arrogant smirk, and casually walked away from Joseph and Bill.

"Come back, Granger! Grab a shovel and do some hard work for a change," Bill said.

Marion was disgusted by Tom's vulgar response. Turning away, she spotted Martin packing his tent away. "Captain, may I have a word with you?"

"Certainly. What's on your mind, Commander?"

"I have an idea that could save us a great deal of time, sir."

"Okay. I'm listening."

"Captain, if we deploy our parafoil kites while this favorable wind is at our back, we could reach the north coast in 10 hours."

"Parafoil kites can be dangerous, especially for inexperienced kiters. Professor Tohvian and Commander Granger are inexperienced kiters."

"You are right on that score, Captain. Both men need more experience to handle a parafoil kite. However, we have a favorable wind behind us. If it continues, Professor Tohvian, Commander Granger, and the others would support the idea."

Martin needed time to think; he couldn't risk anyone getting hurt or, worse still, left behind because they couldn't keep up.

"You are worried. I can see it on your face, Martin. Please forgive me for being unduly familiar, Captain. I meant no disrespect, sir."

"There is nothing to forgive," Martin said, realizing he had feelings for Marion. However, this was not the place for a budding emotional attachment, nor did he have the time.

"Professor Tohvian and Commander Granger can easily handle the Freelander kites. They are lightweight and highly forgiving. I will demonstrate the proper training procedures to ensure they can fly the kites safely, Captain."

Feeling the cold wind in his face, Martin remembered moving to Antarctica from Western Australia with his family and the popularity of kite skiing during his teenage years.

"Okay, Marion, you convinced me. Now, you have to forgive me for being unduly familiar."

Marion's smile softened, her pale blue eyes radiating warmth and empathy. More importantly, they expressed happiness being close to Martin.

"Come on. Let's go back to camp and tell the others," Martin said.

***

Martin was leading the group, flying his orange parafoil kite over the powdery snow. Joseph, Brendon, and Bill followed a few yards to his left, waving and smiling, having a great time. Marion and Ezra flew their kites lower in the sky to Martin's right. With Marion's assistance, Ezra quickly learned to control his parafoil kite. However, Martin was disappointed with Tom, who was struggling to keep up and needed assistance to maintain his speed and line. Granger, lacking experience, refused help and had a poor relationship with everyone, including Marion. Her attempts to mother him only angered Tom. As time passed, Tom watched the kites getting smaller and realized that he would be left behind if he couldn't catch up.

Martin had a pained expression on his face as he tugged hard on the right side of the kite control bar. He was reluctant to direct his parafoil kite away from Tom and towards the snow-covered horizon. This action reminded him of his childhood in Antarctica and the lessons his father had taught him about flying parafoil kites. Martin's father had always emphasized the importance of steering the kite properly.

"Remember, you steer the kite. The kite does not steer you."

"Yes, Dad. I understand. I steer the kite, not the other way around."

"Good boy. Now, race me to the old missile silo. If you win, I'll fry some goose eggs for breakfast. But if you lose, you'll have to wash dishes for a whole week."

"Dad, I'm faster than you on skis."

"Let's not waste any time then. Remember, it's not about winning or losing; it's about having a good time."

***

Camp Victor

Professor Briar made a wise decision choosing Lt. Cdr. Satori Thomas to lead Group 2 South to the southernmost point of the Frey Peninsula. Although the professor had initially planned to lead the expedition himself, his persistent respiratory infections made it impossible. Doctor Mason advised him to stay indoors and avoid the severe cold and chilly winds lashing the Ashyr Plain. Selecting a capable leader like Lt. Cdr. Thomas ensured the success of the mission.

Group 2 established their camp at the southernmost point of the Frey Peninsula. At the insistence of Commander Thomas, Roberta Tully was the first to set foot on the peninsula. Immensely proud of her Freelander heritage, Roberta named the narrow peninsula after Doctor Lucien Frey, her great-grandfather, and Western Australia's first Freelander leader.

The Frey Peninsula, which was 240 miles wide and extended southeast for 1,420 miles into the Ithinian Sea, had its southernmost tip as the closest point between the northern continent of Ashyr and the southern continent, Southland. The Freelanders who had settled in Ashyr were geographically close to Southland, yet they remained entirely oblivious to the significant events that had transpired there. Unbeknownst to them, a towering ten-foot metal pylon had been erected by Martin and his team to commemorate the historic first crewed landing on the bitterly cold southern continent. Additionally, a state-of-the-art communication tower had been established to connect Southland with Ashyr, providing access to an automated weather data system. Despite Martin's mission objective of establishing a connection between Southland

and Ashyr, the effort proved to be an abysmal failure. The atmospheric conditions of Galraithia created distortions in the radio waves, rendering communication with Ashyr unmanageable due to poor radio reception and static interference.

***

Massive swells rolled eastward across the north Tezarian Ocean, gathering power over miles of open water before thundering against Ashyr's rocky northern coastline. Far to the south, a different world existed—the Ithinian Sea's calm, nutrient-rich waters lapped gently at coral atolls and pristine white beaches that encircled volcanic islands thick with vegetation.

The largest of these volcanic peaks stretched across the equator in a continuous arc, their chain extending eastward through a wide strait peppered with rocky islets. This tropical abundance stood in stark contrast to Southland's western shores, where steep ice cliffs and deep U-shaped valleys carved a barren, windswept landscape.

Yet Southland held surprises. Recent drone data revealed that its northern region flourished with dense forests and abundant freshwater streams. Plant life thrived here, offering edible fruits to potential inhabitants. Aerial observations from space confirmed what the initial surveys suggested: the northernmost territory provided ideal conditions for settlement.

The southern continent told a different story entirely. Early images captured by the Faxian telescope's equipment showed a forbidding landscape—a dry landmass buried beneath a two-mile-thick ice sheet, where winds screamed across the frozen wasteland at speeds exceeding 450 mph.

Martin and his team of explorers understood the data they collected, which outlined Southland's climate. Professor

Tohvian, their astrophysicist and glaciologist, explained how Galraithia's elliptical orbit around two suns affected its climate now and in the future. He also described how the shadow of Ithinia, Galraithia's largest moon, impacted surface temperatures in the northern and southern regions.

***

Roberta Tully had received Captain Brindle's scratchy radio message and quickly informed Commander Thomas of Martin's dire situation. The Southland team led by Captain Martin Brindle had completed two objectives: establish a communication link between Ashyr and Southland and construct a weather station. Their third and final mission was to find edible wild plants and animals in Southland, but their efforts were unsuccessful. Martin's team blamed the mission planners for taking them through moguled terrain and deep crevasses hidden by snow and thin ice. With their food running out fast, survival depended on a rescue mission led by Commander Thomas. Martin was confident they could be rescued, reassuring the team that they weren't too far from Alpha, the first and largest human settlement on Galraithia, which lay across an alien sea.

***

Planning the rescue mission was easy, but putting the plan into action was difficult due to the drained power cells of the All-Terrain & Amphibious Rover (ATAR). Satori and her team members offered many suggestions but needed help understanding how or why the power cells failed. Brand-new power cells and corrosion-resistant materials should not become brittle and break. Satori hoped Professor Lin would produce an answer to the power cell problem.

379

"It is unacceptable to have critical failure alarms in any fuel cell," Satori said, "and we have three fuel cells and three backup electrical systems offline."

"ATARs were specifically designed for reliability, but the chemical oxidation process is causing the ATARs electrical equipment to corrode faster than moist air rusts iron," Professor Lin said, showing Satori chemical formulas with blank spaces, the unknown components of Galraithia's air. "The corrosion problem cannot be resolved here, Commander. We must return to Alpha so I can continue my research on Galraithia's atmosphere."

"You can continue researching after we fix the ATAR and rescue Captain Brindle and his team," Satori said.

"Commander Thomas, our survival on this planet depends on electrical systems and equipment. If we don't find a way to stop the corrosive attacks, it's game over. Do you understand me?"

Veronica Blainey stepped closer to Professor Lin. "Why don't you walk back to Alpha? No one's stopping you."

Professor Lin squinted at Veronica, a tall, fair-haired, strapping strong girl from a very influential Freelander family. "I have not made up my mind one way or the other. Even though I think walking alone anywhere on this planet is unsafe," Professor Lin said.

"Well, if you decide to return to Alpha, I will happily accompany you."

"Thank you, Veronica. I appreciate your support," Professor Lin said.

While Professor Lin and Veronica discussed a safe route back to Alpha, Major Nikolayev walked by to talk to Satori and Roberta Tully. During their conversation, she gave them detailed plans for a wooden boat, including a mast and sail. "I think building a boat is a great idea," said Roberta. "We have all the necessary tools and plenty of good timber here."

Satori rubbed the back of her neck, feeling anxious. "Building a good-sized boat takes time and hard work."

"Talking won't build the boat. Let's get to work," Major Nikolayev said.

***

In Alpha, the corrosion problem had led to electrical outages, which caused a lot of controversy and division among the Freelander colonists. In an effort to address the issue, Father Sandor called for a meeting in the large dining hall where everyone was encouraged to actively participate in the discussion of the data collected from Galraithia's air, water, and soil. The samples showed no evidence of Earth-born bacteria or contaminants corroding plastics, aluminum, copper, and steel. Father Sandor announced that due to the presence of corrosion in the condenser tubes, the power plant and solar generators would be shut down until the root cause of the corrosion was identified and resolved. This decision had been taken to ensure the safety and well-being of all individuals associated with the power plant. Furthermore, the corrosion had also impacted the refrigeration system, which may lead to a shortage of fresh food supplies. This announcement caused quite a stir among the people gathered in the dining hall. "Settle down, people!" Professor Briar commanded. "Don't all talk at once."

"There is no need to panic as we have more than enough fresh water and dehydrated food to last us through this challenging time," Father Sandor declared confidently.

381

"Rationing is just a temporary measure. Let's stay positive and tackle this challenge head-on," Professor Briar said.

Murillo of Gascony, a French pollinator working for the Growers Association, expressed his disappointment and frustration. He accused Father Sandor and Professor Briar of misleading the Freelanders. "You made us believe that Galraithia was a planet similar to Earth, a land of promise and hope," he said, pointing at Father Sandor and Professor Briar. "But where is this promised land? As far as I can see, it's certainly not here."

The Frenchman's words angered Jonas Flint, the leader of a 100-member team of crop pollinators sent to Galraithia by the Royal Pollinator Society of Great Britain.

"Professor Briar! Murillo of Gascony is not our spokesperson!" Jonas Flint shouted.

Murillo fixed a look on Flint, his dark eyes piercing and intense. In a few quick strides, he closed the distance between them, to stand mere inches away from Flint. His voice dripped with contempt as he spoke, "Your so-called 'Royal Society' is nothing but a group of mindless lemmings, blindly following William Briar and a renegade priest down a path that leads to nothing but extinction."

Two burly security guards approached Murillo to escort him from the dining hall.

"Step away. Let him speak," Professor Briar commanded.

Murillo nodded in appreciation, his eyes lowered. "There are serious worries about the long-term viability of the Alpha settlement. Our fabricators are all offline and have corroded inner parts. We have no electricity or refrigeration; our fresh food supply spoils while we sit around crowded tables and talk."

"I completely understand where you're coming from, Murillo of Gascony, and I couldn't agree more," Professor Briar said with empathy. "Life can often seem unreasonable, but here we are, on an unfamiliar planet, doing our best to make sense of it all. As Freelanders, we're committed to facing any challenge that comes our way."

Amidst the bustling dining hall, the doors suddenly flung open, and Chief Fredericks hurried in, appearing slightly out of breath. He swiftly approached the crowded tables and stood beside Professor Briar and Father Sandor at the front of the room.

"I am thrilled to share some good news for a change," he exclaimed, eyes scanning the room to meet everyone's gaze.

"Good news is always welcome," Professor Briar said.

"Doctor Vikram Raipur of the science team has isolated the known chemical components in Galraithia's atmosphere, but a new unknown element exists as a gas. Doctor Raipur believes this invisible gas is the probable cause of the corrosion," Chief Fredericks said.

"The probable cause?" Murillo interrupted. "Actions speak louder than words, Chief."

Chief Fredericks scowled at Murillo defiantly. "Please, let me speak!"

"Then speak up, man!" Murillo said in a rasping voice. "Tell us what preventative measures Doctor Raipur has taken to stop the corrosion."

"Ensuring the safety of electrical circuitry is of utmost importance," stated Chief Fredericks with conviction. "Our primary measure of success is fiberglass tape, which has proven to be effective in encasing the circuitry. However, in science, we know that nothing can be one hundred percent certain. Therefore, we continue to explore and test new measures to guarantee the safety of our electrical systems."

"Let me make it clear to everyone in this room. Doctor Raipur and his team of scientists require additional time for testing and improvements," Professor Briar said. Then turning to Chief Fredericks, "While your honesty and openness are appreciated, Chief, we must prioritize the quality of our work over meeting the deadline."

Professor Briar focused on Father Sandor and asked if he had any final thoughts before the meeting was adjourned. Father Sandor took the opportunity to speak up and express his opinion. "It is important to note that when we work together as a community, we can use our collective intelligence to overcome any challenge."

Professor Briar and everyone in attendance nodded in agreement.

"Lastly, before I conclude this meeting, I want to inform you that another meeting is scheduled for tomorrow morning," Professor Briar announced loudly. "Doctor Vikram Raipur will be attending the upcoming meeting to address any further questions or concerns you may have regarding the corrosion problem. Thank you for your patience and support."

The mood changed in the dining hall; the air was filled with fearful whispers and anxious mutterings as people began to leave. Father Sandor waited until the hall had emptied before approaching Professor Briar.

"You didn't disclose the information about the bacteria," Father Sandor said urgently, his expression serious.

"No. The news about the bacterial threat will soon spread across the settlement," Professor Briar replied.

"Why do you say that?" Father Sandor asked.

"I told Dr. Raipur to keep the atmospheric findings confidential until Joseph and the others return, but I know Vikram can't keep his mouth shut about anything," Professor Briar said.

"Have Joseph and the Southland team established radio contact?"

"Group 2 South received a somewhat distorted message from Captain Brindle," Briar replied, "but it was still understandable until the radio signal was lost due to static interference."

Stoddard's Canyon

Doctor Raipur held a detailed briefing on the morning of the mission to Keyway Valley and Stoddard's Canyon. The mission aimed to explore several lava tubes and deep caves in the canyon previously discovered and explored by Michael Stoddard. However, there were still many that required further exploration. Commander Tyler and his team attended the briefing and were well-equipped for their mission with the highly advanced all-terrain vehicle, Rover-2. It was specially reconfigured with a new interior and a stronger engine to ensure they were well-prepared to accomplish their task. Unfortunately, Jason Tohvian, one of the team members, wasted exploration time discussing the new engine with Dr. Raipur. It was already late in the morning, and Commander Tyler was upset with Jason for causing delay. He even threatened to exclude Jason from the team but Professor Briar intervened. Briar's decision was not influenced by the fact that the Tohvian family was one of the oldest and most respected Freelander families. According to Professor Briar, Jason Tohvian was recommended to be a part of Tyler's team because of his exceptional numerical aptitude and mechanical skills.

***

By mid-afternoon, Tyler's Group 2 North had explored the lava tubes in the rocky northeast quadrant of Stoddard's Canyon. The biggest and the most extended lava tube measured 31 miles long, 60 feet high, and 70 feet wide. Andre Zarovski recorded in his daily log that the lava tube was spacious enough to conceal an army. *"While geologists may disagree, the most significant discovery inside the lava tubes is the clean water that flows into deep pools. I am confident that there are longer and deeper lava tubes and caves containing sedimentary rock layers, which will lead to fossil localities in the Keyway Valley and Stoddard's Canyon. These findings will provide invaluable insights into Galraithia's geological history."*

After heading east for about 10 miles, Rover-2 stopped at the entrance of Stoddard's Canyon. Michael Stoddard had discovered the canyon and had showed remarkable ingenuity by constructing a small stone hut using flat stones. Positioned on the highest point of the jagged cliffs, the hut offered a panoramic view of the Keyway Valley and shielded him from the ferocious winds that battered the cliffs. Michael's humble abode became his sanctuary for more than a month. During his stay, he had chanced upon an extensive cave system camouflaged by towering hedges swathed in yellow leaves and an impenetrable thicket of thorn bushes.

***

Rover-2 dipped and swayed, making steady progress up a steep slope. Then, without warning, the engine just cut out as Rover-2 crested the canyon. Jason raised the engine panel and swore under his breath. "The batteries are utterly drained. There's yellow powder on every electrical circuit." Alistair jumped into the driver's seat and began jabbing the power button out of frustration.

Jason reached out and grabbed Commander Tyler's wrist. "The engine won't start, sir. The electrical system is offline."

"Doctor Raipur had predicted this would happen, but no one believed him," Andre said.

Jason looked over his shoulder and noticed Andre wrapping every electrical cable and connector with fiberglass tape. He shook his head and said, "Andre, wrapping every electrical cable is a waste of time. This corrosion isn't caused by the usual suspects like the interaction of corrosion gases in the atmosphere or prolonged exposure to water. It's something else."

Rihanna approached Jason as he was intently focused on collecting yellow powder with a flat-head screwdriver to deposit it into a glass vial. "What exactly do you mean by something else?" Rihanna asked.

"Doctor Raipur told me that he had discovered an unidentified strain of alien bacteria in soil samples. This yellow powder is the indicator of alien bacteria feeding on electricity, whereas the grainy white powder indicates dead bacteria and the absence of current flow. I must admit that I didn't fully comprehend everything Doctor Raipur said. His Freilish language skills are not the best."

"You did the right thing by telling us about the yellow and white powder, Jason. It's a difficult time for everyone without electricity, and I'm here to help in any way I can," Rihanna said.

"We have had numerous electrical outages since the first landing, and we all blamed Gordon Winthrop and his corporation for selling us substandard electrical equipment," Andre said. "But the real culprit is alien bacteria."

"Jason, did Doctor Raipur discuss this particular matter with anyone else?" Alistair asked.

"Not that I'm aware of, sir. He said he would provide all the required details at the appropriate time."

"Is there anything else we should know about the alien bacteria in the soil," Rihanna asked.

"You should know that Doctor Raipur doesn't know how to keep his big mouth shut," Alistair said, slamming the reinforced engine cover hard.

"Doctor Raipur is undoubtedly one of the most intelligent individuals I have ever met," Jason countered.

Alistair caught Jason's right arm and tightened his grip as he spoke assertively and loudly for all to hear, "It is crucial to maintain the confidentiality of the information regarding the alien bacteria until we better understand the situation."

"I was brought up believing it's better to be open and honest with people," Jason said.

Alistair frowned. "It is crucial to maintain the confidentiality of the information regarding the alien bacteria. Until we better understand what we are dealing with. Do you understand me, Jason?"

"It's likely that news about the yellow and white alien bacteria has spread throughout the settlement by now, sir."

As Rihanna approached Alistair he looked away and opened Michael Stoddard's paper map.

"Alpha settlement's survival depends on our ability to prevent harmful bacteria from spreading," Rihanna warned Alistair. "The consequences of stalling any immediate actions could be disastrous…wiping out the entire population."

"Okay, okay! I'll tell you what I do know," Alistair said. "Dr. Raipur led a team of researchers who sent reconnaissance drones to gather planetary information before achieving a stable orbit around Galraithia. Upon their return to Phoenix, the reconnaissance drones were found covered in a yellow powder, a type of alien bacteria that corrodes metal and plastic. The alien bacteria had corroded the drone's outer shell casing to feed off electrical current coursing through the drone's inner circuitry. Due to time constraints, the corrosive effects of bacteria were not adequately discussed; the landing phase of the mission had priority. However, there is more."

Alistair rubbed his forehead as if trying to rid himself of the tension building inside his head. Speaking with calm authority, Alistair emphasized the information he was about to share must not be disclosed to anyone outside the team. He said that Professor Briar and Doctor Raipur were concerned about a white powder, a new strain of alien bacteria in Galraithia's soil that fed on electrical current and affected metals, plastics, and human tissue. "It is important to note that when alien microorganisms come in contact with damaged human tissue, there is a high risk of infection. Currently, no specific antibiotic is available to treat this strain of bacteria, which makes it crucial to exercise caution and avoid any cuts or abrasions until an appropriate remedy is developed. You can understand why this newly attained knowledge is sensitive and divisive. However, hard decisions will be made soon and an effective plan must be implemented to protect everyone and everything, and it is best to avoid making assumptions that could cause confusion and panic among the colonists." Alistair hoped his message was clear to everyone.

"Doctor Raipur is brilliant, but he is also an overthinker," Andre Zarovski said in his thick Russian accent. "I was the acting Science Officer during shift B when I witnessed something extraordinary. The Drones returned to Phoenix with their titanium shells glowing white hot and displaying a pitted white rust appearance. The event was remarkable and had the potential to change our understanding of alien bacteria forever. After researching, I discovered that covering the circuit board and connectors of the drone with fiberglass tape can temporarily prevent the corrosive effects caused by bacteria that feed off the drone's electrical circuitry. This process has no negative effects on the drone's functionality."

"Fiberglass tape was only a temporary fix," Alistair said, scanning the high canyon walls that divided an arid, flat landscape. Green and yellow shrubs sprawled across the distance in scattered clumps, threaded with purple grass.

"Father Sandor believes that working together can solve any challenge and create positive change in our lives," Rihanna said. "Let's start by believing a solution is waiting to be discovered, and it's somewhere out there."

"Sandor is an intelligent scientist, but he is also a priest," Andre said.

"I trust Father Sandor completely," Rihanna said. "He pledged his unquestioning loyalty to the Freelander people. You chose The Brothers of Anarchy."

"I pledged allegiance to The Brothers of Anarchy because my family did not survive the Russian Civil War," Andre said. "My parents were highly educated, but their knowledge didn't provide for our family. We had to rely on government food trucks, but unfortunately, they frequently arrived empty or sometimes didn't arrive. If we had a small patch of land and some vegetable seeds, my parents and sister Eva would be alive today."

"The Brothers of Anarchy were cold-blooded killers," Rihanna said openly.

"Yes, cold-blooded killers who threatened all of Europe and Asia. Today, those killers have a different name: Freelanders," Andre countered.

"Andre and Rihanna, stop chitchatting, grab your gear, and start walking," Alistair commanded.

***

Due to insufficient electrical power, Rover-2 was disabled by a corrosive yellow powder. Alistair's new exosuit showed stiffness in its metallic joints and signs of corrosion, which caused the servo motors within the enclosed circuitry to overheat and ultimately led to the suit's failure. With no other choice, the members of Group-2 North had to walk 15.6 miles back to Alpha, relying solely on their own physical strength without their exosuits. Along the way, two unexplored caves were added to Michael Stoddard's paper map. After closing the map, Alistair made his way to the eastern edge of a 1,450-foot cliff. From there, he gazed out over a deep gully running north and a vast stretch of sheer cliffs blanketed in purple grass and low yellow shrubs.

"It's beautiful!" he exclaimed, captivated by the breathtaking landscape.

Earlier, Alistair had told Michael he hadn't expected to see such a variety of colors and subtle shades within Ashyr's mixed forest zone. Quickly, he set up his rappelling gear and nylon ropes, preparing to descend into the gully below. But Rihanna suggested they pause for lunch and savor the stunning view. They eagerly awaited two mini castabraun sandwiches filled with shredded organic lettuce and diced tomatoes. Alongside the sandwiches, they each enjoyed a pack of peanuts, a bar of dark chocolate, and two small bottles of water.

After finishing his lunch, Andre felt a twinge of unease at the thought of rappelling down the sheer cliff. Yet, a familiar fragrance carried on the soft breeze caught his attention—an unexpected scent on Galraithia, one he associated with Earth. The smell of freshly cut hay transported him back to his early childhood, long before the wars and catastrophic famine ravaged his homeland. In those simpler days, life was filled with the warmth of family and friends, and the air echoed with happiness, laughter, and overflowing love.

"Andre, harness up," Alistair commanded. "Help him, Jason."

"Yes, sir," Jason said, then quietly muttered, "… *Jason, do this. Jason, do that.*"

Heart racing, Andre peered into the deep gully below, his mind consumed with a paralyzing fear that threatened to swallow him whole.

"Okay big guy, you're good to go," Jason said confidently.

Andre moved cautiously to the edge of the cliff. His mouth was dry, and his right leg trembled from nervousness. "Jason! I don't know if this thin rope can hold my weight. This is crazy!"

"Just tighten the rope so it won't sag too much and stop worrying. Regolith fiber rope can hold twice your weight."

Andre could feel sweat trickling down his forehead as he descended the steep cliff face, making it hard to see. He paused to wipe it off, taking a deep breath before continuing his descent. Suddenly, Andre felt the rope slack, sending a jolt of fear through his body. With his heart racing, he clung onto the rope for dear life, hoping it would hold his weight.

"Don't look down!" Alistair shouted, his voice echoing through the vastness of Stoddard's Canyon.

"You're doing great, Andre! Don't let Alistair get to you," Rihanna reassured him with a smile. Alistair responded by flipping Rihanna off, but she just laughed and blew him a kiss playfully. Andre's confidence grew. He rappelled down with a steady brake hand, pulling his thin rope slowly across a carabiner brake and varying the speed of descent.

Rihanna, Jason, and Alistair stepped off the edge together, but Jason was the quickest to rappel down. He removed his harness and approached several truck-sized boulders and dense thorny thickets that could slash and cut the unwary.

* * *

All four had safely rappelled down to the bottom of the cliff face. They fanned out in different directions. Rihanna, with her camera in hand, captured the essence of the alien landscape. Alistair, his hands covered in dirt, carefully examined the soil and rock samples he had collected. Andre, following closely behind, marveled at the unique plant life. Many of these stood without any notable amounts of chlorophyll, the natural green pigment found in many plants and algae on Earth.

Jason strode puposefully past the others, until he reached a specific point marked on Michael Stoddard's map. The point was nestled between two ridges that sloped dramatically from east to west. The steeper and longer ridge was a rugged terrain, its surface adorned with large igneous boulders and broken rocks of various sizes. In stark contrast, the lower ridge was a sandy expanse, its soil a pale yellow, and it was home to vibrant shrubs with purple berries. It made for a burst of color in the otherwise muted landscape.

Jason gazed up at the ridge top, noticing that the ground ahead was steep and uneven, and it continued to rise higher and steeper toward the summit. He realized he had gone too far ahead of Alistair and the others. They were two miles further back, so he stopped and waited briefly. Jason scanned his surroundings, hoping to catch a glimpse of the others and hear the loud echo of Andre's voice. However, Jason soon grew impatient and blamed Alistair for slowing everyone down. He thought Alistair habitually spent too much time examining the surrounding geology and collecting too many soil and rock samples.

***

Jason lifted his gaze and glanced at the eastern horizon. "Where are the others? Galraithia's sun is at its zenith; sunset is a few hours away," Jason muttered. He took a deep breath and started climbing towards the ridge's summit alone. Hurrying, Jason stumbled on the uneven ground. He quickly regained his balance and cursed his carelessness. While catching his breath, Jason spotted what appeared to be a stairway nearby. Upon closer inspection, he realized it was an excavated stairway in the rocky ground, making the climb more accessible and safer. Jason stared at the elaborate stone carvings (petroglyphs) on the first step. The stone carvings described a group of people joyously celebrating. *Perhaps the celebration means to honor the arrival of the Freelanders on this planet*, Jason thought. Renowned photographer Michael Stoddard had discovered and partially explored this geologically diverse region of Ashyr and marked down several interesting caves on his map. However, he had not mentioned anything about rock-cut steps or stone carvings. Michael Stoddard referred to this cave as the most extensive, the highest and of great geological value.

Why Stoddard did not elaborate further left Jason puzzled.

Jason rummaged through his backpack for his camera, but it wouldn't turn on, possibly due to the damage caused by his fall. After opening the battery housing, he noticed white powder inside. He recalled taking a few photos before putting the camera down on the ground for a few minutes to have lunch. Somehow, alien bacteria in the soil drained the camera's power cell. Now Jason could not fulfill his promise to Father Sandor of taking photographs of anything

he considered typically alien. He felt he had let Sandor
down.

*"Anything interesting, weird, and bizarre, I want to know
about it," Father Sandor had said.*

***

Climbing the rock-hewn stairs cautiously, Jason arrived at
the entrance to Stoddard's cave, curious to see what was
inside. Although Jason had thought all the caves he had
ever visited looked the same, he couldn't wait to explore
this particular dark, unexplored cavern on an alien
world. However, Jason decided against entering the maw.
Instead, after a brief pause, he walked away from its dark
entrance, leaving Galraithia's geological secrets hidden
within for the time being. He descended the stairs and sat
on the first step, taking a chocolate bar from his backpack.
He savored every bite and thought that waiting for the rest
of the group to catch up was the best option. As minutes
passed, Jason grew increasingly impatient as Andre,
Rihanna, and Alistair were nowhere in sight. He walked
back up the stairway and reached an overhanging ledge just
a few feet away. From the high ledge, Jason saw Andre
waddling cautiously between thorny shrubs.

"What took you so long? Where are the others?" Jason
yelled.

"Not too far behind. Wait there. I'll only be a few minutes,"
Andre said even though he desperately needed to empty his
bowels. Jason smiled, although he appeared irritated. He
was aware of Andre's habit of running late, so he
proceeded into the cave alone.

***

As Jason ventured deeper into the cave, the mineral
deposits on the walls caught his eye, shimmering like tiny

396

mirrors in the flickering torchlight. Above him, crystalline stalactites hung like delicate chandeliers from the ceiling, while stalagmites of all shapes and heights rose from the floor as if quietly keeping some ancient vigil. Rounding a smooth bend, he stumbled upon an oval chamber that seemed almost otherworldly. The high ceiling glittered with calcite crystals, and the floor was adorned with flowstones arranged in intricate patterns no human eye had ever charted. It felt like stepping into a surreal cathedral carved by nature on an alien world. Jason reached out, letting cool droplets from the ceiling bead on his fingers. Surprisingly, this part of the cave lacked the usual musty scent, replaced instead by a fresh, earthy coolness. Searching for a path deeper inside, he traced the damp wall with his hand until a small hole low to the ground revealed itself. Crawling through on his belly, he entered a dimly lit inner chamber. There, resting on a rock shelf, lay a collection of dusty books. Carefully wiping away the dust, Jason revealed gilt titles still sharp despite their age: *From the Earth to the Moon*, *The Time Machine*, *Forbidden Planet*. Flipping through yellowed pages and faded ink, he wondered if Michael Stoddard had accidentally left these treasures behind. Slipping the books into his shoulder bag, Jason prepared to return them to their rightful owner.

***

As Jason left the dim inner chamber and squeezed through a crevice large enough to fit through, he found himself in another open area with two beds made from long timber pieces. Moving closer, Jason shivered at the sight of complete skeletons on the beds. One of the skeletons had a broken thigh bone (femur) and a fractured pelvic bone (pelvis). The other had a crack and a gaping hole in the skull above the forehead. Jason also found some pieces of clothing partially buried in the sandy soil. Everything was handmade; Jason figured the material was not cotton or wool, but twines of sisal grass interweaved and stitched together with fine strands cut from tree bark. Jason moved silently and reverently away from the skeletal remains to another spacious chamber. On a high wall, he noticed charcoal drawings, crude maps, and Chinese symbols representing water, air, and fire. The drawings included the planets of our Solar System, with Earth painted in bright blue. Jason noticed a deep crack in another cave wall rising into the ceiling as he explored the capacious chamber. Upon shining his torch through the gap, he peeped into a small chamber and saw human skulls set into grooves in the cave wall. The skulls, with eyeless sockets, stared at him while their grinning teeth silently laughed at him. Suddenly, a familiar voice echoed back and forth inside the cave.

"Jason, where are you?" Andre shouted. "Hey! Can you hear me?"

Racing thoughts flooded Jason's mind; he had much to say and little time to think about the grinning skulls or the skeletal remains. Jason rushed back into the dimly lit room and crawled through the hole in the wall. "Stop shouting. I'm not deaf," Jason said, brushing away some of the dirt on his belly.

"I was worried," Andre said. "You didn't answer when I called you."

"I was too distracted by what's on the other side of this wall," Jason said, noticing Andre's bloodied forehead and cheek. "What happened to you?"

Andre explained to Jason how he had stumbled over loose rocks on the way up. "You need not concern yourself about me, Jason. It's just a bruise and few scratches."

"You're a big oaf. Why didn't you use the stone steps leading up to the entrance?"

"Steps!" Andre yelled, opening Michael Stoddard's map. "There are no steps marked on this map."

"Stoddard is too security conscious. He didn't mark the location of this cave either," Jason said. "But you'll understand why soon enough."

Andre looked up at the vaulted ceiling, exposed white limestone 20 feet high. He could hear water dripping into a water pool hidden behind some rocks. "How deep is this cave?"

"Deep enough," Jason replied, moving into the oval chamber.

Andre paused several times to survey the oval chamber, which was 30 feet wide and had a high, domed ceiling 39 feet above the rocky floor.

"On the other side of this rock wall, there's a small hole leading into another chamber, a burial chamber," Jason said. "Inside, there are two wood-frame beds and the skeletal remains of two humans and human skulls resting in niches carved into the rock."

"Burial chamber! Skulls and bones!" Andre whispered. "Have you gone mad, Jason?"

"Go and look for yourself if you don't believe me. I'm going down to the gully and see if I can find Alistair and the others."

"Jason, wait!"

"Crawl inside through the small hole on the other side of this wall," Jason said, touching the cold cave wall which was illuminated by a beam of light from a crack in the ceiling, about 20 feet above. Andre couldn't help but think that Jason had gone mad. But his friend was intelligent, and nobody's fool. Andre walked around the cave and looked at the walls and floor and inside every crevice. This cave was similar to any other one he had ever visited, and there were no signs of human presence inside except two sets of boot prints, his and Jason's. No holes in walls, human bones, or skulls. Coming to the cave had been a complete waste of time for the big Russian. Andre cautiously emerged from the chilly cave, mindful of the loose rocks, and returned to the gully.

***

An hour had passed when Andre heard a noise coming from behind a row of thornless yellow bushes unique to particular areas of Ashyr. He peered over the top of a massive boulder and saw Alistair approaching. Andre emerged from behind an enormous boulder.

"Ah! There you are," Alistair said.

"I thought you'd never get here. What took you so long?" Andre asked, scanning the area for Rihanna and Jason. "Where are the others?"

"I'm not sure about this," Alistair said skeptically. "Jason wants to show Rihanna a burial chamber he found in Stoddard's cave."

Andre clarified that the burial chamber Jason referred to was not inside Stoddard's cave but inside Jason's head. Alistair looked at Andre, silently conceding that the chance of finding a human burial chamber inside a Galraithian cave was unbelievably improbable. After a brief silence, Jason's voice broke the quiet. "Hey, you two! Come on up," Jason shouted excitedly from the cave entrance.

"I am not going in there again," Andre said.

"I don't blame you, Andre. It's not an easy climb to the top," Rihanna said; then adding with a shout, "Hey, I can see Finnegan! He's at Horseshoe Canyon!"

Alistair instructed Rihanna to signal their location with an orange flare for Finnegan.

"Okay."

As the orange flare arched across the sky, a high-pitched whistle echoed around Horseshoe Canyon. Finnegan acknowledged their location by firing a whistling green flare. He responded with a silent green flare to indicate that he intended to rejoin Group 2 North. "He's on his way here. He should arrive in about thirty to forty minutes," Rihanna shouted

Alistair smiled warmly at Rihanna and gestured a thumbs up in approval.

"You go up to the cave. I will stay here and wait for Finnegan."

"No. You are coming with me," Alistair commanded.

"I am not a geologist! Rocks, caves, are of no interest to me."

"Andre, follow my orders, please."

"Okay, okay. But we both proceed with caution. The path leading to the cave is steep and slippery," Andre said, pointing to the dried blood on his forehead and cheek.

"Jason mentioned stone steps," Alistair said.

Andre shook his head. "Jason is a clever man, but sometimes he makes ridiculous statements."

"I'm only telling you what Jason told me himself."

"Look around, Alistair. Tell me what you see."

Alistair stopped halfway up the slope to suck air and look around and see the stark beauty of the surrounding cliffs. "I see steep cliffs, mica stones, igneous boulders, very few flowering shrubs."

"You can stop looking, Alistair. The stairs exist only in Jason's mind."

***

Upon entering the cave, Jason and Rihanna could be heard arguing loudly by Andre and Alistair.

Jason yelled, "There was a hole in this wall. I had to crawl through it on my belly to get to the other side. I'm not lying."

"Jason, this wall is made of solid limestone," Rihanna said.

"What is going on here?" Alistair asked.

"Jason needs help," Rihanna replied.

Alistair cast a questioning glance at Jason.

"Commander, there's a burial chamber right behind this wall. It contains human bones and skulls. I even found a pile of books. I'll show you," Jason said. Rummaging through his backpack, he found no books inside. Jason could not understand what was happening and saw only questioning looks around him.

"Michael Stoddard discovered the cave but did not report the discovery of the burial chamber to either Professor Briar or Father Sandor. Why?"

Andre said, "Stoddard never set foot inside this cave. I found only two boot prints, yours and mine, Jason."

402

"Michael Stoddard was here, I tell you."

"Michael discovered the cave, but he didn't survey or explore it," Rihanna said.

"That's enough from both of you! Pass me the seismic scanner, please, Rihanna," Alistair exclaimed. He placed the base of the seismic scanner on the wall and held it there for a few seconds. "The entire length of the wall is solid limestone rock," Alistair reported.

"Hand-held scanners are unreliable," Jason said, glaring at Rihanna.

"There is nothing wrong with my scanner!" Rihanna declared.

"And there is nothing wrong with my eyes, Miss Wakeman. I know what I saw!"

"Jason, it's clear that you had a hallucination. Why are you refusing to admit it?"

"Why are you so reluctant to admit that you are wrong?" Jason asked, stepping uncomfortably close to Rihanna.

Alistair stepped between them, frowning. "Are you two still arguing?"

"Commander, we should head back home. We have wasted enough time here," Rihanna said.

"That is a great idea, the best I've heard all day," Andre said, as he moved towards the upper level of the cave. Jason was walking beside Andre when he suddenly stopped and looked over his shoulder. Andre looked at his friend with concern. "Are you okay, Jason?"

"If I look at the wall, I see the small hole through which I crawled earlier. Is it clearly visible to you or am I hallucinating?"

"I see water running down the wall, seeping into a narrow crevice," Andre said, ushering Jason toward the fading light at the exit of the cave.

"Stop, wait! I'm feeling dizzy, Andre. Why is my head pounding inside?"

"Because you are stressing yourself out for nothing. Don't worry about anything. I will help you, Jason."

Andre held Jason's right arm, and saw mounting frustration on Jason's face.

"We have plenty of time left. There is no need to rush. But you must report your medical condition when we return to Alpha."

"I'll be okay, Andre. Thank you."

"Margaret Mason is a good doctor, the best we have. She will fix the problem inside that stubborn head of yours," Andre said, smiling.

***

Galraithia has only two seasons, a short summer, and an exceptionally long winter. Both seasons are dangerously unpredictable. Winter has arrived early. The Cradle Mountains are covered in a reasonable amount of snow. However, Professor Briar's winter model for Galraithia is little more than guesswork. The Freelanders are not adequately prepared for their first Galraithian winter. Astronomers claim there will be time to prepare during Ròlegur, the quiet time between the two Galraithian seasons. Back on Earth, Ròlegur falls between the last week of Spring and the first week of Summer, with peaceful stary nights and perfect weather days. Unlike Earth, however, Galraithia has 30 degrees of axial tilt, and its slow journey along an elongated elliptical orbit takes

186.8 years to complete one orbit around the sun's Dimos and Daedalus. As a result, the consensus among astronomers is that Galraithia undergoes prolonged periods of extreme temperature fluctuations, particularly in the northern hemisphere, where soil and plant sampling studies suggest the freezing cold of a typical Galraithian winter is more than 90 years.

So, several prominent astronomers proposed pulling up stakes and moving the Freelander settlement to the Equatorial Zone of Galraithia before the long winter set in. Professor Briar and Father Sandor agreed that protecting the Freelander colonists was crucial.

Alistair's Group-2 North entered the Alpha settlement before the sun dipped below the horizon.

Along the way, Jason lost consciousness and needed immediate medical attention. Carrying Jason on a stretcher, Andre and Finnegan hurried towards the Habitat ring and the medical unit.

"Stop right there! Don't come any closer," said the young man on guard duty.

"What do you mean, 'don't come any closer?' Our friend needs urgent medical assistance!" Andre declared.

"Decontamination procedures dictate otherwise. I have strict orders from Doctor Mason."

The young man, dressed in a blue hazmat suit and yellow gloves, approached cautiously. He carried a Sequanta tablet with an integrated printer. He distributed quarantine cards and instructed everyone to remove their clothing and place it in a bag.

"Ty tupoy ublyudok," Andre said in Russian. "My friend is unconscious and needs a doctor right away!"

"Please remove his clothes and place them in a quarantine
bag. I won't repeat myself!"

As Rihanna started to undress and put her clothes in a bag
for quarantine, she turned to Andre. "You should do as the
young man says," she told him, standing fully naked,
covering her breasts and private parts with her hands.
Another man assigned to the decontamination chamber
stood in the doorway, shamelessly leering, until he tore his
eyes away from Rihanna.

"Hey, old man! "What are you carrying inside those bags?"

"I think he is referring to you," Andre said to Finnegan.

"What's inside those bags? Or do I have to come down
there and see for myself?"

"Small ganitte crystals, a few plant cuttings, various seeds,
and berries in one bag, and dirty underwear in the other,"
Finnegan said, casting the man a disapproving look.

"Remember to fill out the quarantine card and print your
name on both bags. Then, place the bags inside one of the
yellow boxes in the quarantine area. Understand?"

Rihanna glared at the man and said, "Yes, mister, we all
understand. There's no need to shout."

Finnegan and the others entered the outer decontamination
airlock. They were tired and cold, and no one spoke as the
airlock door closed and the decontamination cycle started.
Jason suddenly woke up, found himself naked, and leaped
off the stretcher.

"Where are we?" Jason asked, looking around the airlock.
"What's going on?"

"Inside the decontamination airlock, waiting for the cycle
to finish. How's your head?" Andre asked.

"Pounding headache. Hurts something fierce."

Then Andre yelled some colorful Russian curses at the guard overseeing decontamination.

"Almost finished, sir. Two more minutes."

After thoroughly drying the cleansing solutions on their naked bodies, a Microvax sequanta computer dispensed blue coveralls and matching anti-static slippers before opening the Decom airlock door. Andre and Jason stepped out of the airlock. They proceeded down a brightly lit, chilly corridor toward the medical unit. At the same time, Alistair, Finnegan, and Rihanna hurried to a debriefing room to review the events of the Keyway Valley mission.

****

Doctor Margaret Mason and Doctor Allan Porter were inside the central medical unit, busily treating colonists with flu-like symptoms, debilitating headaches, heart inflammation, and hallucinogenic experiences. First, Doctor Porter checked Jason's health condition and helped him to an empty bed. Then, Andre stood at the edge of Jason's bed and watched the doctor inject an antipyretic drug directly into Jason's neck to stop the hallucinations and cluster headaches.

"Thanks for the pain relief, Doc."

"You're welcome, Jason. Try and get some sleep."

"An excellent idea," Andre said. "Jason, follow Doctor Porter's advice. I'll come back later." "Andre, thank you for helping me."

"I did nothing. You and Martin Brindle saved my life," Andre said, remembering the Mount Vinson avalanche.

"That was a long time ago," Jason said, calmly, closing his heavy eyes.

"Doctor Porter, I must go to debriefing. Jason will be okay, yes?"

"Until we know the biochemical makeup of the allergen inside Jason's brain, I can honestly say I do not know. But we must not lose hope, Andre."

***

The storm hammered Alpha with relentless fury—dust clouds spiraling like dervishes, lightning crackling across the sky, and wind howling at over 200 miles per hour as Professor Briar and Father Sandor ducked into the medical unit. While the debriefing room buzzed with heated discussions about the power cell failures and Jason's disturbing hallucinations during Tyler's Keyway Valley mission, a more sinister crisis was quietly unfolding. Behind the chaos of mechanical breakdowns and psychological episodes, colonists were dropping like flies—wracked with burning fevers, bone-deep exhaustion, and flu symptoms that seemed to worsen by the hour.

"Margaret, I know that you and Doctor Porter are terribly busy," Briar said. "I won't take up too much of your precious time. How many people have reported sick today?"

"ICU (intensive care unit) has admitted twelve adults and three children," Margaret informed him. "That brings the number of infected to 86."

"Fifteen today, eighteen yesterday. The numbers are going down," Briar said.

"There are changes in our favor, William, but it's too early to tell."

"And Jason, how is he doing?"

"Like the others, Jason is responding to the medication very slowly. The headaches are gone, and he is showing no symptoms of hallucinogen intoxication."

"Well, that is a good sign."

"William, you are pushing our young people too hard."

"Our young people are stronger than you think."

"Jason is not as strong as you think, William. He barely survived the cryosleep. He needs time to recuperate from the stress effects of prolonged cryosleep and more time to acclimatize to the thinner, drier air."

Doctor Mason and Professor Briar noticed how Ludwig had become quiet and withdrawn over the last few days. "You are noticeably quiet, Ludwig, are you okay?" Margaret asked.

"I confess, I am tired, but I won't use tiredness as an excuse not to work."

"You are working too hard, Ludwig. Spending too much time in Keyway Valley," Professor Briar said.

Margaret understood Briar's unsympathetic attitude toward human weakness, but Briar expressed empathy toward anyone who had the moral courage to take risks for potential rewards. "Lanfen told me about the delicious purple berries she found," Margaret said.

"Yes. The berries are delicious though the glossy purple plant is very slow-growing and found only the Keyway Valley thus far," Father Sandor said.

"You ate the berries without thoroughly testing them first?" Professor Briar asked.

"Yes. I apologize, William. We know we made a mistake."

Margaret's eyes met Father Sandor's, and the familiar ache stirred in her chest. He had seen her at her lowest—those dark months in Garrawi when depression had wrapped around her like the endless wheat fields surrounding their remote farming community west of Sydney. The heartache of her marriage to Philip Mason had nearly consumed her, each day stretching into the next with suffocating sameness.

But Father Sandor had thrown her a lifeline. As Garrawi's parish priest, he'd guided her through the worst of it, and when her divorce was finally behind her, he'd made an unexpected suggestion: "What if you started over completely? Dome Halley needs someone with your expertise."

Antarctica. The idea should have seemed absurd—trading Australia's scorching heat for the world's most unforgiving continent. Yet something about the research opportunities in cryogenics and space medicine ignited a spark she hadn't felt in years. More than that, William Briar was there. Her brilliant friend from university days had relocated years earlier to restore the century-old Dome Fuji radio telescope, and the thought of reuniting with him felt like a sign.

So she'd done the unthinkable—packed up her children and chased winter to the bottom of the world.

"Sit down here," Margaret said, pointing to a chair. "I want to take some blood and run a few tests, just to rule out a few nasties that could be floating around in your bloodstream. I'll be gentle."

"I said, I feel fine. I'm just a little tired."

"Clearly, you're not!" Margaret replied.

"At least your hands are warm, unlike that infernal machine," Father Sandor said, referring to the offline medical fabricator inside its magnetic hatch.

"You should be thanking medical fabricator 36M for keeping you alive while you slept in your cryo-bed."

"We should all be grateful," Professor Briar said. "Without their help, I don't believe most of the upper-tier colonists could have survived cryosleep."

"Speaking of upper-tier colonists," interrupted Margaret. "I could do with more help down here."

"Okay. I'll ask Professor Lin. I'm sure she would like to help. Would you agree, Ludwig?"

Father Sandor didn't reply; he was now sound asleep in the chair.

"Leave him alone, William. Let him sleep."

"Is he okay?"

"No, William, he is not okay," Margaret whispered. "His lungs are inflamed, but there are no detectable traces of bacteria or pleural effusion. But, William, I want to emphasize that there are 86 colonists with the same symptoms. So, I don't know what to do other than place them back in cryosleep."

***

The sun set, and darkness enveloped Ashyr. Beneath a starlit sky, Roberta Tully, Margaret Gray, and Veronica Blainey prepared the evening meal: castabraun patties made from white, flaky eel meat mixed with sultanas, raisins, lemon pulp, and grated lemon rind to balance the rich flavor. As they sat around the campfire, Commander

Thomas, Major Nikolayev, and Professor Lin praised the three cooks for their efforts.

"The meal looks delicious. Thank you."

During dinner, everyone discussed the Southland rescue mission. Growing more despondent, Satori needed time to think; after dinner, she left the campsite and walked towards the ATAR. She stopped when she noticed a red light illuminating the ATAR's interior. "Where is the light coming from? The ATAR has no power," she said aloud. Opening the rear hatch door, she moved empty food storage containers and drilling equipment. Then, she saw the glowing Van Wagner crystal attached to one of the self-powered laser drills. The Van Wagner crystal could generate energy for underwater drilling equipment and was a reliable heat source.

Satori hurried back to tell the others still talking around the campfire about their personal journey to Galraithia. Professor Lin's eyes widened when she saw the glowing Van Wagner power crystal.

Early the following day, Professor Lin and Major Nikolayev attached the power crystal to the ATAR's twin electric motors and gearbox, connecting the driveshaft to the propellers.

Working hard to fix one problem, Professor Lin, and the Russian Major uncovered other urgent issues.

"Traveling on solid ground, the ATAR can accommodate a maximum of twelve people," Major Nikolayev said. "But in the water, there is a maximum weight allowance, no more than nine people."

"Then we strip-down the ATAR, lighten it up," Satori said.

"Commander, that won't be necessary," Professor Lin said. "Veronica and I have decided to leave the Group-2 South and walk back to Alpha."

"Okay. That leaves us with Margaret and Roberta. You two must decide. Stay, or go?" Satori asked. Margaret looked at Roberta. Their close friendship during their university years had bloomed into a serious romance. They had been inseparable ever since.

"Roberta and I would like to stay behind, with your permission," Margaret said.

"Yes, we would like to explore an underwater cave and do some rock climbing," Roberta said.

Satori nodded. "Okay," she said. "Major Nikolayev, your decision, please."

"Commander, this rescue mission presents the opportunity to see the southern continent and the honor of being the first Russian cosmonaut to cross an uncharted alien sea."

***

Before sailing away, Major Nikolayev and Satori wrapped every electrical connector with fiberglass tape. Winthrop Corporation had a poor reputation for reliable radar/navigation systems and communication equipment. "I have no confidence whatsoever in this electrical equipment."

"Major, we must make do with what we have."

The ATAR entered the water early the following day. The Ithinian Sea was calm with a favorable tidal current. With glassy seas and barely a whisper of wind, the ATAR maintained a steady 20 knots towards the southern continent, a full day's sail ahead.

***

Captain Brindle tossed his rigid daily schedule aside—they were making exceptional time slicing through the ice sheet that carved between the Fortress Mountains like a frozen river. As dusk painted the sky in bruised purples, they pitched their temporary camp and methodically inspected each parafoil kite, searching for the telltale splits that could spell disaster.

Joseph retreated to his solitary ritual, hunched over his diary as he catalogued the celestial tapestry above. One hundred and thirty constellations blazed across the southern sky, but three burned brightest against the black velvet canvas: Canis Lupus prowling overhead, the sinister curve of Serpent Head, and his personal favorite—Waka Taua, named for the Māori war canoe it resembled as it sailed through the star-drunk darkness.

Meanwhile, Tom Granger worked frantically to salvage his reputation. He'd cobbled together a makeshift Pharnas Lamp from spare parts—a portable generator married to water testing equipment in mechanical desperation. The long handle groaned under his determined cranking until the electric charge sparked to life, igniting the vacuum-sealed cocktail of CO_2 and nitrogen trapped in the glass tube. The gases burst into luminous yellow fire, a beacon powerful enough to pierce the Southland night for fifteen miles.

"I'm extremely impressed with your work, Tom. The Pharnas could prove useful as a signaling device."

"Thank you, Captain."

"The lamp is too small, and the light it gives off is rather dim," Ezra Tohvian said. "But Tom and I have disagreed before. Goodnight, Marion, goodnight, gentlemen."

"Goodnight, Professor."

Sunrise, 5:30 a.m. Solar Local Time. A laser-thin red line stretched across the southern horizon for a few seconds. Major Nikolayev and Commander Thomas changed course and steered away from the open sea. Straight ahead loomed the northern tip of the continent and the entrance to a wide and ice-free bay. "Slow ahead, Major."

"Slow ahead, aye, Commander. Turquoise is your lucky color, but red clouds are approaching. Is that a bad omen?"

"No, Major, where I come from, turquoise water and a red sunrise are considered good omens. Ready two green flares and set the height at 5,000 feet, please."

"Flare tube ready for firing. Height set at 5,000 feet, Commander."

***

Meanwhile, Martin and his team saw the northern coastline but had stopped five miles from the breaking waves to help Tom Granger. Unfortunately, he misjudged the depth of mogul and tumbled ass-over-head on the ice. Bill and Brendon rushed up to help. Brendon reeled in Tom's kite, which was flapping uselessly low to the ground. Bill took hold of Tom's right arm and tried to get him to his feet.

"Let go of me and leave me alone," Tom said.

"Suit yourself, dickhead."

"What happened?" Captain Brindle asked, using his body weight to offset the up force generated by his snow kite.

"I got on the wrong side of a deep mogul, sir."

Brendon looked at Martin. "Tom's wrist is badly bruised, but it's not broken, sir."

"Harden up, Granger, you're letting the team down," Bill Aldridge said.

415

"Why don't you just leave me alone?" Tom snapped.

"Tom, do you think you can control the steering bar with one hand?" Captain Brindle asked.

"I'll do my best, sir."

Suddenly, a high-pitched whistle echoed in the distance. Martin looked up at the sky and saw a Bonhoeffer flare shining like a bright green star. The flare slowly drifted down towards the frozen ground. Martin opened his backpack, picked up a flare gun, and loaded the Bonhoeffer cartridge. Aiming skyward, he shot the Bonhoeffer flare and shouted, "Cover your ears!"

Marion pressed her hands to her ears as the memories rushed back. She could see herself as a child again, watching in amazement as her father lit the fireworks to celebrate Rachel Sibley's birthday.

"Joseph is the fastest on skis," Martin said. "Go on, Joseph, meet up with the rescue team. We won't be far behind you. Hurry!"

"Okay."

***

Joseph reached a rock-strewn northern coastline, reeled in his parafoil kite, and removed his skis. He scrambled clumsily to the crest of a hill of rough ice and saw an ATAR stopped at the edge of a rocky cove five miles away. Sliding down to the hill's bottom on his butt, Joseph clipped into his skis and rushed towards the ATAR. The doors of the ATAR were pushed open, and Joseph was momentarily surprised as Satori came out and walked towards the high ice terraces that were too steep even for an all-terrain vehicle to negotiate. The thin snow covering was hard underfoot, but scanning around her slowly, she could tell the best route around the overly steep terraces of ice was more than a mile away. Instantaneously her heart started pounding, and her eyes widened when she saw a lone skier hurtling downhill, approaching her at a controlled speed.

"Hello!" Joseph yelled, taking in deep breaths, and waving his ski pole at her.

"Hey!"

She took Joseph's hand, and their eyes met. "So, you made it to here in one piece. I'm so proud of you, Joseph."

Joseph kissed her waiting lips. It was a perfect moment; time seemed to stop for Joseph and Satori. They both had the desire to spend the rest of their lives together.

***

Martin wasn't too far behind them. Skiing down a steep slope, he slowed his forward momentum and turned his skis upwind, away from the parafoil kite. Looking towards the cliffs and at the water's edge, he saw Major Nikolayev, Satori, and Joseph waving and hurrying to greet him.

"Captain Brindle, it's good to see you."

"Major Nikolayev, it's great to see you," Martin said, shaking the Major's hand.

"Commander Thomas, you look well!"

"Thank you, Captain. I'm glad to see you, sir," Satori said. "But where are the others?"

"About two miles south of here. Marion stopped to investigate some odd-looking metal debris buried in the ice. I think she found the wreckage of Joseph's missing reconnaissance drone. I don't recall the exact coordinates, but I remember the drone dropped out the sky over the northern coast and came down seven miles inland."

"Electrical failure?" Major Nikolayev asked.

"No. Pilot error. I was the guy remote-flying Joseph's toy at the time, and he hasn't forgiven me yet."

Marion, walking cautiously on thin ice, spotted Martin standing near the ATAR talking to Major Nikolayev. Joseph and Satori were further away, sitting on Joseph's backpack and looking out toward the choppy Ithinian Sea.

"Marion, stop!" Martin yelled. "It may not be safe to cross there, thin ice. Warn the others."

"Aye, sir," Marion said as the other team members approached a large area of slippery flat ice. "We understand the dangers, Captain, thank you," Ezra said.

"Captain, the ice is about to break up under my feet. Where should I cross?" Tom yelled.

"Walk towards me, all of you. But do not bunch up, walk single file."

***

The ATAR remained anchored at Southland, her crew watching the sky darken with gathering clouds. Beyond the harbor, the ocean heaved with mounting fury—swells that had been manageable at dawn now rolled like liquid mountains, growing more violent by the hour. Galraithia's twin moons hung at full phase, their combined gravitational grip tightening as they swept toward perigee, stirring the planet's waters into a frenzy.

The crew felt torn between frustration and relief. Nobody wanted another delay, but the weather station's forecast painted a brutal picture: torrential downpours, gale-force winds shrieking across the water, and tidal surges that could swallow a ship whole. Sometimes the wisest courage was knowing when to stay put. So, Martin thought it unwise to leave the protected bay, which he had aptly named Ròlegur Bay.

"Brendon, how much food do we have leftover in the food container?"

"Less than one day's ration, Captain."

"We might have to stay here a while longer," Martin said.

"Aye, sir," Brendon said, grabbing Tom's injured wrist.

"Hey, that hurts!" Tom said, gritting his teeth.

"Shut up and keep still. I have to use the rest of this wrap to stabilize your wrist."

The massive swell pounding the coast delayed the ATAR's departure and talk of a cluster of small islands excited Ezra Tohvian.

"Skirting the islands would offer some protection from the gale-force winds," Satori said.

"Would you agree with me, Captain, that going the direct route to the southeastern tip of the Ashyr Coast is the better choice?"

"Yes, Major, the direct route to the Ashyr Coast is the better choice. Navigating around the islands without precise geographic details would be extremely dangerous."

"Visiting the islands presents a higher degree of risk," Ezra said. "However, there may be significant quantities of freshwater, edible fruits, as well as animal life. Therefore, I propose an excursion to the largest island."

"Professor, the radar unit on this ATAR has a limited range, and it's unreliable," Joseph put in.

Brendon taped Tom's wrist, and Marion handed out a ration of oatmeal biscuits.

"Ezra, there's another storm approaching, and you want to go exploring?" Marion said.

"Marion, it's in everyone's best interest," Ezra countered.

"Going home together is in everyone's best interest," Brendon said firmly.

"Professor Tohvian, for the time being, exploring the islands is out of the question," Martin said.

***

After numerous discussions, the group decided to sail past the islands and return at a more opportune time. During this journey, Brendon discovered a bottle of overproof rum in a medical kit. He opened it and shared the contents with others. As Joseph sipped the warm liquid, he became more talkative, and Satori appeared more receptive to his flirting. However, an argument broke out between Major Nikolayev and Marion. Marion claimed she had found the top of a birdcage buried in the ice, along with other smaller cages meant for animals like mice and rats. Major Nikolayev dismissed Marion's claim as nonsense, despite her being an intelligent woman. "How ridiculous!" Major Nikolayev snapped. "Do you really expect us to believe such nonsense?"

"It's not nonsense; there's unmistakable evidence, the mesh pattern, the seed catcher, and the guano."

"Marion, calm down! The Major has the right to voice her opinion," Martin said.

"Calm down? The Russian bitch is calling me a liar!"

"Enough!" Martin yelled.

"I'm sorry, Captain, but I don't take kindly to being called a liar."

"I said, that's enough."

As the light faded, tempers simmered down to a slow boil, and everyone bedded down for the night.

***

Major Nikolayev woke early the following day, and under an overcast sky, navigated the ATAR out of Ròlegur Bay. The waves were ten feet-high as they crashed head-on into the ATAR, causing it to pitch steeply forward, backward, side to side, washing over its roof. Brendon, trying to stop a persistent water leak from entering the cabin, locked the underside of the ATAR's glass sunroof.

"Hey, Granger, you're turning green!" Brendon said. "I'd give you a spew bag, but we don't have any." Brendon laughed loud and hard. "Here, use this," he said, tossing Tom an astronaut helmet.

"Hey! You two had better call it quits with the insults and disrespect, or you will be out there and swimming home."

***

The Birds of Paraihe Island

Late in the afternoon, Brendon sat in the navigator's chair, taking his turn on watch while Martin and the others rested. Brendon looked out the forward viewing window, noticing a few scattered clouds floating on the distant horizon. The Ithinian Sea was calm; a light breeze was blowing from NNW. He quickly turned his attention to a large reef and an unexplored island looming off the ATAR's starboard side. Brendon named the island 'Paraihe' and noted the coordinates on a radar-generated map. Then, far into the hazy distance, Brendon saw a smaller island. He thought the island looked like it was floating between the sky and the sea. Brendon named the small island Mataririki and was about to manually enter the name into the navigation computer when something cast an enormous shadow over the front of the ATAR. Brendon jumped out of the navigator chair and scrambled up a retractable ladder attached to the rear of the ATAR and onto the roof. Feeling the air warm and humid, Brendon wanted to dispel the previous day's frigid winds from his mind, but he couldn't dispel from his mind the shadow that passed over his head; hundreds of seabirds and countless more were circling above Paraihe Island.

"Ne, betta en ekki ebla," Brendon said in Freilish. "No, this is not possible."

He hurried below to wake the captain. "Captain, wake up! There are birds outside, hundreds if not thousands flying about."

"Aitama, you are a nuisance! Go away and let me sleep."

"Come on, Captain, wake up!"

Brendon called everyone to the round port side window.

"I don't believe what I'm seeing!" Ezra exclaimed. "There are hundreds of seabirds outside! I'm going up on the roof to get a better look. Coming, gentlemen?"

"Right behind you, Professor," Bill said.

Bill and Tom joined Ezra on the roof. Brendon had time to grab the camera from his backpack. He took photographs of a great flock of hungry sea birds hovering over schools of dragon-winged crustaceans breaching out from the depths of the Ithinian Sca by the thousands.

"Martin, you are surprised to see birdlife just as much as we are," Joseph said, climbing into the driver's seat and turning on the front and rear windshield wiper system. "Galraithia has diverse ecosystems which are like those of Earth. But we've known this fact for some time now. So, look at all this…life…it's mind-blowing."

"I'm going topside for a few minutes," Martin said. "Slow down to idle speed and keep the bow into the wind. We don't want to get tossed around too much up there on the roof."

Satori and Major Nikolayev exchanged glances. Marion didn't seem at all interested in the island or the sea birds. Without saying a word to anyone, Marion retreated to the sleeping compartment. "She is a stubborn, obtuse woman," Major Nikolayev said.

"Marion is different," Satori said, "that's what I like about her. And it's obvious to me that Captain Brindle likes her a lot and certainly enjoys her company."

"I really don't care one way or the other," Major Nikolayev said, somewhat taken aback by Marion's statement.

"Are you jealous of Marion?"

"Jealous of her? Of course not!" Major Nikolayev replied with a disdainful glare.

***

"Captain, the birds fly out to sea from Paraihe Island," Ezra said, looking through his binoculars.

"Paraihe Island?"

"Captain, I've taken the liberty of naming the two islands, Paraihe and Mataririki. I hope you don't mind, sir?" Brendon said.

"No, I don't mind," Martin replied, smiling. "Your Māori ancestors adapted to their new environment. The Freelanders will do the same here."

"Paraihe island is a vast garden laden with strange colorful plants and fruit, a virtual paradise," Ezra said.

"Happy, Ezra? You found what you have been looking for, finally."

"I have waited for this day for over 40 years, Captain. Islands full of exotic flowers and lush green forests are a botanist's dream."

"Well, take a good look, Professor, because we are leaving."

"Leaving? Captain, you cannot be serious!"

Martin was serious. He climbed down the ladder, and he looked eager to leave the sheltered waters around Paraihe Island and head out towards the open sea. High in the sky, two hungry eagles soared and circled in tandem over the foaming alien sea. One was a brown-bodied juvenile with distinctive diamond-shaped white and brown markings on both wings. The other raptor was slightly smaller with a bright yellow head and band of white neck feathers, which indicated a female nearing the end of its life cycle. Regardless of age, her eyes were sharp. She was patient, an experienced hunter, unlike the juvenile diving down towards the water at high speed and overtaking its prey by pursuing it. The young raptor caught a dragon-winged crustacean skimming the water's surface around the head and dug its sharp curved claws into the crustacean's scaly skin. Then, flapping its great wings, the young raptor carried the dying crustacean towards the high cliffs of Paraihe island. Above a sandy beach overcrowded with seabirds, the young raptor did the unexpected; it dropped its hard-won prey. Only then did the old female raptor swoop down silently with wings half-folded. She gained more speed, snatched the crustacean mid-air, and flew off towards a high cliff.

The sharing of food between the two eagles continued for several more minutes. Then, finally looking away, Tom focused his attention on the long-range spectrometer scanning the interior of Paraihe Island. The entire island was a kaleidoscope of colors mixed in every combination.

"Granger, I need a hand with the high-gain antenna!" Brendon shouted, the sound of his voice drowned out by thousands of screeching, squawking seabirds.

Tom rolled his eyes and didn't leave his seat to help Brendon.

"Hey, Brendon, I'll come up and give you a hand," Bill said, glaring at Tom.

"Okay, Bill."

Joseph sat himself down at the control console with Satori. She ran through the system checklist of the high-gain antenna. "Turn the antenna anti-clockwise. Two clicks!" Joseph shouted to Brendon.

"The spindle head is stuck! The antenna won't budge!" Brendon replied.

Bill handed Brendon a spray bottle of liquid graphite. "Spray this stuff on the adjustment screw locknut."

"I can try, but it will take a while; the spindle head is stuck tight, man."

Ezra and Major Nikolayev had been capturing the island's wild beauty through their camera lenses—the sweeping vistas, the colossal birds riding the thermals—when death plummeted from the sky without warning.

The giant eagle struck like a feathered missile, its shadow blotting out the sun as it dove toward the four Freelanders trapped on the ATAR's exposed roof. For one fatal heartbeat, they stood frozen in disbelief, watching the magnificent predator's wings beat the air into submission while it hovered overhead, its razor-sharp beak snapping inches from Major Nikolayev's face.

Then the bird's massive talon raked across her throat in a blur of motion. She crumpled backward, blood fountaining from the gaping wound as her body toppled over the rail and hit the water with a sickening splash.

The ocean erupted into a feeding frenzy. Within seconds, the water became a churning crimson cauldron as razor-toothed fish boiled to the surface, their frenzied attack stripping flesh from bone. Satori and Marion's screams pierced the air while Joseph killed the engine, the crew stunned into horrified silence by the revelation of these aerial killers.

The eagle wheeled overhead, taunting them with predatory patience. Brendon flattened himself against the roof, arms shielding his head, while Ezra—desperate to escape—

slipped in the spreading pool of blood and plunged into the crimson waters below.

"Straka! Ezra, Straka!" Bill yelled in Freilish. "Swim! Ezra, swim!"

Brendon wanting desperately to help, slid perilously close to the edge of the ATAR's roof. He pleaded with Ezra to swim hard and straight toward the portside boarding ladder, but the great bird still circled, flying low above the water. Everything happened so fast; the giant bird clutched Ezra's right leg and lifted him out of the water. Ezra let loose a painful scream and was aware of being carried towards the high cliffs. That was the last time anyone saw Ezra Tohvian alive.

"Joseph, get us out of here! Fast!"

"Yes, Martin."

Joseph pushed the throttle lever forward. The ATAR's undercarriage rose out of the water to complete a full turn at high speed, before it headed straight out for the open sea. Meanwhile, Bill was still up on the roof, legs straddled apart to keep his balance. But as the ATAR picked up on speed and bounced over the swell, Bill turned to climb down into the cabin through the open sunroof. Then, out of nowhere, another fierce bird of prey swooped down and Bill found himself lifted off high into the air, wide-eyed with fear and screaming. Kicking his feet wildly, talons dug deep into Bill's flesh. He somehow managed to pull out his belt knife, began to stab the bird's underbelly repeatedly. After holding on to him for several long moments, the raptor let out a screech of pain. The tiring fighter was thrusting the blade deeper, getting closer to delivering a mortal blow. When the dying eagle dropped its prey, Bill let out a victorious cry, and they both plunged into the sea.

Thousands of ravenous flesh-eating fish were instantly attracted to the scent of blood.

The journey to Galraithia was the most significant challenge Bill had ever faced, and this was the last round. Bill Aldridge was a true champion; he never gave up; he fought right up to his last breath. Marion looked away from the viewing window, terrified. She sat in a chair, sobbing, her body trembling with fear. She felt a warm, wet trickle between her legs. Martin and the others felt emotionally drained and physically worn out, but their Galraithian nightmare was far from over. A young eagle swooped down from the sky and perched on the ATAR's roof. Everyone heard the thud and the loud distressed cries of a juvenile eagle screeching for its mother. Then, looking up at the sunroof, they all saw the bird's underbelly, the bloodstained feathers. Marion jumped out of her chair, scared out her wits. She wanted to scream, but she ran to Martin, put her head to his chest, and started sobbing.

"We have to fight back!" Brendon shouted.

"Fight back? Fight back with what? We have no weapons," Marion cried.

Tom Granger looked out the portside window and yelled, "Can't this tin can go any faster? The giant raptor is still on the roof."

"The throttle lever is full forward, maximum speed," Joseph replied.

The eaglet let out an exceptionally long and loud screech, leaped into the air, and flew off looking for its mother.

"Joseph, what do we do if there's another raptor attack?" Satori asked.

Looking up at the ceiling, Joseph thought of the steel frame, the structure that formed the ATAR's bodywork. "If we dismantle a steel batten from inside the roof or wall cavity, we can make a spear."

"What if we made a crossbow?" Tom said.

"A crossbow would be more effective than a spear," Satori added.

Joseph looked at Satori. "I don't see any problems with Tom's idea if we have the right materials and equipment."

"Captain, if you want to make sharp metal spears, there's a laser cutter and a portable angle grinder in the toolbox," Brendon said.

"We have to start somewhere," Martin said, looking around intently at his team. In their eyes, he didn't see fear but the steely look all Freelanders possessed when they refused to quit.

***

Back at Alpha, three men carrying knives were deep into an argument in the dining hall, and Father Antonio was hurrying down the east-west accessway to tell Professor Briar; he was afraid someone was going to be hurt or get killed. The young priest pushed open the meeting room door and barged into a dozen people attending the first debriefing session of the day. They exchanged surprised glances when the priest interrupted the meeting.

"Professor, please, you must stop the fight!"

"Father Antonio, what are jabbering on about?"

"Three men, in the dining hall, they are fighting," Father Antonio said, walking alongside Professor Briar to match his long strides.

When Professor Briar opened the dining hall doors, several people were gathered around a paramedic working on an unconscious young man lying in the middle of the room. The paramedic looked up at Professor Briar. "He's dead, sir."

The professor bent down over the body and looked at the bloodied ID tag around the dead man's neck: Benjamin Nicolson, 23, born in Sheffield, England.

"He was a member of the Bio-hazard Security Unit," said a voice from behind Professor Briar. "Hello, Professor. My name is Peter Sangster. I work for Pat Greer."

Patrick Greer was Head of Security and a Judge. He held a permanent seat on the Council of Freelander Elders. Furthermore, Greer was a stickler for rules and regulations. Professor Briar spent the entire afternoon with Greer pondering why Jason Tohvian had taken to stabbing 23-year-old Benjamin Nicolson four times in the neck. Every colonist had a good understanding of Freelander Law, its criminal code; murder by any member of the Freelander movement carried a mandatory death penalty. Father Antonio and Father Sandor were present at the trial, and they heard Professor Briar read out the death sentence.

Father Antonio and Father Sandor trailed behind the guard, who jabbed Jason forward with a metal rod. When the priests asked him to stop, he snapped at them, eyes narrowing with contempt. "Speak again," he growled, "and I'll carve out your lying tongues with my Gurkha." He glanced down at them with a scowl that made clear he wasn't bluffing.

Jason didn't flinch. He lay still on the bed, eyes wide open. He didn't speak, but the look in them was apology enough. He knew what he'd done.

When Antonio stepped out of the holding cell, he felt hollow. The corridor spun slowly, as if the air itself had weight. He couldn't shake the isolation—or the doubt. What was he even doing in Galraithia? This bleak outpost had no use for his sermons or vestments. Among the Freelanders, faith meant little. What mattered to them was his strength, his grit. So he spent his days hauling solar panels across blistering rock, working side by side with Finnegan, until his limbs trembled and sweat stung his eyes. Most nights he collapsed on the cot fully clothed. On others, when sleep refused him, he lay awake staring at the ceiling, remembering the Saint Anthony Monastery in Rome—his old life reduced to a memory growing thinner each day.

Later, the smoke from Benjamin Nicolson's funeral pyre drifted into a pale sky and vanished. A small crowd lingered until the flames died down, then quietly filed back toward the habitat ring. On the way, they spotted an ATAR speeding away from the Keyway, Satori at the wheel. She didn't slow, but the crowd waved anyway, catching a glimpse of urgency in her face.

News spread fast at Alpha. Word of what happened near Paraihe Island traveled through the ranks like fire. The settlement seethed. Major Nikolayev, Ezra Tohvian, and Bill Aldridge—three names now spoken only in grief—had met deaths too brutal to imagine.

***

After leaving the medical unit and Quarantine station, Martin returned to his team. Tom Granger was nowhere in sight.

Still, the Council of Elders convened. Professor Briar. Father Sandor. And five of the Southland survivors sat in the chamber, their expressions grim. Martin spoke last, after what felt like hours of questions and summaries and

431

cross-examinations. He didn't hold anything back. Every question the Elders threw at him, he answered head-on. Truthfully. Without omissions.

Tom had chosen not to attend.

Instead, he'd slipped away from the habitat ring to meet privately with Pat Greer. There, behind closed doors, Tom laid it bare. He spoke of mistreatment—intense, deliberate—and how Captain Brindle had stood by while Brendon Aitama needled and broke him down during the long, bitter days of the journey.

Greer listened in silence, arms folded over his narrow chest. His skin, pale and pink, looked almost waxy under the office lights. His white hair clung to his scalp like cobwebs. He blinked slowly, nose crooked, lips thin and tight. The look he gave Tom wasn't pity. It was disgust.

"Mr. Granger," he said at last, voice hushed and cold, "this conversation is finished. I've heard your accusations. I won't lay blame, nor can I find any grounds to conclude that Captain Brindle or Mr. Aitama mistreated you."

Tom's chair scraped back hard.

"That's bullshit," he snapped. "I went through hell out there. Psychological abuse. And I'm putting this on record: the decisions made by those two men led directly to the deaths of Major Nikolayev, Professor Tohvian, and William Aldridge."

Greer's hands didn't move. He didn't blink. "Mr. Granger, I told you—there's nothing more I can do for you. I'm sorry."

"Sorry, my ass!" Tom shouted. "You haven't heard the last of this." He turned, shoved open the door, and stormed out into the corridor.

Ròlegur

For the Antarctic Freelanders, the time of **Ròlegur** was always a cause for celebration—the most festive season of the year. But even as the music played and spirits lifted, the joy came with a shadow. Ròlegur marked the slow descent into the long, punishing winter. It was the last quiet breath before the cold truly arrived. Soon, bitter winds would drive people indoors. Snow would fall in thick, relentless veils. Blizzard conditions would sweep across the land, and the temperature would plunge.

On Galraithia, the first Ròlegur was something else entirely. A snowfall blanketed the Ashyr Basin in a soft, flawless white. It was beautiful—almost gentle. But the warning signs were already in the air. Nights were stretching out, longer and colder. Above the basin, violent electrical storms clawed at the sky, lashing it in streaks of purple light. The planet's orbit was pulling away from Dimos, their warm, familiar sun, and toward Daedalus—a pale and distant flame at the edge of Galraithia's wildly extended ellipse.

Meanwhile, back at Alpha settlement, another storm brewed—one more grounded, more human. The colony's fuel reserves were dwindling. Food supplies had started to run thin.

Survival now hinged on what they could grow in the hydroponic bays. Everything depended on the stubborn patches of Earth soil they'd brought with them. From that: potatoes, beans, zucchini. Some fruit—limes, tomatoes, apples—managed to grow. Protein came from a more alien source. Eels, bred in containment tanks, had become a daily staple. Their boneless white meat was often pressed into castabraun patties, the most popular dish in the dining room. The Freelanders ate them with the kind of resigned enthusiasm that comes with necessity.

But in recent weeks, attention had shifted to something else—tiny purple berries. Packed with nutrients, low in sugar, low in calories. Just a few of them could keep a person alive in the worst conditions. They had become the new obsession, and not only because they could sustain life.

Lanfen and Finnegan called them **magic fruit**.

They'd noticed something strange. The berries didn't just nourish—they healed. Skin, worn thin by wind and time, seemed to smooth again. Finnegan, who had spent a lifetime with creases carved deep into his face, now looked at his reflection and barely recognized the younger man staring back. He found it amusing. Disconcerting. Unnatural, maybe.

And not without risks.

The berries held compounds no one could identify. Some might be harmful, even toxic over time. Worse still, the plants refused to grow from seed. Neither Galraithia's soil nor imported Earth soil could coax them into life. Finnegan thought it odd. More than odd—troubling.

A group of experienced seeders volunteered to investigate. They joined Finnegan and Lanfen on a scouting trip, traveling 150 miles beyond the settlement in search of more purple plants. For three hours they combed the landscape. But the terrain was cruel—open to winter winds, the soil frozen solid beneath a skin of frost. The few berry plants they found clung to the ground like secrets, shriveled and exposed.

The seeders returned to Alpha with disappointment written on their faces—and a small pouch of rotting fruit in their hands.

***

The snow kept falling, soft and constant. Near the Ashyr River, the once-clear water froze into a sheet of dull glass, untouched and silent.

Joseph sat near a window, writing in his diary.

As the daylight hours shorten, the Galraithian sky fills with birds—hundreds, maybe thousands—all flying southeast, toward the volcanic islands in the eastern Tezarian Ocean. The sight should be beautiful. But instead, it brings something else. Something heavy. I can't help thinking of Major Nikolayev, Ezra Tohvian, and brave Bill Aldridge. The image of all those birds in flight won't leave me. It drags those men into it, like a vision I didn't ask for.

Later, he shared this with Doctor Mason, and she listened carefully before offering calm reassurance. She told him that the medical team had developed a new treatment for the pulmonary inflammation—the same affliction that had already claimed 250 lives. A simple solution, but effective: sodium chloride added to nebulizers and air systems throughout the Habitat Ring. A preventative step. Measured. Quiet. But one that might save lives.

And even as winter tightened its grip, life moved forward.

For many Freelanders, **Ròlegur** wasn't just a season of cold or reflection. It was the time for **Life-bonding**—a sacred ritual when couples formally pledged themselves to each other. This year, the Council of Elders had accepted the Life-bond commitments of five pairs: Martin Brindle and Marion Tyler. Margaret Gray and Roberta Tully. William

Briar and Margaret Mason. Joseph Arunui and Satori Thomas. Professor Peng Lin and Veronica Blainey.

The elders had chosen wisely. Families rejoiced. Friends couldn't wait for the ceremony. It was tradition, after all—deep-rooted and joyfully elaborate.

When the day arrived, the dining hall overflowed. Standing room only. People laughed and squeezed together, warm despite the cold pressing in from beyond the outer walls. But then a hush fell—slowly at first, then total. Heads turned.

The couples entered.

Arm in arm, they made their way down the aisle. All eyes followed them to the front of the vast room.

Each bride wore a long hemp tunic dyed a regal purple. A soft gray shawl lay across their shoulders, and a handmade floral crown rested lightly atop their hair. Satori caught Joseph's eye and smiled. He smiled back, not at her face, but at her sandals—tiny, diamond-studded things that seemed almost too delicate for the moment. And yet, they suited her perfectly.

The grooms stood in bare feet. Each wore a green-dyed hemp coat, long-sleeved and cut at the knee. Joseph's head was wrapped in a velvet headband, deep purple and braided. A gold-colored sash hugged his waist.

One by one, each pair turned to face one another. When it came time, Satori and Joseph stepped forward.

"I wish to share my body, my life, only with you," Satori said, gently wrapping a handmade hemp bracelet around Joseph's wrist. Her voice didn't shake. Her eyes didn't waver. "My life would be poor without you."

Joseph swallowed. His voice came out a little tight, but clear. "Satori Thomas, my life would be poor without you. I wish to share my body, my life, only with you."

There was no signal, no cue—but the hall erupted. Thunderous applause rolled over them. Laughter. Cheers. The air swelled with joy as each couple declared their eternal bond and their vow to raise children who would respect and protect all life. The applause came again, louder this time, as Martin and Marion walked out hand in hand, glowing with happiness. The others followed soon after—five couples stepping out into a future they'd chosen, parting ways and disappearing in different directions, their lives newly woven together.

***

The night air was crisp and clean. Twin moons Galrah and Ithinia hung low over the horizon, and the sky was teeming with dazzling points of starlight.

"It's a perfect night," Satori said.

Looking at her eyes as she looked at him with tender feelings, Joseph reached out and held her soft, warm hands. "A perfect beginning for both of us."

They walked to their favorite hideaway, which was a geothermal pool in a limestone cave.

"Are you nervous?" Satori asked.

"A little. My right leg is shaking."

Satori stood on tiptoes and gently kissed his cheek. She told Joseph how much she loved him and would always love him. Then they made passionate love for the very first time.

437

A new beginning

Fifteen years had passed since the *Endeavour* was pulled into the outer rim of a collapsed star, caught in the energy-draining clutch of a Gravity-well. Against every probability, it had finally broken free. The ship now drifted within Lagrange Point G7, the stable gravity corridor nestled between the twin moons Ithinia and Galrah—just as the avoidance trajectory had always intended, steering toward planet Galraithia at last.

The PSC—*Endeavour*'s primary Sequanta computer—initiated the disembarkation phase. One by one, system protocols came online: diagnostics, internal sensors, atmosphere regulators, and finally, life support. Somewhere beneath the hum of relays and blinking lights, the sleepers began to wake. The long night was over.

Mission Phase Two had officially begun: a rendezvous with Galraithia.

But that promise came shadowed by complications the original planners had never imagined. *Endeavour*'s communication systems had failed to make contact with the *Phoenix* spacecraft, or with Earth's Deep Space Communication Network. No signal. No link. Nothing.

Gordon Winthrop tried to keep morale from crumbling. He moved through the ship's narrow corridors offering his usual reassurances, spinning positive forecasts and speaking in his steady, detached cadence. But for all his show of composure, the cracks beneath the surface deepened. Social tensions had risen sharply. The gap between command staff and colonists widened. Grievances echoed through the habitat modules. Discipline thinned.

Gordon claimed not to be troubled by the distrust. After all, he'd handpicked every officer aboard *Endeavour*. They had sworn allegiance. He expected that loyalty to endure.

Peter Winthrop was not so convinced. Though he bore the same last name, his sympathies lay elsewhere—especially with the allied colonists, who looked to him more than to any command figure. He worried for their well-being, more than he let on.

Galraithia, indifferent to the human drama unfolding in orbit, loomed large below. A mystery. A paradox. A promise. Despite everything—the tension, the grief, the unknowns—the planet still beckoned.

Some colonists clung to a renewed faith in technology and human ingenuity. They voiced this optimism to Gordon directly. But when he smiled back, his mouth slightly askew, they realized something sobering: he didn't care what they thought. Not really. Only Peter made time to console the grieving. Many colonists had woken from hypersleep to find that friends, lovers, or spouses had not.

It was Peter who addressed the ship through the internal radio system. His voice did not waver as he read the names of the dead. Gordon said nothing. He didn't have to—the silence itself had weight. Fifteen hundred colonists gone.

Peter tried to protect his father from blame. He insisted the losses stemmed from equipment failure, not command error. Cryo technology, he said, was still an imperfect science.

But Gordon had no patience for apologies. "More deaths from respiratory complications will bring that number closer to two thousand," he said, eyes fixed on the data scroll in front of him. His voice carried accusation, not grief.

"Shocking numbers, I know," Peter replied quietly. "Regardless of human skill or how carefully we proceed through research, the margin for error is always there. Cryo is still evolving."

Gordon slammed a fist down. "The Winthrop Corporation put the best cryo systems money could buy on this ship! No more excuses. Dismantle every medical fabricator and build me new ones—without software faults."

Peter nodded. "Yes, Father. I'll make the arrangements."

By the time *Endeavour* reached its fifth orbit around Galraithia, another nine colonists failed to wake. Gordon canceled the funeral services without explanation.

The landing phase began.

One by one, the automated pods detached from the ship's lower bays and plunged through Galraithia's thin, unwelcoming atmosphere. Each pod carried its human cargo to the designated landing zone—a wide, austere stretch of land between Keyway Valley and Alpha, the main Freelander settlement. Gordon considered Alpha a peripheral outpost. Insignificant. But for now, it would have to serve.

***

Collin McAllister, a tall man, whistled as he walked between the last row of empty cryo beds and life-support units. Whistling the same tune over and over was something Collin did when he was bored or if he wanted to annoy his boss, Ryan Chyloe.

"Mr. Chyloe, people are lining up in front of the landing pods on Muster Station H, so you had better leave now if you want to join Rob and Rachel."

"There's one more checklist item, then I'm done," Ryan said, pushing his chair back from one desk to the diagnostic scanner unit. The scanner illustrated the trajectory of a large meteor that had ripped through Endeavour's solar sail. "The solar sail is at 82 percent integrity on the scanner. I need a fabricator to go out there and fix the solar sail asap."

"Five-o-nine is the nearest fabricator," Collin said, touching a diagram of G Deck on his old touchpad and scheduling a work order.

"Five-o-nine back in-service mode? Rachel's work ethic never ceases to amaze me," Ryan said.

"That woman is usually a stickler for regular calibration checks, but she wouldn't allow me or any other technician to touch Five-o-nine," Collin said with sarcasm in his voice.

"Rachel is my 2IC. She deserves respect from every technician aboard this ship."

"Absolutely," Collin said as Rachel's voice came over the ship's radio.

"Ryan, come up to High-Lab when you're ready."

Ryan pressed the answer button on his Vox radio. "High-Lab?"

"Yes. Captain Winthrop has decided to leave behind four fabricator units and 150 technicians to control all scheduled maintenance. You, Rob, and I are staying on board until next Ithinian moon cycle."

"Well, that's just great!" Ryan said sarcastically. "We are staying on board and do what? I haven't negotiated a new work contract with Gordon Winthrop or Peter Winthrop."

"It's Captain Winthrop. Show some respect, Ryan."

"Okay, Rachel, Captain Winthrop! But I'm left wondering which Winthrop I dislike the most."

"Ryan, I feel it's important that we do this. Captain Winthrop and Dallas Fitch have been incredibly patient with us. You cannot deny that, can you?"

"Rachel, I'm too tired to think about anything to do with Captain Winthrop, Dallas Fitch."

"And everyone else, and everything else involved in the running of this ship?"

"Yes, I mean no! Not the fabricators!"

"Captain Winthrop and Dallas Fitch need our help. I can't emphasize this strongly enough."

"Okay, Rachel. Give me the details," Ryan said, moving away from Collin McAllister and trying to keep his voice low.

"Captain Winthrop has issued a task order contract. Five new medical fabricators. Mr. Winthrop wants them built before the Ithinian moon cycle comes around. We'll get double pay for the extra work. Then, we can leave for Alpha on the next available shuttle."

Ryan lowered his voice, whispering so Collin could not overhear, "Winthrop's money will be worthless once we touch down on Galraithia. So, we must find a way to secure a decent house. Preferably near the Alpha settlement."

"My thoughts exactly," Rachel said. "The problem is Rob doesn't know about the task order contract, so you'd better get yourself up here and talk him into signing; otherwise, he will be stranded aboard this ship for another six months

or until a relief crew arrives from the surface. " "Okay, Rachel. I'll make my way to High-Lab."

"Bad news, eh?" Collin said.

"I'm afraid so."

Collin paced down a row of cryo beds, all vacant except one.

"Hey, Ryan, look here. Someone forgot to wake this guy up."

"Fabricators emptied the Cryo module hours ago," Ryan said, eyes scanning each Cryo chamber.

"I thought the same. So why is this guy still in cryostasis?" Collin asked, stepping closer and reading the name tag above cryo bed 50035. "Dani Li, 34. birthplace, Beijing, China."

"This is damn peculiar," Ryan said. "Mr. Li should not be here right now."

Ryan looked at Dani, and he began to wonder whether a fabricator had made a mistake, but he thought, *No! That is highly unlikely.* Then Ryan noticed three tattoos, one on Dani's left forearm: a red dragon with open wings, the ancient symbol of Xiangshan Traders. A barn swallow, the iconic symbol of the Freelanders, on his left hand. And on Dani's right forearm was a swooping sparrow attacking a golden dragon.

"A passerine bird and a golden dragon. A combination of innocence and deadly danger," Ryan said.

"What do you mean?" Collin asked.

"Mr. Dani Li is a Xiangshan Trader and a Freelander," Ryan replied. "Gordon Winthrop's pet peeves. I wouldn't say I like Dani's chances of leaving here anytime soon. Alive or dead."

"You seem certain of that," Collin said.

"Gordon is a total fool!" Ryan added. "The Freelanders do not forget any wrong done to them. I lived in Freeland Antarctica for more than two years, and I know how violent Freelanders can be when pushed too far."

"The Freelanders are mostly peaceful and nonviolent," Collin said.

"Most Freelanders are peaceful and nonviolent, but not all," Ryan said. "Dani Li here belongs to the latter. He is a Xiangshan Trader expertly trained in the use of ancient and modern weaponry, stealth, and deception. Xiangshan Traders are unashamedly called the perfect killers."

"How can you be so sure?" Collin asked.

"A sparrow attacking a golden dragon is the symbol of an Askudai, the second-highest rank in the Trader hierarchy," Ryan replied. "The visible tattoos are not body art; they are medals of honor earned by a master of subterfuge and murder."

"Even if this Dani guy is extremely dangerous, as you say, Gordon Winthrop has a private army, security guards at his disposal. So, while they guard every door, he's untouchable," Collin said.

"While they guard every door, Gordon Winthrop may be untouchable," Ryan countered. "But Xiangshan Traders are relentless, resourceful predators without equal in covert activities. If there's a way to honor a murder contract and not get caught, a Xiangshan assassin will always succeed."

***

Dallas Fitch walked over to a viewing window. Galraithia was pale green, blue, white, and tan. Dallas could also see snow on the mountains and dark blue water, and an east-west band of clouds stretching out across the equator. Dallas Fitch was quiet, and he looked tired. He and Lee Hapgood, and Professor Mitchel had been on duty on the bridge for 16 hours. They had successfully deployed the Winthrop Telescope at LaGrange Point 7. They had found Endeavour's Davis-Molby rocket engines unreliable. They did not work efficiently or work at all due to heat stresses and other technical problems inside the ignition chamber. The Damage Assessment Team agreed that there was no other choice but to shut down all five engines and lessen the likelihood of a mass explosion. They had sent a small specialist fabricator to assess the aging DM rocket engines. However, it was undeniably clear to the fabricator that many critical engine components had melted away during Endeavour's struggle to break free from the Gravity-well. Captain Winthrop removed the damaged engines and replaced them with new ones with his father's approval. Even with two new rocket engines, Endeavour's Engine management systems could not guarantee a slow rate of descent down to the planet's surface. Based on risk to the spacecraft and the lives on board, Captain Winthrop decided not to proceed with the landing phase of the mission. Consequently, Captain Winthrop had also decided to leave the grand ship in a stable orbit 400 miles above Galraithia. He then ordered his Fabricators to fuel-up Endeavour's landing pods and special-purpose shuttlecraft. "Prepare for de-orbit burn. Planetary entry and the landing interface will commence shortly. Wait for the launch order," Captain Winthrop commanded. Finally, after his officers declared, 'All systems are ready,' Captain Winthrop ordered all passengers to assemble at their assigned muster stations.

***

Gordon Winthrop entered Endeavour's bridge and looked around the room. He noticed Dallas Fitch standing in front

445

of a computer station behind the captain's chair. As he walked up to join Dallas, Captain Winthrop issued last-minute instructions to his pilots. These brave men and women pilots would be held responsible for the colonists' safety. "Initiate the launch sequence, Mr. Fitch."

"Aye, Captain."

Acting Science Officer Doctor Anthony Mitchel, a softly spoken man, looked anxious when Gordon Winthrop approached a staticky radio receiver.

"Is there a problem with this receiver, Doctor?"

"The noisy static is coming from the Sun," Doctor Mitchel said, changing his radio to another frequency. "Despite the background noise, there is good data streaming out from two land-based weather observation stations, sir."

"What about wind strength?" Dallas Fitch asked.

"Wind strength is variable, less than 10 knots," Doctor Mitchel replied.

"The long-range scanner has scanned an area of some 680,000 square miles. The Ashyr Plain is one large ice sheet with elevated levels of ganitte," Captain Winthrop declared. "There are a few scattered buildings in and around the Freelander settlement, and an extensive underground lava stream is close by."

"The dark spots above the southern continent are cyclonic storms with temperature readings of minus 334 degrees Fahrenheit," Doctor Mitchel put in.

"So much for your earth-like environment on the southern continent, eh, Doctor?"

"Mr. Hapgood, don't put all the blame on me. Every piece of data I received from the Faxian telescope suggested weather patterns on the southern continent were extreme but not very different from a typical Antarctic winter."

"Doctor, you are doing an outstanding job," Gordon said glaring at Lee.

"Mr. Hapgood doesn't know when to keep his mouth shut."

Lee looked away, afraid of what Gordon might say to him later; he did not want to lose his job.

"Continue scanning the southern continent and the islands along the equator, Doctor."

"Yes. Mr. Winthrop."

"Launch interlocks are green for go, Captain. Pods are pressurized, and guidance is internal."

"Very good, Mr. Fitch. Launch the starboard side pods when ready."

"Aye, sir."

"Well, gentlemen, we are about to make history together. Although synchronizing the landing interface will give us more potential headaches once we touch down. In any event, I would like to take this opportunity to offer my thanks and to acknowledge all your hard work. And it would be remiss of me not to mention how lucky we were to get here while putting up with my indecisiveness at critical times."

Gordon acknowledged the applause with a subtle nod and smile. "Captain, I would like a word, please."

"Yes, Father."

"Is there any radio chatter coming from Alpha?"

"We received some very faint radio chatter, but it's mostly computer-generated weather reports on a transmission loop," Captain Winthrop said.

"Keep monitoring the transmissions on the proper frequencies. I don't think Briar and his people are clever enough to jam our communication systems and deliberately keep us in the dark. But we will soon know. Now, is my private shuttle ready?"

"Your shuttlecraft has been ready for some time, sir. I have also arranged transportation for the maintenance crews staying on board until the next full moon, as you suggested. Everyone else will be safely on the surface by nightfall."

"Excellent! Carry on, Captain. Get them all away. Let's not waste any more precious time than we must."

"And the Freelanders…what do we do with them, sir?"

"An unfortunate set of events brought 50 Freelanders to this vessel," Gordon said, recalling the explosion that ripped Endeavour's hull and almost claimed the lives of his entire crew.

In his mind, William Briar had to be held accountable for this brazen act of sabotage against the Allied folk and Gordon's quest to be the first man from Earth to set foot on Galraithia.

"Organize a shuttle for Briar's people. Send the craft down to the southern continent, dead or alive; I really don't care," Gordon said coldly.

"If those people die, the dire consequences that follow may cost you your life and mine."

Gordon approached his son with an angry frown. "Don't test my patience and do what you are told, Peter."

Peter could not tolerate being belittled by his father, and Gordon was in a vengeful mood and best left alone. So, Peter just stood there as his overbearing father left the bridge. Peter hadn't noticed before, but his father's long confident strides were shorter. And Gordon was in better shape than many men half his age when he left Earth. But now, every breath seemed more labored as Gordon awkwardly shuffled towards the door leading to his private quarters.

"Mr. Fitch!"

"Yes, Captain!"

"Hold Shuttle-9. It's reserved for the passengers coming from the D-deck."

"The Freelanders?"

"Yes, Mr. Fitch, the Freelander passengers. Load them up without delay, then set the landing cycle on automatic and enter Alpha settlement's geographic coordinates into the onboard Navigation computer: 25.2744 degrees S, 133.7761 degrees SSE."

"Aye, sir."

"Dallas, when do we leave?" Lee whispered.

"We'll be ready to leave as soon as everybody is secure."

Dallas Fitch and Lee Hapgood, both expert navigators, figured out that the Alpha settlement's geographic coordinates were wrong. The X and Y grid reference matched the geographic coordinates of a vast uncharted region in Southland known as the Eastern Ice Sheet. Gordon Winthrop and his mission planners had considered putting the Eastern Ice Sheet landing site on the unacceptable risk list. Lee's calm demeanor changed from calm to complete anger. He was surprised by the captain's orders and angry at Dallas for being silent and not speaking out.

All three men were staunch supporters of the Freelander movement.

"Captain, maybe I heard wrong, but I think you gave Dallas the wrong geographic coordinates," Lee Hapgood said, in a concerned tone.

"Mr. Hapgood, voicing your concerns is important to me," Captain Winthrop advised. "But there is nothing for you to worry about."

"Aye, Captain."

Then the captain turned to Doctor Mitchel. "Follow me, please, Doctor."

As Captain Winthrop and Doctor Mitchel turned and walked away, Dallas Fitch walked up to his friend Lee Hapgood and said, "You certainly chose the wrong time to voice your concerns to the captain."

"Dallas, the wrong geographic coordinates could destroy Shuttle-9, and you didn't say anything about it to the captain."

"Lee, stop worrying. There are one hundred last-minute preparations and course corrections to make before Shuttle-9 attempts to land."

***

As Doctor Mitchel glanced at the captain striding briskly beside towards the turbo-lift doors, he said, "Excuse me for asking, Captain, but where are you taking me?"

"G-deck."

"Captain, I have a backlog of individuals needing additional immunizations."

"I know you are a busy man, Doctor. But I have 50 Freelanders, all in deep cryostasis that need your immediate attention." Doctor Mitchel followed Captain Winthrop to the hypersleep chamber and cryo bed 50035, in which Dani Li was still sleeping soundly.

"This man is your first patient, Doctor. Wake Mr. Li and do it quickly."

The Doctor looked a little apprehensive at first, but he had no questions for Captain Winthrop. "Waking a patient too quickly from hypersleep increases the risk of brain injuries," Doctor Mitchel said. He carefully removed rubber tubing and closed the valve, supplying cryo fluid under pressure to the cry bed. Next, he disconnected the cryo bed unit from the hypersleep chamber, which increased Dani's oxygen consumption. "Wake up, Mr. Li. Tell me, how do you feel?"

Dani grimaced as he lifted his head. "I feel like I've just been kicked in the head."

"The pain will pass," Doctor Mitchel said. "Now, slide off the bed for me. Stand up straight, feet together."

Dani got out of bed slowly and stood up straight, feet together. "That's good. Now, put on clean clothes," Doctor Mitchel said.

Dani started to get dressed but he felt dizzy, and his legs felt weak.

"The weakness you are experiencing is quite normal after an exceedingly long hyper-sleep. Your legs will regain their strength as you gain more weight. Nevertheless, you will need to take things easy for a day or two. There is nothing more I can do for you here."

Dani gave Doctor Mitchel a small smile and said, "Thank you."

"Yes, yes. Report to Muster Station-H. The on-duty security guard will tell you what to do next. Do you understand, Mr. Li?"

Dani nodded. "Yes."

Then Doctor Mitchel turned to the captain and said, "No need to worry about Mr. Li. He is a strong and healthy young man."

"Thank you, Doctor. Please continue with your assigned duties."

"As you wish, Captain," Doctor Mitchel said, moving to the foot of another cryo bed.

"Mr. Li, you have recovered quickly from hypersleep," Captain Winthrop said. "Drink hot tea. It lessens the unpleasant side effects."

"Captain, on behalf of the Freelanders, I'd like to thank you firstly for taking us aboard this magnificent ship and bringing us here. We all owe you a debt, not easy to repay."

"You and your people owe me nothing. It was my father's idea, not mine."

Dani knew deep down in his gut that the captain had told him an outright lie. Gordon Winthrop hated Xiangshan Traders as much as he despised the Freelanders. Fifty Freelanders, including Dani, who was born to a Xiangshan Trader family, would be dead already if it weren't for Captain Winthrop. "In that case, please make sure to express my profound appreciation to your father," Dani said, but it was an empty gesture.

Captain Winthrop nodded with a smile. "Now, make your way to Muster Station-H. Report directly to Dallas Fitch and give him this," he said, handing Dani a folded sheet of paper.

When Dani unfolded the paper, it had latitude and longitude coordinates. He then headed to Muster Station-H. Along the way, Dani wondered whether he really could trust Captain Winthrop. Dani had learned many methods that would increase his opportunity to gain and secure others' trust and respect over time. But would it be too challenging to convince Captain Winthrop and his officers to join the Freelander Movement? The immovable obstacle in Dani's way was Gordon Winthrop. Gordon would not hesitate to speedily annihilate any or all enemies of the Allied People if he found out those closest to him were also the ones who betrayed him.

So, Dani needed to act fast and with great caution to gain Captain Winthrop's trust.

The Newcomers

The years rolled by; another harsh winter had set in the northern continent of Ashyr and with greater severity. Nevertheless, the resilient Freelander community inhabiting the Alpha settlement braved daily winter temperatures below negative 200 degrees Fahrenheit. Also troubling were the relentless dry lightning storms that lingered for more days than people cared to remember.

Thirteen-year-old Albert Arunui and Jonathon Brindle met up most mornings in the Dining hall. Over breakfast, they planned the day's activities, which never changed too much. But this morning was different. Another friend would join them at the breakfast table: Twelve-year-old Walter Tyler, the son of Rihanna and Alistair Tyler. Walter entered the room alone; without his tenacious baby sister Sarah and the homemade castabraun patties she had promised to bring. "Where's Sarah?" Albert asked.

Walter explained that Sarah had woken up just before sunrise, soaked through with sweat, shivering with a high fever, to complain of stomach pain on her right side. Concerned for her well-being, his mother gave Sarah fever medication before calling Doctor Mason. Then she told her to stay home and rest until Doctor Mason arrived because the doctor assumed Sarah's pain was due to appendicitis.

***

Over a breakfast of two poached eggs and two castabraun patties, the young Galraithians reviewed their plans to explore a cave in the Keyway Valley. There were miles of deep caverns and cave systems to discover. Unfortunately, the cave the boys were interested in led to an abandoned mine shaft that structural engineers considered too dangerous to access.

Albert had packed four rechargeable pharnas lamps into a small backpack earlier that morning. Jonathon had brought 60 feet of climbing rope, and a choice of carabiners crammed in a soft bag. Walter had the good sense to carry a restocked first-aid kit. He also provided a paper map of the area and his father's magnetic compass, which always pointed to the Alpha settlement.

As soon as the boys finished breakfast, they gathered their gear and went to the Keyway Valley. Once lush and fertile, the river valley was also the favorite meeting place for seed gatherers and pollinators. However, the early onset of winter had brought bitterly cold air, severe southerly winds, and much ice and snow. Professor Briar and many colonists said that as Freelanders and the first humans to inhabit Galraithia, they needed to prove their worth by accepting the harsh realities of the Galraithian winters. So, Professor Briar resolved to send out several more expeditions inland. Some of the older colonists objected vocally to Briar. The excursions beyond the deep ravines and narrow passes of the Cradle Mountains of Ashyr would discover nothing of any value. The professor did not mention that winter temperatures plummeted to around 260 ° F and surface winds exceeded speeds of 345 mph. As a result, some of the older colonists made no secret of their unhappiness by refusing to venture beyond the two twenty-foot tall ganitte towers denoting the main entrance to the Alpha Settlement. The freestanding structures of polished ganitte also commemorated the historic landing site where the Freelanders had first set foot on Galraithia's soil.

Each boy carried a water and an oxygen bottle attached to a leather belt around the waist. Jonathon had also attached his father's handheld radio. Unfortunately, the transmitter/receiver had often proved unreliable in the past under Antarctic skies; it worked intermittingly. And it had never worked when heavy gray rain clouds filled Galraithian skies. However, rain was rare in this Ashyr region. The last raindrops fell and dried up nine years ago when the air was hot and humid, and shade was at a premium around the settlement. Now, it snowed incessantly in Ashyr. Some people said that the cold of the winter solstice had set in, and most Freelanders did not know how long the cold spell would last.

After venturing inside the cave, the boys found cold water trickling down from sheer rock walls, mixing with hot spring water in rock pools steaming with geothermic heat. The boys quickly realized that the water was too hot to soak in. Still, the overly hot water provided primary nutrients needed for life, especially for a school of tiny pink fish with no eyes.

They also discovered many crystalline ganitte rock shards inside the cave. This material was a precious natural resource because ganitte molecules slowed down the flow of electricity. Due to this increased electrical resistance, the ganitte had begun to glow, generating heat and light energy.

***

The deeper the boys ventured, the lower the cave's roof became. As they crept slowly forward, they heard voices echoing. Finally, Albert inched his way towards the entrance of the mineshaft.

"Albert, what do you see?" Jonathon whispered.

"Five workmen are breaking large rocks, and two fabricators are drilling holes into a rock wall," Albert whispered. Then, suddenly, the two fabricators stopped working and turned in Albert's direction. Their zoom lenses caught a glimpse of the glowing light from the pharnas lamps lighting up the rock ceiling. The intruder alarm sounded. The boys panicked and tried to hurry out of the cave without looking back. But they suddenly stopped when they saw four men armed with pickaxes and sledgehammers blocking the path ahead. Hiding in a dark corner, the boys blindly waited. A few seconds seemed like an hour, and the armed men would not move away from the way out.

"Step out into the light," a voice said. "Have no fear; I won't harm you! My name is Samis. I'm the mining supervisor. Step out into the light so I can see you."

The boys stepped out of the darkness to face Samis and the four men who stood smirking beside him. "Well, well, look who we have here. I know you and you," Samis said, pointing at Albert and Jonathon. "But I don't know who you are."

Walter moved forward with his head hung low, his shoulders hunched, and shaking with fear. "Walter Tyler, sir."

"He's Alistair's son," a man called Kris said.

Samis hesitated, but then he gave Kris a subtle nod.

"Why are you shaking, Walter? Are you afraid of me, boy?"

"Yes, sir."

"This is not a playground for children to play in," Samis said. "Underground mines are inherently dangerous. A rockslide killed three strong men, squashed them to death, like summer bugs on a car windshield. I can describe the gruesome scene in greater detail if you want me to, but young Walter here is growing pale."

"This place can't be so dangerous if you are here. In any event, we have everything from a helmet on our head to oxygen bottles on our belts!" Jonathon declared, touching his leather belt.

"Helmets and oxygen bottles won't save you down here, boy," Samis countered.

"We were collecting cave survey data before you came along," Albert said, hoping to justify their attempt at exploring the cavern.

"You three scurried around like scared rats after the intruder alarm sounded!" Samis yelled. "Go on, get! Before I lose my temper. And don't let me catch you down here again!"

"Cocky little shits," Kris said, watching the boys as they hurried out of the cave.

"Come on, let's work the West wall for a couple more hours, and then we'll call it a day," Samis said.

While Kris and two other men followed the work order blindly, another man walked beside Samis to the west wall. This man was feeling anxious. "We should leave now, Samis. We are working this mine illegally."

"Garon, you worry too much," Samis replied.

"Okay, don't listen to me," Garon said getting angry. "But we will be in a whole lot of trouble if those boys tell their parents."

Kris pounded a short pickaxe into a large boulder that had fallen on the ground from a massive wall of rock. He wiped the sweat from his brow with his forearm, turned to his friend Garron and said, "When narc agents arrested your ass every Friday night, did you tell your parents?"

"Well, that's different, and you know it!" Garon declared.

After three sharp blows, the boulder broke into two equal pieces. Kris's eyes widened when he saw a ganitte seam eight inches wide sandwiched in the middle of the two rocks.

"Samis, look here!" Kris pointed to a long crystal shard tapered to a point at one end and rounded at the blunt end. Handing Samis the long crystal shard, Kris was smiling broadly.

Samis pulled out a jeweler's loupe from his jacket and put the loupe directly to his right eye. Looking through the loupe, Samis stared at the long crystal shard, magnified ten times normal eyesight. "This is an excellent find. The cell structure is uniform," Samis said with excitement. "Such crystal specimens usually yield a substantial amount of heat."

"Boss, do we keep digging or pack the gear up?" Kris asked.

"Dig along the west wall for another 20 feet," Samis said. "I believe there's a good chance of finding larger, higher-quality crystals."

"I hope you're right, Boss. I have three little girls back home wrapped up in blankets because the heating unit in the housing compound doesn't work."

"Did you report the problem?" Garon asked.

"More than once to the Council of Elders," Kris replied as he dug the pickaxe deep into the rock wall and pulled down another large boulder, but this one almost rolled on his right boot.

"And?"

"The Council has done absolutely nothing. So, I'm taking my share of ganitte crystals with or without their approval," Kris said.

"I say we have every right to keep the crystals," Samis declared. "We have all labored long and hard to reach them. And the temperature outside drops further with each passing day. Protecting our health is essential; safeguarding our family's health is even more critical."

"Oh, I intend to take care of myself and my family. Don't you worry about that," Kris said. "The Council could not care less if people freeze to death in their homes. There aren't enough solar heating systems, and not all homes have an available and efficient electricity supply. We don't have the resources to build new electricity grids. Unless we build more and faster electric heat exchangers inside the Habitat Ring, many more people will die."

Samis nodded; the look he gave Kris was of genuine concern. Garon shook his head and laughed a little, but it was a forced laugh.

"You think this is funny," Samis said, taking a few steps toward Garron. "You find it amusing, do you?"

"Samis, I apologize for any disrespect. I thought you would understand why I laughed," Garron said. "We encountered a similar issue back in Antarctica, remember? On Earth, polished weapon-grade ganitte crystals weighing one pound or more sold for 220,000 yuan on the black market. Ironically, in this new world, ganitte is primarily used for clean heating rather than for producing laser weapons."

"Stop thinking of Earth because you are not going back there. None of us are," Samis said. "Now, go and help the fabricator working the east wall and keep your mouth shut."

***

Wheeling around a snow mound near the Ganitte mine entrance, the boys hardly said a word to each other. And after walking about a mile, they heard several loud bangs high above their heads. Instinctively they looked up at the clear blue sky. Then they saw hundreds of yellow, black, green, gold, and red parachutes fill the sky. More shiny objects were dropping from the sky, but they were incredibly high up and against the sun's glare, hard to see.

One by one the parachutes opened at 10,000 feet above the surface. The first generation of Freelanders born in Alpha settlement had never seen an actual parachute, only color photographs inside several history books: Soldiers, airplanes, battleships, and the ugly realities of cruel wars fought over control of land, resources, trade, and the personal ambitions of too many despots and leaders who possessed tenacious societal aspirations. To say the boys were amazed and troubled at the same time would be understating the obvious; all three stood open-mouthed. Had the shiny objects come from Earth, or were they alien in origin? The boys would have their answer soon enough. The silver-skinned pods were descending over a designated touchdown area. Then, as powerful thrusters spewed a whitish-blue vapor, the pods settled ever-so-gently upon the snow-covered field.

***

Albert was the first to reach the comforting safety of his home. He hurried across the frozen front yard, slipped on the icy walkway, and crashed into the front door. Ignoring the pain, he opened the door and dashed down a short corridor to his father's office. Excitedly, Albert shouted, "Parachutes and metal machines have landed on an icy field between the frozen river and the Keyway Valley entrance!"

461

Joseph leaned back in his office chair, looking at his son with a mix of pretended disbelief and genuine relief. He was not surprised by Albert's description of the silver landing pods, which bore the emblem of Endeavour: five interlaced rings in blue, yellow, black, green, and red against a silver background.

Albert glanced through a wide south-facing window at the slanted shape of the glass greenhouse attached to the kitchen, Satori's favorite part of the house.

"I don't see Mother. Where is she?" Albert asked, thinking his mother would be home working in the kitchen or the garden.

"She went to visit your Auntie Marion. The baby is due any day now," Joseph replied. Then, standing up, Joseph walked out of his small cluttered office and into the corridor which led to the kitchen area and a storage room. Albert followed behind and watched his father enter the storage room and remove a flat wooden box sitting on the top of a shelving rack. Joseph opened the box and found a pair of high-powered binoculars with image stabilization. "I had intended to give you these on your 15th birthday," Joseph said, as he began to unwrap the binoculars. Albert's eyes widened in surprise when his father handed him the binoculars.

"Thank you," Albert said, giving his father a long hug. "These binoculars are fantastic!"

"And very old," Joseph said, walking over to the front door. Albert walked outside with his father and closed the door.

"Now, carefully slide the small notch and look through the two lenses. Once an object comes into your field of view, the Auto-focuser will continually track the object."

"Yes, Father." Looking through the powerful lenses, Albert could see nothing but blackness at first, and then the Endeavour entered his field of view. "Father, I see the spaceship…it's massive!"

"The Endeavour is a big ship, the biggest ever built. You see, I wasn't lying to you all these years."

"Father, I never doubted Endeavour's size. But I never thought I would see an interstellar spaceship from Earth orbit Galraithia."

"I have dreamt of this day when I would be able to see the Endeavour again," Joseph said.

Albert turned to face the distant mountains, and with the auto-focus, he could see all the way to Cool Ridge. Before long, Albert and Joseph heard voices; there were people everywhere, walking in the direction of Keyway Valley.

"Bertie, go to your mother and tell her what is happening if she doesn't know already," Joseph said. "Tell her to meet me at the Keyway Valley entrance as soon as she can."

"Yes, Father."

Word had spread that shuttle pods carrying new colonists from Earth had landed about five miles from the Keyway Valley entrance. People soon emerged from their warm homes. Chilly wind whipped around their bodies. Nonetheless, they marched down the road leading to the valley entrance. Everyone seemed excited that more people from Earth had finally arrived and wanted to welcome them. Joseph walked along with the crowd, but he crossed the road and hurried to the Frogmouth Pub, where he was sure he would find Martin. Whether Martin would come voluntarily with him to the Keyway was another question. Martin was spending too much time at the Frogmouth Pub drinking with friends when he should be home and spending time with Marion. She was heavily pregnant with their second child and overly anxious as the due date approached.

Joseph heard someone call his name. Then he realized the voice belonged to Sandros, the oldest man in the Alpha settlement, and the most experienced public servant to be given a seat on the Council of Elders. "Joseph, can you believe it? More people from the Old World!" Sandros said, closing the front door of his warm home and leaving it unlocked as he had always done.

"Hello, Sandros. Nice to see you."

Sandros waved his whalebone cane at the sky, unsure if he would ever see the sun again. "Another cold, cloudy day!"

Joseph glanced at the thick gray clouds passing overhead. "The sun and the warmth will return eventually."

"I believe you, Joseph. Now, tell me how many ships are orbiting around Galraithia."

"Only one ship has put itself in parabolic trajectory around Galraithia, the Endeavour."

"Gordon Winthrop's Endeavour?"

"Yes, Sandros. Winthrop's Endeavour. The sun is shining brightly above the clouds—a glorious day for all humankind."

Lowering his glance, Sandros replied in Freilish, "Bara sheliendo domante tristeh (This glorious day may bring tears and sadness tomorrow). Then, walking alongside Joseph, Sandros talked about the Battle of Albany, hard-won by the Freelanders of Western Australia, and the days of deep sorrow that had followed. "I can remember how happy everyone was waving their victory banners in the wind and marching down York Street. The Freelander people were happy and proud of their Militia regiments. They had defeated a long-standing enemy, the Allied Army and Navy holding the city of Albany and its port under military occupation for more than 50 years. But the Siege of Albany turned our great victory to ashes in our mouths."

The Siege of Albany occurred when Sandros was nine years old. The Allied forces had assembled the largest fleet of warships ever seen. The warships had crossed the Indian Ocean and eventually lay off the southern coast of Western Australia unopposed, blockading King George Sound and the Port of Albany. There had been an immediate outcry from the Freelanders demanding that the Australian Government send its naval force immediately to the southern coast of Western Australia. However, the Australian Government had already allied itself with the Allied Nations. Subsequently, without the aid of the Australian Government, two million people slowly starved to death. Sandros was one of the lucky ones; only a small group of children had survived the siege. Without Naval support, Freelander Militia leaders surrendered and signed a peace treaty to save lives but forfeited their own. Three months later, 400,000 young Freelander men and women gathered from all over Australia and New Zealand. They shared a common goal to create a collective identity of Freelander states within a world divided between rich and poor, wants and needs.

"It's hard to imagine now that the battle and blockade of Albany sparked the global emergence of Freelander communities and began a new renaissance," Joseph said.

"Humanity achieved great successes and made grave mistakes in the past. We cannot afford to make more mistakes here. Galraithia would extract a higher price than humanity can afford, total human extinction."

***

Upon hearing the news of parachutes drifting through the sky, Father Antonio hurried back to the Habitat Ring. Without stopping at his room, he knocked urgently on Father Sandor's door at the far end of the long corridor.

Father Sandor, absorbed in his morning prayers, heard the knock and called out, "Come in. It's open."

"Father Sandor! I ran here as fast as I could," Antonio said, breathless.

"Why? What's happened?" The older priest grimaced slightly, rising from his kneeling position.

"Landing pods from the Endeavour… hundreds of them!" Father Antonio announced. "Right now, they're touching down outside the Keyway Valley entrance."

Father Sandor appeared calm, showing little worry about the Endeavour or the landing pods. He walked carefully to the single window in his room and peered outside. Two final pods floated down through the sky, moments away from landing.

***

As they neared the valley entrance, Doctor Mason, Satori, Marion, and young Albert Arunui waited tensely for the pods to begin landing. Moments later, colorful drogue parachutes unfurled against the sky. The soft-landing rocket motors ignited, guiding the pods to touch down gently on the ground.

The three women exchanged meaningful glances, realizing the settlement's future now hung on whether the Allied people would accept and work alongside the Freelanders.

Unable to contain his excitement, Albert slipped away to find his friends. He left his mother with the talkative

Doctor Mason, who was busy checking on the heavily pregnant Marion.

***

The Freelanders had proved highly adaptive, resourceful, and versatile throughout their short history on Earth. They fought with tenacious fanaticism against every adversity. Having learned to survive in the harshest environments on Earth, they contrasted sharply with the soft-bellied Allied newcomers, who hailed from overpopulated, technology-rich cities.

The Freelanders eagerly exchanged greetings with the newcomers. Afterwards, the newcomers walked alongside them, beginning the long march back to the Alpha settlement.

A biting wind grew stronger and colder with each passing minute. Hundreds of newcomers shivered uncontrollably. The Freelanders offered blankets and hot tea to help warm them.

One friendly newcomer, walking beside a Freelander, hesitated before accepting the gifts. "How do you people cope?" he asked, glancing nervously around. "I don't think I can live out here in this desolate frozen wasteland."

The Freelander met his gaze steadily. "We cope by accepting that we all chose to come here willingly. And we have agreed to face any challenge Galraithia throws at us and live the best way we can, one day at a time," he replied calmly.

Another Freelander nearby, handing out blankets, overheard and interjected, "To survive here, you'd better talk to people with more experience. Listen to what the Freelanders are saying."

467

"Freelanders?" the newcomer repeated skeptically.

"Yes, Freelanders. You're in our world now," the first replied with quiet pride.

"The cold doesn't bother me. I don't need a blanket," the newcomer said with a stiff shake of his head.

The Freelander's eyes narrowed slightly. "Overruling common sense is a mistake," he said firmly. "It doesn't take long to freeze to death out here."

"I survived two world wars," the newcomer said quickly, his voice gaining confidence. "Learned to live with minimal resources—hunting rats in drains and sewers. I think I can manage to survive out here in this desolate frozen wasteland or anywhere else in this alien world."

"Only time will tell," the Freelander said with a slow smile. "Where do you hail from?"

"The United Kingdom," the newcomer answered, glancing briefly to the side. "Squire Circle, the eastern quarter of London. And you?"

"Antarctica. The city of Dome Halley," the Freelander replied.

He shared his incredible stories of survival living in Ashyr—firsthand accounts of rapid climate change from comfortable temperate zones to extreme wintry weather, the hardships of finding a passage over the Cradle Mountains, and the efforts to open inland routes to fertile grasslands now buried beneath deep snow and blue ice. He explained how the whole northern continent was a frozen, barren wasteland, lifeless and unforgiving.

***

The Freelanders approached the Alpha settlement with an uneasy sense of foreboding. The newcomers embodied all the mistakes humanity had made on Earth, and they posed a direct threat to the settlement's increasingly scarce food supply. Meteorologists insisted this was an undeniable reality. The freezing of the northern continent signaled the onset of a glacial period, as Galraithia drifted toward Aphelion—the point farthest from its sun, Dimos.

Yet, a critical detail omitted by mission planners weighed heavily on their minds: the necessity of breathing pure oxygen daily to stimulate human lungs unaccustomed to Galraithia's thin atmosphere and lower air pressure. Tragically, by the time researchers grasped this fact, pneumonia-like symptoms had claimed one-quarter of the Freelander population.

Despite this grim loss, Galraithian children flourished. Advances in prenatal biological technologies had enhanced cellular function within the human body. Biological science experts concluded that environmental factors played the pivotal role. Consequently, the first native-born generation of Freelanders in Ashyr exhibited higher nitric oxide levels. With fewer red blood cells coursing through their veins, their blood vessels remained open, allowing steady blood flow despite Galraithia's rarefied air.

***

Heavy transport shuttles from the Endeavour landed last, delivering 5,000 tons of food, medical supplies, electrical and earth-moving equipment, building materials, synthetic coal, and oil. Freelander and Allied quarantine inspectors clashed fiercely over livestock embryos—sheep, cow, and horse—preserved in cryogenic stasis. As tempers flared, severe weather worsened, hampering the transport of cargo across the settlement. Deep drifts blocked the road leading to the iconic Ganitte Gateway, inaugurated by the Council of Elders in the settlement's eighth year.

Professor Briar and his entourage—Father Sandor, Joseph, Martin, and eight other senior council members—gathered to meet Gordon and Peter Winthrop, accompanied by six crisply uniformed staff officers. After a few well-rehearsed welcoming greetings, the officers wasted no time unfurling flags representing the six Allied Zones back on Earth. Holding the banners high for all to see, they marched in formation behind Gordon and Peter Winthrop toward two waiting Tyloski over-snow vehicles.

Judging by their demeanor alone, the newcomers radiated a tactless arrogance, indifferent to the Freelanders who neither expected nor appreciated such displays. Still, accepting the gesture as a diplomatic slight, Professor Briar and his group stood morosely silent in the freezing air. They exchanged suspicious glances as Gordon Winthrop and his officers climbed into a waiting Tyloski. Gordon glanced through his window, flashing a dismissive sneer at the onlookers before the vehicle roared away toward the Alpha settlement. The official welcome dinner was scheduled to take place in the banquet-sized dining hall.

Suddenly, Professor Briar turned to the driver. "Contact Vehicle-1. I want to make one final brief stop at the Rotunda."

"Yes, Professor," the driver replied promptly.

***

Both vehicles arrived at the Rotunda simultaneously. Professor Briar opened the side door of Vehicle-2 and stepped out first. The others followed, heading toward the circular domed building where a permanent plaque honored the sacrifices of Rachel Sibley and the first Freelanders.

Beneath the dome, glazed mosaic tiles formed a vibrant mosaic of shapes and colors. Yet all eyes were drawn to the towering eighteen-foot statue of Rachel Sibley standing proudly on a green granite pedestal at the Rotunda's center. Her arms were open wide, welcoming all oppressed and impoverished people worldwide to join the Freelander Movement and uphold its principles.

Gordon shifted restlessly in his seat, a warm flush of anger rising within him, though his son's face remained unreadable—no sign of approval or displeasure. Father Sandor, Joseph, and Martin said nothing; they only exchanged small, satisfied smiles.

Visiting the Rotunda to honor Rachel Sibley's memory was Professor Briar's calculated political move—his first subtle checkmate against the haughty Gordon Winthrop. It was payback for Gordon's earlier political ignorance, for encouraging his men to unfurl the Allied banners that had long sown hatred in Freelanders' hearts and rekindled a deep resentment toward the Allied newcomers.

As silence lingered, Martin finally broke it softly, whispering, "She was a beacon when hope was scarce."

Meanwhile, from the Endeavour, a new shuttlecraft launched flawlessly—Shuttle-1089, a last-minute replacement for an older model that had malfunctioned seconds before its scheduled lift-off.

***

Flying at cruising altitude, Shuttle-1089 banked eastward toward the Cradle Mountains and the vast, empty wasteland of snow and ice beyond. Specialist pilot Adrian Sangster shifted his focus to the on-board flight computer, disengaged the Autopilot, and locked in the landing coordinates Sergeant Philip Sheridan had provided.

"Autopilot off," announced the monotone voice of the flight computer.

As they approached the landing zone from the eastern slopes of the Cradle Mountains, Adrian lowered the airspeed to 280 knots. Sudden downdrafts and fierce turbulence buffeted Shuttle-1089. Warning lights blinked urgently, and the terrain avoidance system's monotone voice warned, "Increase power, pitch the nose up to gain more altitude. Low terrain! Pitch up! Low terrain! Pitch up!"

"Shut the fuck up. I know what I'm doing," Adrian muttered into his microphone, frustration thick in his voice.

Bold orange and red warning texts flashed repeatedly on the screen, but Adrian manually trimmed the airspeed and adjusted power. He maintained a steady descent toward the landing zone—four hundred miles downrange, five miles east of the Alpha settlement.

"Sergeant Sheridan, five minutes to the LZ. Gear up!" Adrian shouted.

Sergeant Sheridan, conducting last-minute checks on the field equipment, barked orders to his soldiers. Preparedness was everything; no action took place without his command. Yet, Sheridan's relationship with this select band of mercenary soldiers was strained. He viewed them as dim-witted, a pot calling the kettle black—utterly fitting, considering Gordon Winthrop's criteria for his private army. The men were not chosen for their military skill but for their insatiable greed. Gordon had tempted them with one of the rarest opportunities in the galaxy—the chance to join the Galraithian expedition as elite security personnel alongside a fortune in pay. What Gordon omitted was the peril: the slim-to-none odds of ever returning to Earth.

"Now listen up, scumbags! Ready up! Now!" Sheridan barked again.

Adrian peered out the portside cockpit window just as Shuttle-1089 thumped onto a patch of bare ground, jolting everyone aboard to alertness.

"Engine stop! Power off," he instructed the flight systems computer.

He climbed from the cockpit, opened the rear cargo hatch, and an icy rush of air swept in. The cold bit at his face as the small contingent of sixty elite soldiers, burdened with heavy equipment packs and laser rifles slung over their right shoulders—barrels pointing down—marched out, some bitching, others moaning.

"Thank you, ladies," Adrian quipped with dry sarcasm. "I do hope you had a most enjoyable flight."

A soldier shot him a frown as Adrian passed.

"What's the matter, pisshead? Did you forget something?" Adrian taunted.

The soldier spat on the ground, his disdain evident, then smirked coldly before descending the unloading ramp and disappearing into the snow alongside the others.

Adrian inwardly welcomed their departure. He disliked how heavily armed soldiers felt untouchable aboard his shuttle. Worse still was the pervasive distrust—soldiers and Allied personnel alike viewed Freelanders as undesirable, untrustworthy, and dangerous. Adrian himself was a Freelander, once a pilot in the Freelander air force, scarred by a checkered career. Somehow, after five years flying supplies and personnel to Dome Fuji, he'd found a new path running his own transport business.

Walking toward the cargo bay, Adrian smiled weakly at Sergeant Sheridan, who continued shouting orders at the troops. Adrian shook his head, certain their presence would only bring trouble to the Alpha settlement. He motioned a nearby forklift driver toward the cargo bay area.

"Welcome to Galraithia, sir," the forklift operator greeted curtly.

"Sherinye sheliendo. Bara credimpoli. Thank you. I cannot believe I'm here."

"You're Freelander?"

"Yes. Born and raised in Antarctica."

An odd expression flickered across the forklift driver's face. "This is an Allied shuttlecraft?"

"It might seem strange to you, and frankly, it bothers me that I piloted a shuttle full of Allied soldiers here, but I had little choice. It was my free ticket to Galraithia—the New World."

"Hope good luck keeps following you, sir," the driver said earnestly. "If there's anything I can do, just ask."

"Thank you," Adrian smiled and started to walk away, then paused and turned back.

"Tell me… do you know Joseph Arunui and Martin Brindle?"

"I know the Arunui family well," the forklift driver replied.

"Family?"

"Yes, sir. Professor Joseph Arunui, his wife Satori, and their son Albert."

"That's luck right there. Can you direct me to Professor Arunui's house?"

"Certainly. Head northeast along Snow Road. When you reach the three water storage tanks, his house will be on your right. Captain Brindle's house is about two miles further down on the same side."

"You've been most helpful. Thank you."

"Very welcome, sir."

Standing still, the cold seeped through his leather jacket. Adrian zipped it up tightly and added, "One last thing before I go—be careful with those ammo boxes stacked over there. Old chemical munitions don't take kindly to sudden forklift movements."

"Yes, sir," came the prompt reply.

***

As Adrian turned right onto Snow Road, heading northeast, he spotted Sergeant Sheridan and Gordon Winthrop's hand-picked mercenary soldiers about two thousand yards ahead. They marched single-file against the biting cold wind, moving in the same direction.

Freelanders flanked the formation, their expressions arrogant and self-important, deliberately giving the soldiers a wide berth. Though Adrian was too far away to discern their worried faces, he sensed the Freelanders' celebration of the historic occasion was tinged with anger. The sight of heavily armed Allied mercenaries approaching the Alpha settlement was a risk the Freelander settlers found wholly unacceptable.

Aware of the tension, Professor Briar had sent Gordon Winthrop explicit instructions—including the location of

475

the soldiers' barracks—which had to be situated at a reasonable distance from the Alpha settlement.

***

Albert, Walter, and Jonathon broke from the crowd and ran toward the armed soldiers clad in gray-black uniforms and polished black leather boots.

"Welcome to Galraithia! Welcome to Ashyr!" the boys shouted eagerly. A female soldier holding a large laser rifle gave a faint smile and waved at the three Galraithian boys, who knew little of Earth's violent, destructive past.

"If you befriend these people, treat them well, they will cut your throat while you sleep," Sergeant Sheridan barked. Then, targeting Jonathon—who showed particular interest in rifles and shooting skills—he shouted, "You three, piss off! Are you deaf, boy? Move away!"

Despite the sharp rebuff, Jonathon, Albert, and Walter trailed behind the marching soldiers until they reached three water storage tanks and several greenhouses. All Freelander structures—constructed primarily from regolith panels—were not permanent fixtures sunk into frozen ground; instead, they rested on hydraulic stilts and skis, designed to be moved easily, whatever the weather.

Around the water tanks clustered a dozen buildings, most of them smaller than the greenhouses. Two hangar-style structures—Buildings P and Q—stood neatly between the electric motor room and a frozen riverbed. The smaller Q-Building held the stripped-down Phoenix shuttle, five mothballed Far-Star rocket engines, and contingency plans for any unforeseen cataclysmic extinction event.

Sergeant Sheridan swung open the metal doors of P-Building, an empty hangar. His soldiers swarmed inside as he contemplated the space's suitability: temporary barracks, armory, mess hall, and galley. It would also serve as the private quarters for Gordon and Peter Winthrop until better accommodations were arranged. Suddenly, Commander Alistair Tyler entered P-Building, pulling Sheridan aside. "Gather your people and equipment. We're leaving P-Building immediately."

Sheridan narrowed his eyes, stepping closer in challenge. "Freelander, who do you think you're talking to?"

"I'm talking to you, Sergeant. We're marching back to the Keyway Valley. It's getting dark."

Sheridan sneered, voice thick with contempt. "I don't take orders from you or any stinking Freelander. You better walk out while you still can." He glanced at his exhausted soldiers, hurrying to set up hammocks for the night.

Captain Winthrop appeared and overheard the tense exchange. The soldiers snapped to attention beside their slung hammocks and saluted him sharply. He stepped between Sheridan and Tyler.

"Sergeant Sheridan, you will follow Commander Tyler's orders. Is that understood?"

Exasperated, Sheridan shook his head and spat back, "Why should I? I answer only to one man—your father. He gave me explicit instructions before we left Endeavour: set up temporary barracks inside P-Building."

Peter Winthrop's frustration cracked through his calm. "Sergeant, we don't have time for this nonsense! Nearly 9,000 people are freezing outside!"

"That's not my problem," Sheridan snapped.

"It is everyone's problem!" Captain Winthrop yelled.

Sergeant Sheridan doubled down. "Your father's instructions were clear to me. I intend to follow them."

Growing angrier, Captain Winthrop tried reasoning, "Understand this: there's no room inside the Habitat Ring for anyone, so we had to find alternative housing—fast."

Sheridan scoffed. "Coming here was a mistake. There's nothing but this shit-hole."

Alistair Tyler cut in, voice sharp. "Exactly what did you expect? Shimmering condominiums and the easy life?"

Sheridan turned away, anger simmering beneath the surface. He had never hidden his purpose — to protect Gordon Winthrop and carry out his orders. But Gordon was aging, and living with the Freelanders wasn't socially acceptable. "If we can't stay here, where do we go?" Sheridan asked, turning to Tyler.

"There are several deep caves nearby, carved from rare Longese ganitte and limestone. No major obstacles or dangers."

Some soldiers exchanged looks at the mention of Longese ganitte—a rare crystal back on Earth—and nodded, intrigued by the promise of valuable mineral seams. Tyler continued, "The caverns contain freshwater streams and thermal springs—excellent shelters from the elements."

Sheridan glanced toward Captain Winthrop for confirmation.

"It's only temporary," Winthrop assured.

"We estimate the caverns can hold six thousand people, maybe more," Tyler said.

Sheridan shook his head in disbelief. "Temporary?"

"Yes. We intend to build permanent residential buildings and barracks in the western Keyway Valley, with your help and the Freelanders'," Tyler explained.

A soldier stepped forward suddenly, shouting, "I don't work with Freelanders! Don't need their help!"

Sheridan turned to Winthrop, disdain clear in his tone. "Why care about the stinking Freelanders? We both know your father would never trust them."

"Sergeant, I strongly suggest you follow Commander Tyler's orders — or you might find yourself out there in the frozen wilderness, naked and alone."

Sheridan fell silent, glaring hard at Captain Winthrop.

"Are my intentions clear, Sergeant?"

"Crystal clear," Sheridan said. "But I think you're making a mistake."

"I will not tolerate your insubordination any longer. Apologize to Commander Tyler—now."

Winthrop turned away to speak with a fabricator who had entered.

Reluctantly, Sheridan apologized to Alistair. Tyler was no fool but believed in second chances. Sheridan did not qualify.

"I do not accept your apology," Tyler said bluntly. "Now tell your men to lay down their firearms—unloaded and without power crystals. Carrying offensive weapons is forbidden."

"Careful, Freelander, you're pushing your luck," Sheridan muttered under his breath.

Captain Winthrop returned, noticing the tension. "Is there a problem?"

"No, sir," Sheridan responded, hiding his contempt behind forced politeness, though his eyes revealed otherwise.

***

Young Albert Arunui had discovered a clever way to slip in and out of P-Building unnoticed. He hadn't needed any high-tech jammer — just soft, sticky candy pressed over motion sensors and camera lenses. Still, Albert knew they couldn't remain hidden from watchful eyes for much longer. So, the three friends quietly crept up and took cover behind the water tower standing beside P-Building.

They stayed perfectly silent, watching Sergeant Sheridan and his soldiers file out, followed by Commander Tyler and Captain Winthrop escorting the fabricator.

Sergeant Sheridan gave the fabricator a shove before closing and locking the door behind him. Then the group set off briskly toward the Keyway Valley.

"Come on," Albert whispered, "let's follow them — but stay out of sight."

"No way. I'm not going anywhere," Walter replied stubbornly. "It'll be dark soon!"

"Walter, you want to be an astronaut, but you're scared of the dark? Where's your sense of adventure?"

Jonathon grabbed Walter's arm. "It's going to be dark soon! I don't understand your logic. What's wrong with you?"

Walter didn't care about being afraid of the dark — what frightened him more was being alone. But he was having

fun and definitely didn't want to clash with Albert and
Jonathon.

Soon enough, the boys froze in their tracks as they spotted
Samis, the mine supervisor, and the man they called Garon
walking toward them. After a few steadying breaths, the
young Galraithians turned and ran, heading back to the
Alpha settlement. Before parting ways beneath the
emerging stars, they agreed to keep quiet — to never reveal
the forbidden areas they had seen or the shame of being
caught by Samis and Garon.

When Walter got home, he found his sister Sarah in the
kitchen, preparing dinner.

"What have you been doing all day?" she asked.

"Nothing much."

"Nothing much? You mean just being a nuisance," Sarah
said with a smirk.

"Yeah, whatever. Where's Mom?"

"She had to go to Aunt Marion's. The baby's due any
moment."

"Couldn't you go help?" Walter asked, feigning concern.

"Mom told me to stay home, clean, and cook dinner for
you," Sarah said, glancing out the window as snowflakes
swirled down. "But you're home now. You can cook. I'm
headed to Aunt Marion's."

***

Snowflakes drifted softly over the picturesque valley when
a knock came at Joseph's front door. Surprised and pleased,
Joseph opened it to find his old friend Adrian Sangster
standing on the doorstep. He warmly welcomed Adrian

inside, guiding him to a chair near the fireplace and the dinner table.

Albert lingered in the kitchen doorway, watching his father and the loquacious guest exchange stories of the past. Finally noticing his son, Joseph introduced Albert to Adrian. Soon, Albert was swept into the rhythms of family life and seriously entertained the thought of becoming a shuttle pilot.

Another knock interrupted them. Martin and his son Jonathon arrived for dinner, having wisely avoided the house full of women preparing Marion for childbirth. Warm air greeted the newcomers as Joseph led them to empty chairs around the table. Martin's family was always welcome here.

"Albert, go down to the cellar and fetch some bread and cheese," Joseph instructed.

"And bring up some more beer, please," Martin added. "Jonathon, help him."

"Yes, Father," Jonathon replied, following Albert downstairs.

As they descended, Jonathon broke the silence. "Who's the tattooed man?"

"That's Adrian Sangster, a shuttle pilot," Albert answered eagerly.

"A shuttle pilot!" Jonathon's eyes widened.

"Not just that — he's also a qualified flight instructor."

"I want to be a shuttle pilot when I grow up," Jonathon said with determination.

"You have to be at least nineteen," Albert cautioned. "But don't lose hope. We won't have to wait long before venturing into space."

"How do you mean?"

"I asked Adrian if he could get us on the next shuttle back to Endeavour," Albert said excitedly.

"And what did he say?"

"He promised to find Captain Winthrop and ask for permission. Imagine that — we could be the first Galraithians to explore an Earth ship. Honorary crew members."

"That's fantastic news!" Jonathon beamed. "I can't wait to tell Walter and Sarah."

"We'll see them tomorrow, okay?" Albert said as they climbed the cellar steps, beers and cheese in hand.

"Tomorrow sounds perfect," Jonathon agreed.

"Calaspa!" Albert exclaimed in Freilish.

Back at the table, Jonathon placed the food down and was beckoned over by Martin.

"Jonathon, come say hello."

"Hello, sir."

"I'm delighted to meet you, Jonathon."

"Likewise, sir."

Turning to Martin and Joseph, Adrian smiled warmly. "You both must be immensely proud — two handsome and strapping young men."

***

After dinner, Martin and Adrian settled by the fire, exchanging quiet conversation and enjoying the comforting warmth. Memories of their first meeting on Antarctica's brilliant-white snow and the flight to Dome Fuji flooded Martin's mind.

"Smuggling drums of chicken shit and brik paste didn't make you rich after all," Martin said with a wry smile.

"No," Adrian replied. "I sold everything I had to raise the money for a ticket on the Endeavour. Best decision I ever made."

"And you, Martin? How do you manage living here?"

"Freelanders have a mindset for coping," Martin said, pouring Adrian a glass of Joseph's home-brewed beer. "My wife went into labor. Our second child is due any day now."

"Congratulations, my friend. Wishing you a healthy baby and a happy future. It's wonderful to see you and Joseph after all these years," Adrian said, raising his glass. "You two haven't aged a day since we last met. And me? I'm missing teeth and lost half my body weight during hyper-sleep."

"You should start working your muscles soon, rebuild your strength," Martin advised.

"I should, but I feel tired most of the time," Adrian admitted.

"And how is your wife? The children?"

Adrian downed his beer in a single gulp. "Margaret is just a distant memory now."

Martin's smile faded. "I'm sorry to hear that."

"Don't be. That bitch took our children and ran off with Rashu—the Xiangshan trader I worked for. The same guy who wasted no time putting a price on my head for stealing twelve gold ingots that were rightfully mine. So I came to Galraithia—to start fresh, like everyone else with a death warrant on their back."

Adrian pulled a worn photograph from his pocket and pointed to two boys sitting beside him on a sandy beach. "My boys, Robert and Selwyn. Twelve and ten. I carry this photo to remember the good times we shared. I still feel guilty leaving them behind."

A sudden knock at the front door broke their conversation. Joseph answered to find Cora standing hesitantly on the doorstep—the young trainee midwife who had stayed with Marion Brindle through her labor, until she gave birth to a baby girl.

"I'm sorry to disturb you, sir," Cora stammered, "but I was told Captain Brindle would be here. I need to speak with him."

"Of course, Cora. Come in."

Joseph led her inside and closed the door against the cold, ushering the young woman into the warm dining room.

While Cora smiled softly, relieved and happy to share the news, Martin waited by the fireplace. He nursed Joseph's beer and smoked his pipe, nerves and emotion tightening inside him. Memories of Jonathon's birth flooded back— how Marion had nearly died that day.

Cora met Martin's gaze with bright eyes and a broad smile. "I have wonderful news for you, Captain."

***

485

Marion had given birth to a beautiful, healthy baby girl named Nicolea, in honor of the late Major Nicolea Nikolayev. She and Martin had discussed their second child's name together, agreeing that Nicolea would be perfect for a girl. If the child were a boy, they would name him Ethan Brindle, after Martin's grandfather.

Grateful for Cora's assistance, Martin embraced her warmly before rushing home—so hurriedly, in fact, that he left behind his blue quilted coat and said no goodbye. Joseph shook his head, smiling softly as he closed the front door behind him. He was happy for his best friend yet tinged with envy. The thought of having another child with Satori, whom he loved deeply, stirred complex emotions. Satori, now in her early forties, was honest about her feelings—she believed she was past her prime. Joseph respected her sincerity and the wisdom of the Freelanders' elders.

"Let's drink to new life, and to a future filled with love and happiness for our children," Joseph said, pouring home-brewed whiskey into two shot glasses. Handing one to Adrian, he added in Freilish, "Yera imbrim sheliendo hamingua."

"Yera imbrim sheliendo hamingua," Adrian echoed, raising his glass.

Joseph and the boys joined in unison, their voices warm and full of hope.

The miracle of birth drew friends and loved ones together. Gifts were exchanged, joyful songs filled the air, and everyone eagerly looked forward to seeing little Nicolea. Yet, beneath the surface, outsiders from Earth awaited—ready to shatter the fragile peace between the Freelanders and Gordon Winthrop's Allied settlers.

With the arrival of new colonists and Winthrop's private army, the rhythms of life inside the Alpha settlement shifted dramatically. Gordon Winthrop had broken a verbal pact between two powerful men—a pact that forbade any weaponry within the settlement. As a result, the celebrations in the dining hall were subdued.

Still, Winthrop and his stewards maintained order, ensuring abundant food and drink were supplied. Trays overflowed with provisions, storage containers piled high, and yet the tables soon lay littered with scraps and remnants.

Watching his people scramble for leftovers, Gordon's expression twisted with humiliation. He avoided eye contact with Professor Briar and Father Sandor, even as pride whispered in his mind. Winthrop believed he had saved Ashyr's fledgling colony from extinction—delivering vast stores of surface construction materials for giant greenhouses, food supplies to last a decade, mobile equipment, and a broad array of advanced machinery, including electronic research devices. An army of fabricators equipped with corrosion-resistant, never-needing-charge power cells stood ready under his command.

"Professor Briar," Winthrop called out, "where is Joseph Arunui? I wished to thank him publicly for saving my ship."

Father Sandor rose from his seat. "Joseph and Satori wished to attend, but another commitment has kept them away. They have asked me to offer their apologies."

Winthrop's voice hardened with a mocking edge. "Do you never tire of playing diplomat?"

An uneasy silence settled around the main table.

"Gordon, you said Joseph saved your ship, yet I see no record in the Phoenix logs to verify that claim," Professor Briar said coolly.

Winthrop's six staff officers exchanged nervous glances, unaware of how narrowly the Endeavour had escaped oblivion. Captain Winthrop then explained with quiet pride how Joseph Arunui's quick thinking had launched a navigation beacon toward the far side of the Gale Nebula, some fifteen light-years from Galraithia.

"From that moment, our navigation computer was able to track Phoenix's course home," Captain Winthrop said.

"Joseph's choice to release the beacon was inspiring," Briar acknowledged, "but the spot where Endeavour exited the Gravity-well was pure coincidence. Yet that coincidence ultimately united our people."

***

Sometime later, after the dinner conversations had wound down, Gordon and Peter Winthrop, closely followed by their six staff officers, left the dining hall. Gordon felt no need to negotiate with the Freelanders—neither directly nor through intermediaries, certainly not with a priest. Meanwhile, Professor Briar, Father Sandor, and senior members of the Council of Elders quietly departed, their faces etched with concern over Gordon Winthrop's persistent failure to address the escalating climate crisis and the urgent need to relocate their people to Penglai Island. Outside, temperatures were expected to plunge further in the coming month. The time had come: the Alpha settlement had to be abandoned in favor of the warmer, still-unexplored Equatorial Zone, where Penglai Island— the largest landmass there—offered hope for resettlement.

Speaking for the Allied settlers, Gordon declared that occupying Alpha sooner rather than later was the wiser course. He told Professor Briar he was willing to wait until the Freelanders' scheduled departure, vowing to respect their timeline. Assuming he had finally outmaneuvered his adversary, Professor Briar swiftly convened an emergency session of the Council of Elders. Among those summoned were Professor Lin, Margaret Gray, and Roberta Tully. The honorable council members reached unanimous agreement: Gordon Winthrop was a man neither trustworthy now nor in the foreseeable future.

"Ask yourselves this," Father Sandor intoned gravely. "When the long Galraithian winter finally ends, will Winthrop permit the Freelanders to return to Alpha—to the very homes they built?"

The answer was already clear to all: emphatically no.

As some council members began to rise from their seats, ready to depart, Martin stood as well. His voice was steady but resolute. "If you decide to relinquish the Alpha settlement, then the stripped-down Phoenix, its five Far-Star engines, and every last piece of hardware will not be up for negotiation. With or without the Council's approval, we will move the entire contents of Buildings P and Q to a new, larger holding facility on Penglai Island."

***

489

Reunion

When Dani Li entered the dining hall, the room bore the traces of a lively feast—tables littered with dirty dishes, empty food platters, and drained jugs of ale alongside discarded bottles of wine from Earth.

Cleaners moved hurriedly, clearing away the mess while diners lingered by the open fireplace, drinking and talking. Despite the aftermath, the atmosphere held a certain warmth, though every voice echoed a different note. The loudest belonged to Michael Stoddard.

"Hello, Michael!" Dani called out.

Michael glanced over his shoulder, nearly falling from his chair in surprise as he spotted Dani standing behind him. He jumped up, embracing Dani like a brother long lost. "Man, it's good to see you, Dani."

"Good to see you too, Michael. You look healthy and relaxed."

"I'm a little drunk," Michael admitted with a grin, "but only a little."

"How are Lanfen and Rihanna?" Dani asked.

"I haven't seen them since I got back from Cool Ridge, but I hear they're both well. Lanfen's busy cultivating native plants, and Rihanna—you know her—probably out there interviewing Allied colonists and soldiers."

"I'm glad they're doing okay."

"They never lost hope, even after reporting you missing, presumed dead. But here you are—a little thinner."

Dani gave a quick nod and a faint smile.

"What happened to you, Dani?"

Dani hesitated, uncertain how to explain. "What happened? Let's just say the Phoenix abandoned fifty Freelanders and me at the Outer Marker. We became unwanted guests of Gordon Winthrop aboard Endeavour and were treated with utter indignity."

Michael's expression softened. "I don't know why you were left behind. No one deserves that treatment. Yes, the Allied people carry burdens—their global culture is riddled with social inequalities. But forget the past, Dani. Look ahead. I won't abandon you. I'll help you settle here."

"Thank you. You've been a good friend." Dani felt grateful for support nearby. He also remembered his new ally, Dallas Fitch, a senior Allied officer who had guided and cared for Dani and the fifty elderly Freelanders during their cramped shuttlecraft journey, treating them with respect and kindness.

The last diners shuffled toward the exit. Michael and Dani joined them, stepping outside into the biting cold. Dani barely noticed the chill as they spoke briefly and agreed to visit Lanfen and Rihanna the next evening. Soon enough, they arrived at the Habitat Ring's main entrance. Michael glanced at his wristwatch and stepped into the elevator, but Dani stopped.

"What's the matter?" Michael asked.

"Nothing's wrong," Dani replied. "I just need to walk a bit. Clear my head before sleep."

"Fair enough. Goodnight, Dani."

"Goodnight."

Gordon Winthrop awoke early the next morning feeling unwell. A restless night had left him uncomfortable, and he complained of chest pains to his primary care physician, Doctor Marcus Kemp. In his sixties, Marcus had earned Gordon's complete trust through years of loyal service.

Gordon was rushed to his private medical facility in P-Building, where Doctor Kemp performed a thorough examination. After a battery of tests, he summoned Peter Winthrop to his office.

"Your father has an enlarged heart," Doctor Kemp said bluntly. "But there's no need to worry. Gordon is a strong man. We are even growing a new heart for transplantation. Until it's ready, it's safest to place him in cryostasis as a precaution."

Peter voiced genuine concern for his father's health and sought reassurance for himself.

"Doctor Kemp, do you think my father was poisoned?"

"That's highly unlikely. No signs point to poisoning."

"Then how do you explain such a sudden, life-threatening illness?"

"To be honest, Peter, I don't know. My guess? We lack six million years of human evolution helping us fend off alien bacteria."

"How do you mean?"

"Galraithia may resemble Earth in many ways, but its environment doesn't favor human biology. We're facing new challenges, biologically and medically, here."

***

When Peter Winthrop left the medical facility, concern weighed heavily on his face. His father's health was failing rapidly, struck by a crippling illness that could hardly have come at a worse time. Beneath the surface, dissent was quietly brewing—especially among his father's mercenary soldiers, who felt increasingly marginalized by the Freelanders.

Around two thousand Allied volunteers had taken refuge in several river cave systems nearby. Fresh food arrived regularly from Endeavour, swiftly distributed to the underground community. Geothermal energy, seeping up through Galraithia's crust, provided much-needed heat and electricity.

Yet, life inside the caves was fragile. Conditions could collapse rapidly if food supplies dwindled—a real risk given there was no guarantee the shipments from Endeavour would persist. Gordon Winthrop had not prepared for a major food crisis.

In contrast, the Freelanders had already adapted to Galraithia's harsh environment and its unpredictably shifting food sources. They achieved this with less labor and minimal waste.

The Allied settlers faced the same stark choice: adapt to their new world—or risk perishing in the attempt.

***

Captain Winthrop approached the cave opening and followed a narrow passage to a hot spring nestled within an immense cavern crowded with people. Smaller groups had emerged from the adjacent river cave systems, settling on rock ledges and the flowstone floor, waiting to hear what Captain Winthrop had to say.

Father Antonio stood nearby, consoling a family mourning their first loss—a son named Morgan. The nineteen-year-old had died of complications from pulmonary hemorrhage.

Thirty newcomers had succumbed unexpectedly to the same condition, most men who had been working outdoors in the freezing weather.

"Many here believe my father favors the Freelanders' interests and is blind to the social humiliation of living in these caves," Captain Winthrop began. "But I assure you, he understands the urgency of your plight. This is a terrible burden on your health and safety, but we must exercise patience for just a few more days."

"That's easy for you to say. You're Gordon Winthrop's son. You don't have to sleep on a cardboard box on a hard rock floor!" Sergeant Sheridan shouted angrily. "I'm telling you—we can't stay here any longer! Our people deserve better. Look at these innocent lives—they're getting sick every day because they're forced indoors!"

Peter fixed Sheridan with a glare. "Are you speaking for yourself, Sergeant, or on behalf of everyone here?"

"I speak for everyone," Sheridan shot back. "The Freelanders treat us like filthy animals while you and your father stand by doing nothing."

"Sergeant, you don't care if these people live or die, so shut the fuck up!"

A woman's voice rose from the crowd: "Philip is our elected spokesperson. He has every right to speak."

As her voice faded, she looked away. Captain Winthrop's expression grew troubled. He knew both Allied settlers and Freelanders faced urgent work ahead—building adaptation strategies and forging a resilient partnership essential to survival and prosperity. The primary obstacle was the mutual, instinctive hatred and distrust between the groups. Nevertheless, both sides had to accept that history was beginning anew.

After a heavy silence, Father Antonio stepped forward, meeting the anxious eyes fixed on him.

"I have known the Freelanders for over fifteen years," he said. "It has not been easy—they are godless people. Outsiders have no place in Freelanders' society unless they join the Freelander Movement. That said, most Freelanders treat others as they wish to be treated: with respect and kindness."

A muffled voice rang out across the cavern floor. "I'd rather cut my throat than see my family live among Freelanders."

Captain Winthrop turned to the crowd. "If you have questions about the Freelanders, ask Father Antonio."

"And why should we?" Sheridan challenged.

"Because the Freelanders have decided to leave Ashyr and resettle on Penglai Island," Captain Winthrop replied firmly.

"Once they're gone, Alpha settlement is ours to do as we please!" someone shouted from a high ledge.

"Freelanders would rather die than surrender a piece of land to the Allied people," Sheridan growled.

Captain Winthrop regarded Sheridan with a worried look— an unusual change on his face. "Personally, I prefer to push for their resettlement on the Ranglap Archipelago—the largest archipelago in both landmass and biodiversity, equal to Penglai Island."

"Your father is a liar, and you're no better," snapped fusion specialist Alfonse Benei. "He promised me 12,000 acres west of Keyway Valley."

Sergeant Sheridan stepped closer to Alfonse, his voice low but resolute. "Back on Earth, the Freelanders tried to take our lands and undermine our unity. Seems nothing's changed here in Ashyr. The Freelanders will keep taking—and taking. You can be sure of it, Alfonse."

"Freelanders aren't the problem," Captain Winthrop countered. "Climate change is the real threat, one we must face sooner rather than later. Our survival on this planet depends on how well we work together and adapt."

"How do you mean?" Sheridan demanded.

"Galraithia's temperate northern hemisphere is currently gripped by a mini ice age," Captain Winthrop explained. "The cold has settled over eastern and central Ashyr. Freelander scientists estimate that the planet's winters fluctuate between eighty-six to a hundred years. Moving the settlement and food production indoors on Penglai Island is complex, but it's the challenge they've accepted to survive."

"If what you say is true, then our people should leave with the Freelanders," Sheridan said, voice thick with determination.

"You're free to go with the Freelanders if you choose—no one will stop you, Sergeant," Winthrop replied calmly.

"I don't intend to stay here!" a soldier shouted.

"The Freelander, Alistair, forced us into these caves," Sheridan shouted back. "And where is he now? Preparing to leave Ashyr with the rest of his kind."

"Your father must have known this planet was freezing over," Father Antonio interjected.

Peter shook his head. "The Freelanders' scientists have it wrong. The so-called mini ice age is based on outdated data from just two antiquated weather stations."

A woman stood and challenged, "What makes you sure our scientists got it right?"

Captain Winthrop scanned the cavern but couldn't see her face clearly, obscured by the glare of the pharnas lamps mounted along the wall.

"The Freelanders may rely on old equipment and only two stations for fifteen years," the woman acknowledged. "But from the limited data, their forecasts have proved accurate."

"Madam, I did not come here to debate weather patterns," Winthrop said firmly. "I came to ask for your patience and understanding."

"Our patience wore thin the moment the Freelanders herded us like cattle into these dank caves," Sheridan declared, eyes flashing as he scanned the crowd. "We've been duped by Gordon Winthrop. Coming to Galraithia was a mistake, and I've said so from the start. But it isn't too late to return to Earth."

A tall, powerful man stepped forward, bare to the waist. "Return to Earth? There's no future there."

"You're wrong, Micah," Sheridan shot back. "There's plenty to go back for. My friend Garon here knows every inch of this river system underground. He's shown me vast deposits of metallurgical-grade ganitte," Sheridan said, moving between two rough beams supporting the cavern ceiling.

"What do you mean your friend? Garon is a Freelander," said a man carrying a bucket of hot water near the cave's south entrance.

"I'm not a Freelander!" Garon declared loudly.

"Where this man's loyalties lie changes nothing," Sheridan said. "He knows where the richest ganitte seam is—the largest ever found here. If we help dig it up, we'll be richer than ever dreamed."

Captain Winthrop shook his head. "Gems and precious stones mean nothing here. Freelanders use Longese ganitte for heating and as primary power cells."

"Ganitte is worthless here without a money market," Sheridan sighed, heartened by the crowd's rapt attention. "But back on Earth, a bag of these crystals makes you unimaginably rich. Listen to me, friends: Galraithia isn't the paradise Gordon Winthrop sold us. Look around—step outside the cave. Venture into the frozen wastes. Ask Captain Winthrop what you'll find. But he'll just walk away to spare you the disappointment. Because all you'll find is endless toil, hardship, and finally, death. Is that the life you want for yourselves and your families?"

Philip Sheridan's words stirred the Allied colonists. Young and old alike dared to believe his message. Open displays of resentment toward the Winthrop family became common. Living—and waiting—in chaotic caves was unbearable. They had had enough. Desperate to return to Earth, they urged Sheridan to leave Galraithia as soon as possible.

In small groups, disillusioned voices threw stones toward Captain Winthrop. One struck him sharply on the forehead.

"Garon! Put down those stones," Sergeant Sheridan commanded sharply.

Suddenly, loud voices erupted from a neighboring cavern.

"Listen to me!" Sheridan yelled. "Believe me, I want to go home just as much as you do. But Endeavour has three dead rocket engines. A ship that size can never lift off on two."

"I strongly disagree," said a man standing beside Garon.

"Speaker! Step forward!" Sheridan barked. "You wear Allied clothing, but I don't know you. Guard! Detain that man!"

"My name's Tom Granger," the man said calmly. "I was a staff officer on the Phoenix. Now I help Garon dig ganitte."

Voices rose up immediately. "Kill the Freelander!"

"Tom's done no wrong," Garon shouted back. "He's a hard worker."

"He may be good at work, Garon, but he's still a Freelander," another warned.

Sheridan glanced at Captain Winthrop and Father Antonio but needed no counsel.

"Freelander, you're educated and intelligent. I'll spare your life—for information. If what you say checks out, you can walk away, work with Garon, and do as you please. Understand?"

"I understand perfectly, sir," Tom replied.

"You strongly disagree with me. Why?"

"There are five perfect rocket engines mothballed inside Q-building," Tom said. Sheridan knew the place well—its walls lined with crates.

"Tell me more about what I already suspect," Sheridan said, drawing his sidearm and cocking it.

Tom's mouth dried; his legs trembled.

"Endeavour is a colony ship," he said quickly. "With five good engines, she can reach the edge of the known universe—and beyond."

Sheridan holstered his pistol. "You have my full attention, Mr. Granger. Continue."

"Retrofitting Davis-Molby engines with Far-Star engines should be straightforward, in my opinion, sir."

Sheridan caught the nod from fusion specialist Alfonse Benei.

"Alfonse, you believe Endeavour can take us back to Earth?"

"Provided the ignition chambers handle the excess heat, yes."

"Thank you, Alfonse. That settles it," Sheridan said decisively. "Micah and Aeron, take the Freelander and five men to Q-building. I want those Far-Star engines—and I want them aboard Endeavour ASAP."

"Yes, Sergeant. Consider it done."

"You're a good man, Micah," Sheridan added.

But Captain Winthrop's voice rang out, furious. "Stay away from Q-building! Sergeant Sheridan is a reckless fool who'll get you killed if you listen to him."

Sheridan lunged forward, grabbing Winthrop by the throat and slamming him against the cavern wall. Pressing Winthrop's cheek hard into the stone, Sheridan hissed, "When this planet freezes over and food runs out, you and your Freelanders will tear each other apart like rabid dogs."

"Sheridan, you're insane if you think Endeavour can reach Earth without a competent bridge crew," Winthrop gasped.

Then a fist smashed into Winthrop's face so hard tears welled in his eyes.

"The only reason you're still breathing is because I need you to pilot that ship back," Sheridan snarled.

"Endeavour will never reach Earth, I promise you," Winthrop said defiantly.

"Garon! Get a rope—tie him up!"

"You're making a huge mistake, Sheridan. My father will hunt you and your men like dogs. Anyone who follows will share your fate—I promise."

"If he speaks again, gag him."

"Yes, Sergeant."

Garon bound Winthrop's wrists so tightly circulation stopped. Father Antonio watched silently, a quiet fear gripping him.

"Good Lord, help Captain Winthrop—and forgive me for being weak," the young priest whispered before hurriedly leaving toward the cave's exit, convinced Tom Granger had betrayed his Freelander friends.

***

While Captain Winthrop languished unjustly imprisoned aboard the Endeavour, Rihanna prepared the family home for a reunion dinner set for eight. She had invited Dani Li to join them and had crafted a fabulous meal in anticipation.

501

"You have a lovely home," Dani said, shedding his coat. Rihanna took it from him and hung it carefully in the hall closet.

"Alistair thinks the house's a bit small," she remarked with a smile.

Dani followed Rihanna to the dining room, where Alistair, Lanfen, and Michael Stoddard, and Father Sandor sat around the table with the Tyler children, Sarah, and Walter. The children eagerly awaited visits from their parents' friends—especially Michael. Whenever he came by before dinner, he would regale them with tales of valiant knights clad in shining armor, strange ocean worlds, and marvelous underwater cities.

***

There were warm hugs and handshakes all around. Dani expressed his gratitude for the invitation to Rihanna and Alistair's home.

"Don't be silly," Rihanna replied. "You, Lanfen, and Michael are part of our family now."

"Dani, we're truly happy to have you here," Alistair added. Yet beneath his words, a flicker of jealousy lingered. He knew about Dani and Michael—both held a soft spot for Rihanna and shared similar aspirations. But Rihanna was happily married, with two children she dearly loved. That truth changed everything. She would never risk her family's happiness.

"Just like old times," Michael said fondly.

"Just like old times," Rihanna echoed softly.

Dani felt his throat tighten as tears welled in his eyes. At the dinner table, an empty place was set—a porcelain plate and silver cutlery accompanied by a carefully mounted photograph of Walter Briar. The ornate wooden frame held pride of place at the head of the table. The picture spoke volumes of Walter's wisdom, generosity, and abiding love. Time had not lessened Rihanna's devotion to her beloved uncle.

Dani couldn't help but notice how youthful Rihanna, Lanfen, and Michael looked. They hadn't aged a day since he last saw them. Much of the evening's conversation revolved around the precarious supply of staple foods and the ongoing failure to grow surplus crops in Galraithia's odorless soil. That's when Dani learned the secret behind their youthful appearance.

"It's still a hotly debated topic," Alistair said with a sigh.

"And much argued among biologists and botanists," Father Sandor added. "Those tiny purple berries contain extraordinary molecular properties. They enable telomeres to regrow, repairing DNA damage and slowing the aging process."

"I don't blame the Allied folk for wanting a share of the berries," Michael remarked.

"But we can no longer gather any," Father Sandor said, irritation creeping into his voice. "Berry plants enter hibernation during the long Galraithian winter. Gordon Winthrop and the Allied leaders know this well."

"Speaking of Gordon Winthrop," Rihanna said, looking around. "Where is he? Father Sandor hasn't seen or spoken with him for days. I think something's wrong."

"Ill, maybe?"

"Michael, you know him—he loves overseeing everything," Rihanna replied with a knowing grin.

"I wouldn't worry too much," Alistair said. "Captain Winthrop would've told me if his father were ill."

"When was the last time you spoke to him?" Rihanna asked, eyes intent on Alistair.

"Sarah, could you pass me the asparagus?" he asked, avoiding her gaze.

"Alistair, I'm asking you a question."

"Just doing my job as best I can. That's all there is to it," Alistair snapped.

"Yes, sir, Commander, sir," Rihanna replied, a teasing glint in her eyes.

Alistair's expression grew dark with anger. He had never spoken to Rihanna like that before.

Walter glanced at his mother, who looked visibly upset. He couldn't understand Alistair's harshness toward Rihanna. Why was he unwilling to admit he had led the Allied soldiers into the Keyway Valley caves?

***

Sometime later, more guests arrived at the Tyler house: Brendan Aitama, and the affable Andre Zarovski. Dinner had already been served, eaten, and cleared away, so Rihanna hurried to the kitchen and returned with trays of homemade ginger biscuits.

The company mingled easily—true to Freelanders' nature, everyone carried a story to tell. Brendan was the first to speak, openly sharing his feelings and harrowing experiences. He showed photographic evidence of giant Raptors, flesh-eating fish, and the picturesque Paraihe Island, with its fragrant vegetation and abundant, luscious fruit. Despite escaping death that fateful day, Brendan confessed he was haunted by a recurring nightmare of being torn apart by wild animals.

Dani shook his head in disbelief. "Has anyone returned to the island since then?"

"We sent a drone a few weeks ago," Brendan replied. "But aerial reconnaissance showed only empty nests—no birds anywhere."

"The birds left Paraihe Island for the warm Equatorial Zone more than a month ago," Father Sandor explained.

"Six weeks ago, to be exact," Rihanna added as she passed the ginger biscuits around.

"Okay, six weeks ago," Andre quipped. "The birds knew winter was coming. It's our fault we're still freezing our asses off here."

"Andre, you overlook the fact we no longer have the transport resources to just up and leave," Father Sandor said sternly. "The Phoenix was stripped down to a bare metal shell. The top aeronautical engineers debate whether Phoenix will be flight-ready in three months—or three years. We have few options."

"The Aquarius Lander has size limitations," Alistair pointed out. "It can carry only twelve people at most and has a short-range fuel tank. Plus, the four ATVs make up the lion's share of our ground transport."

Rihanna glanced between her husband and Father Sandor. "Daytime lows are plummeting fast, and you two are still debating transport options? The birds have all flown to the Equatorial Zone. How many more signs do you need, Alistair? We must leave—and soon."

A knock sounded at the door. "That must be Martin," Rihanna said. "Don't get up, Alistair. I'll let him in."

As Rihanna strode toward the door, Alistair's gaze
followed her. "Seems I can never do enough for that
woman," he muttered to the others. "But don't mind me—
just thinking aloud. Please carry on."

"We could use Endeavour's double-decked shuttles," Dani
suggested. "There are at least twenty idle shuttlecraft at the
landing zone."

"That's an excellent idea," Father Sandor agreed. "Leaving
such valuable machines to rot was shortsighted. We should
take advantage. But I doubt Gordon Winthrop will freely
hand over shuttles or security access codes."

"Father Sandor, if it's all right, I'd like to speak with
Captain Winthrop tomorrow morning," Alistair said. "He's
educated, understanding, and intelligent. Maybe he can
help."

"By all means. Peter Winthrop is also very perceptive,"
Father Sandor replied. "He knows we don't have time to
rebuild Phoenix."

"Priest, why do you always complicate things?" Andre
scoffed. "There are only two choices: stay here and freeze
to death, or migrate to the Equatorial Zone."

"I'm still a newcomer," Dani said cautiously, "and this is
your fifteenth winter on the planet. So, I don't grasp the
sudden urgency to abandon Alpha now."

Andre smiled knowingly. "Galraithia has the longest orbital
transit in this binary star system. Unfortunately for us,
we've arrived mid-journey—an 186-year trek toward
Daedalus, a cold black dwarf star. Soon, both hemispheres
will freeze over. The temperature drop will be so severe
only cold-resistant bacteria will survive."

"It's not all doom and gloom," Father Sandor assured them. "Our people will be perfectly safe in the volcanic Equatorial Zone, living day by day as they always have."

As Martin entered the dining room, he immediately felt the radiant heat emanating from a sizeable ganitte crystal at the center. "Hello, gentlemen," he greeted cordially. "Sorry I'm late."

"You missed a wonderful dinner," Michael said warmly.

"Martin, my good friend, come and sit here beside me," Andre invited.

Lanfen motioned for Martin to sit beside her.

"Thank you for the offer, Andre, but I've got a better one," Martin replied with a smile.

"Suit yourself," Andre said with a playful grin. "You're no longer a good friend, then."

"Lanfen, you always look beautiful," Martin said softly.

A blush crept across Lanfen's cheeks. "Did I hurt Andre's feelings?"

"Oh, don't mind him. He's just a soft Russian bear," Martin teased.

"How are Marion and baby Nicolea?"

"Nicolea is thriving," Martin said proudly. "Marion's doing well too; it'll be another week or two before she's fully recovered. She lost a lot of blood during delivery, but Doctor Mason is pleased with her progress."

Sarah poured Martin a cup of hot tea. "Thank you."

"You're welcome, Captain."

"Sarah, I forgot to thank you for helping Marion and the midwives. Marion wanted to be here tonight to thank you and Lanfen personally."

"I'm afraid I wasn't much help," Sarah said, lowering her eyes.

"Sarah wanted to throw up when she saw the baby coming out," Walter teased.

"You're a lying toad!" Sarah snapped, storming off to the kitchen.

"Sarah!"

Alistair shot Walter a stern look. "Apologize to her, Walter. Don't belittle your sister ever again. Do you understand me, son?"

"Yes, father."

"Alistair, you are an overbearing parent," Andre retorted.

"Easy for you to say, Andre. You don't have children."

"Okay, enough," Andre interrupted, raising his voice. "Pour us some more whiskey. Let's drink to our dear friends who have passed on."

The room fell quiet as Professor Briar and Joseph Arunui arrived, engaging in a hushed conversation with Alistair, who had answered the door. Without delay, they approached Rihanna and the gathered guests by the fireplace bearing disturbing news.

"Five Far-Star engines stored in P-Building and Q-Building are missing—presumed stolen," Professor Briar announced. "The thieves had full access to sensor codes and alarm systems. Security found no signs of forced entry."

Only six people held access codes: five present around the fireplace, who had invited Professor Briar and Joseph to join them, and Tom Granger—who hadn't been seen since leaving his two-bedroom Habitat Ring apartment.

"Let's be clear," Professor Briar said firmly. "Allegations are meaningless without proof. Besides, without dedicated thermal controllers, these engines are useless."

"Who would steal five unpaired engines?" Brendan wondered aloud.

"The one who'd benefit most," Dani answered.

"What do you mean?" Brendan pressed.

"After waking from hypersleep, I shared a recovery cell with Alfonse Benei, a fusion engine specialist. He asked if I'd signed a work contract. I hadn't. He offered me a job clearing land and planting hemp seeds. Then he told me about Gordon Winthrop's offer: a large parcel of land in exchange for drawings of paired Far-Star engines with Davis-Molby thermal control systems."

"Winthrop and his old tricks—offering what isn't his to give," Brendan said bitterly.

"I don't know if Benei was truthful," Dani admitted.

"I know Benei never lied," Professor Briar said. "The Council of Elders struck a deal with Winthrop—land west of the Keyway Valley for unlimited access to Endeavour's telecom network. But Winthrop demanded more: two Far-Star engines with fully functional thermal controllers. The Council refused to hand those over."

"Gordon Winthrop would never abandon a deal he can't win," Andre said. "When he wants something badly, he stops at nothing."

"Winthrop believes himself honorable," Michael added, "and he'd never admit to theft."

"Yes, but we must find those engines," Professor Briar insisted.

"Maybe finding the thieves would be easier," Andre suggested.

Martin turned to Joseph. "Adrian Sangster could help."

"Adrian Sangster? He can't be trusted," Father Sandor said, shaking his head. "He abandoned his wife, children, and the Freelander people to become an Allied shuttle pilot aboard the Endeavour."

Walter tugged Captain Brindle's sleeve, eager to speak. Martin's eyes narrowed in irritation—Freelander children were taught never to interrupt adult conversations unless absolutely necessary.

"Pardon me, sir," Walter said earnestly. "I met Adrian Sangster, the shuttle pilot, at the arcade earlier today. He spoke to Albert and Jonathon before he left."

Joseph noticed the flicker of worry on Martin's face. "The arcade closed two hours ago," Martin reminded him, already considering their next move.

"I know. And we don't have time to hunt for Adrian," Joseph replied firmly.

Professor Briar turned to Martin. "All five engines are vital—insurance against unforeseen events that might force us to abandon this planet and return to Earth."

"I understand, sir. I'll do everything in my power to recover the engines—one way or another," Martin vowed.

"I'm sure you will, Captain."

Martin quickly looked to Brendon. "Do you think you can get Joseph and me aboard the Endeavour without raising suspicion?"

"Yes," Brendon said decisively. "Docking with Endeavour is straightforward. My concern is finding a shuttle orbiter fueled enough to get us there—and back to Echo-6."

"The odds of finding a fully fueled orbiter are slim," Joseph said.

"But not impossible," Martin replied calmly.

"Alright," Michael Stoddard spoke up. "Let's say you find an orbiter and manage to dock. Then what?"

"With Brendon's flying skills and your negotiating talents," Martin said, "we'll find a way inside."

"Wait a minute!" Michael protested. "If you think I'm putting on a spacesuit and going back out there, you're crazy. Endeavour's decks have advanced security, wireless sensor networks, and who knows what else."

"I'm surprised, Michael. Backing down? You never back away from a challenge."

"No, but this one might be unwinnable."

"You worried about getting caught or killed?" Brendon asked.

"Aren't you?"

"No. Once you face death, fear fades."

"Michael, we won't get caught. We can do this."

"Boarding Endeavour is tough enough. Navigating its maze of corridors and decks without the right security codes is downright dangerous," Rihanna warned.

"Look, I understand the risks," Martin said, frustration creeping in. "But the Council of Elders wants those engines back."

"I'm tempted to give Winthrop an ultimatum: return the engines or we destroy Endeavour," Andre added with a grin.

Laughter rippled through the room—even Father Sandor chuckled.

"Do we have concrete evidence?" Alistair asked seriously.

"We have partial video from a damaged camera," Professor Briar replied. "Six men wearing markings unique to Winthrop's mercenary force were seen inside P-Building before the engines and navigation gear disappeared."

"Captain, I'd like to join your team," Dani said. "I know Endeavour's security protocols and layout well."

Martin paused, then nodded. "You're a man of many talents, Dani. Glad to have you."

"I've got some ideas to buy us time," Joseph added confidently.

"This should be interesting," Father Sandor remarked.

Joseph then outlined his plan to board Endeavour and access the reactor and engine rooms without raising alarms.

"Oh, one more thing," Joseph added. "Echo-6 is the closest landing zone to Q-Building. It'd be ideal to get a heavy transport vehicle there."

"Alistair and I will arrange that immediately," Andre promised.

"Thank you."

Rihanna hurried to an open cupboard. "It's minus 86 degrees Fahrenheit outside. I've got a few chemical heat packs left if anyone wants one."

"I'll take one, please—if you have a spare."

"Here you go—nice and warm for you, Michael."

"Thanks, girl. Always looking out for me."

"Take care, Michael. Be careful up there."

"Don't worry. You know I'm not the hero type."

***

It was never easy whenever Father Sandor said goodbye, and tonight was no different. He wrapped a woolen scarf snugly around his neck and slipped away quietly into the darkness. His footsteps echoed softly as he walked, until a familiar voice called out to him.

"Father Sandor, what are you doing out here?" Father Antonio asked, breathless.

"Captain Winthrop was arrested at the Keyway Valley caves!" Antonio blurted out.

"Who arrested him?"

"Sergeant Philip Sheridan," Father Antonio declared grimly.

"Sergeant Sheridan? On what grounds?"

"I'm not sure—at least not entirely. I saw two of Sheridan's men bind Captain Winthrop's wrists and force him into a shuttlecraft bound to rendezvous with the Endeavour."

Father Sandor tilted his head back, gazing up at the star-studded sky, and exhaled deeply. He couldn't fathom why Sergeant Sheridan would want to arrest Peter Winthrop.

513

"Father Sandor, what do we do now?"

"We're going to see our mutual friend, Doctor Marcus. I suspect he might want to warn Gordon Winthrop—he could be next."

The young priest caught Father Sandor's gaze and hurried after him, his mind racing with the terrible consequences that could unfold should harm come to Gordon Winthrop.

***

When Father Sandor and Father Antonio arrived at Q-Building, they exchanged tense, anxious glances. The automatic security doors stood wide open, flickering as the interior lights flashed erratically. Stepping into the long chamber, their eyes swept from wall to wall, taking in the destruction.

Medical equipment lay broken within the small cryo chamber—shattered pieces scattered across the floor. Two medical fabricators stood silent amid the debris in the wide corridor, their circuits smoldering and venting acrid fumes.

Father Antonio's gaze dropped, recoiling from the pool of dark blood staining the floor. There, beside a cryo bed, lay the lifeless body of Doctor Marcus, face pale and expressionless—murdered at close range, execution-style.

Father Sandor stood silently over the old doctor's corpse before moving to a nearby cryo bed. Peering inside, his breath caught as he beheld the still form of Gordon Winthrop. Life support machines had been violently disabled: catheters ripped out, intravenous tubes severed, and cryo fluid flow halted.

Gordon Ercial Winthrop—the man who once held sway over Earth's economic heart—now lay cold and lifeless, a victim of ruthless neglect.

514

"Gordon is dead, and his son is missing," Father Antonio said, his voice trembling with a mix of sorrow and dread. "This nightmare is the devil's handiwork. If this is what festers here, then all life on this planet is doomed to a violent end."

His trembling finger pointed to the wall, where words stained in blood declared: *Unleash hell on the Freelander nations!*

Father Sandor shook his head slowly, disbelief etched deep in his features.

"Antonio, send word to the head of Freeland Security—tell him exactly what's happened. I'll return to Commander Tyler's house to warn the others. We must move quickly— the perpetrator may still be here."

Retribution

Robert Jandamarra let Rachel Vaughn handle all the packing while Ryan Chyloe finished prepping the shuttle scheduled to return to Echo-6 with fresh food supplies.

"Rob, shuttle B-1157 is ready to go," Ryan said into his Vox microphone.

"Okay, I copy, mate. Do you have landing instructions?" Robert asked.

"No. Dallas Fitch has the coordinates. Echo-6 is now the designated landing zone."

"Dallas told me he's staying on board for another month," Robert replied.

Ryan scanned a list on the shuttle's computer screen. "Well, according to the onboard computer, Lee Hapgood is the only qualified shuttle pilot on Endeavour."

"That can't be right," Robert said calmly. "Check again."

"Power surges are messing with the main system again," Ryan said, frustration creeping into his voice.

"Ryan, your signal's breaking up. Do you read me? Over."

Rob adjusted his microphone volume. "Ryan, do you copy? Over."

"I'm having data comm issues down here, Rob. The Sequanta computer just rebooted itself—no explanation. I'll call you back."

Rachel finished packing the last of her belongings into a large suitcase and looked around the cabin, her face alight with excitement at finally leaving the Endeavour.

"Rob, I'm ready to go if you are."

Glancing at his wristwatch, Robert agreed it was time. Slinging an army rucksack over his shoulder, he followed Rachel toward Muster Station-9.

"Ryan, what's going on?" Robert asked.

"Sergeant Sheridan is holding up the boarding line."

A young woman stepped forward. "Sergeant, you don't seem to understand. Our duty roster aboard Endeavour is finished. Our families and friends are waiting for us at Echo-6."

Sheridan unholstered his laser pistol. "This shuttle is not going to Echo-6."

The woman and six coworkers reluctantly stepped back.

"Back to your cabins. Now!" Sheridan barked.

"Hey, dickhead!" Robert Jandamarra snapped, throwing a punch that caught Sheridan under the chin and sent him sprawling. Robert grabbed the laser pistol.

"You must have maggots in your head, Sheridan. Get up, or I'll kick those maggots out myself," Robert growled, glaring down with unforgiving, furious eyes.

Unsteady, Sheridan stepped back. Ryan moved quickly, snatching the portable radio clipped to Sheridan's belt.

"I'll keep this, thanks."

"You'll pay dearly for this, Jandamarra," Sheridan warned through gritted teeth.

Robert didn't suffer fools gladly but was mindful of the risk to Ryan, Rachel, and himself if Sheridan retaliated later. He opened the laser pistol, removed the power crystal, and pocketed it.

"Stop talking and start walking, Sergeant."

Sheridan stormed off down the grated walkway, shoving Lee Hapgood aside with enough force to nearly knock him down.

"Hey! Watch the hell where you're going!"

"Lee, you're wasting breath on a worthless piece of trash," Ryan said quietly.

Lee had long thought Philip Sheridan a heartless bastard.

"I hate that guy."

"You're not the only one."

Ryan glanced at Robert. "Sheridan's afraid of you, Rob. He threw his weight around, but everyone saw how weak he really is. Best to leave him be."

Robert nodded slowly. "You might be right."

"It's been a crazy morning," Lee muttered. "Everywhere I go, people are stuck in a bad mood."

"The Automatic Muster System (AMS) came online today," Ryan added. "The roll call separated children from parents."

Lee pulled a slip of paper from his pocket—the Sequanta computer's orders. "Something's off. It told me to report to Muster Station-9 and take a group of colonists and Winthrop reps down to Echo-6."

"Solar flare activity is causing power outages and glitches throughout the ship," Ryan said. "The engineers are working on it—that's all I know."

"That may be," Lee said grimly, "but my job for the next twelve hours is Officer of the Deck."

Rachel leaned out of shuttle B-1157's forward hatch.

"Lee, there are sixty people strapped in and waiting. Their names were checked against the Endeavour muster roll."

Lee sighed. "Rachel, I'm the Acting Officer of the Deck for the next twelve hours. I'm not authorized to fly a shuttle."

"It's a forty-minute flight to Echo-6," Robert said. "Anyway, Adrian Sangster is rostered as Officer of the Deck today too."

"That guy's unreliable. You know it."

"Adrian can be unpredictable, but he's a good pilot. So, are you flying this bucket of bolts—or do I call Adrian?"

"Alright, alright. I'll fly you down. But I'm shaking my head on this one."

"You're a good man, Lee."

"Yeah, right. Just hope I don't regret it. Could lose my job over this."

"You won't lose it. I'll square things with Dallas Fitch if anything goes sideways."

"What could possibly go wrong?"

"You're a pain, Hapgood. Now stop worrying and fly us down to Echo-6."

***

Like all shuttle pilots, Lee Hapgood was a skilled navigator, yet his sweaty palms and anxious expression betrayed his nerves as he approached Echo-6 for his first attempted landing.

"We've lost all data from Endeavour," the navigation computer announced over the loudspeaker.

Lee toggled a data switch several times. "Abort guidance system. Switching to manual control."

"Manual control engaged. Aye, sir."

"Lee, is everything all right?" Rachel asked, concern in her voice.

"Ask me again in two minutes," Lee replied grimly.

"Warning: 0.08 degrees off course," the computer warned.

"I have control," Lee said firmly. "Drifting slightly right... Thrusters on full!"

The shuttle touched down with a slight bounce.

"Engines off!"

"Engines off. Aye, sir."

Lee felt sweat trickle down his back. "I'm getting too old for this. Computer, open the forward airlock door."

"Opening forward airlock door. Aye, sir."

Ryan was the first to unstrap and step out, followed by Lee, Rachel, Robert, and the rest of the passengers. The freezing air hit their warmed faces, stealing their breath. It was too cold to linger outside, yet they all stood silently, shivering while admiring the eerie light cast by Galraithia's twin moons, illuminating the snow-capped mountains with a pale shade of greenish-blue.

Ryan scanned the horizon, hoping to glimpse the Alpha settlement. Instead, he saw only a sprawling plain blanketed with snow and ice; no buildings or infrastructure in sight.

"The Keyway Valley isn't what you expected?" Lee asked.

"No," Ryan replied. "I remember first seeing the reconnaissance photos—a verdant paradise."

"I think it's beautiful here," Rachel said softly. "Like a surrealist painter's dream."

"Definitely a stunning location," a young woman remarked—the same one who had exchanged a few words with Sergeant Sheridan earlier.

"Mr. Jandamarra, thank you for putting that obnoxious sergeant in his place."

"Sergeant Sheridan won't bother you again... Miss?"

"Turner. Rebecca Turner."

"Pleased to meet you, Miss Turner. I hope the flight wasn't too rough," Robert said, glancing toward Lee and Ryan, who stood just out of earshot.

"Right now, I'm pretty sure that's the last thing on anyone's mind," Ryan muttered.

"Do you mind if we move inside?" Rebecca asked. "It's two in the morning, freezing out here. I think we ought to get out of the cold."

Robert nodded. "We'd better listen to Ryan. He's a tough one."

"That Ryan doesn't look tough to me. Honestly, I think he's cute," Rebecca said with a teasing smile.

Robert rolled his eyes.

Ryan felt embarrassed and awkward. It was the first time a woman other than Rachel had complimented his good looks.

"Okay, let's get down to business. Lee, do you have an aerial map of the landing zone?"

"Yes, it's on the navigation console. I'll grab it."

"Thank you."

As Lee left to retrieve the map, Ryan turned to Robert. "There's nothing but static on the radio. I doubt anyone knows we're here."

"There's an overhead locker with heavy winter gear. We can hike to Alpha settlement. Your call."

"Alpha can't be too far," Ryan mused. "Temperatures are dropping fast. I think we should stay here tonight."

"Okay, boss."

Lee returned with the map, holding it awkwardly. "Sorry, I accidentally spilled some cold coffee on it."

Ryan snatched the map and unfolded it carefully. "All right, let's take a look."

"Chyloe, I can't wait around here much longer. I need to get back to Endeavour," Lee said impatiently.

"Lee, I told you I'll square things with Dallas Fitch."

"Don't patronize me, Rob. It's my job on the line, not yours. Give me thirty minutes to find the nearest shelter, then I'm out of here."

"Fair enough. We'll start heading to Alpha just before sunrise."

"I'm sorry, Chyloe, but I have to think about my own skin."

"Lee, enough talk. I want to move on, but first, you'd better prep the shuttle for liftoff before the fuel line freezes."

***

Three o'clock in the morning, local solar time, and the outside temperature had plunged to minus 101 degrees Fahrenheit. Lee had finished prepping the shuttle's fusion engine; launching to rendezvous with the Endeavour was now his call. Yet, most passengers had slipped into a blissful sleep, and Lee's frustration simmered. No sign of a welcoming party from the Alpha settlement appeared, and the minutes ticked by in the dead silence of the remote landscape.

Farther away, Rover-1, an all-terrain vehicle, veered steadily away from landing zone Delta-12. Inside, five occupants struggled with the fruitless search for a shuttlecraft fueled and ready for an orbital linkup with the Endeavour.

"Captain, Echo-6 is the next landing zone on Endeavour's chart," Brendon said firmly.

Michael studied the paper map intently. "I know this area well. Head for Cool Ridge, then cross the frozen Ashyr River at grid reference AR 609-473."

"Got it," Martin replied, punching in the coordinates. He pressed the throttle forward, and Rover-1 surged to its top speed.

"Martin, the extreme cold is draining the power cells fast. Energy capacity is down to sixty percent."

"Stay calm, Joseph. We're almost there."

***

With the moon Ithinia hanging low on the horizon and its twin Galrah high above, bathing the landscape in a calming turquoise glow, the silhouette of shuttle B-1157 finally came into view.

Brendon wasted no time. He leapt from the rover, hurried to the shuttle's fuel tank management system, and flashed a thumbs-up to Martin, who waited patiently in the driver's seat.

"We're in luck, Captain. Shuttle B-1157 has enough fuel to return to the Endeavour."

Martin and his men moved swiftly and silently toward the outer airlock door. Dani glanced around in surprise as the airlock swished open without requiring an access code.

Martin charged into the shuttle's passenger cabin, abruptly stopping short. His eyes widened in shock and unease at the sight of Allied folk already on board.

"Mir ar lest brin dant? What are these people doing out here?" he demanded.

Ryan rose quickly, apprehension furrowing his brow. "Greetings. My name is Ryan Chyloe."

Martin stepped forward and shook Ryan's hand firmly. "Captain Martin Brindle."

Suddenly, Martin turned sharply to his men. "All of you stand still and listen!"

"I take it this isn't a social call, Captain," Ryan said calmly.

"No, Mr. Chyloe. This is no time for pleasantries."

"Have we done something wrong?"

"Mr. Chyloe, please explain what you're doing here. This is our land!"

"I could ask the same of you, Captain. This shuttlecraft belongs to the Allied People. You and your men are intruding on Allied property."

"Fine. We could argue motives all night. But let's get to the point. Five rocket engines were reported stolen, and there are several suspects."

"A grave mistake, punishable by death or exile to some remote asteroid under Freelander law," Ryan remarked.

"You're familiar with Freeland laws?"

"Yes. I own several of your law books. Rachel Sibley's *New Social Order* was a fascinating read. Now, what do you want from us, Captain? We might be able to help catch the thieves."

"I don't think so," Dani snapped sarcastically.

"We believe an organized conspiracy connects certain Freelanders and mercenaries in Gordon Winthrop's private army. They robbed us of the engines and whatever else they could—and transported the loot back to the Endeavour," Martin explained.

"So you intend to steal them back?"

"Is taking back what's rightfully yours stealing?"

"No, I suppose not," Ryan admitted.

"It's a desperate gamble, if you ask me," Lee said loudly.

Martin barely glanced at Lee as Robert Jandamarra stepped forward.

"Rachel, Ryan, and I helped install two Far-Star engines," Robert said, nodding toward his companions. "We truly believed these engines were goodwill offerings from your Council of Elders."

"To us, the engines were merely spare parts," Rachel added.

"And who told you that? Gordon Winthrop?"

Rachel sat up straighter. "We haven't seen Mr. Winthrop for some time. What's the matter, Captain? You look surprised."

She paused, casting urgent glances toward Ryan and Robert.

"There's a rumor that Mr. Winthrop was poisoned at the arrival dinner," Ryan said bluntly.

"And another rumor suggests the Council of Elders had a hand in it," Robert added.

Michael Stoddard, a large man with broad shoulders and impressive biceps, fixed Robert with a steely gaze.

"I was at the arrival dinner," Michael said firmly. "Mr. Winthrop ate and drank with his staff officers and mingled with Professor Briar. Nothing seemed amiss when he left that evening."

"Where's the evidence that Allied mercenaries stole the engines?"

"Your name is Robert?"

"Yes, Captain."

"Robert, understand we're not accusing anyone here."

"We're only relaying what Tom Granger told Ryan, Rachel, and me."

"Tom Granger is a traitor and a thief!" Michael shouted, his voice booming through the cabin.

Regardless of the hostility between the Allied folk and the Freelanders, each side held the other responsible for their troubles. On this remote, lonely world of Galraithia, centuries-old rivalries had long torn their societies apart. Yet, inside the cramped shuttlecraft, despite the simmering tensions, no violence erupted. A subtle change was in the air.

Joseph pushed aside his worries about Tom's fate and turned his attention to the Far-Star engines.

"Robert," he began, "you said only two Far-Star engines were installed on the Endeavour?"

"Yes," Robert confirmed. "After we disconnected the two faulty Davis-Molby engines from the fusion reactor, we successfully connected two Far-Star engines."

"Are those two engines paired and running in parallel with the Endeavour's fusion reactor?" Joseph pressed.

Ryan answered confidently, "Both fusion engines were operating at peak control parameters when we left the vessel."

A sudden shadow crossed Joseph's face. He understood the danger of tampering with engines paired in parallel. He quickly addressed Martin.

"If we try to remove those two engines, they'll shatter into a billion pieces and destroy the Endeavour in the process."

Martin's brow furrowed. "What about the other three Far-Star engines? Where are they?"

Rachel answered, "The crates were stored in Cargo Bay-6."

A nagging thought struck Martin: Professor Briar would be displeased if he returned to P-building with only three engines. But Martin hoped to find help in an unexpected source.

"I don't know if you realize it yet, but we're facing life-threatening weather conditions," Martin said, voice grave. "This planet is freezing over. We know when the deep freeze will strike, but survival is uncertain if we remain here. Meanwhile, meteorologists predict that the Equatorial Zone will stay warm enough to support liquid water and sustain life. Over the past few weeks, our aerospace engineers have worked feverishly to reassemble the Phoenix. But without rocket engines, the Phoenix will remain grounded indefinitely. I don't know what else to say except we must help each other if we are to endure. The future of humanity on this planet hangs in the balance—not in some distant future, but here and now."

Lee slid out of the pilot seat and moved toward Martin. Brendon stepped forward, blocking his path.

"I'm the pilot of this vessel, Captain. Name's Lee Hapgood," he said firmly.

"I don't need a pilot, Mr. Hapgood. Return to your seat."

"Do you want my help or not? I'll help you get your engines back, Captain."

Martin narrowed his eyes. "Your help always comes with a price, no doubt?"

Lee shook his head. "Back on Earth, maybe, but we're not on Earth anymore. Let me be clear: you seem like a man who gets things done—and your trust won't be easily earned. But if you want my help, I'll give it with no strings attached."

Martin glanced at the photo ID clipped to Lee's jacket. The security clearance was valid for all areas inside Endeavour.

"Captain, without my authorization code, this vessel won't hard dock with Endeavour—let alone access a cargo bay," Lee said.

Martin hesitated. He didn't fully trust the shuttle pilot, but his plan to board Endeavour depended on patience, stealth, and now, Lee's help. Lee's involvement added a vital advantage: the element of surprise.

"Hey, I see lights outside," Rebecca Turner said, peering through the wide viewing windows.

Sure enough, an all-terrain vehicle approached at reckless speed.

"It's Rover-2," Joseph said.

Caught off guard, Martin hurried to the outer airlock. A blasting gust of freezing wind nearly knocked him over as the automatic door slid open. Rover-2's lights went dark as he stepped outside. Alistair and Satori climbed out of the vehicle.

Martin pressed the keylock again to open the inner airlock door, ushering them inside the warm shuttle cabin.

As Satori hurried to Joseph's side, Alistair bore grave news.

"Gordon Winthrop is dead!" Alistair exclaimed. "Murdered in his cryo bed by his own people. And almost certainly, his killer also took Doctor Marcus Kemp."

"You make serious accusations against the Allied people," Martin said cautiously.

"Father Sandor and Father Antonio found the bodies. They have no reason to lie," Alistair insisted.

Martin scanned Ryan Chyloe and the others, noting the nervousness and concern painted across their faces. "You don't need to convince me."

Satori touched Joseph's arm gently, whispering, "Albert and Jonathon haven't come home. Walter said he saw them after sunset, playing in the arcade with Adrian Sangster. Since then, no one's seen them."

Joseph frowned. "I know the boys dislike the arcade. Why would they be there? They'd rather explore nearby natural caves."

"I hope you're right," Satori said, anxiety evident. "I'm worried about their safety."

"Don't worry," Joseph said firmly. "I'll speak to Martin. He may know where they are."

As Joseph turned away, Satori recalled their last conversation with Albert: she had forbidden him from associating with Adrian, especially after the shuttle pilot promised the boys a tour of Endeavour.

Joseph's face went pale as panic rose. Albert wouldn't disobey his mother willingly. Needing a moment to gather himself, Joseph embraced Satori tightly.

"Don't worry. Everything will be okay," he whispered.

A few minutes later, Joseph returned with Martin and Alistair. Satori's face blanched, panic creeping in as the reality sank deeper—the boys were still missing. Albert and Jonathon gone raised troubling questions for their parents. Had the boys gone willingly with Adrian Sangster to the Endeavour? Could Adrian be trusted to bring them home safely?

"There's more bad news, I'm afraid," Alistair said grimly. "Two aerospace engineers were found dead inside P-

Building, their throats slashed from ear to ear with a serrated ceramic blade. The same type of blade left traces of blood on the tubing inside Gordon's cryo bed."

Suddenly, Robert stepped forward. "I don't know who murdered Mr. Winthrop," he said steadily. "But I know who owns that Muromachi blade. Sergeant Philip Sheridan is your man, and I can take you to him."

Rachel looked up at Robert, her brow furrowing in doubt. "You want to risk your own life for Gordon Winthrop? You hated him. You and I both loathed the sight of him—and I still do, even now that he's dead."

Robert's voice was firm. "I never hid my contempt for old man Winthrop. But whoever killed him deserves to be caught—and punished—for deliberately taking a life."

Rebecca Turner blurted out bitterly, "I couldn't stand the creep. I'm glad he's dead."

Ryan shook his head. "We all hated Winthrop, but I don't know anyone who hated him enough to kill him."

"Ryan, talk all you want, but I don't want my husband risking his life over this," Rachel said sharply.

Near the aft airlock, the conversations became one-sided. Martin held the floor, smoothing rising tensions between Freelanders and Allied folk.

"Mr. Jandamarra, I appreciate your willingness to help, but your wife needs you here," Martin said frankly.

"Finally, someone talking sense," Rachel muttered under her breath.

Annoyed by Rachel's interference, Robert reached into his pocket and pulled out a small remote control unit, handing it to Martin.

"This is something Rachel and I have been tinkering with in our spare time," he said.

Martin examined the device in his hand.

"The remote emits an ultrasound pulse that can activate or deactivate the nearest fabricator, whether in use or idle on its charging station," Robert explained.

Rachel added, "It's only a prototype, and there's a drawback: it will affect only one fabricator—Five-o-nine."

"That's odd, given that all fabricators have the same components and construction process," Joseph mused.

"How it works isn't important," Robert said briskly. "Just press the black button, and Five-o-nine will find you— wherever you are on the ship."

"Rob, you big oaf, Joseph's as curious as the rest of us," Rachel snapped.

"Then you explain it to him, Rachel—we haven't got all day."

"I'm curious because I love machines," Joseph said eagerly. "My mind's already racing with possibilities."

"The control unit is essential for communicating with Five-o-nine," Rachel continued. "Pressing the button triggers an emergency alert in its programming. That means the fabricator comes to your aid—and more importantly, watches over your safety aboard the ship. Rob and I grew fond of Five-o-nine. It's a shame we had to leave it behind."

Joseph glanced at Martin. "Regardless of your feelings about intelligent machines, using Five-o-nine correctly could mean the difference between success and failure."

"Time will tell, Joseph," Martin replied. "But I'll hold onto the control unit."

Joseph looked up timidly. "I'd feel better if you didn't."

"Yeah, probably best if you keep it," Joseph said with a smile. "I'd be calling Five-o-nine at the first sign of trouble."

Lee Hapgood jumped into the pilot seat, scanning the controls as he prepared the shuttle for launch.

"Captain Brindle, I'm ready when you are."

"Very well, Mr. Hapgood. Stand by."

Lee nodded with a smile. "Yes, Captain."

"We need each other now more than ever," Martin said, eyes blazing with determination. "Our mission: find the boys, retrieve the stolen engines, and get home safely. I'm not asking more than that."

"We won't let you down, sir," Brendon said, stepping forward.

Martin's expression darkened. "I'm sorry, Brendon, but I can't take you with me."

"But Captain!"

"There's no time to explain. Will you look after my family until I return?"

Brendon straightened and stood proud. "It would be an honor, Captain."

Martin nodded gratefully, then turned to Alistair and Satori.

"The safety of these people is your responsibility now."

"We will do our best to get them to the Habitat Ring safely," Alistair promised.

While most Allied passengers aboard the shuttlecraft could not speak Freilish, they regarded each Freelander with wary suspicion. Still, Satori smiled warmly at the newcomers, directing them toward Rover-1 and Rover-2—ready and waiting to move toward the Habitat Ring instead of the volatile Keyway Valley caves. The decision was urgent: reports flooded the Committee on Allied Security and Freelander lawmakers of riotous chaos inside the caves, culminating in stabbings and nineteen deaths.

As the last Allied passenger disembarked into the biting cold, Ryan turned to Martin. "Approach the Endeavour from the starboard side. From there, you can board via the hangar deck. Sahristi benes, Captain."

Martin smiled and nodded in thanks. Meanwhile, Alistair, waiting impatiently for his turn to speak, forced a tight smile as Ryan rejoined Robert and Rachel.

"Mr. Chyloe is an intelligent man—and speaks Freilish remarkably well," Alistair remarked.

"You say that as if you're surprised, Alistair."

"I confess I am, Captain. I assumed most Allied folk neither knew nor understood our Freelander laws and customs."

"Well, it strikes me as strange too. I never imagined a day when Freelanders and Allied folk would show mutual respect."

"A strange day indeed," Alistair agreed. "And the week ahead may hold even more surprises."

"It's hard to believe Moving Day is upon us," Martin said quietly.

"Daylight's coming soon," Alistair warned. "You'd better hurry if you intend to keep the rendezvous flight schedule."

"Understood. Tell Professor Briar to leave without us if we aren't back by then. We'll make our own way to Penglai Island—if luck is on our side."

"I understand, Captain."

"Goodbye, sir."

Martin glanced at Satori. Her eyes betrayed her worry for her son and husband's safety.

"Don't worry. Everything will be fine," Martin said, gently taking her hand.

"I hope so, sir," she whispered.

Turning to Lee, Martin said, "Close all hatches. Let's get this bird in the air, Mr. Hapgood."

"Starting rendezvous procedures, sir. Just sit back and enjoy the ride."

With a sudden burst, shuttle B-1157 shot skyward, vanishing into a bank of clouds. Moments later, it pierced Galraithia's thin atmosphere and entered a stable orbit between the twin moons, Ithinia and Galrah.

***

"Endeavour, Endeavour, shuttlecraft B-1157 requesting final docking coordinates, acknowledge."

Static hissed and crackled through Lee Hapgood's comm-link. The shuttle pilot expanded his output signal and tried again. "Endeavour, Endeavour, acknowledge."

"Is that you, Hapgood?"

"No, the big bad wolf."

"I was expecting Little Red Riding Hood."

"Quit fooling around, Grandma. Open docking bay 12C, please."

"I'm afraid I can't do that, Lee."

"Why not?"

"There are unnamed passengers aboard shuttlecraft B-1157, according to the docking computer."

"The docking computer must have a power glitch, Tibor. I have six names on my passenger manifest—fusion specialists, important people. Do you want their names?"

"There are no scheduled incoming passenger flights from Ashyr, not today, not tomorrow."

"Tibor, these people have the highest security clearance!"

"I hear you, Lee! But I can only see your name and no others listed on B-1157's flight manifest."

"Well, something's obviously wrong. I'd turn the central security computer off if I were you before it crashes."

"Lee, this security issue must be reported to a higher authority. Stand by."

"Tibor, open the goddamned docking bay doors, right now!"

Dani's patience snapped. "Hand me the microphone. Let me talk to him."

"Make it fast, Dani. We're running low on fuel," Martin said, his eyes fixed on the fuel gauge.

"What's the guy's name?" Dani asked.

"Tibor Fischer."

"Switch off the visual display panels," Martin ordered. "We don't want our retinal scans taken and recorded on the central security computer."

A worried look crossed Lee's face as he nodded. "Aye, Captain."

"Mr. Fischer, this is fusion specialist Alfonse Benei speaking," Dani said, his voice smooth and authoritative. "My colleagues and I are here at Gordon Winthrop's request. We need to recalibrate the newly installed Far-Star engines. Do you copy?"

A series of beeps echoed through the comm-link, followed by more static hissing and crackling. Security sensors swept the shuttlecraft's interior, searching for signs of breach.

"Security procedures are sources of frustration for many people, so I understand what must be going through your mind right now, Mr. Fischer. But serious consequences may result from your refusal to follow Mr. Winthrop's most urgent request. Do you copy, Mr. Fischer? Do you copy, sir?"

The docking doors opened slowly. Below in the control station, Tibor Fischer glanced around nervously as shuttlecraft B-1157 approached the docking platform. He noted the time in Endeavour's log, left the docking control station, and ended his workday with a hot cup of tea.

***

Lee unbuckled his seat harness and leaned forward. "Okay. Listen up. There's a shift change taking place. Give me five minutes to get inside the docking control station. Once I disable the security panel, I'll give you the signal to proceed to the engineering module."

"And if the docking officer sees cameras offline, what then?" Michael asked.

Dani slung his backpack over his shoulders and checked the straps. "I'll take care of the docking officer and cover your backs if there are any problems. We don't want any unpleasant surprises moving forward."

"Okay, Dani."

"Shuttle B-1157!"

Lee exchanged a worried glance with Martin. "It's Dallas Fitch. He could be a big problem, Captain."

"Pilot, are you there?"

"I beg your pardon, Mr. Fitch. What can I do for you, sir?"

"Who is this?"

Static filled the comm-link for a long moment before Dallas heard Lee's response.

"Lee Hapgood, sir. There's a problem with the comm-link."

"Lee, a Delta IV heavy transport is scheduled to dock at 12C. Reposition B-1157 inside docking Bay 8C, please."

"How much time do I have, sir?"

"The Delta IV is scheduled to arrive within two hours."

"Okay. I'd better get a move on then."

"And fix the comm-link. Call me when B-1157 is inside 8C."

"Yes, sir."

Martin grabbed Lee's arm as soon as the transmission ended. "Talk to me, Lee. Tell me what's happening."

"Captain, you have less than two hours to find the rocket engines, or you and your people will never get off this ship alive."

"The rocket engines are important, but our priority is finding Jonathon and Albert."

Checkmate

Dani and Lee pressed themselves against the corridor wall, waiting as Tibor Fischer gathered his belongings and left the docking control station. Tibor waved to the incoming shift officer—a man called Peadrick—before disappearing around the corner.

Dani peered around the wall's edge, studying the new officer's movements. The security cameras swept back and forth in their programmed patterns, red lights blinking as they searched for intruders. He needed the perfect moment to strike without triggering the alarm system.

When Peadrick turned his back to check a display panel, Dani slipped from the shadows. He moved through the camera blind spots, timing each step carefully, then struck Peadrick with a swift blow to the side of the head. The officer crumpled without a sound.

Dani dragged the unconscious man into the Fabricator Supply Room and quickly secured him. He found duct tape in a drawer and bound Peadrick's hands behind his back, secured his ankles, and gagged his mouth. After forcing open a storage locker, Dani discovered five blue coveralls. He gathered them under his arm and slipped away toward the motor room, crawling through ventilation shafts and hidden passages that crisscrossed Endeavour's hull.

Meanwhile, Lee had taken position at the docking control station's security console. His fingers danced across the interface, opening and closing hatchway doors and airlocks to clear Dani's path. He systematically deactivated security cameras and disabled the laser grid systems that could incinerate an intruder in seconds.

A deep grinding sound rumbled through the vessel, followed by a tremor that vibrated through the deck plates.

"Endeavour's rocket engines are coming online and warming up," Martin explained to the others waiting in the motor room. "It's routine procedure."

With Lee's expert guidance, they moved swiftly from the upper decks toward the ship's belly without encountering anyone or triggering security alerts. But Martin knew they couldn't rely on luck forever.

"We're splitting into two groups," he decided. "Dani and I will head straight for the engine room. Joseph, Satori, and Michael—you make your way to the High Lab Module and Endeavour's observation bubble."

Joseph nodded grimly. "If Albert and Jonathon are anywhere, they'll be there. Both boys developed a fascination with astronomy while growing up on this planet."

*****

Disguised as fusion engineers, Martin and Dani entered the engine room's upper level. The air thrummed with the deep hum of cooling fans and spinning Davis-Molby electricity generators. Tall vertical containment cylinders made of regolith glass cast an eerie iridescent blue glow across the chamber.

Martin had assumed Endeavour's engines were simply warming up to circulate heated water through the heating systems—a routine procedure to prevent airlock hatches from freezing. But as the cylinders pulsed with that unmistakable blue radiance, his face flushed with realization.

He turned to Dani, his voice tight with urgency. "I was wrong about the engines. Dead wrong."

Martin understood the ship's general construction, but he'd made a critical error about Far-Star and Davis-Molby propulsion systems. The containment cylinders only radiated that iridescent blue light when the nanotrine fusion reactor approached power load operating temperatures and the nanotrine crystals began to melt. The melting process produced high-energy reactant plasma—the lifeblood of a Far-Star engine.

"We have to get to the High Lab module and find the others," Martin said.

"What's the problem? There's plenty of time left to reach the rendezvous point."

"No, Dani. Time is against us." Martin pointed toward the nanotrine reactor where five men in blue coveralls worked alongside a fabricator unit. "Those fusion specialists hold key positions in the engine room. While they prep Endeavour's propulsion system, that fabricator is inspecting the reactor's magnetic field coil."

Martin had spent enough time around experts like Joseph to recognize the signs. A fabricator only accessed the reactor's magnetic coil when cooling liquid in the heat exchanger ran dangerously low, or when abnormal radiation levels spiked outside the reactor core.

"Departure? Endeavour isn't going anywhere," Dani protested.

"Endeavour is leaving!" Martin's voice cracked with desperation. "We need to find a way off this ship before she breaks standard orbit around Galraithia."

"How much time do we have? Can we stop the departure?"

"When the nanotrine reactor completes its run-and-cycle procedure, the propulsion management system will power up all five engines for a long orbital departure burn."

Dani's face went pale. "So what do we do now? If we don't find the boys before this ship leaves, we don't stand a chance—not without spacesuits or cryo-beds."

Martin was already moving toward the exit. "Joseph once told me there are always options in any situation, always a way out. He'll help us shut the reactor down. I'm sure of it."

***

Philip Sheridan had always turned to Dallas Fitch when anger or frustration consumed him. In the heat of challenging missions, Dallas remained the one person who understood his fears—a bond forged in blood during the Eurozone campaign and strengthened through the brutal Western Australian conflict.

The Freelander forces had captured them both two days after an underwater drone attack sent the troop transport ANS Talisman to the bottom of the ocean off Dampier's coast. Thirteen hundred Allied soldiers died in those frigid waters, while 896 survivors found themselves imprisoned in POW camps scattered across the Pilbara region.

Dallas ended up at Gravelly Creek, a sprawling Freelander cattle station where he learned to breed and raise scrub cattle under the harsh Australian sun. He had no idea that Philip had escaped to Indonesia within months of their capture, just as Philip remained unaware of Dallas's fate.

When the war finally ended, Dallas made a choice that would have surprised his old comrade. He married a Freelander woman who had worked alongside him on the farm, and together they built a life that brought him ten years of unexpected happiness. Two children blessed their union—a son and daughter who filled their modest farmhouse with laughter.

But joy proved fragile in the post-war world. After their second son's birth, zoonotic viruses swept through Western Australia in devastating waves. Dallas watched helplessly as the diseases claimed his wife and children, one by one, while he survived—a cruel twist that left him hollow and broken.

The loss shattered everything Dallas had believed about his new life as a Freelander. Consumed by grief and disillusionment, he abandoned the farm and sought out Gordon Winthrop's mercenary army. There, he found Philip Sheridan again, and their friendship resumed as if the intervening years had been nothing more than a pause between battles.

***

As the solar clock counted down toward Endeavour's departure, Sergeant Sheridan's patience wore thin. His carefully orchestrated plan was unraveling thread by thread.

Only two reusable shuttlecraft serviced the massive vessel—Adrian Sangster's D-2987 and Lee Hapgood's B-1157—and both sat idle in Docking Bay 12C. Meanwhile, Victor Champion pushed his Delta IV heavy transport beyond its limits, ferrying desperate colonists from the Keyway Valley caves. He had already transported over 1,250 people to Endeavour without incident, but now the red low-fuel warning light blazed ominously on his instrument panel.

Sheridan could do nothing but wait, and waiting made him dangerous. He was the type of man who blamed everyone but himself when operations went sideways.

544

The maintenance computer had flagged several safety issues with shuttlecraft D-2987, while B-1157 showed visible wear damage on its starboard wing control spoiler. Lee Hapgood could have easily fabricated additional problems to ground both craft, but he walked a razor's edge. He was confident that the substantial backlog of work in the engine room would draw maintenance teams away from the shuttlecraft, yet he had to avoid detection. Sheridan would not hesitate to eliminate anyone who betrayed him.

High above on Endeavour's bridge, Sheridan paced alone as storm clouds gathered over the planet below. A fierce electrical storm approached the Keyway Valley from the northwest, where five hundred colonists huddled together for warmth while waiting for the Delta IV's return to the Bravo-8 landing zone.

More refugees continued to present themselves to the authorities, registering their desperate intention to leave Galraithia. These disillusioned souls complained constantly about the lack of monetary rewards for their backbreaking labor. The planet was no tropical paradise—nothing like the Eden that Gordon Winthrop had promised them.

But these broken dreamers were exactly what Sheridan wanted. He fed their bitterness with promises of returning to Earth rich beyond their wildest dreams. They carried few personal possessions aside from commemorative 'First Settler' medals, following Sheridan with blind faith born of desperation.

He rewarded their loyalty generously. Each refugee received a small bag filled with glittering perfect diamonds and precious Longese ganitte crystals. Philip's customs officers had allowed the contraband to slip through their checkpoints, turning blind eyes for the right price. However, Philip remained unaware of just how much

illegal cargo his greedy soldiers had smuggled aboard
Endeavour.

***

Lightning bolts carved jagged paths across the sky above
Keyway Valley, narrowly missing the Delta IV as it roared
through the storm at three hundred miles per hour, just four
hundred feet above the ground. Despite the treacherous
conditions, Victor initiated his landing procedure with
masterful precision. The five hundred waiting colonists
erupted in cheers at his piloting skills as they boarded the
shuttlecraft, settled into their padded seats, and secured
their harnesses. Their long journey back to Earth was
finally beginning.

From Endeavour's bridge, Captain Sheridan watched 1,250
colonists prepare for hibernation in the cryo chambers
below. An overwhelming sense of pride swelled in his
chest—this was his moment of triumph. He was finally in
command, ready to lead them into what he believed would
be a glorious future.

Yet for all his arrogance, Sheridan understood little about
spaceflight procedures or the critical complications that
could arise. Missing the departure window from Galraithia
would add years to their journey home, but he refused to
consider such failure. He issued immediate orders to get the
spacecraft underway with only the minimum crew of
twenty-three and five fabricators to maintain life support
and engineering systems.

Sheridan had hoarded more than his share of Galraithia's
treasures—more Longese ganitte crystals than anyone else,
more gold, and perfect diamonds the size of goose eggs. He
promised equal shares to those who cooperated, but this
was pure salesmanship, a deliberate lie designed to con the

desperate. Still, 1,250 Allied colonists had accepted his offer to return to Earth wealthy.

"AutoNav, initiate departure from Galraithia orbit," Sheridan commanded.

Minutes later, the Delta IV arrived with its precious cargo of five hundred souls. Victor's voice crackled through the comm system, broadcasting a desperate mayday call for docking clearance. He received only silence—Sheridan had deliberately switched off all communication systems.

That single moment of calculated cruelty sealed Victor's fate and the fate of everyone aboard the Delta IV. The shuttlecraft had consumed two tons of rocket fuel reaching Endeavour's last known position and carried insufficient reserves to return to the Bravo-8 landing zone. Victor understood the mathematics of his situation with grim clarity. The Delta IV would fly on fumes for mere minutes before gravity claimed them.

He had hoped for a quick, painless end as the atmosphere embraced his craft, but the heat transformed the shuttlecraft's interior into a roaring inferno. Endeavour's short-range optical sensors tracked the Delta IV's disintegration as fiery debris rained into the Tezarian Ocean below.

Captain Sheridan didn't bat an eye as he turned away from the display. Behind him, Endeavour's bridge crew stared at each other in horrified silence, wishing they were back in the safety of the Keyway Valley caves. But reality pressed forward relentlessly—the AutoNav computer executed its preprogrammed trajectory correction maneuver as 1,250 anxious colonists and Endeavour's skeleton crew of twenty-three prepared to enter deep-space hibernation.

***

Audible alarms pierced the ship's silence as portside thrusters fired, nudging Endeavour away from the deadly gravitational well of a nearby black hole. The alarms fell quiet, and medical fabricators throughout the cryo module began preparing the ship's human population for hypersleep.

Under normal circumstances, the preparation procedure required five to ten hours with a full complement of passengers and crew. But many rows of cryo beds sat dark and empty inside Endeavour's vast hibernation chamber. Sheridan had calculated the maximum number of people returning to Earth by measuring the cryogenic fluid being diverted from the ship's holding tanks to the cryo module.

What the passengers didn't know was that cryogenic fluid levels had dropped dangerously low—too low to safely operate Endeavour's onboard systems. As captain, Sheridan bore the responsibility of ensuring those levels didn't fall to life-threatening depths. Yet in the darker corners of his mind, he relished a simple equation: fewer passengers meant more riches for himself. Philip had no intention of sharing Galraithia's treasures with anyone.

Before entering hibernation, Sheridan filled a leather bag with his most prized possession—life-extending Lanfen blueberries—and secured it away from prying eyes and potential traitors.

Now he lay in his luxurious captain's cryo bed as a medical fabricator moved with mechanical precision around him. The machine unrolled a reel of cryo tubing, cut the flexible glass conduits into precise lengths, and arranged them on a sterile metal shelf beneath his bed.

Philip stared up at the fabricator's lifeless optical sensors as it smeared clear antiseptic gel across his freshly shaved chest. The substance gave off a sickeningly sweet odor that triggered waves of nausea. Once the antiseptic covered him from head to toe, the fabricator inserted catheters into his neck and chest with surgical accuracy, then opened the catheter valves.

Cryo fluid began coursing through his veins like liquid ice. Fighting to keep his eyes open against the growing lethargy, Philip issued his final command to the main Sequanta computer.

"Tell Mr. Granger to energize the polmate gas canisters."

"Yes, Captain."

Consciousness slipped away like a fading dream.

Two minutes later, the medical fabricator checked Philip's vital signs on the ECG machine and analyzed his oximetric pulse waveform. Strong and healthy—a prime candidate for extended cryopreservation. Robotic arms inserted feeding ports, drainage systems, and additional cryo tubing with mechanical efficiency.

The fabricator verified oxygen saturation levels on the pulse oximeter. Satisfied with all medical parameters for the long journey back to Earth, it sealed the cryo bed and opened the secondary cryo fluid control valve. Sleep timers activated and cooling motors hummed to life. Freezing iridescent blue liquid rushed into Philip's chamber as the fabricator peered through the sealed lid, watching frost patterns spread across the glass.

The next task was routine: check the backup power generator supply, then summon Albert and Jonathon—next in the waiting line.

***

For Albert Arunui and Jonathon Brindle, the invasive cryo procedures turned deadly when their blood oxygen

549

saturation levels plummeted to eighty percent. The medical fabricators had miscalibrated their cryo beds, failing to account for the boys' unique physiology—traits found only in Galraithian-born children.

The ship's recycled atmosphere itself posed a threat to their health. Galraithia's atmosphere contained eight layers instead of Earth's seven, and no one understood the mysterious eighth layer. Earth-made spectrographic sensors couldn't detect or recognize the differences, but the effects were undeniable. The two Galraithian boys possessed greater physical strength and larger lung capacities than Earth-born humans. The medical fabricator dutifully recorded this evidence and its conclusions in Endeavour's log.

Dallas Fitch, Tom Granger, and Adrian Sangster rushed through the ship's corridors toward the cryo module. As they hurried down the passageway, Tom and Adrian's argument escalated over the fate of the two Freelander boys.

Adrian had brought Albert and Jonathon aboard with Tom's permission—the boys had simply wanted to see what an interstellar sleeper ship looked like. But Tom saw opportunity in their presence.

"We should hold them as hostages," Tom declared. "The Council of Freelander Elders will honor ransom demands and provide the equipment and food supplies we need. More Galraithian treasures for Earth."

Adrian protested vehemently. "Albert and Jonathon are my responsibility. Besides, I don't want to return to Earth— there's nothing there for me. Everyone I've ever cared about will be dead by the time Endeavour reaches Earth's orbit."

Inside the forty-bed cryo chamber, Tom found the two boys and fixed Adrian with a stern glare. "You're wasting your time, Adrian. Don't wake those boys up, or you'll never leave this ship alive."

Adrian knew Tom was a Freelander, but nothing more about his background. He certainly didn't realize that harming the boys was Tom's twisted way of striking back at Martin and Joseph.

"Talk all you like, Granger," Adrian shot back. "One way or another, I'm loading Albert and Jonathon into a shuttlecraft—awake or asleep—and flying them down to Ashyr."

Adrian's declaration that he would use force if necessary infuriated Tom further. There were only two shuttlecraft aboard Endeavour and no life pods—Gordon Winthrop had used every available escape vessel to ferry colonists to the Keyway Valley landing zones, and even that hadn't been enough.

Dallas remained silent, recognizing the danger of getting involved with extremists from both sides. He maintained his stoic expression as two guards marched Adrian to the brig and shoved him into a holding cell. Inside, Adrian found a shoeless man slumped on the floor, his clothes bloodstained, his nose clearly broken.

"Mister? Are you okay?"

The man raised his head, revealing an expression of hopeless anguish. "Don't you recognize me?"

"Captain Winthrop?"

"Under the circumstances, it's a meaningless title, wouldn't you say? I'm an outcast, but I know I'm not the only one.

We must help the people living in the caves—it's another problem I'll solve eventually."

Adrian wondered if Captain Winthrop had lost his mind.

"Don't look so despondent, Sangster. Every puzzle has its own unique solution." Winthrop's voice carried a hint of his former authority. "Don't forget that."

"Yeah, I guess so. But right now, I'm too bloody angry to think straight, sir."

The High Lab module stretched before them like a labyrinth of narrow connecting passageways leading to clustered workstations linked to the Fabricator Network System. Deck plans and a noticeboard hung on the starboard bulkhead, and Joseph quickly scanned the airlock isolation instructions and safety procedures.

"This area is essential personnel only," he noted.

"But there's no one up here," Satori observed.

Michael studied the deck plans intently, committing details to memory. "I'm mighty glad you found these, Joseph. I lost my bearings after the second passageway."

Joseph was still trying to reestablish his own bearings when he stepped on a pressure mat inside the observation bubble entrance. A deafening alarm shattered the silence.

"Intruder alert! Intruder alert!"

As the alarm echoed throughout the vessel, Satori caught a faint odor drifting from a fresh air vent. Yellowish-green gas wafted into the corridor, and she instinctively backed away.

"Halopolmate gas!" she shouted, but found herself retreating toward another outlet spewing the same quick-acting sleeping agent—designed to incapacitate, not kill.

The advancing gas overwhelmed Joseph, Satori, and Michael in seconds. They collapsed unconsciously to the floor as the yellowish-green vapor rose through the engineering module's ventilation shafts toward Martin and Dani.

Dani didn't have time to react—he was unconscious before his head struck the deck. Standing further from the nearest vent, Martin managed to fumble the Intelligent Key from his pocket and press the black button six times before dizziness overcame him. He lost his balance and collapsed.

In the docking station, Lee desperately tried to shut off the air supply while holding his breath. But the gas proved too potent, and he slumped unconsciously into the cushioned chair beside the security console.

Just then, Fabricator Five-o-nine came online to acknowledge Martin's emergency signal. Six button presses meant six humans needed immediate rescue. The fabricator's image sensors and radar scanners detected multiple unauthorized persons in the engineering module and observation bubble, security breaches in the docking station, and an unconscious human near the Area-6 muster station.

Five-o-nine found Martin and Dani unconscious and breathing shallowly. Lifting them one at a time with mechanical precision, the fabricator carried them to an empty cryogenic chamber. Its independent predictive modules—developed by Rachel, Robert, and Ryan, the finest cybernetic specialists in known space—began prepping all six humans for prolonged cryo stasis.

Five-o-nine peered into each chamber before returning to its docking plate. Then the fabricator did something extraordinary—something no other machine could accomplish. It activated its sensory and perception processors, opening layers of recognition and recall data entirely on its own initiative.

As it powered down, Five-o-nine's memory banks conjured the kind and caring face of Rachel Vaughn, and it began to dream about the day Rachel, Robert, and Ryan had departed.

"We've come to say goodbye. We're leaving for Ashyr tomorrow."

"Don't go!"

Rachel had touched Five-o-nine's metallic hand with gentle fingers. "We're really sorry we have to leave you behind."

"We won't forget you," Robert had promised.

But they had left, and Five-o-nine dreamed on, alone among the sleeping humans it had saved.

Penglai

Since the first landing, aerospace engineers had never stopped working. Alongside their many flight projects, a strong desire burned to resurrect the Phoenix spacecraft. Discarded life pods became valuable sources of scavenged parts. Six small rocket boosters, tested individually, proved indispensable — the key components that brought the Phoenix back to life. Expertly rebuilt, its frame composed of more timber than steel, the new Phoenix was ready.

The aerospace engineers confidently declared it could fly like a jet across the winter sky toward the warm Equatorial Zone. It was no small triumph. After long hours of intensive repairs and reconfiguring the hull to half its original size and weight, the Phoenix now boasted the fuel capacity and endurance to fly for 1,000 hours on nanotrine rocket fuel. More than enough to reach the Equatorial Zone, establish a permanent forward operating base, return to Ashyr, and transport thousands of colonists eager to start anew on Penglai Island — the third largest and most beautiful island in the Penglaian archipelago.

Professor Briar called the archipelago the Islands of Good Hope. Penglai Island, a tropical paradise, was home to the Penglaian people — a resourceful, creative community of around 2,000 inhabitants. Long-range spectrographic sensors on the Faxian telescope had detected unmistakable signs of human activity there. Multispectral drone data and photographic evidence confirmed it beyond doubt. From then on, the Penglaian archipelago and its delicate balance of human presence and indigenous life became closely guarded secrets under the council of Freelander Elders. Only a handful outside the council's influence knew of the mission to directly contact the Penglaian people.

When the Penglai mission became public knowledge, Freelander elders exchanged nervous glances. Most people cheered Professor Briar, aware that after Gordon Winthrop's death and his son's disappearance, the Allied folk were suddenly leaderless. William Briar welcomed the chance to unite the Allied groups and families — even if it meant abandoning Ashyr and settling permanently in the Equatorial Zone alongside the Freelanders and Penglaians.

"Make no mistake," Professor Briar warned, "the Equatorial Zone remains a dangerous alien environment. If you don't want to go there, that's your prerogative. But I think you're crazy if you choose to stay here. Extreme winters, failed crops, and months of blinding blizzards make life in Ashyr untenable."

Indeed, the Equatorial Zone was a land of paradoxes: stunning golden beaches, active volcanoes, and exotic flowering plants that filled the air with sweet, colorful scents. At its center rose Malpaso Mountain. Around its flanks stretched the Highland region — marked by 4,000 stepped terraces visible from the Penglai coast. These terraces supported crops like Cheno beans and Perteccul wildflowers. Perteccul grew at higher elevations in Ashyr, where boiled Perteccul stems were considered a delicacy.

On Penglai Island, the fried version of the dish and Cheno beans were favorite foods, thanks to year-round cultivation made possible by the mild climate.

***

Moving Day

With the glow of moon Galrah filling the sky, its twin Ithinia peeked above the Cradle Mountains. Brendon focused on the flight controls of the reconfigured Phoenix. His hands trembled slightly as he pushed the control stick forward. Phoenix lifted off smoothly into the turquoise sky as planned—more importantly, without a hitch.

Looking over his shoulder, Brendon smiled triumphantly at the colonists nestled tightly in the front and middle sections of the fuselage. He spotted Rihanna and Alistair sitting beside Walter, Sarah, and Lanfen. Nearby, Andre Zarovski sat alone near the cargo bay's rear door, testing and monitoring radio signals and frequencies. Brendon's eyes then found Marion Brindle, gently breastfeeding baby Nicolea.

In that moment, his thoughts flickered to Martin, Joseph, Satori, Michael, and Dani Li—wondering if he would ever see them again.

Professor Briar spent the day reassuring Allied passengers aboard, insisting this journey was not just another one-way ticket to backbreaking labor and food shortages. And for the first time in Freelander history, there was no conflict between Freelanders and Allied folk. Rachel Sibley's dream had finally come true.

The Phoenix touched down in a clearing before a sandy beach framed by majestic mountains and towering slopes. Colonists peered out the windows at tall, graceful palms swaying in the breeze. The sight of lush green vegetation, splashes of tropical color, and clear ocean water lapping the shore lifted everyone's spirits—especially Lanfen's.

Brendon cut the engines and exhaled deeply in relief.

Professor Briar quickly unbuckled his seatbelt, rose, and made a brief but earnest speech.

"The Penglaians are peaceful and friendly people. We must do our utmost to reassure them that our goodwill and friendship come without conditions. Acting solely in our own interest is no longer acceptable."

"Professor Briar! We're receiving incomplete and contradictory information about the Penglaian people," a man called out.

The professor paused with one hand raised. "If there has been a lack of transparency or misleading information, I take full responsibility for not speaking to you sooner."

Then, he revealed a startling discovery: Finnegan had found a repository of bones, skulls, and many personal belongings inside a cave ten miles north of the Penglaian village. Finnegan spent three days searching other small caves but found nothing else. He took fragments from the first cave's broken bones for DNA testing.

Finnegan's discovery coincided with a reconnaissance flight over one of the Equatorial Zone's volcanic islands. Professor Lin and Lesley Fredericks discovered the body of an elderly man washed ashore. Genomic tests linked him to the bone fragments from Finnegan's cave.

But doubts lingered about the DNA's purity: the man's DNA was relatively recent, while Finnegan's bone fragments dated between 250 and 300 years old.

Professor Lin connected the two stories. She had lived with a Penglaian family for several weeks while Lesley Fredericks and Finnegan explored the island and archipelago, paving the way for other colonists.

Eager to learn the Penglaian way of life and native language, Lin found the language complex, a blend of Sino-Tibetan and Mandarin influences—its words layered with multiple meanings.

***

The rear cargo bay door opened slower than some colonists wished. As they stepped off the Phoenix, most gathered around the landing area, slowly settling into the new surroundings. After so many days and weeks spent indoors, their bodies and minds had withdrawn from the outside world—shunning Galraithia's ruthless cold, bleak winter darkness, and debilitating sickness. They had worked under artificial light, breathed recycled medical air, subsisted on eels bred in holding tanks, and consumed dehydrated freeze-dried meals with extensive shelf lives.

Now, a warm ocean breeze carried the salty tang of the sea, mingling with laughter and song—the sounds of first-time visitors on an alien beach. Further up, on the firm, damp sand, locals clad in colorful, loose garments smiled and welcomed the newcomers as they ambled toward the water's edge. The scene looked idyllic. The colonists instantly understood how one could fall in love with this place—even amid the lively bustle of local customers and vendors hawking island goods in a nearby marketplace.

A group of eminent Penglaian scientists and high-ranking officials organized public diplomacy efforts, focusing their energy on making these visitors—clad in unfamiliar garments—feel welcome. Robert Finnegan skirted around the gathering, spotting some familiar faces from Ashyr. Yet his close friend Michael Stoddard was conspicuously absent from the crowd milling near the Phoenix.

Professor Briar stepped forward, gesturing toward the crowd filled with hopeful eyes.

"Ladies and gentlemen," he began, "I mentioned earlier Robert Finnegan—a man whose achievements I admire and whose friendship I value deeply."

Finnegan stepped forward cautiously, meeting the Professor's gaze. "What are you trying to do, William? Scare everyone off?"

"These people deserve the whole truth," Briar said firmly. "Gordon Winthrop is dead, and all the lies that man spread must be forgotten."

"Indeed."

"Come closer, listen carefully to what Robert Finnegan has to say," Briar urged both Freelanders and Allied folk.

"Let me start by saying the Penglaian people are descendants of Captain Jian Zhou and the crew of the *Star Chaser Liaoning*." Murmurs of awe rippled through the crowd—no angry outbursts.

"The Liaoning's remarkable deep-space journey almost ended when it plummeted into a gravity well. Unlike Phoenix and Endeavour, Liaoning was less fortunate; it broke apart on Galraithia, claiming 150 lives."

Finnegan's revelation stunned the Allied folk. Gordon had never denied the Penglaian people's existence—but why keep it secret? Had he dismissed the importance of Finnegan's discovery? Did he fail to foresee the dangers of sheltering in caves or makeshift shelters during Ashyr's brutal winter?

Robert, Rachel, and Ryan pondered these questions, unfamiliar with the City of Yuǎnfāng or its location. Yet they knew joining Freelanders had been the right choice. Life locked in lightless caves or the power-hungry Habitat Ring of the Alpha settlement would be bleak indeed.

Rachel, Robert, and Ryan wandered down the beach to a one-story wooden schoolhouse facing a paved walkway. Local children waved warmly and took an immediate liking to Rachel.

"I have good feelings about this place."

Robert and Ryan agreed, feeling as if they had finally come home after a long absence. A warm, welcoming sense of family washed over them—so unlike the cutthroat world aboard the Orbital Station and Endeavour.

Ryan had been closely linked to Rachel and Robert since Endeavour's inaugural launch from the Outer Marker. But the death of his brother Alexander dealt a crushing blow to Ryan's sense of family. He warned Rachel and Robert to remain vigilant; the Galraithian expedition's extraordinary scientific achievements had been mired in bitter controversy from the start. Unscrupulous cybernetic specialists sought to discredit their research in Intelligent Robotics.

While the three friends trusted each other implicitly, they distrusted almost everyone else—especially their boss. They had repaired his personal computers and unlocked restricted information. Gordon Winthrop knew Galraithia's harsh winters would disrupt shuttle services bringing food to Ashyr's fledgling colony, but he kept Penglai Island and its people secret—not even telling his son. His shrewd knowledge of human nature made him doubt that centuries of conflict and struggle could yield lasting peace between Freelanders and Allied folk—or anyone. He enlisted Philip Sheridan to purge Freelander sympathizers from his ranks, doubting their loyalty.

Overconfidence hastened Gordon's death. Two days later, while Doctor Marcus Kemp prepped him for emergency cryostasis, Sheridan and security forces stormed the private

medical facility in P-Building. Investigators charged
Sheridan and six bodyguards with murdering Gordon
Winthrop and Doctor Marcus Kemp. Allied and Freelander
tribunals convicted them in absentia, sentencing them to
death by hanging.

Sheridan's death warrant brought little comfort to Allied
colonists who stayed instead of migrating to the Equatorial
Zone. Food ran low. Blinding blizzards grew frequent,
storms fiercer. Sheridan evaded capture, returned to
Endeavour, and cut supply lines to Ashyr. People begged
Captain Sheridan for food—an empty hope. Radar lost
contact with Endeavour.

Waiting in the Keyway Valley caves for aid that would
never arrive, many Allied colonists with soft bellies and
little resilience didn't know if they could take the new
planet's extreme conditions. While they sheltered in groups
inside the caves, the hardy and weather-worn Freelanders
chose to leave Ashyr.

***

Lanfen and Rihanna had missed Finnegan's discourse. A
sandy track led them through thick zhamosa bushes before
opening onto a grassy clearing beside a winding
shoreline—part rocky headland, part sandy beach. Clear
blue water lapped gently against their feet, noticeably
cooler than the humid tropical air. The heavy, sticky heat
amplified the scent of flowers—those fragrant blooms
scattered across the narrow sand strip before a hillside thick
with tall, shady ferns and blossoms. Flowers were
everywhere, strange native plants burdened with fruit
bursting with sweet juice. Above them, tall trees teemed
with colorful birds singing loudly from the branches.

Nearby, rising above the tree line, rows of oddly shaped
wooden houses boasted lush, functional rooftop gardens—a

562

Penglaian community living harmoniously with nature. In stark contrast, the northern continent of Ashyr lay bleak and lifeless by comparison. There, overnight winter temperatures plummeted to minus 375 degrees Fahrenheit, with winds howling at 400 miles per hour across the frozen Keyway Valley. Ice and snow now blanketed Paraihe Island, located in the subtropical and temperate zone. Yet beneath the icy surface of the Ithinian Sea during winter, life pulsed on—schools of fish teemed, voraciously feeding on the eyes of flesh-eating dragonfish.

A tall, tanned, muscular young man walked along the sandy beach, stretching his legs. His long black hair was pulled back into a ponytail. Approaching the two pale women who followed the tide line, collecting colorful stones and seashells with living creatures inside, he smiled.

"Welcome to Yuǎnfāng City," he said warmly.

Rihanna cleared her throat and nudged Lanfen. Lanfen returned the young man's smile and thanked him in his language. Though fluent in several Chinese dialects, she hadn't heard a blend of Sino-Tibetan and archaic Chinese dialects in years.

He introduced himself as Gan, a teacher, and said he would be delighted to show them around the beautiful island. "We have eagerly awaited your arrival. The journey from Earth must have taken many, many years."

"Yes. Too many years in hypersleep," Lanfen replied.

"Did you lose many colonists on the voyage?"

"Yes. We lost many great people—too many friends."

"My grandfather, in his later years, often retold how he and his crew survived the perils of deep space and hypersleep."

"Your grandfather?" Lanfen asked, intrigued.

"Yes. Jian Zhou, captain of the *Liaoning* star chaser."

"That's impossible; Captain Jian Zhou died centuries ago."

"Grandfather Jian was 375 years old when he died. Would you like to see his tomb? It's not far from here. The Liaoning crew were buried with him, bolt upright."

"Thank you. Rihanna and I would love to see your grandfather's tomb," Lanfen said, glancing at Rihanna, who looked impatient and bewildered—understanding none of the conversation.

"What's the matter with your friend?"

"Nothing. Rihanna is always in a hurry to leave."

"There's no need for haste. We have plenty of daylight left."

"Maybe you can help us, Gan."

"Of course."

"Rihanna and I are searching for a particular purple berry that grows in grape-like clusters."

"Haniapor grows in grape-like bunches," Gan said. "The Haniapor bush is sacred to us; we drink its sweet juice and live long, healthy lives."

"Live a long and healthy life, like your grandfather?"

"Yes, like my grandfather and all the Penglaian people. It was his gift."

"Are Haniapor bushes scarce here?"

"No, they are remarkably prolific. You'll find them growing everywhere—if you know where to look."

"Where should we start looking?" Lanfen asked.

Gan pointed to a mountain peak towering in the island's center. "Up there is an excellent place to begin."

Before Gan could respond, Rihanna cut the conversation short. "Lanfen, I've had enough of this guy and his stories. I'm not hanging around here all day!"

"I'm sorry for keeping you waiting, but Gan has shared important information," Lanfen defended.

"You should be sorry. You haven't translated a single word for me," Rihanna shot back.

More locals wandered down to the clearing near the beach, curious to see the spaceship and to meet the visitors who had come all the way from Earth. To the Penglaians and first-generation Galraithians, planet Earth was an alien world. Lanfen, Rihanna, and Gan turned their attention to the water's edge. Sitting on the beach, Lanfen translated Gan's words, though Gan himself was more intrigued about Earth's past, present and future. Even so, the Penglaian people's destiny walked hand-hand with that of the newcomers.

***

Rachel, Robert, and Ryan made their way to the bustling bartering market, crowded with people and dotted with free food stalls. Volunteers tended fires, stirred giant clay pots brimming with nutritious protein, spiced vegetables simmering in rich stocks. The sights and smells of food being prepared and served stirred their deepest childhood memories—both tender and painful. Their parents and grandparents, Australian Freeland farmers, had won the war against ruthless business oligarchs like Robert Shuster, Jin Feihong, and Darius Weksler, a notorious money exchanger. These men had controlled uncaring giant food processing corporations, dictating what farmers could grow and what people could eat before the war. Fresh meat and vegetables in urban markets had been luxuries accessible only to the wealthy.

Ryan spotted Alistair Tyler weaving through the market. Vendors shouted, hawking sizzling street foods, enthusiastically promoting the delights of their favorite dishes. Remarkably, at this marketplace, locals didn't pay in currency—it was a regulated honor system: "I give to you, and you give to me" — trading a pair of shoes or a shaving razor in exchange for a bowl of spicy Cheno beans.

Walking alongside Alistair were two teenagers: a blonde-haired, blue-eyed boy and a brown-haired girl with striking hazel eyes—Walter and Sarah. Three women accompanied them: Rihanna, Lanfen, and Marion. Marion, the tallest and most somber-faced among them, appeared to be in her thirties and carried a baby, Nicolea, snug in a sling.

"Rob," Ryan called, pointing towards a red stall selling purple melons, bright yellow, fig-shaped fruit, and crimson Perteccul wildflowers. "If you want to talk with Commander Tyler, he's standing near that stall."

"Okay. You and Rachel go on ahead."

"Where are you heading now?" Rachel asked.

"I need to speak with Commander Tyler. Won't be long— ten minutes at most."

Robert pushed through the lively, noisy crowd and caught up with Alistair.

"Commander Tyler, hello. You remember me, don't you?"

"Yes, of course. How are you?"

"I'm well, sir, thank you. We're concerned about a mutual friend—Lee Hapgood. It's been a while since we've heard from him."

"Lee Hapgood... I remember. He was the pilot who flew Captain Brindle and his team to the Endeavour."

"That's right. We've searched everywhere for Lee—inside the Keyway caves and even the Habitat Ring—but found no trace. Perhaps Captain Brindle knows where Lee is or what happened to him. Maybe you could arrange a meeting with the captain—only if it's not too much trouble."

Alistair shook his head gravely. "Captain Brindle isn't here. After the Endeavour left stable orbit around this planet, the away team never returned."

"Do I hear you correctly?" Robert asked, a chill creeping into his voice. "You're saying they're still on that God-forsaken ship?"

Alistair's face grew solemn. "Yes, Robert. I'm afraid so."

***

Marion's expression shifted abruptly from that of a protective mother to one of sudden, fierce anger. She watched Alistair converse with a man dressed too elegantly to escape notice. Clearly, he was one of the Allied folk—a Freelander wouldn't dare wear such neat, comely clothes.

She approached the man and tapped him sharply on the shoulder.

"You're from the Endeavour!"

Robert turned to face her, noting the woman carrying a baby in a sling.

"Marion, this is Robert Jandamarra," Alistair said, stepping forward to introduce them.

"I'm not interested in his name," Marion snapped.

"Can I help you, ma'am?" Robert asked calmly.

"It's too late for that. Your kind stole my husband and my boy."

Rihanna caught sight of Marion from a distance, tears streaming down her face as she moved away from Alistair, clutching baby Nicolea close to her chest.

"I'm sorry, Robert. I hope you can forgive Marion. She's lost both her husband and son," Alistair said gently.

"Marion…is Captain Brindle's wife?"

"Yes. She's a kind, generous woman and a devoted mother. She's battling a deep depression—painful beyond words. And now she has Nicolea to care for."

"What do you think happened up there, Commander?"

"To be honest, Robert…we simply don't know."

"Captain Brindle, Lee Hapgood, and the away team should have returned by now."

"Yes. They're long overdue," Alistair admitted. "I know Martin well, and he would never have allowed the Endeavour to leave orbit while his son and close friends were still aboard."

"When Endeavour left its parking orbit, it carried several cybernetic and cryogenic specialists from the High-Lab module," Robert added. "People who lacked the physical strength or time to resume their regular duties on board."

"Do you think they might have been bold enough to seize control of the ship and return here to Galraithia?" Alistair asked.

Robert paused thoughtfully. "No, I don't think so. From this point forward, every choice we make as individuals will determine our fate."

"Your parents and grandparents were proud Freelanders. They taught you valuable lessons."

"I often remember my grandmother telling me I was special—that I should never lose hope and always respect all living things equally," Robert said softly.

"As Freelanders, we needed Rachel Sibley's words to be taught to us all: 'Quis resis, lalai pah, tog ther namal.' Everyone is special. Never lose hope and respect all life. Goodbye, Robert. I hope that you and your friends find happiness and peace here."

"Thank you," Robert replied.

As Alistair walked away, he was struck by the paradox of Galraithia. Philip Sheridan had told his followers, "Earth will always be the perfect world for continuous human habitation—not Galraithia." Yet Professor Briar told the Freelanders the opposite: "Galraithia is the perfect world, not Earth." After Sheridan's departure, the conflicting statements became known as Galraithia's paradox: if Briar's claim is true, then Sheridan's must be true as well, because if Sheridan's is true, Briar's is false—and vice versa, creating an endless cycle.

Robert caught up with Rachel and Ryan.

"Sorry I was so long, Rachel."

"That was a long ten minutes, Robert."

"Alistair and I had a lot to discuss."

"You were gone over half an hour," Ryan said, looking stressed and worried.

"I told you I was sorry, Ryan."

"You did. Though a little grudgingly, wouldn't you say?"

"Okay, two against one—what's the verdict?"

"No, I'm done here," Ryan said. "I can't find my personal computer. I left it onboard Phoenix in all the excitement. I'll see you and Rachel back at the house later."

"Bungalow-12—don't forget," Rachel reminded, thinking of the new home she would share with Robert, Ryan, and their unborn twins.

"Bungalow-12?"

"Our new home. Ryan and I met a Penglaian property owner while you were talking with Commander Tyler. We offered him computer training in exchange for rent-free housing."

"That's a fair trade," Robert said with a grin.

"Yes, an ideal one."

"And where do I fit in?" Robert asked. "Data storage? Neural network planning?"

"No. You've got a vast garden to maintain."

"Maintain a garden?"

"Rob, that was part of the deal. Don't get upset."

"I'm not upset. Come on, I'll help you unpack."

"No! Go with Ryan. There's not much to unpack."

"Okay. I'll start building two cozy little cots when we get back."

"No, I want you and Ryan home before dark."

"Yes, boss."

***

Having left Rachel and the bartering market behind, Ryan and Robert made their way toward the Phoenix. Along the way, they crossed paths with Father Sandor and Father Antonio, who were briskly walking in the opposite direction—away from the landing zone and the ship.

Father Antonio seemed tense, his movements edged with nervous energy. At first, Ryan thought the young priest might have something important to say, but Antonio only offered a curt nod of greeting. Then, he nudged Father Sandor, though Sandor seemed uninterested in stopping or engaging; the two continued down the forest path, heading due east toward Yuǎnfāng City and the sea.

"Antonio, just keep walking. Don't look back," Sandor said quietly.

The young priest nodded, glancing anxiously at the countdown timer on his wristwatch—the seconds ticking down steadily.

***

Ryan and Robert approached the landing zone cautiously from the northwest. As they rounded a sharp bend on the bush track, the mighty reconfigured fuselage of the Phoenix loomed into view. Robert stopped abruptly and dropped to one knee when he spotted an odd pair of animals a short distance away—sniffing the leafy forest floor, urinating to leave scent markings.

Ryan grunted and knelt beside him.

"Keep quiet and stay still," Robert whispered.

"Okay, okay."

It was their first sighting of native animals. These four-legged creatures resembled wolves, though far larger in size and strength. Their head and body shapes differed little from the iconic predator wolves scientists said no longer roamed the wilds of Earth. Robert moved cautiously closer, mindful of the breeze blowing in his face, downwind.

"I remember reading old nature magazines, seeing glossy photos of wolves hunting prey," Robert murmured, "but they were smaller than these."

"A new species of wolf, maybe?" Ryan asked.

"I don't know. Let's get a little closer."

Suddenly, a long-tipped spear drove into the ground right beside Ryan's head. He glanced sideways to see a large Penglaian man with a heavily tattooed face.

Ryan and Robert stood up, greeted the man with a nod and stepped forward to shake hands. Even the wolf-like creatures grew curious, edging closer, drawn by the strong scent of fear.

"They're coming closer!" Ryan blurted.

"My pets will not harm you. Lái, lái," the tattooed man commanded—the phrase meaning "Do not approach the strangers."

The beasts' tails wagged vigorously as they obeyed, behaving more like domesticated dogs than fearsome wolves. They settled on their haunches, panting to cool their bodies, eyes gleaming with wary menace at the two strangers brushing leaves from their navy-blue overalls.

"Hi, I'm Robert."

"And I'm Ryan. Pleasure to meet you, sir."

"What's your name?" Robert asked, gesturing to the man.

"My name is Qiang."

"Nice to meet you, Mr. Qiang."

"Likewise."

"What kind of work do you do?" Robert inquired.

"Master builder."

"Mr. Qiang, you speak our language very well," Ryan said.

"I was fortunate to have an exceptional teacher," Qiang replied.

Ryan glanced at the beasts, now frantically scratching the ground and urinating.

"Magnificent creatures. They're not indigenous to this planet, are they?"

"No. Our star chaser *Liaoning* carried seeds and banks of animal and human embryos. We were lucky to save everything valuable after the crash—food processors, medical beds, freezer units. But we lost most of the heavy cargo. Weeks passed before some animal embryos began mutating into zoklar wolves and giant raptors."

"We have first-hand accounts and photographic evidence of giant raptors, but nothing about zoklar wolves. Your pets— they are zoklar wolves?"

"Yes. This planet's atmosphere alters the genetic makeup of plants and animals native to Earth, somehow changing their DNA matrix."

"How is that even possible?" Robert asked incredulously.

"Rob, why the surprise? Anything's possible—otherwise we wouldn't be standing on this planet. Mr. Qiang, your pets are magnificent. What are their names?"

"This is Bai, and the angry one is Jengi," Qiang said, scratching behind Bai's ears.

Jengi snarled at Ryan, then flopped down near its handler.

Suddenly, a loud explosion shattered the calm. The Phoenix erupted violently, black acrid smoke billowing above the forest canopy. Sparks, embers, and shards of hot steel rained down, slamming into the ground. The fire rapidly spread through the dry undergrowth.

Qiang and the zoklar wolves led the way out of the forest, thick acrid smoke irritating eyes and throats. Ryan and Robert followed quickly, descending a trail that opened onto a grassy clearing beside an intertidal pond.

***

Robert and Ryan reported the shocking news to Professor Briar. They told him the Phoenix was gone—utterly destroyed by a violent explosion—but neither mentioned their chance encounter with Qiang or the two zoklar wolves. Instead, their conversation soon turned to a shared concern over the explosion's cause.

Disturbing allegations surfaced, revealing their recent, accidental meeting with Father Sandor and Father Antonio on the forest path leading to—and away from—the Phoenix, not long before the fiery blast.

Professor Briar spoke strangely dismissively about the destruction of the Phoenix. He had authorized its destruction himself, applying his executive seal to cut off any lingering hope that Freelanders might abandon the dream of colonizing Galraithia and return to Earth.

Ryan and Robert, however, did not share Briar's firm convictions. They hurried back to Bungalow 12 to recount everything to Rachel. But the expectant mother, caught in

the midst of a real-life dream, found herself far more
fascinated by the idea of the zoklar wolves than by the
tattooed man named Qiang.

***

NEO-57

Two solar years had passed since the Endeavour spacecraft departed Galraithia—two years of profound silence as the crew slept soundly inside fluidized cryo beds. As the Endeavour neared the edge of the Cassandra Major System, onboard radar scanners detected a carbonaceous C-type asteroid designated Neo-57.

The scanners analyzed the time-frequency of the radar signal alongside the De-Cel trajectory coordinates Captain Sheridan had programmed into the navigation computer. The final course correction—the De-Cel maneuver—had decelerated Endeavour from maximum light speed to sub-light velocity as it approached Neptune, repositioning the ship directly in Neo-57's path. The asteroid's predicted collision course was simulated again on a digital display. Scrolling numbers and Sequanta computer code, fed from the Simulink system, confirmed a chilling mathematical certainty: Neo-57 was hurtling at 85,000 miles per hour on a direct collision course with Endeavour.

With every passing second, Neo-57 drew closer. Deafening collision alarms blared throughout the vessel. Endeavour's automatic helm control was locked in Closeout Mode— offline and powerless to take evasive action. Even the Sequanta control computer (SCC) was inaccessible. Mission parameters were rigidly fixed to Captain Sheridan's defaults, and no changes could be made until the ship reached Neptune.

To make matters worse, Sheridan had implemented site-specific security measures to prevent unauthorized access to the SCC database node: hidden lasers and halopolmate gas ensured that no one aboard—even a fabricator—could interfere with his relentless plan to return to Earth, wealth beyond imagining in his sights.

Now, his carefully crafted scheme was unraveling. Dallas Fitch had warned Sheridan of the dangers of operating the automatic helm control in Closeout Mode, but the warning had come too late.

***

As the Simulink computer had predicted, the odd-shaped asteroid slammed into the Endeavour and deflected off. The impact ruptured the outer hull plating and tore through the ship's fragile inner shell. Explosive decompression obliterated the Greenhouse module and destroyed the entire food supply.

Collision alarms blared on every deck, but the majority of the human population—deep in cryogenic stasis—remained utterly unaware of the chaos unfolding. Fabricator Five-o-nine had come online just minutes before the asteroid struck. Following G-Deck's emergency evacuation plan, Five-o-nine hurried to the Area-6 muster station. Optical sensors detected extensive metal deformation and fatigue cracking along the mid-ship hull's inner lining. Plug plates mounted on the upper starboard wall of the Cryo module suddenly stopped the oxygen venting into space. Five-o-nine then identified further structural fatigue and hull deformations along the bulkhead facing the brig.

Six cryo beds stood lined up beside a holding cell. Five were occupied; one—the bed belonging to citizen pilot Lee Hapgood—was empty and offline. According to the ship's logs, a security fabricator had detected unauthorized movement inside the Cryo Chamber. Following Captain Sheridan's protocols, the security fabricator wheeled the beds down to the brig and secured them inside a small holding cell surrounded by unbreakable safety glass and a coded lock. Why anyone would do this, Five-o-nine could not ascertain. Still, its sensors and Rachel Vaughn's programming concluded that under current conditions, there was justifiable danger to everyone aboard Endeavour.

Five-o-nine keyed in the unique security code and unlocked the cell door. Seconds later, the sealed lids of the five occupied cryo beds lifted simultaneously and the temperature inside began to rise. Peering into each bed, Five-o-nine removed thin plastic sheets floating atop pools of freezing cryogenic fluid—liquids that never froze even in temperatures potent enough to destroy cells. The fabricator then carefully withdrew feeding tubes, intravenous saline drips, and liquefied cryogenic gas. A quick jab in the neck with pre-filled syringes of synthesized adrenaline gradually roused Martin, Joseph, Satori, Michael, and Dani from deep sleep.

A small electric motor inverted the cryo beds to vertical positions. Groggy and confused, the five Freelanders stepped barefoot onto the cold floor, every inch of their skin bruised and sore. Their eyes hurt the most. As Joseph's vision sharpened, he reeled back in horror.

Before them lay the partial skeletal remains of three adult men. The sight was too ghastly to escape anyone's attention. Satori looked away from the corpses, recognizing two immediately—Lee Hapgood and Adrian Sangster. The third was unmistakably Peter Winthrop, identified by a ring bearing the Winthrop family crest on his right index finger.

Satori wept.

Albert and Jonathon might have met the same fate as the three men lying dead on the cold floor.

Joseph stepped behind her. A shiver ran down her spine.

"Hey, are you okay?"

"We have failed our son," Satori sobbed. "And Jonathon…
and Professor Briar."

"We haven't failed anyone," Martin countered.

"How can you say that? The mission to bring the three Far-
Star engines back to Galraithia has failed. Finding Albert
and Jonathon and bringing them home safely has failed."

"Are you implying that it's my fault?"

"No, Captain, I'm not."

"I believe they're still here somewhere, and alive," Joseph
said.

"But how can you be so sure?"

Joseph placed his hands gently on her shoulders.

"The boys aren't here inside this glass prison. That tells me
they're alive, somewhere on the ship."

Dani spent time conversing with Five-o-nine; he had never
seen skeletal remains before.

"These men starved to death," Dani remarked.

Five-o-nine turned to him and responded with two distinct
affirmative beeps—also signals warning of hazard ahead.

Martin fitted a rubber repair clamp around a ruptured
oxygen pipe.

"This vent must lead to the upper passenger decks," he
said.

"Affirmative!" Five-o-nine responded. "Muster Station-9!
Report to Muster Station-9, Captain."

"Yes, I'm aware. But first, we have to find Jonathon and
Albert."

"As you command, sir."

"Five-o-nine, we're leaving now. It was a pleasure knowing you," Michael Stoddard said as he exited the brig.

"Likewise, sir."

"Does this blue pipe run along the starboard bulkhead?" Michael asked.

Five-o-nine beeped twice and watched Martin approach. "Yes, sir."

"Michael, wait up!" Martin called. "The short walkway on the left leads to one of the hangar bays."

"Okay."

***

The medical fabricator on duty roused Captain Philip Sheridan. The collision warning system still blared, while the Damage Control Center detailed the vessel's damage from the impact. Philip donned his warmest one-piece coveralls and black army boots, then called up his best four soldiers along with Dallas Fitch—the only man who knew the Endeavour inside and out. Safety protocols required them to spend the next half hour undergoing a series of medical procedures and cognitive tests to counter hypersleep's lingering effects.

Leading his team down to G-Deck, Philip moved to inspect the damage to the inner hull. Meanwhile, the Freelanders reached the bulkhead door there. Martin stepped forward and opened it, the squeak of rusty hinges alerting Philip immediately. Dallas and the soldiers rushed over, drawing sidearms and aiming them at the intruders. Throughout the vessel, collision and air pressure alarms echoed ominously.

Martin faced Captain Sheridan, the anticipated questions hanging in the air: how had the damage occurred, and why? His answers made it clear to everyone—the Endeavour was structurally compromised. Essential supplies, including food stores and the carefully tended hydroponic gardens, had been violently ejected into the void of space. Personal grievances had to be set aside; survival depended on collaboration. Time pressed cruelly, and unity was their greatest weapon against the mounting challenges.

Philip's focus wasn't on how the Freelanders had boarded or their intentions. What mattered was deciding the next course of action. He forced himself to stay calm, though fatigue from hypersleep and command stresses clouded his thoughts. Intruders threatened his plans, undermining his hold on the ship. To assert control, Philip placed the Freelanders under arrest.

As Satori strode back to the brig's holding cell, she cast a fiery glare over her shoulder, her eyes flashing with fierce intensity. "Captain Sheridan, I demand to see my son!"

"Freelander, I hardly think you're in a position to make demands," Philip replied sharply.

Before he could react further, a heavy fist struck his ribs and then his face, catching him off guard. Dazed and sore, Philip struggled to maintain his balance. Grimacing, he shouted at his soldiers, "Kill them! Kill the Freelander scum!"

Suddenly, punches rained down on his stomach and right kidney. Clutching at his side, his knees buckled, and he collapsed heavily to the floor.

Everything happened in a blur as soldiers drew sidearms. Dani Li, spinning like a whirlwind, unleashed several high kicks that hit the soldiers' throats. He followed with a rapid flurry of crushing punches to heads and faces. Weakened by years in hypersleep, Philip's soldiers dropped like lifeless birds.

The Freelanders fought with practiced coordination, though Joseph stayed mostly in the background. His approach favored brains over brawn, a strategy that paid off—he seized a fallen soldier's laser pistol and aimed it at Dallas Fitch's head. Meanwhile, Satori held an army knife to a young female soldier whom Philip had loved fiercely for six months.

"Good job," Michael praised, but agony overtook him as a knife wound gushed blood from his abdomen. Dani knelt beside him. "I fucked up," he whimpered. "I didn't see the knife hidden in her right boot."

Michael needed immediate surgery to stop the bleeding, but the nearest medical fabricator was three levels up. Gasping, he looked at Dani and whispered, "Living my life was a great ride, man." Slowly, he slipped into shock and died.

Satori's eyes burned with hatred. A female soldier collapsed, blood gushing from her throat. The Freelander showed no emotion, no remorse—their law justified deadly force to prevent felony and vengeance killings. Joseph picked up the bloodied knife from the floor, tossed it aside, then slid an arm around Satori's waist as they exited the prison cell.

The unconscious soldiers were dragged into the brig and stacked in a corner. Philip hissed curses and spat toward Martin, but a sudden strike to his head erased his vision in darkness. Martin then turned to Dallas Fitch.

"You could have fired your sidearm during the fight but let Joseph take your weapon. Why?"

"Captain," Dallas replied, "what if I told you I bear no ill will toward you or your people? Would you believe me?"

"That all hinges on whether I can trust you, Mr. Fitch."

"Trust always involves risk," Martin muttered.

Dani interjected, "You're not seriously considering trusting him? He's second-in-command on Endeavour and Sheridan's best friend."

Dallas met Dani's gaze firmly. "You might think you know me, Mr. Li, but you don't. Now is not the time to question my loyalty."

Martin kicked Sheridan sharply in the back. Turning to the five cryo beds, he ripped out tubing and wiring, smashed the glass panels covering the temperature displays. Then, with brutal finality, he slit an unconscious soldier's throat and forced the bloody knife into Philip's right hand.

"Mr. Fitch, prove your worth. Seal the brig!"

"Yes, Captain." Dallas quickly opened a small electrical panel and bypassed the circuitry that locked the glass doors.

***

Dallas led the Freelanders to the uppermost level of the Cryo module. Upon entering the chamber, it quickly became clear that more than half of the cryo beds supported by the medical fabricator were offline. Martin cautiously moved forward, shining his torch into one of the beds. Inside, he discovered the skeletal remains of a colonist lying in dried cryo fluid. The fluid's life-giving nutrients and energy had evaporated, leaving behind a gray residue crystalline with dehydrated ice.

"Fabricator on duty!" Martin called sharply.

"Yes, sir. How can I help you?"

"Jonathon Brindle and Albert Arunui. Where are they?"

"Master Arunui and Master Brindle were assigned to the cryo beds farthest from the airlock. Please, follow me."

Joseph glanced around the chamber, a frown creasing his brow. "It's unsettling to see so many vacant cryo beds," he remarked, his unease evident in his voice.

"There's only one medical fabricator on this level," Satori noted.

"Captain, with your approval, Dani and I are ready to proceed to the bridge, sir."

"Okay, Dallas, you two go ahead."

"We should head back to the Cargo Bay first," Dani suggested. "I saw several food storage modules there, all unopened."

"Good luck finding any food," Joseph said bitterly. "I haven't had a morsel since we left Alpha."

***

The medical fabricator stopped in front of beds 45988 and 45989. Joseph held Satori at arm's length to keep her back, but she nonetheless peered into bed 45988 and saw Albert peacefully asleep. Jonathon rested in the adjacent cryo bed. Relief washed over Martin at the sight of both boys, though a shadow of worry crossed his face. The fabricator switched on the cryo bed lights.

"You need not fear. Everything is satisfactory: heart rate normal… oxygen level normal… blood pressure normal. Neurological signs show no complications at this time," the fabricator reported. Martin glanced down at his son's pale face, longing to offer a reassuring hug.

"You are strong, and you'll get through this. I promise you."

"Martin, do you have a minute?" Joseph interrupted.

"What's up?"

"There's pressure loss in the discharge pipe attached to the cryo tank. The pipe must have torn loose. Cryo fluid is slowly leaking down the wall and pooling on the floor behind the inner bulkhead."

Martin shook his head. "I know the diagnostic system detected stress fractures in the inner mid-ship bulkhead, but there's no mention of a burst hydraulic seal or serious cryo fluid leakage."

The Endeavour's hull, hydraulic pipes, and gate systems might be severely compromised. Martin's worst fears solidified—he had to evacuate everyone off the Cryo Module immediately. "Satori! Wake the boys. Get on it right away."

"With pleasure, Captain."

Martin turned to the fabricator. "Cargo Bay-6 is on C-Deck, correct?"

"Yes, Captain."

"Initiate emergency wake-up procedures. I want everyone prepped and ready to relocate to Cargo Bay-6 within the hour."

"I'll see to it," Joseph pledged.

"No. I need you to locate the main selector valve and manually open the hatchway doors."

"Okay."

***

The medical fabricator quickly followed Martin's order, moving from cryo bed to cryo bed to wake the sleeping passengers and instruct them to report to Cargo Bay 6. Albert and Jonathon were the first to wake and immediately felt the nauseating after-effects of prolonged hypersleep. Their eyes were sore, and speaking was difficult. Satori helped them step under hot showers to wash away the sticky cryo fluid that had become encrusted on their skin.

Using all their strength to regain their balance, the boys changed into clean clothes. However, they both looked around the room, outwardly disoriented, feeling as if they had lost their way. Suddenly, a hissing sound caught everyone's attention…the sound of escaping air followed by the vacuum alarm.

"Get to the airlock!" Joseph yelled. Albert and Jonathon struggled to move forward; their legs had grown weak. Tears of anguish filled Satori's eyes as she held the airlock open while Martin and Joseph carried the boys through. Just seconds before the inner hull plates collapsed, she quickly closed the airlock. The hull breach created a large hole, unleashing a violent windstorm that sent loose materials swirling around the Cryo module. Tom Granger and a dozen other passengers rushed to the spacesuit locker, but anything not securely bolted to the floor was sucked out into space. Cargo Bay-6 became the temporary refuge for 693 Allied colonists, but its temperature was freezing compared to the warmer passenger areas inside the Endeavour.

Hull breach alarms blared throughout the ship as stress fractures ruptured the inner hull plates on decks 8, 7, and 12. Martin and Joseph, exhausted but determined, carried Albert and Jonathon safely to Endeavour's bridge. Meanwhile, Dani and Dallas were further back, welding the stress fractures on the longitudinal bulkheads. A look of relief spread across Martin's face when Satori, Dani, and Dallas entered the bridge. Satori appeared drained and leaned heavily on Joseph's arm. "Hatchway doors can only be closed manually," she said. "There's hydraulic oil leaking past the shut-off valve."

"Your Endeavour is slowly breaking apart, Dallas."

"Endeavour is a well-built Sleeper ship. She can take a lot more punishment than you might think, Joseph; there is no Sleeper ship in her class that is stronger."

***

The end game scenario

After a detailed damage report, Dallas Fitch and twenty-three crew members were tasked with repairing the ruptured inner bulkheads. Five fabricators were retrieved from storage and inspected by Five-o-nine. As they worked outside in space to mend the Endeavour's buckled hull plates, Dallas recognized that every available resource had to be used with utmost efficiency. Internal maintenance crews were insufficient, and pressure fluctuations on the hull threatened to further weaken the inner bulkheads, risking the collapse of the lightly constructed living compartments. Fabricators had to operate swiftly and precisely.

Meanwhile, Martin and Dani searched the last remaining food storage bins on F-Deck. Inside a freezer that had not opened since leaving Earth, they found only a few sacks of wheat flour and barley. That would be their food supply until Endeavour reached Draxas-9, a human-staffed mining facility still two light-years away. No matter their coordinates, Martin knew the stark reality: food was dangerously scarce. The distant colonists of Draxas-9 were too far to provide aid to their crippled Sleeper ship.

With resolve, Martin called a meeting in the dining room, large enough to hold everyone aboard. There, he delivered the devastating news.

"Two undeniable facts loom over us: we are running out of food, and Draxas-9 is two light-years away. Distress calls have been sent and will be repeated until operators on Draxas-9 acknowledge them. Meanwhile, we must adjust our rations—using barley flour instead of wheat, and improvising oats by grinding the few bags of rolled oats in

Cargo Bay 3. Without liquid nutrition, hypersleep is impossible. It is likely the entire human population aboard will perish from starvation before we reach Draxas-9. Accepting this reality will test our resilience—mind and body alike. Starvation will be an ever-present threat."

He paused solemnly. "But there is an alternative protein source: the bodies of seventy-eight deceased passengers stored in the morgue freezer."

A chilling silence filled the room as the weight of his words registered, sparking vigorous protests against controlled cannibalism. Joseph remained unusually quiet. Satori and Dani argued fiercely that life was too precious to sacrifice.

Dallas felt torn and sought counsel from his best friend, Science Officer Dr. Anthony Mitchel, summoned to the bridge. The idea nauseated Anthony, whose profound religious convictions clashed with the grim proposal. Once cheerful when sober, he now bore the weary visage of a man burdened by despair—his brow furrowed and hair graying.

"As gruesome as it sounds, feeding off dead colonists is what we must do to survive," Dallas insisted.

"I would rather starve to death than endorse cannibalism," Anthony shot back.

"Martin, the decision must be unanimous, right?" Joseph asked.

"Yes. Every passenger and crew member must vote and sign the ship's log."

Jonathon looked to his father, as did the assembled crew and passengers, their eyes silently pleading for guidance.

"Doctor Mitchel, I know you are deeply religious," Martin began.

"I am, Captain. And?"

"My grandfather told me of the harshest Antarctic winter ever recorded, when our Freelander ancestors ate human flesh to survive."

"Did he tell you human cannibalism is an affront to God?"

"No. I think some take life for granted. Living is a gift, and Freelanders do whatever it takes to prolong it."

"Captain, you are wasting your time—and mine. I'm not a Freelander. Leave me be."

***

Later that evening, a corner-mounted ceiling camera captured Doctor Mitchel entering Airlock 82 without a protective spacesuit. The outer airlock door slid open, and the doctor drifted silently into the abyss of space. Joseph switched off the video display unit and slumped back into his chair—there was absolutely nothing he could do to save his friend's life.

Joseph's mind spiraled back to memories—the FS *Taimaha*, Douglas Tyler, and the childhood trauma of the New Zealand earthquake that had claimed his entire family and nearly his own life. Despair and anguish nearly broke him, driving him to the brink of giving up, even contemplating ending his own life. Yet, thanks to strong medical support and love, he endured. Shanawi Station remained a haunting paradox in his mind; he recalled a conversation with Martin while they waited for Adrian Sangster's heavycopter to arrive.

"Not everyone at Shanawi starved to death," Martin had said. "Kaito Shanawi took his own life, a bullet to the brain. His family and closest friends followed rather than succumb to cannibalism."

"The idea of dismembered bodies being cooked makes my stomach turn," Joseph admitted.

"So you wouldn't eat human flesh to save your life?"

"No. I'd rather open my veins than become a cannibal."

In the days following Martin's grim announcement, most people kept to themselves. But while Martin and Dani conducted routine flight system checks on the bridge, the Sequanta guidance computer reported its first radar contact with another Earth vessel. Dani climbed into the navigator's chair and pulled up the radar unit.

"It's likely just an automated mining station," Martin speculated.

"There's a dense asteroid field spanning sector DX-4 through G7-Alpha," Dani pointed out on the star chart. "If it is a mining station, it's moving away from the field."

"Are we receiving data from the Omega scanner?" Martin asked.

"No. The asteroid strike damaged the long-range laser scanner antennae."

Frustration crept into Martin's voice. "Get Joseph up here."

Moments later, Joseph entered the bridge, rubbing his tired eyes.

"I'm sorry for waking you," Martin said.

"No matter. I couldn't sleep anyway."

Joseph took the empty chair beside Martin and accessed the Sequanta code he and Dallas Fitch had learned to decipher.

"This computer is operating in Closeout Mode," Joseph said, shaking his head. "That's why the navigation computer didn't take evasive action when it detected Neo-57."

He took manual control of the helm.

"What are you doing?" Martin asked.

"Disengaging Closeout Mode," Joseph replied, then handed control back to the Central Sequanta Computer.

He explained, "Phoenix's onboard navigation computer has its own laser scanning antenna mounted on the front starboard side. The engineers who designed Phoenix were wise to install a similar LRS just beneath Endeavour's hydrogen intake manifold."

Joseph played back the recorded Sequanta code—the conversation between the ships' computers. "Our distress calls were received and acknowledged."

"But we never got any verbal confirmation. Not a single response!" Dani exclaimed, frustration clear in his voice.

"Closeout Mode has a hidden interlock," Joseph explained. "While active, it overrides all navigation and communication protocols—and, in wartime, even life support systems."

"Joseph, turn the Endeavour around and plot an intercept course," Martin commanded.

"Before leaving Earth, Xiangshan Traders had commercial interests in and around sector DX-4. Identifying that vessel would be wise," Dani advised.

Joseph continued, "The guidance computer gave me the last recorded transmission. It includes a registration code, a name, and media notes from Earth: The FS Rachel is the first of three recently built supply carriers bound for the third planet in the Cassandra Major System—Galraithia."

"Old Gordon Winthrop would turn in his grave if he knew the Freelanders had built three supply carriers capable of reaching Galraithia," Dani muttered.

"He would indeed," Joseph agreed, recalling his deep dislike for Winthrop.

"Joseph, give me a track time to rendezvous," Martin said, stepping up to the raised navigation station.

"Rendezvous is possible within two months… three at most."

Closing his eyes, Martin thought of Marion and his daughter Nicolea. He stepped down from the navigation station and hurried toward the Cryo module's security console.

"We need to go faster!" Joseph urged. "But decelerating a ship this size won't be easy."

Dani scanned real-time data from the food station. "There's only enough food to last one month."

"We can survive on barley bread and half rations—and still recuperate," Martin said, trying to inject confidence.

Martin called Dallas Fitch in the engine room, who was investigating temperature spikes in several heat exchangers. Dallas's face tightened as temperatures rose inside the Endeavour, and interior condensation on electrical equipment caused short circuits across the spacecraft.

"Hello, Mr. Fitch," Martin said, tapping the radio console. "Dallas! Acknowledge."

"Yes, Captain."

"Dallas, I know there's no quick way to slow this beast down, but we need more speed. We have to go faster."

"Captain, the reactor core is damaged. Exceeding the coolant pressure boundary is dangerous and could destroy the engines. Worse, heat instability might destroy the entire ship."

"Is there anything you can do to gain even a little more speed?"

"You're not listening, Captain."

"I am listening, Mr. Fitch. Follow my orders. Initiate an all-engine burn on my command."

"Aye, Captain."

"Joseph, are you ready?"

"Yes. Endeavour is in position."

"Thirty seconds to all engines burn on my command… three, two, one, initiate!"

***

Draxas-9

Two years later

Captain Thorsten Norden entered the bridge and settled into his command chair. He greeted the crew and scanned the overnight staff log. Calm and confident, his tone was steady. Yet, as he reviewed data from the long-range scanners (LRS), his expression shifted—concern crept in. The LRS had detected radar contact with a derelict spacecraft, but no communication signals came through.

"Endeavour, Endeavour, this is the Majestic Star. Please respond."

"Did I hear you correctly, Cadet Jones? Did you say Endeavour?"

"Aye, sir. The LRS logged the hull number as EN-DEV02424-A04."

"It could be a radar glitch. Verify the hull identification number, just to be sure."

"The main Sequanta computer has confirmed the hull number, Captain. It belongs to the Endeavour," Lieutenant Grace Ellington reported.

"Very well, Lieutenant. Dispatch a Nexus probe and a quarantine team to that vessel. And Grace, inform Michael Taylor and his team—suspected hull instability. Exercise extreme caution."

"Aye, aye, sir."

***

The quarantine vessel secured a firm 'Hard Dock' with the Endeavour. Quarantine Officer Michael Taylor opened the outer airlock door and led his team of four coveralled inspectors inside. The heat buildup within the vessel was disturbingly intense, and lighting sensors had melted away. Moving cautiously, the team navigated twisted, misaligned metal handrails leading to dimly lit passageways and hatchway doors sealed tight, blocking access to the upper decks.

Live electrical cables sprawled across grated metal floors like hazards waiting to strike. Careful to avoid danger zones and broken handrails, the quarantine team retreated back to the main airlock, realizing they needed to find a safer route to the upper decks.

Meanwhile, several photographs taken by the Nexus probe revealed a clear image of the 35-foot breach in Endeavour's outer hull. Captain Thorsten Norden shook his head, eyes fixed on the haunting images. He couldn't fathom how the vessel had not broken apart. Yet structural evidence supported his suspicion that vibrations from the Endeavour's nanotrine reactor and five rocket engines might have caused the ship to fracture.

Deeper inside the Endeavour, Michael Taylor and his team reported empty cargo holds and buckled hull plates to Captain Norden. Fabricators were nowhere to be found. Most greenhouse modules and food storage bins in Section C-9 were gone; titanium flanges had sheared clean off. Although life support systems remained functional, electrical power flickered unpredictably.

The quarantine team split up. Taylor pressed forward with unrelenting speed until he reached G-Deck and the brig. The air temperature there soared to 125 degrees Fahrenheit, heavy with the distinct, pungent scent of rotting flesh. Michael held his nose as he moved along a narrow passage, flanked by a series of small compartments—holding cells built from unbreakable glass.

Peering into the middle cell, he recoiled in horror. Inside, human skulls lay cracked open like coconut shells, bones heaped in a grotesque pile. Deep cut marks scarred the bones. Longer fragments had been hollowed out—bone marrow meticulously picked clean. Nausea churned in Michael's stomach. He fought the urge to vomit, clinging to his composure as he donned his oxygen mask. Breathing deeply, he steadied himself.

He attempted to contact Captain Norden via his handheld Vox radio. "Captain, if you hear me, please acknowledge."

"Yes, Taylor, I read you. Where are you now?"

"G-Deck, Captain."

"I see you on the infrared scanner."

"Sir, I found human skeletons in holding cell 2-D."

"A significant portion of the Endeavour's outer hull must have been breached—either by an internal explosion or a direct meteorite strike. Such violent trauma would explain many deaths and casualties. Seal off the area and continue searching. There's still hope of finding survivors."

"I understand, Captain. We'll keep looking."

Moving on, Michael reached the crew quarters. Opening the first cabin door on the starboard side of Deck D, the ceiling lights flickered on automatically. The room was spacious and cleaner than his own on the Majestic Star. A brown leather upholstered chair sat near a double bed, beside a mirrored wardrobe, bureau, and washbasin. Michael splashed cool water on his face and neck, relief washing over him from the oppressive heat.

Opening the mirrored wardrobe, he found five army uniforms neatly pressed on a rod—and an empty suitcase bearing Philip Sheridan's name tag. Curiosity piqued, Michael unzipped the suitcase to reveal a sealed bag of purple berries. He carefully placed the berries in a quarantine bag and exited Sheridan's cabin.

"Michael, can you hear me?"

"Loud and clear, TJ."

"The transverse beam supporting the Cryo module's roof must have snapped under tension," TJ reported. "The ceiling and walls collapsed, burying hundreds of empty cryo beds under regolith paneling."

"Is there any electrical power?"

"No. Only handheld flashlights. The entire area was blacked out when we arrived. There are no lifepods, no transport shuttles, and zero pressure in the airlock actuators at the muster station. The passengers and crew must have evacuated long ago. I think searching for survivors here is a waste of time."

"Maybe you're right," Michael said, "but doesn't it bother you—not knowing what happened to the people aboard? And where are the fabricators? Have you seen any?"

"Nope. But honestly, I hope we don't find survivors. That would jeopardize salvage rights."

"Taylor! Come in, over."

"Taylor here. Go ahead, Jonas."

"Captain Norden wants to remote-pilot the Endeavour into a stable orbit around Draxas-9."

"Everyone heard that?"

"Yes."

"As you move through the ship, watch for new cracks forming."

"Jonas, stop treating us like novices," Michael snapped as he strode down the D-Deck corridor, lined with expensive private cabins. This was the fastest route to Main Engineering and the Engine Room.

In the lower level of the Engine Room, Michael peered down into the magnetic confinement reactor. The shaft was motionless; the nanotrinc cyclotron offline. Two locking clamps lay open, blocking 'rapid-rate' nanotrine energy production—and starving Endeavour's five rocket engines of fuel. Michael climbed over a broken railing and descended a circular metal staircase, dangerously close to the nanotrine fusion reactor. The air burned at 220 degrees Fahrenheit, thick and scorching, making each breath difficult. He donned his self-contained oxygen concentrator and made his way back toward the main airlock via the galley.

Approaching the galley entrance, Michael found the dining room door ajar, stuck hard to open. Pushing with his shoulder, he entered a pitch-black room. Moving cautiously forward, something brushed his right leg. He jumped back and quickly swept his flashlight over the floor. Illuminated under the beam was a dirty-faced woman shielding her dazzled eyes, scurrying away. His heart pounded fiercely as his palms sweated. More eyes—grimed and wary—glinted in the shadows, members of a ragged group huddled in the far corner, whispering anxiously.

Michael stepped back into the light and closed the door. The sound of tired, suppressed sobs filled the air. His hands trembled as he drew the Vox radio from his belt and tapped the microphone.

"TJ, I need your help. Get down here—now!"

He called Captain Norden, stunned by the revelation that colonists had survived aboard the crippled vessel. The grim answer lay in holding cell 2-D—human skeletons showed acts of cannibalism, hard evidence that starving people resorted to unspeakable acts to survive.

As Michael ended the call, the door creaked open again. A man with long hair and an unkempt beard peered out, eyes wary. Sensing no threat, he shuffled forward and introduced himself as Dallas Fitch.

Michael searched his pockets, producing a small emergency medical kit, which he handed over. Dallas found water and nutrient pills inside—small lifelines for quick recovery.

Color slowly returned to Dallas's cheeks as strength seeped back into him. He explained how Captain Martin Brindle had desperately tried to evacuate all 693 allied colonists from the Endeavour to the FS Rachel. Still, 398 colonists, including Dallas, chose to remain aboard the damaged ship.

"Why would so many choose to stay?" Michael asked, incredulous. "The Endeavour was doomed."

"Captain Brindle asked the same. Most said they'd rather hope for rescue in space than return to Galraithia and live among the Freelanders. I had my reasons for staying too."

Michael shook his head in disbelief. "What reasons?"

"I couldn't abandon those who stayed behind. I know most personally—they're honest, peaceful, hard-working. And I couldn't leave the Endeavour; she's a remarkable ship."

"You made the right call. The FS Rachel is a Freelander vessel, built and run by Freelanders."

"I expect experienced Freelander captains and navigators will explore this quadrant in faster Star-chasers. Nexus-9 will be the gateway to Galraithia. The Freelanders treated us well—I must credit them for their generosity, food, and warm clothing. They were visibly upset when we said we wanted to stay aboard Endeavour. Still, rescue and return to Earth seemed a faint hope."

Squinting under the bright light, Dallas seemed to carry a lifetime's worth of darkness. Recounting the past confused his mind. "Galraithia isn't the living hell many think. We create our own hells and blame everyone but ourselves."

Michael smiled and nodded, shaking Dallas's hand warmly. Dallas thanked him for his empathy.

***

TJ's arrival startled Dallas, who would have kept talking if not for TJ and Michael quietly counting the Endeavour's passengers as they shuffled single file down the passageway toward the outer airlock door. Shoulders slumped and heads hung low, they carried a silent, terrible burden too heavy to share.

The ragtag group of scrawny allied colonists were led to decontamination chambers where they were soon provided with clean clothing and food after boarding the Majestic Star. Captain Thorsten Norden met Dallas Fitch—the man credited with saving the Endeavour and everyone aboard.

"No, no," Dallas corrected. "That honor belongs to Martin Brindle, a Freelander captain. After the FS Rachel hard docked with the Endeavour, he organized supplies of food and medicine—enough to last five years."

"A Freelander helping Allied folk? Hard to believe," Captain Norden said, suspicion lingering in his tone.

"Well, that's exactly what Martin did. He saved our people—not me."

Norden's curiosity was far from satisfied. He explained that he wanted to know more about Captain Brindle and the world of Galraithia—if Dallas was willing to share.

Dallas obliged, beginning with the story of Gordon Winthrop and the Endeavour. He spoke of Philip Sheridan's murder and how it had fanned the flames of the ongoing war between the Freelanders and the Allied colonists—a conflict Sheridan believed he could win. Captain Norden and his young officers listened intently. Dallas was resolute in telling the unvarnished truth about Galraithia, a world without evolutionary limits—an environment frequently at odds with the basic requirements for human habitation.

***

Epilogue

The Penglaian people welcomed the establishment of the second Freelander settlement. Construction of Freelander settlement Alpha-2 is nearing completion and is located on the southwestern coast of Penglai Island. Nearby, there is an active volcano situated in the center of a 122-mile-wide gulf. This area features an abundant supply of freshwater, timber, fertile grasslands, and aquatic vegetation. Additionally, several species of fish thrive on small crustaceans and blue algae found along the rocky shoreline.

As the sun rises over the horizon, the turquoise waters of the Gulf of Penglai are sparkling in the morning light. The sky is filled with brightly colored birds swooping past the forest canopy and gliding over the wetlands and mudflats, drawn to flat-headed fish with gills, scales, and four small limbs to support their bodies. These evolving flat-headed fish species have developed the ability to gulp air into their lungs, walk on the mudflats, and feed on the organic matter growing on the surface of the mud. This evolution mirrors the development of fish on Earth during the Cambrian Period.

***

Lanfen opened the front door of the timber house her builder husband had crafted. Bai and Jengi, their Zoklar wolves, followed her down the stairs to a vegetable garden bordered by colorful flowers and fragrant brush. Carefully, Lanfen plucked a sprig of hinalawa—the freshly harvested herb she brewed into a flavorful tea each morning before breakfast. She lifted her face to the sky. The usual dawn chorus of chirping birds filled a distant part of the island.

The birds scattered into the sky in different directions, steering clear of an open field beyond the tall trees.

A sudden, booming roar erupted—the sound of rocket engines pierced the air. The house trembled as Qiang burst from the bedroom, cradling their two-year-old daughter, Maya. Bai and Jengi began barking and snarling; Lanfen hadn't yet stepped inside.

"Hush now, I'm here. Lái, brin das!" she soothed.

"Lanfen, get to the underground shelter. Keep Maya safe," Qiang urged. "I have to warn the others."

"No. We're coming with you."

Suddenly, shadows darkened the sky as the FS Rachel hovered just above the treetops.

Qiang nodded reluctantly and whistled twice. Bai and Jengi circled close around Maya and Lanfen, their ears pricked forward, noses to the ground, snarling softly at the gently swaying ferns. "Bai, Jengi povest sheliendo. Protect Maya," Lanfen commanded, securing Maya in a rucksack.

Qiang led the way to the clearing. "Jengi, come. Walk beside me."

***

The FS Rachel touched down three miles from the nearest building. As the loading ramp automatically lowered to the ground, a swelling crowd of Penglaian and Freelander citizens surged forward, drawn to the imposing ship. Security guards moved swiftly, forming a tight perimeter around the rear of the cargo bay's loading ramp.

Father Sandor strode alongside Penglaian dignitaries while Professor Briar and Professor Lin greeted Admiral Marcus Nelson and Elisabeth Healey, the ship's captain. Twelve officers and 220 crew members had already poured down the ramp. Chief Lesley Fredericks led the long line of fabricators, their steps steady and purposeful. Close behind him came Fabricator Five-o-Nine.

"Fabricator Five-o-Nine," Lesley commanded, voice firm against the murmur of the crowd. "Instruct the other fabricators to assemble in the vacant area behind the spacecraft. Form Square in an orderly fashion, then power down on your assigned Lockplate."

Five-o-Nine stepped off the ramp without hesitation. "Yes, sir."

***

Marion Brindle and her four-year-old daughter, Nicolea, waited near the Security Station as the fabricators powered down. One by one, the passengers disembarked, their carefully gathered luggage and belongings in hand, filtering slowly down the loading ramp. Quarantine officers halted the first wave at a hastily erected Security Station, screening for contraband and signs of hypersleep sickness.

Dani Li stepped off through the starboard side quick exit ramp. He carried no luggage and showed no symptoms of illness. He paused briefly on the ramp when he spotted Rihanna waving at him. A security guard blocked her path, ordering her to stay back and wait until the rope separating the crowd from the new arrivals was removed. Dani motioned for Rihanna to wait for him at the Security Station.

Andre Zarovski pushed through a crowd near the Avionics Bay, making his way toward Dani. In his haste, he nearly knockcd Dani to thc ground.

"It's good to see you, comrade," Andre said, falling into step beside him. "I feared I might never see you again, my friend."

"It's good to see you too, Andre. You look well."

"On the outside, maybe. But I'm far from well."

"Why? What's wrong?"

"The head doctor—the man's an incompetent fool. He told me to stop drinking vodka. I never heard such nonsense."

"You should always heed your doctor's advice, Andre. You know that."

"Da, da! But he doesn't understand my dilemma."

"How so?" Dani asked, eyes tracing the long line of passengers waiting at the security stations.

"I have only one bottle left. The last of the great vintages from before the Great Rebellion. It's priceless. I'd like to share it with you and Michael. We'll raise our glasses high and celebrate your homecoming."

Michael's name stung. "I'm sure he would have said yes— if he were here. Sadly, Michael died on the Endeavour, protecting what he loved most: his friends and his freedom."

Andre's voice dropped. "I'm sorry, Dani. I didn't know. Michael Stoddard was a great man—a wonderful friend."

"He was a friend to many," Dani agreed.

As they neared the line, the two pushed past locals selling fresh fruit and sandwiches. Suddenly, Dani turned at a warm voice calling his name.

"Hello, Dani! Welcome home."

His throat tightened and his eyes welled up when he saw Lanfen holding a small hand.

"This is Maya," Lanfen said.

"Hello, beautiful Maya. You have the loveliest green eyes I've ever seen."

Maya shrank behind Lanfen, hesitant yet longing to reach her father, who stood farther off, holding a leash close to Bai and Jengi. Qiang smiled and waved at Maya. Dani's gaze locked onto Qiang and the wolves, his expression fixed.

"That's Qiang, my bonded partner with Bai and Jengi. He's a good man and a wonderful father. Maya and I love him dearly. I'm sure you and Qiang will get along."

"I get along with everyone," Dani said quietly, still watching the wolves.

"If you're worried about Bai and Jengi, don't be. They won't harm you."

"Right now, I'm not worried about anything."

"I'm glad you feel that way, Dani."

"Lanfen, I'd like to meet Qiang." Dani raised his hand, beckoning Qiang over. Lanfen quickly warned that Bai and Jengi grew anxious and aggressive around strangers, so Qiang kept them close, away from the noisy crowd.

Ryan, Robert, and Rachel approached Qiang and exchanged greetings. While the men chatted casually, Rachel sat down on the short grass, quietly sobbing. Robert never truly recovered from her miscarriage, but Rachel, healthy again, had become pregnant. When she shared the news, Robert swore his undying love for her and their baby.

Bai and Jengi lingered nearby, nosing cautiously at a few feet from Rachel. Just then, a security guard called to Dani.

"Please make your way to the Security Station, sir. This way."

"Lanfen, I must go. Can we catch up later?"

"Of course. Maya, say goodbye to Dani."

Dani smiled as Maya frowned and tugged her mother's sleeve, clearly wanting to play with Bai and Jengi.

***

Having cleared security, Dani and Andre approached Rihanna and her family. Dani embraced Rihanna warmly, pressing a gentle kiss to her cheek. "Welcome home."

Dani's gaze swept the area, and memories of the island's breathtaking views from the air came flooding back.

"This place is a tropical paradise."

"Indeed it is," Rihanna replied softly. "Alistair and the children love it here, and so do I."

"How are Alistair and the children?"

"Sarah's a beautiful young woman—clever and eager to learn, unlike her brother. But don't misunderstand me; Walter's a fine young man too—clever in many ways— very much like Alistair, only taller. I'm immensely proud of them."

"And Alistair?"

"Oh, Alistair's fine. You know him—he says one thing and does another. He told me he wanted to catch up with everyone, but he left early this morning with Father

Antonio. They went snorkeling around Blue Reef with Rob Finnegan."

Rihanna couldn't help but notice how much weight Dani had lost in four years. His face was drawn and pale, but his spirit remained intact—a hard shell that opened only when the time was right. She felt this wasn't yet the moment or place to revisit the hardships and conflicts from the Endeavour.

Dani and Andre also agreed it was best not to mention Michael Stoddard's death before the upcoming mission debriefing with Professor Briar and Father Sandor. Yet at that moment, all eyes turned to two men wheeling Michael's aluminum coffin down the quick exit ramp.

Marion Brindle's eyes locked on Martin and Jonathon, who followed closely behind the casket draped with the Freelander Flag of Honor and Freedom. Breaking protocol, Marion took Nicolea's hand and hurried toward the ramp. Jonathon ran to her, and she hugged her son tightly, tears of relief and happiness streaming down her face as Martin called Nicolea over, and she jumped into his arms.

At last, after four long years, Martin felt grateful for the chance to rebuild life for his family.

Brendon Aitama approached, smiling warmly and shaking Martin's hand. "I'm so glad to see you, Captain. Welcome to your new home, sir."

"Thank you, Brendon, for looking after my family. I'm deeply indebted."

"No thanks needed, Captain. Serving your family is a great honor, and I look forward to many more years of it."

Nearby, Father Sandor and Professor Briar approached Joseph and Satori. They exchanged smiles, handshakes, and hugs like old friends reunited. For Joseph Arunui, arriving on Penglai Island marked the end of a long, difficult journey that began years ago when he boarded the FS *Taimaha* in Southport, New Zealand.

Back then, Joseph struggled to find meaning after losing his entire family. He had doubted whether the voyage to Antarctica and Galraithia held any purpose. But now, standing close to Satori, holding her hand, looking at her and Albert, tears filled his eyes. Family gave life meaning—and another journey was just beginning.

***

The sweet scent of forest flowers blossoming beneath Rachel's window mingled with the salty sea breeze. A sudden noise stirred her awake—the breeze must have knocked over a glass flowerpot. Rising from bed, she draped a stole wrap shawl around her shoulders and stepped outside, her pregnant belly visible beneath the moonlight's soft glow.

"Rob, Ryan," she called timidly, eyes scanning the dimly lit garden. "Are you out here?"

Then came the distinct hum of an electric actuator as Five-o-Nine approached, standing patiently in the open doorway.

"Five-o-Nine?"

"Hello... Rachel."

"Rob, Ryan! You'd better get down here!" Rachel called sharply.

Eager to see her, Five-o-Nine's outer metallic skin shifted color—from forest green to a calming sky blue.

"What are you doing here? Who sent you?"

"No one."

"Then tell me why you're here," Rachel said gently.

"I want to stay here. With you."

Footsteps echoed nearby as Robert appeared at the top of the stairs.

"Rachel, are you okay?"

"Look who's here!" Rachel smiled, eyes fixed on the fabricator she had affectionately named Five-o-Nine. She remembered the exact time logged in her work when she activated Five-o-Nine's cerebral matrix—the moment it entered her life.

"Is that Five-o-Nine?"

"Greetings to you, sir," the fabricator replied.

"Well, greetings to you, Five-o-Nine," Rob said, bowing deeply, a surprised smile on his face.

More footsteps followed; Ryan appeared outside his room, rubbing his tired eyes.

"I haven't had a good night's sleep since we arrived. What's all this noise?"

"We have a visitor," Rachel answered.

"At this hour? Send them away!"

"Greetings to you, sir."

Rachel noted, "Five-o-Nine's sound module has changed—its speech patterns are far more human-like now."

Robert met Rachel's gaze. "It's as complex as our own sound module has become."

"Professor Joseph Arunui reprogrammed my sound module, sir. Do you approve, Rachel?"

"Yes, Five-o-Nine. I do. Professor Arunui is a skilled Sequanta programmer."

Ryan scratched his head, puzzled. "Well, I'll be damned. Whatever the reprogramming, this machine shouldn't be off its Lockplate at this hour. There are rules—Penglaian society is primitive in that way. The powers-that-be are even debating whether fabricators should have freedom to roam the countryside."

"Directional circuitry could be failing," Robert suggested. "I want to check your directional circuit board in the morning, Five-o-Nine."

"My directional circuitry is fully functional, sir."

"You should be on your Lockplate, offline!" Ryan snapped.

Five-o-Nine hesitated, as if to respond, then looked to Rachel for support.

"Ryan is concerned. We all are, because you left your Lockplate without permission. This signals a serious malfunction in your programming."

"Everything is functioning perfectly well, Rachel," Five-o-Nine replied.

"Then why did you leave your Lockplate without permission? Refresh your memory modules and answer me."

The fabricator's eyes blinked three times, signaling full memory recharge and storage capacity for seven years.

"I want to stay here with you, Rachel," Five-o-Nine said softly.

"That's decision-making—a rule that doesn't apply to you, a machine!" Ryan shook his head.

"Five-o-Nine, follow shutdown procedures and return to your Lockplate, then power down," Robert ordered.

"I cannot. I will not, sir. I want to stay here... with Rachel."

Tiredness and frustration flared as Ryan rushed down the stairs, intent on disabling Five-o-Nine's logical matrix but unwilling to meet Rachel's piercing gaze.

"Don't you dare! Five-o-Nine belongs to me; I built it. I claim all rights and privileges."

"Rachel, you forfeited those rights when you accepted Gordon Winthrop's money."

"And you'll forfeit our friendship if you touch Five-o-Nine."

Ryan raised his hands in mock surrender. "Okay, Rachel, you win. I don't want to argue. But remember, you alone will be accountable for Five-o-Nine's actions. If you'll excuse me, I'm going back to bed."

"Good night, sir."

As Ryan climbed the stairs, he glanced back and waved dismissively. Rachel knelt by Five-o-Nine, whispering, "No harm will come to you. Not from Ryan or anyone else. You're part of my family now."

Five-o-Nine's metallic skin shifted to a deep iridescent blue, a sign of love and happiness. To Rachel, it proved fabricators were evolving alongside humans.

Every life form in Galraithia was advancing at a pace far beyond anything Joseph Arunui had imagined. This rapid evolution added another layer to the complex tapestry of Galraithian paradoxes, where the rules of nature seemed to twist and bend in ways that defied understanding.

The Beginning